D1241524

I, John Mordaunt

Also by Virgil Scott

THE SAVAGE AFFAIR

THE HICKORY STICK

THE DEAD TREE GIVES NO SHELTER

I, John
Mordaunt

Virgil Scott

Harcourt, Brace & World, Inc.
New York

For
JOHN HAROLD WILSON
who taught me more than a technique

and for
JOSEPHINE MORSE
who led me out of the valley of the shadow

and for
JUSTINE
who does not have to be told why

ᛮ *Foreword* ᛮ

The writer who attempts to recapture in a story another time, another place is probably rushing in where angels fear to tread, and this is doubly the case with *I, John Mordaunt.* For in committing myself to a first-person narrative, I have assumed the challenge not only of accuracy in background detail but accuracy in depicting the "psychology"—and, within limits, even the stylistic flavor—of another age. Moreover, all characters in the novel except two (Andrew Harris and the Indian girl, Nina) are historical rather than imaginary, and their characterizations are based not alone upon my imagination but upon hints dropped in the various journals, diaries, histories, and collections of letters of the time. Naturally, in a novel running to nearly two hundred thousand words, I will have committed errors in fact or interpretation; and I can only say in my defense that *I, John Mordaunt* is as accurate, as "truthful" as five years of research can make it.

With one major and one minor exception. John Mordaunt's activities during the Commonwealth, his conspiracies, marriage, and trial for high treason, are all matters of record, as is his arrest in 1654 for his implication in the Gerard conspiracy. But the years between 1654 and 1657 are blank. There is no record that he took part in the Penruddock rising, that he was transported, or that he went through the Santo Domingo campaign. Neither is there any record that he did *not*, but if he did not, dozens of loyalists like him did. And my purpose here has been something other than fictionalized biography;

it has been to create a character and a story which will be representative of all those who from 1649 to 1660 resented and resisted a new set of masters and who for ten years or more risked comfort, estates, and lives out of loyalty to an exiled king and to the concept of kingship and constitutional government.

Beyond this, I have in one place taken minor liberties with historical fact. The Penruddock rising was originally planned for St. Valentine's Day, 1655, and, in fact, two hundred did gather on that day and rode to within sight of Salisbury before dispersing. But the Penruddock rising did not in fact occur until early March.

Finally, a word about vocabulary. Throughout the novel I have Americanized the spelling of a few common seventeenth-century terms—"humor" for "humour" (meaning, most commonly, "whim" or "inclination"); "lieutenant" for "leftenant"; "sennight" for "se'ennight" (meaning "week"). I have also used a number of terms which may be foreign to most modern readers. Thus, the word "an" is most often used in the sense of "if." A "badger" was a cattle dealer. The "brotherhood" was the fraternity of highwaymen. A "composition" was a fine imposed upon a man's estates by the authorities, and "sequestration" was the outright seizure of his property by the state. "To cover" meant to wear a hat, and "to uncover" meant to remove it. "Cozen" was the current slang term which meant "to cheat"—the modern equivalent is "to con." A "cull" (or "gull") was a fool or "sucker." A "malignant" was any person who opposed the established government. An "ordinary" was the main dining hall in an inn. A "papist" was, of course, a Roman Catholic. A "Cavalier" was an adherent of either Charles I or his son, and a "Roundhead" was an adherent of the "parliamentary party." If we use the term with absolute accuracy, the "Rump" was that portion of the Long Parliament which survived after Colonel Pride "purged" it of all its "disaffected" members; however, the term was loosely used throughout the Commonwealth for any parliament which suffered exclusion of any of its elected members. A "saint" was the Cavalier's term for a religious fanatic. A man was "trepanned" if he was lured into a plot against the state and then betrayed. Finally, the term "forlorn" is, in seventeenth-century military parlance, a group of men, sometimes volunteers, sometimes chosen by lot, who went ahead of the army proper as scouts; its modern equivalent is, perhaps, "reconnaissance detail," but the term "vanguard" would be an inaccurate substitute, since the front regiment of the army proper was then called the "van."

I cannot hope to mention here the books, articles, journals, diaries, or collections of letters and state papers which I have consulted in the writing of this novel. But I have written it with Gardiner's *History of the Commonwealth and Protectorate,* Firth's *Last Years of the Protectorate,* and David Underwood's *Royalist Conspiracy in England, 1649-1660,* within constant reach. And beyond the dozens of scholars and editors whom I have met only through the pages of their books and articles, I wish to acknowledge my debt and express my gratitude to these: To all those anonymous librarians at the Folger, Harvard, and Huntington Libraries who obtained miles of microfilm for me, and particularly to Henry Koch and Richard Chapin of the Michigan State University Library for their tireless bibliographical help and for the hundreds of items they have added to the library at my request. To Professor Lawrence Babb for his careful reading of the manuscript and for his correction of a number of inaccuracies, and to Professor Clyde Henson for his suggestions. To Arthur Hudd of the British Museum, who ran down and microfilmed a dozen contemporary accounts of life in seventeenth-century prisons as well as two manuscript journals of the Santo Domingo campaign, a copy of the very rare history of the Barbados by Richard Ligon on which I have largely based my account of indentured servitude in the colonies, and two transcripts of Mordaunt's trial. To Professor John Harold Wilson, who, with only six months' time for a project of his own, still devoted a week while in England to some of my problems, and who therefore deserves mention here as well as on my dedication page. Finally, I wish to express my gratitude to Michigan State University for several research grants, a Research Professorship, and a sabbatical leave which gave me a free year to finish this novel.

East Lansing, Michigan
July, 1963

I, John Mordaunt

ξ◁ *Prologue* ▷ξ

Spring stole softly into the south of England this year; it followed a mild winter unobtrusively, almost stealthily. In years past this land of mine has known its share of bitter winters and violent springs, but this winter of 1675 was not bitter and the spring has not been violent. Here in Surrey the frost never went deep enough to support the weight of a horse and rider, and in March the rain that drifted across Hampshire was gentle, and now, by April's end, the trees are in leaf and the cowslips in bloom. It is almost as if, after the ague and the chill, the purging and the bleeding, the fever that once lived in this land has at last died and the sweat has broken and the breathing has become calm again.

Or so I would have thought were this last month and not this.

For it is a quiet spring in a quiet year, but there lies behind it the violence. There are still men abroad in the land who can recall the bitterness of other years. Of '52, say, when the March gales swept down out of Northumberland, and men came suddenly and fearfully awake in the darkness of pre-dawn, and over the crash of broken shutters they heard the scream of trees out on the grounds like women in a sacked town, and there in the darkness and the warmth they offered up thanks to God that this year they had escaped pressment in My Lord Protector's navy. Or of '58, when this time the tempest was September born, and in the heart of it the manor, built two hundred years ago and sound every inch of it in timber and mortar and stone, trembled and complained, and then, in the one un-

3

bearable flash of lightning and clap of thunder like the unalterable and final pronouncement of Almighty judgment, the tyrant died.

There is this violence which some in this land can still remember, and there is another violence. They remember the years when the hand of brother was turned against brother, and father betrayed son, and the time came when a man learned to distrust his own shadow striding before him in the sun. They remember a January morning twenty-five years ago when a king emerged with slim and erect dignity into the frosty air without Whitehall and laid his head upon the block, and the axe flashed in the cold sunlight, and the mob groaned aloud, and anarchy was born. They remember interrogations for no other cause than a passing look, arrests for no reason a man could name. They remember fines for a single, impulsive oath, imprisonment for but walking abroad in the fields of a Sabbath afternoon, deportations for a rash word against My Lord Protector, the striking off of a right hand for the tumbling of a wench. They remember the taxgatherers who descended like locusts upon the villages come market day, and the cold-eyed troops marching along dusty summer roads, and plans whispered in the secret rooms of evil alehouses, and betrayals and arrests and interrogations before the rude, mechanic fellows who were now our justices and our judges. They remember the proclamations and the edicts, the fines and the deportations, the compositions and the sequestrations and the decimations. They remember tyranny.

There are some who yet remember and I one of them—I, John Mordaunt, Baron Mordaunt of Reigate in Surrey and Viscount Mordaunt of Avalon in Somerset. Though I had thought the violence over and done with, though it has been fifteen years since a man named Cromwell died and a king came home and Englishmen once again knew government under law, I remember. For I have just returned from London.

I awoke early this morning. Early waking is a habit of mine, but this morning the sun was not yet a yard above the horizon, and the household at Carey Place was not yet astir, and the waking had been out of an evil dream. For just before opening my eyes, I had again been on shipboard bound for the Barbados; so vivid was the dream that I could feel the sway and dip of the ship, and even after I opened my eyes I could see the gape of the ship's hatch above me,

4

and through it the sun a great copper disk in a terrible blue sky. And so for a little I must lie quiet and breathe deeply against the pounding of my heart. Then I turned my head, and my wife was beside me, and for a moment, before I remembered London, God was content with me again and the world smiling.

She was still sleeping sweetly. A curl had escaped from under her cap, and her face was softly flushed in the morning light, and her lips were faintly and very prettily parted, and her gown had slipped down off one shoulder. I lay there, watching the delicate heartbeat in the hollow of her throat, the modest rise and fall of her bosom; I was thinking that even a gown which tacked twelve yards of Irish lace about the neck and forty yards of ribbon between collar and waist could not disguise her sex. For a moment, thinking that, I almost reached for her. But rather I slipped cautiously from the bed.

The clothing I had worn the night before was flung over the back of the blue velvet chair in the far corner of the chamber. The suit was my silver and black, and the shirt was my best holland, and both were fitter for a London tavern at midnight than for a stroll abroad of a dewy April morning. Nonetheless, I donned shirt and breeches and hose, and then, half dressed like that and my boots in my hand, I stole from the chamber and along the length of the portrait gallery and down the great stairs. I stood at the foot of the stairs a moment, listening to the first stir and clatter of life out in the kitchen, for Friday was baking day at Carey House and fires to be laid in the hearth under the ovens. Then I slipped out of doors into April.

There is, beyond Andrew's gardens, beyond the stables and kennels and orchards of Carey Place, a wood. It is a small, wild place of chestnut and larch, where in winter the bracken grows high and dry and amber brown, and holly berries gleam against the snow like tiny live coals, and redwings chatter in the oaks; where in July the smell of honeysuckle and dog violets is thick and sweet, and where in September a man can find blackberries the size of his thumb. It is a place I love and a bone of contention betwixt Andrew and me. Andrew is the finest gardener in Surrey, and he holds the conviction that God intended the earth to be laid out in neat walks and trimmed turf; and had I not stayed his hand, he would long since have cleared the wood of underbrush and briar. But Andrew, I thought, as I came out of the orchard and squeezed through the gap in the

5

pleached hazel hedge and strode up the path to the wood, Andrew could never understand many things, among them a Mordaunt crossing his fields at five in the morning without coat or periwig or hat.

There was bracken in the path with stiff, green, curled fronds, and to the edge of the path the dog violets were in bloom, and ahead of me, bordering the wood, a white line of wood sorrel. Then I rounded the turn in the path, and I was in the shade of the wood, and the bluebells were in flower. They were everywhere the eye looked and as far as the eye could travel. At my feet they were as deep a blue as a sea I had known off Santo Domingo, and when I lifted my eyes, they faded into a misty blue-gray, like the slate of a Northumberland sky in November. I stopped there, under the great forward oak which marked the beginning of my wood, and followed them to where the path faded into the shadow, and for a moment there fell about me the quick and startled silence you sometimes meet with when you come upon a wild and secret place of an April morning. Then, in the branches above me, I heard the cry of a wood wren, first the sharp nervous twitter, then the long shivering trill. And standing there, I thought, *No, Andrew. While I am master of Carey Place, no man will lay hand to this corner of this land, will hack out the hazel coppice or brick the path or prune the chestnut or lay axe to the larch. For I am recently returned from London,* I thought, *and I have known the hand of man, and here is one spot on earth where the hand of God hath been spared that hand. For here the past is like a dream, vague and distant and dimly remembered even at the moment of waking, even while the sweat is still cold on the lip and the terror still clamped around the heart. For I have known the violence,* I thought, *and mayhap I shall know it again. But here, if only for the moment, a man can find peace.*

I stayed in the wood until the sun was high above the trees. Back at the manor, I caught sight of Andrew at the south corner of the orchard; he was on his knees, tamping dirt about the roots of another new fruit tree, which meant that he, at least, was content this morning. I climbed the stile and walked down the row of trees to him.

"Well, Andrew?" I said. "Another plum?"

"Flemish cherry, M'lord," he said, and got to his feet. I am not unduly tall, but Andrew still looked up at me when he touched finger to forelock; out of Cornwall, Andrew was, and his forebears had been fishermen, and there were men in his family had taken themselves brides in Carmarthen and Cardigan, and so the blood of the coast people showed in him, short and thick and black. "They will bear us cherries in three years," he said, "an the weather hold until they root."

"I venture a prophecy," I said. "The weather will hold this year."

"Why, I hope you are a prophet, M'lord."

And I too, Andrew, I thought, I too. And briefly I felt the small stab of doubt, of weary, nagging fear.

He read that in my face, I think, for his eyes dropped out of mine. "Master Charles is home," he said.

"Charles?" I said. "Charles home? From Oxford?"

"You will find him in the garden, M'lord. With M'lady."

I smiled. "I am taking you from your work, am I?"

"Nay," he said. "Nay, I did not intend that meaning—"

"I know you did not, Andrew," I said, and put a hand briefly on his shoulder. We have our differences, Andrew and I, I thought, but never on aught that makes a difference, and affection for this man welled up in me on the sudden. "You are in the right," I said. "I had best go greet them."

At Carey Place the garden to the back of the manor is bounded by a high wall with a single wrought-iron gate in the southeast corner. When I laid hand to the latch of the gate, I saw my wife. She sat on the stone bench beside the central path, her back to me, and facing her, one hand on the stone into which the seat was fitted, was Charles, and my beloved's hair was immodestly loose and waist-long and glinting pale gold in the morning sun, for it was early yet and she was in the privacy of her own garden. I do not know of what they spoke; I only know that as I laid hand to the latch, Charles was smiling down upon her. Then she briefly moved the hand in her lap, and it was as though there was some secret communion between them, for Charles dropped his hand from the bench and took a single step and bent over and kissed her full upon the lips.

I did not lift the latch and swing open the gate and enter the garden.

I have been called a wit in my time. But I am none of your poets or glib courtiers, and I have not the gift for words which I need here. How then do I explain it, the sudden and awful significance of this moment; how do I explain why a man, coming into his garden of a

7

fair spring morning, will pause on the sudden and drop his hand from a latch and catch his breath, hoping in that same instant that his wife did not note his approach, that she did not hear his hand to the latch, that she will not turn and discover him and a moment forever gone. I do not know how you explain this.

This only do I know. I have known my share of significant moments in my eight and forty years. I have lain stapled to the stone floor of Newgate's condemned hold, with the squeak of rats in my ear and the stink of a sewer to my right hand and the gaol fever raging in me and the certain knowledge that I was a dead man to keep me company—gaol fever or a Tyburn rope, it were all one and God about to collect a debt—and later I have walked out of Newgate Gaol into Phoenix Court a free man, and that was a moment of significance. I have sailed in the hold of a ship, and the ship a fortnight under a blazing tropic sun, and the hatches battened down, and the smell of sick and dying men so thick it were miracle if you did not gag against it, and I have come up out of that hold alive, and that was a moment of significance. I have endured the lash, and afterwards, face down in a Barbados compound, with the fingers of an Indian girl delicate and cool on my flayed back, I have vowed that I would not die, and that was a moment of significance. I have marched forty miles through tropic jungle, with no water and no food save green oranges that doubled a man up with stomach cramps, and at the end of that march I have crawled to the edge of the stream and plunged my face into water, and that was a moment of significance. And I have stood before My Lord Protector's High Court of Justice and looked up into the eyes of the Lord High Commissioner of England and heard him pronounce me not guilty of high treason, and that was a moment of significance. But no moment to compare to this moment; I have learned that in time some memories can grow dim, like dyed linen left out in the rain. But I do not think that this memory will fade.

It is for most, I know, a simple thing, your son, almost a man now, kissing his mother upon the lips. But it was not a simple thing for me. For it was as if all the other moments I had known this morning—a moment when I had awakened from a dream and my wife asleep beside me, a moment in a wood when a wren had burst into song, a moment when I had laid a hand to Andrew's shoulder and smiled down into his eyes—it was as if all those moments had become this moment, and on the sudden my whole life and all my memories had fallen away from me, and London or no London, I had come face to face with peace.

For it had not been ever thus.

ᶓᴵ *One* ᴰᶚ

It was not thus in another year, another April. It was not thus on that April day in 1654 when Henry rode down the Priory lane and looked insolently down upon Andrew and me through the gray slant of rain, and then dismounted stiffly and commanded Andrew, in the way Henry had of commanding a man, to unsaddle and bed down his mare.

I had not been abroad early that morning. I awakened that morning in a chamber bereft of everything save my bed and one frayed and soiled velvet hanging against the north wall, for Reigate Priory had, in ten years of civil war, known two most exquisitely courteous visits by Roundhead militia, both of them led by My Lord Monson. Each time, Monson's troopers had departed with hangings and furniture and linen and plate—everything, indeed, save what lay under a ton of hay in the stable, or what would not lend grace to My Lord Monson's own dwelling, or what, like this hanging, was hardly worth the trouble of carting off to auction.

I awakened that morning in that chamber and into a thin, gray, despairing light which told me that it was still raining, that out on the grounds the sogged and patient trees were standing sad and bleak and dripping as they had stood for a week now. I knew as well that it was past seven of the clock and the household astir below. But it was warm in the bed, and I had little heart for throwing back covers and stepping forth, in half shirt and drawers, into a room

10

that knew no fire. So I lay quiet awhile, listening to the sounds of life out in the courtyard, the ring of a small axe on larch logs, the clatter as one of the kitchen boys brought out the great copper kettles for rinsing, the protest of the windlass on the pump. Then I sighed and slipped out of bed, thinking as I did so of better days at the Priory, when the second son of the Earl of Peterborough would not have had to rise until his man had blown up a fire and laid out his clothes and then stood by to dress him. But this was another year, I thought, and the times out of joint, and as I crossed the chamber, I cursed dispassionately the Roundhead dragoon who had thrust the stock of his musket through the casement pane on our last visit from the present protectors of English liberties.

One blessing, I did not have to devote a third of a morning to the selection of clothes for the day. Of the twenty suits I had once owned, all but two had long since been sold, along with my fine holland shirts and my silk hose, my Spanish leather boots and my beaver hats, to pay a servant's wages or to help Henry meet the latest fine on the Peterborough estates. The one I chose was a plain buff; the coat was frayed and the breeches in need of new points, but it was dress suitable to this month's climate. I donned shirt and breeches and hose and boots, sweating a little in the attaching of points to hose and again when I pulled on my bucket-topped boots; and when I clapped on my hat, I reflected that it was just as well that my hair was my own. For there was no money to spare in the great chest out in the mews for periwigs, and no servants left at Reigate with skill to comb one if there were.

Downstairs, in the withdrawing room off the great hall, my mother was at her desk. I stood in the doorway a moment, studying the Countess Dowager's back, thinking that she was looking older these days than her fifty years. Partly, I thought, it is the damned Presbyterian dress she affects, high at the throat and all a single and unrelieved gray, and partly it is the times, and partly, I suppose, it is her two sons, who have proved a trial to her. Then she turned, and I crossed the room, skirting the battered table with the four soiled gilt chairs, and bent over her hand.

"Well, John," she said. "You are a slug-a-bed this morning."

"Aye," I said, a trifle shortly, for something in her tone reminded me of years ago, when my tutor would chide me for stumbling over a Latin sentence. I straightened and pulled at the bell rope above her desk. When I looked back down at her, she smiled hesitantly, and I thought, At least her eyes are young.

"John," she said, "John, I fear we must lay in some linen. For sheets and pillow-beres. They can supply us in the village with holland for one and six the yard." She read my eyes, and her voice faltered. "John," she said, "we *must* have sheets. We cannot sleep 'twixt flannel in the heat of July."

"Can we not, Mother?" I said. "Can we not, now?" I crossed to the table and kicked out a gilt chair which, like its master, had seen better days. When I sat down, I kept a shoulder to her. I should remember that she is my mother, I thought, I should remind myself that a certain respect is due her. But I had awakened to another rainy day, and I had dressed without help in a damp and cheerless chamber, and in the fumbling with points, I had thought briefly on better days in this land of mine, and now my mother, dressed like some damned London merchant's wife, must choose this time to harp on our need for sheets. "In God's name," I burst out, "are they all asleep and snoring in the kitchen that no one can fetch me my morning draught?"

"Patience, John," she said. "They are short-handed—"

"Patience," I said bitterly. "Patience. It is what I have lived by these five years, patience."

She leaned toward me. I still kept a shoulder to her, but I could sense her lean in her voice. "We could manage with forty yards of holland," she said. "What think you, John?"

"Why, I think," I said, speaking very carefully, "I think that holland sheets at one and six a yard will not wear well this year. I predict they will not wear a month."

"I do not follow your meaning, John," she said. "You well know—"

Now I did turn to her. "My meaning?" I said. "Why, my meaning is this. An we lay in fine holland sheets, they will be gracing the bed of the first ranting, eye-rolling, crop-haired rogue of an Anabaptist trooper that chances to ride this way."

"In God's name, John, lower your voice."

"Aye," I said. "I was forgetting that even the walls have ears these days," and then, almost as if to prove me there, Mary was in the doorway, a tankard in her hand, and behind her Andrew.

"Good morrow, Mary," I said. "Come in, Andrew."

"Good morrow, Master John," Mary said. In the gray light, her round face was the color of bread dough and very near as shapeless, and as she came toward me, her enormous breasts, unfettered under the linsey-woolsey smock by any stay or corset, swayed heavily. She set the tankard before me and then smiled down on me; I had always been fond of Mary, and I knew that of all the Mordaunts, I was her favorite. "Would there be aught else, Master John?" she said.

"Could you fetch Andrew one, too? Before the morning is out, that is?"

She ceased smiling. "We be short-handed in the kitchen these days, Master John, and seventy stone of beef to be salted down—"

I grinned up at her. "Why, Mary," I said, "I was but jesting." I came forward in my chair and slapped her hard on what was probably the greatest expanse of buttock in all the county of Surrey. "Come," I said. "A smile, wench. Tell me we are still sweethearts, eh?"

She smiled, but it was mere obedience to my whim. "We be sweethearts, Master John," she said. "But I would your jests were less cruel."

I looked to Andrew. He was standing nervously in the doorway, watching us. "Come in, man," I said.

He advanced a pace into the room and then stopped. "I ha' the accounts for the week, sir," he said. "They be high, I fear. I laid in both beef and pork."

"High, Andrew?" I said. "How high?"

"High," he said miserably. "One and nine a stone Tom Braithwaite charged for the bullock. I would ye had given me leave to ride over to Redhill—"

"Why, we are fair game at Redhill as well, Andrew. Ye could ride the forty miles to Guildford, they would still know you were a Mordaunt man, and fair game."

"Aye," he said. "Aye, damn them." His eyes flicked to my mother. "Your pardon, M'lady," he said. "But would ye not think they could forgive and forget? 'Tis five years since they murdered the king, and—"

He broke off, while one of the kitchen boys sidled around him and set a tankard on the table. I kicked out a chair. "Come," I said. "Join me in a morning draught, man."

He shifted uncomfortably from one foot to the other. "Why,

13

thankee," he said, "but I ha' had my morning draught, Master John."

"Have another, then. If I can plow shoulder to shoulder with you, you can drink with me, can you not?"

"Aye. An such be your will, Master John." He advanced a final pace and sat down on the very edge of the chair. I watched his face as he sat down; I was thinking that My Lord Protector and our present parliament had their work cut out if they were of a mind to make every man in this land an equal. It will take more than their damned weekly proclamations, I thought, and then Andrew's hand was straying toward his cap.

"Nay," I said. "No ceremony, man. No need to uncover."

He dropped his hand. From his expression you would have thought I had just put him to the rack, and I grinned. "Come, man," I said, "have ye not read the times aright? Up to London they are interpreting ceremony as treason these days. You must train that hand not to stray to your forelock, man. England has been given its liberties now, and the times upside down, and all the masters men now and all the men masters. By weekly proclamation before Whitehall. So no ceremony. Particularly," I said, flicking a look at my mother, "particularly no ceremony if ye serve Mordaunts. For one of us fought to establish these liberties we now enjoy, and I would honor his memory," and I glanced again at my mother to see if the shaft had gone home, and her lips tightened, and then she rose from her chair.

"Wilt excuse me, John?" she said. "There is work for me in the stillroom."

I came to my feet. "Why, yes, Mother," I said and watched her leave. She was a tall woman, and she had been thought beautiful in her day, and there was yet, in the straight line of her back, a dignity that would never desert her, and I felt a twinge of admiration for her, and along with it a flash of shame because I had had to awaken with a devil in me this morning. For it is not her fault, I thought, that we Mordaunts have no luck. No fault of hers, I thought, that my father had had the bad grace in '44 to declare for parliament, nor that he had imbued her, ere he died, with his own Presbyterian principles. And none of her doing neither that seven years later her elder son had had the even worse judgment to declare against that same parliament, to join another Charles on another field at a time when London 'prentices and Gloucester weavers had discovered for champion a fanatic with a genius for the military, a certain Oliver Cromwell. No, I thought, no fault of hers that we Mordaunts have no luck, and as I dropped back into my chair, I knew a brief, tired anger at myself for treating her as I had this morning.

"I do not jest," I said. "The rogues are in the saddle these days, Andrew. Up at Whitehall—"

"I do not live at Whitehall, sir," he said. "And I am none of your damned Levellers. I am a plain steward at Reigate Priory." He looked up at me from under heavy black brows, and now there was heat in his eyes. "I am none o' your parliament rogues, Master John. Ye know that well."

I read the warning in his eyes, and it was time to call a halt to the banter. "Aye," I said. "I know it well, Andrew."

"I was with your brother at Worcester," he said. "I carried him off the field that day, and I nursed him a fortnight in a hayloft, with nought of food nor drink save the milk we stole from a cow below, and when he could travel again, 'twas I got him across the land. Swarming over the land like locusts, the Roundheads were, looking for Charles Stuart in every barn and cellar 'twixt Worcester and the coast, but I got Master Henry to Dover and aboard a ship—"

"Andrew," I said, and put a hand over his. "Nay, Andrew, I had not meant to impute—" I waited until the heat went out of his eyes, and then I withdrew my hand and reached for his accounts. "'Sblood," I said, "uncover if it will put you at your ease, man."

His hand went to his cap. I watched the cap come off and the black forelock fall toward his eyes and the relief steal into his face. I smiled, and he returned it. Then I gave my attention to his accounts.

The list was written in the large, blunt, childish hand of a man who had taught himself his letters and his sums, and our outlay had indeed been high this week. Eight pounds, thirteen shillings, fivepence Andrew had laid out this week, and as I ran my eye down his neat and painful columns, I wondered how long he must have crouched over the table in his chamber, copying and adding this list. I also offered up a prayer that over at Guildford, My Lord Desborough would not choose this month to quarter a Commonwealth troop on the Priory, for the great chest out in the mews would not stand another such outlay before next Michaelmas, when rents would come in again.

15

At the bottom of the sheet Andrew had written, "Att hande, from Mr J^nne Mordante this 7 daye of Aprile, £15 O s. O d. Balence this 14 daye of Aprile £6 6s. 7d." I looked up from the sheet, and his blunt fingers were playing with the bill to his cap. "Ye had best add my figures again, Master John," he said.

"I have yet to catch you in error, Andrew."

He shook his head stubbornly. "I ha' no head for sums. And no hand for making fair copy. I am plain gardener, like my father afore me."

"You have the best head there is," I said. "And the best hand. For you are an honest man, and a loyal one. A man can ask no more these days." I thrust the paper into my doublet. "I will provide you money against the new week, if you will give me a hand with the flooring in the mews."

"I ha' six pound six left," he said. "I shall make it do till the month be out."

"You are to pocket five pounds."

He shook his head. "Nay, I ha' no need—"

"Aye," I said, "you do have need. When was the last money you had from my hand?"

"Why, five pounds. And that last Lady Day."

"Five pounds," I said. "Five pounds against the twenty ye had due you. And afore that, five pounds last Michaelmas. Ten pounds in a year, against the forty we agreed on—"

"Why, a man hath little need of money these days, Master John. An a man hath money, he must tithe in support of the Reverend Richard Parr and his Solemn League and Covenant service—"

"A man always has need of money," I said. "God's blood, let it out to a London goldsmith at eight per cent. Or run up a score at the Swan. Or go up to Southwark when the roads are again passable and spend it on a wench."

His eyes were still stubborn. "There be fines these days for frequenters of taverns. And as for the wenches"—he looked down at his right hand and opened and closed his fingers appreciatively—"I still ha' some use for this right hand o' mine."

"Bah," I said. "Roundheads or no Roundheads, wenches are still tumbled in England and bastards still born. This is one thing not even your fanatic can stamp out, man."

"They can do what they have a mind to. And 'tis a law on their

16

books. Death for adultery, a right hand struck off for fornication."

I pushed back my chair and stood up. "Andrew," I said wearily, and now it was stubbornness meeting stubbornness, Mordaunt will against Cornish will, "Andrew, will you give me a hand with the flooring?"

He looked up at me from under those heavy, black brows. "Aye," he said. "I can give Tom Adams a pound—"

I placed my two hands flat on the table and put my weight on them and stared down at him. "Why?" I said. "Will ye tell me why?"

He looked up at me, his expression innocent and puzzled. "Tom has not had a shilling in six months—"

"That is not my meaning."

"What is your meaning, then?"

"You are the finest gardener in all Surrey. And My Lord Monson has offered you sixty pounds a year—"

"Lord Monson." He made a mouth as if to spit on the floor. "Lord Monson. Would ye ha' me gardening for a damned regicide, Master John?"

"Sixty pounds a year. Yet you stay on with me at forty—"

"A man works for something besides wages," he said. "A Harris has served a Mordaunt since my grandfather left the sea. This is my family, Master John."

"Ah," I said. "Is that the reason of it?"

"Aye." He studied my expression. "Why did your brother join the king at Worcester? He knew 'twas a lost cause—"

"Very well," I said. "You have given me my answer." I straightened. "Will ye pocket the five pounds, Andrew?" I said softly. "Whether ye have need of it or not? For the sake of Mordaunt pride?"

For a moment his forehead wore a crease, and then it smoothed out. "Why, yes," he said, and his voice equally soft. "An ye will forgive me my thick wits." He got heavily to his feet. "I will gi' ye a hand wi' the flooring," he said.

I rested a hand briefly on his shoulder. Then, out of the corner of my eye, I caught the shadow in the doorway, and I turned, and Mary was back.

"Begging your pardon, Master John," she said, "but there is a rider at the head of Workhouse Lane and riding this way. The kitchen boys just spied him."

17

ᘒᐃ *Two* ᐅᘖ

The import of her words did not strike me immediately, and so, as I dropped my hand from Andrew's shoulder and turned, I threw her but a single, careless glance. But it required no more than that glance to read her face. There have been times when I have found Mary's face expressionless, but there was expression on it now and to spare; now, beneath the bland circle like the face of a child's snowman, the cast of her mind was as plain to be read as the mark of the signet ring when you press it to the hot wax on the letter.

"A rider?" I said.

"Aye." Her voice had the thin, breathless quality of someone who has just run a pretty distance. "On Workhouse Lane."

"Alone?"

She shook her head. "I know not. The kitchen boys said they had spied a rider."

"His horse? What of his horse? Fresh?"

"It is raining out," she said. "And more nor an English mile to the top o' the lane, Master John."

I swung about. Andrew had started to rise as Mary came into the doorway, but he had interrupted the motion, and now he was frozen there, half sitting, half standing, and the look was stamped on his face, too.

"If his horse be a fresh one," I said, "he is not an hour away, Andrew."

"The roads hereabouts are a mire," he said. "If he hath ridden but

18

from Dorking, his horse will not be fresh." He was on his feet now.
"It could be a friend," he said.

"A-horseback?" I laughed shortly. "Who among us have they left
a horse?"

"Mayhap he is not for here."

"Mayhap. Shall we take the chance, Andrew?"

"Nay," he said. "Ye are in the right, Master John." He turned to
face Mary. "What o' the meat?"

"The beef is in the barrels," she said. "But the pork is yet on the
dresser. We ha' yet to touch knife to it."

"Can ye put down twelve stone of pork within the hour?"

She shook her head. "Ye know we cannot, Andrew. Not properly.
Pork is to be soaked in brine a day—"

"If ye deal with it as beef, how long would it stay sweet, think
ye?"

"That is not how ye deal with pork, Andrew. Spoiled pork—"

"Damn it, woman," Andrew said, and his voice was like the edge
of a knife, "we lack the time for lengthy instructions on the proper
treatment of pork. How long if we but salt it well?"

"A fortnight," she said, "an the weather kind to us."

"Butcher it, then. But save out a side. A side should stay sweet
three days. If our visitor take his leave within then, we shall celebrate his going with a side of pork."

"And if he do not, Andrew?" I said. "If he plans a lengthier stay?"

Andrew's eyes returned to mine. A moment ago there had been
an uncertain fear in them, but what was in them now was not fear.
"Why, then," he said softly, "we shall have a side of rotten pork on
our hands, Master John."

"At one and six the stone," I said.

"Why, as to that," he said, "there are sauces Mary knows can cover
a multitude of sins."

No, I thought, it is not fear in his eyes. "Tell me," I said, "ha' ye
ever seen a man has eaten of rotten pork, Andrew?"

"Why, yes," he said, and his voice still soft. "Twice."

No, I thought, it is not fear, and as I held his eyes, I was thinking
that he hated them worse than ever Henry or I did. He has suffered
less at their hands, I thought, but his hate goes deeper than ours,
and for a second time that morning I knew a dry bitterness at what
had come to pass in this land of mine, I felt a tired anger that a single

rider coming toward us on a spring road could make a man like Andrew propose murder, and that as coolly as he would propose the readying of a guest chamber.

I stared at him. "Ye are doubtless aware," I said, "that what ye propose would be like taking a stick to a hornet's nest. Let one of the bastards die on our hands—"

"Name me one thing ye can do these days," he said, "will not bring them yapping at a man's heels like curs. Suppose they choose to fork aside a ton of hay in the stables. Or take an axe to the floorboards in the mews. 'Sblood, Master John, all ye need do is incline your head in divine service, and the next ye know, ye are clapped to for a papist."

"All right," I said, for he spoke truth, and anything a man chose to do these days was but pissing to windward. "Save out a side of pork, then," I said to Mary. "Offering up a prayer as ye do so that our guest plans but the briefest of stays." I turned back to Andrew. "Let us see to the beef," I said.

He nodded, and we followed Mary across the great hall and down the long, cold, dimly lighted corridor to the kitchen.

The kitchen was a shambles. To speak truth, I know not what else I had expected, for I had had twenty years and more experience with kitchens on butchering days, and so I knew what it would be like. I knew that the four barrels of salted beef would be standing next the meat block; that across the kitchen, next the door into the pantry, the great copper kettles would be filled with brine, waiting the pork; that the hearth would be piled with discarded bones, still shining wet, only now beginning to sizzle from the heat of the smoldering fire laid there; that the flagstoned floor would be shining with grease from scraps of suet trod underfoot; that the block and dresser would be smeared with blood. I even knew, I think, that the kitchen would be deserted save for Tom Tyler, standing at the block before the side of pork, the knife idle in his hand until someone told him what to do with it. I knew all that, and yet, coming on the sudden out of the corridor, I felt the despair catch in my throat like a sob.

Behind me, Andrew cursed softly. Across the kitchen, Tom looked up and smiled that foolish, empty smile of his and then ducked his head. Poor, crazy Tom, I thought fleetingly, too foolish to desert this ship which is the Mordaunt fortunes with the rest of them, and then I was brushing past Mary and striding across the kitchen and through the scullery.

The two boys were standing in the middle of the courtyard, their bare heads shining in the light, ceaseless rain, their eyes on Workhouse Lane. "You, lads," I shouted. "In here, and quick."

They turned wide and startled eyes on me. I swung about and strode back to the kitchen without waiting for them to spring into a run. Andrew was by now at the barrels, waiting for my hand with them. Mary still stood uncertainly in the middle of the kitchen, her expression like that of a clubbed ox.

"How many hands can we muster here?" I said.

She paused to count, while I bit my lower lip with impatience. "Six," she said. "Eight, an we count you and your mother."

Eight, I thought, eight hands to do the work of twenty, and one of them a poor, shuffling, silly idiot and two of them mere boys. Behind me I heard the sound of running feet in the scullery, and I threw the order over my shoulder as they burst into the kitchen. "One o' ye run and fetch Miss Agnes," I said. "She is abovestairs. If my mother be with her, fetch her, as well. Tell them we require their instant presence in the kitchen." I looked again to Mary. "When Miss Agnes comes below, put her and my mother to work on that block and dresser; I want not a trace of even last year's blood left on it to betray this morning's business. Set Tom to raking out the hearth; the bones should be buried behind the stables. Put the boys to work on this floor; it must be swept of every scrap of meat and then freshly sanded. When Andrew and I have these barrels stowed in the mews, we will empty the kettles of brine and rinse them down. You, Mary, are to quarter and salt the pork. And tell my mother to break out a gallon of her lilac water; the rogues have keen noses as well as sharp eyes. And bear in mind that we have at best little more nor an hour."

"She is gentle born, Master John," Mary said. "She is blood relative, though poor."

I was on my way to Andrew at the barrels. "Who?" I said, over my shoulder. "Who is gentle born?"

"Miss Agnes," she said. "I doubt she will fancy the work of a scullery maid."

I was in full stride, and I cut it short and swung about. For a mo-

21

ment I could only stare at her, speechless, while the fury flared within me. "Is she, now?" I said. "Is she indeed, Mary?"

"Aye," she said. "And she will take orders only from Milady, your mother."

The fury in me was like a hand at my throat—a fury not at Mary but at a cheerless waking to a cheerless morning, at a quarrel with my mother over holland sheets, at a strange rider out there on the road to the village and riding this way, at I know not what. The fury lay there, not here, and so I should have kept my voice sweet and reasonable, I should have put cajolery into it. And yet I could not. "Mark me, Mary," I said, "and well. There is a rider on Workhouse Lane. We do not yet know his identity, but since he is not afoot, I will wager a pound to a ha'penny that he is on the side of the saints in this fair republic of ours. I would also guess that the odds favor a troop of pious and hungry Roundheads two miles behind him."

"I know that, Master John," she said. "I—"

"Do ye, now?" I said. "Well, know this, too. An there be any betrayal of butchering when they arrive, ye can lay to it that a troop of horse will dine fat this night and that neither you nor I will experience aught save the taste of porridge between now and the next assize." I leaned toward her, and I doubt that my face was as pretty as it had been known to be on easier occasions. "An Miss Agnes betrays any reluctance to touch hand to stone and water," I said, "convey her that message. Now shall we blab away the rest of this morning about the niceties of the proper duties of waiting maids gently born? Or will ye rather do me the courtesy of setting to here while there is yet light of day to work by and that pork still sweet?"

She did not reply. Rather, she turned away from me, and as she did so, she made a small gesture with her right hand, as if she intended to raise it to her eyes. It was the gesture a child might make when it has been scolded unjustly, and seeing it, I felt for a second time that morning the shame in me. For the love of God, John Mordaunt, I thought, this is Mary ye are speaking to. They have all the rest of them deserted the Mordaunt fortunes, I thought, the stewards and the wardens and the masters of the horse and the other sixty servants who were once at Reigate, they have all taken service with Surrey families whose politics smell sweeter in the nose these days than ours, and the only ones left us are one down-at-heels relative, and Mary here, and Andrew, and poor Tom, too silly in the head to read the times aright, and in God's name, John Mordaunt, is it Mary ye speak thus to?

"Mary," I said gently. "Mary."

"Aye?" She would not meet my eye.

"Mary," I said, "I should not have spoken to ye so."

" 'Tis all right. Mayhap there was cause."

"No," I said. "Or if there was, it is Miss Agnes I should ha' spent my anger on, not you."

" 'Tis all right," she said, and now she did meet my eye. " 'Twas not you speaking, Master John. 'Twas the times instead."

Aye, I thought, the times. We live in a republic now, I thought, where tyranny has been dethroned, and every man is equal, and justice prevails, and all by weekly proclamation nailed before the entrance to Whitehall. This land of mine, this England, is without kings and lords and bishops now, I thought, and law is whim these days, and the rogues jostle for position in the market place, and knavery is rewarded and thievery honored and pious hypocrisy crowned, and if a man cannot quickly learn to look another level in the eye and lie in his teeth and never a tremor in his voice, why, then, the devil take the hindmost. Ye are not abroad now, John Mordaunt, I thought, ye are home in England, where, if a man spies a rider on the road out of the village, it behooves him to look to his beef. Aye, Mary, I thought, it is the times all right, and as I turned from her, I remembered another time, when there was yet a lawful king at Westminster, and a man was tried by a jury of his peers; a time when there were still men abroad in the land who thought honor worth the dying for; a time when other riders rode toward Mordaunt gates and other preparations made for them, in kitchen and stillroom and guest chamber.

I turned from her and started for Andrew. "We had best see to the beef," I said.

He nodded and stooped and put his arms around one of the barrels. The barrel weighed fifteen stone, but he lifted it clear of the floor as easily as I might swing a chair away from a table. I bent and got a hand under it and eased him of the full weight of it.

We were to the scullery door when I thought of something else. "Mary," I said, "when Tom gets the hearth raked, set him to fetching wood. Damp wood. Have him pile the hearth high. Let us have a roaring blaze in it ere Andrew and I return for that last barrel."

23

"In God's name," Andrew said, "why a roaring blaze, with wood as scarce this season as Newcastle coals? I doubt ye have in mind the comfort of our visitor."

"Why, aye, Andrew," I said, smiling. "Aye, I had that in mind."

"Ye jest with us," Andrew said. "And this no time—"

"No jest," I said. "I merely lack faith in my mother's lilac water. But if we build a blaze and then close the damper to that hearth, I doubt that even My Lord Monson has a nose sharp enough to smell fresh beef in here."

And there, I thought, looking into Andrew's sudden grin, there are the times speaking, too. And for a third time that morning I thought of my father, and now I wished him alive again to view the work his hands had wrought. I do not think my father was a knave; what he did he did in good conscience, and I do not begrudge him his sudden death of fever that summer of '42. But on that April morning in 1654, I begrudged him it. That morning I knew bitterness and to spare for the inheritance he had left me, a world where rogues jostled with rogues for high position, where rude and mechanic fellows flaunted titles and abused power, where law was whim and freedom a mockery, where cobblers and hawkers of pots and pipkins and unlettered button makers interpreted Scripture for us. That morning, as Andrew and I lugged four barrels of beef across the swamp which was our courtyard, or as we worked at the floorboards in the mews and sweated and cursed as we lowered eighty stone of beef into the hole, I most heartily wished my father alive again, I most fervently wished him back in a world where you prepared for a guest by hiding your provisions and planned his entertainment by leaving out a side of pork to spoil.

The mews at Reigate Priory had been built fifty years ago, by my great-grandfather, the Lord William Howard, Earl of Nottingham and Lord High Admiral under Elizabeth; and my grandfather had added to them until mews and kennels formed a long, low rectangle, stoutly built of ship's timber, shining white in a summer sun for the rider who came across Earlswood Common and through the park and up to the manor from the stable side. But that had been years ago, when England still had a king and falconry was still in fashion, along with honor and manners and courtesy, along with long, fair, uncovered hair on a woman and clothing that was other than the color of today's skies. And now the mews and the kennels stood sad and gray and neglected under the sad, gray sky. Now the paint had peeled from stout timbers, and the stones were eroded and dirtied by time, and the doors hung crazily on broken hinges. Now, when a man stepped foot in the courtyard, no terrier yipped and no hound bayed him an answer. Now, inside what had once been the finest mews in Surrey, the oak flooring gave way underfoot, and the cage doors stood idly open, and nothing left of dog or hawk or crane or varnel or swivel save old, dry, chalk-white droppings and a few scraps of furniture—a rotted jess and a rusted luring bell still hanging on the wall, a ripped hood kicked into a far corner, a single hawking glove forgotten in a cage.

But the mews still served a purpose. In the midst of civil war, Andrew and Robert Squire, Henry's falconer, ripped loose a section of flooring here and spaded out a hole shoulder-deep and six feet square and then relaid the floor, cunningly. And here we kept the great chest with its Dutch lock containing the rents that still trickled into Reigate, and here Andrew and I stored the barrels of beef and pork.

By the time we had lowered the last barrel and replaced the flooring, the rider, I knew, had had time to flounder from the village to the head of Priory Lane. Hence, when we came out into the courtyard again, Andrew walked around the Priory to the north and looked anxiously off toward the village.

"He is alone, at least," he said. "He is no scout for a company of soldiers."

I looked up the half mile of Priory Lane to the turn; there was a grove of beeches there, and I tried to follow the line of road from the trees to the village. But it was raining harder now, a steady, gray, slanting curtain of rain, and so the road into the village could have had an army on it and me no more the wiser.

"No company," Andrew said. "But he is for the Priory, that is certain."

Which meant that he had turned into Priory Lane. But though, at the end of that half mile of ruts and mud and small, treacherous gullies, I could just make out the beeches at the turn, I could still make out no rider.

Andrew might have been reading my thoughts. "He is behind the trees," he said. "And his mount all but spent. An 'twere I, I should be walking her."

It was a slow minute before the rider emerged from among the trees. I was thinking, as I watched him, that Andrew had indeed been right about the horse; it was plodding forward in the way of a horse that has been ridden not hard but steadily, its head down until its nose well nigh touched ground, its feet sinking into the mud at each step and then straining and lurching free. Then I was looking at the rider instead of the horse. There was something vaguely familiar about the way he sat his mount; I have seen weary riders, riders who have ridden from dawn to dusk, sit a horse that way, and I have seen wounded men ride off a battlefield that way. And I have also, I thought, I have also—

Andrew interrupted the half-formed thought. His curse was soft and indistinguishable, for it was muttered between his teeth, but there was the sound of relief in it. "We have wasted our morning, Master John," he said. "Our rider is your brother. It is My Lord Henry."

He rode up the long lane on the spent mare, sitting his horse in that slouch which Nicholas Armitage, my father's master of the horse, had never been able to cure him of, a short, thickish man with full red lips and a blond beard that could not hide the long, puckered scar, from temple to chin, which he wore in memory of Worcester. For a moment, coming through the overcast, he was looking down at us with a kind of weary but amused arrogance, and then he was swinging stiffly out of the saddle, the scar livid in the gray light as he turned his left cheek to me. He yet dismounted a horse as awkwardly as he sat one, and when he found his feet and looked up at me, it was with the cold and insolent blue eyes that brought to mind our boyhood together.

"Well, John," he said.

"In God's name," I said, "what brings you from Bedfordshire?"

"Why?" he said. "Am I not welcome then, brother?"

"You are welcome," I said briefly.

He looked shrewdly at me. Then he laughed. "You were ever a poor hand at dissembling, John."

"Nay," I protested, though without, I fear, overmuch conviction,

26

"it was only that Andrew and I could have been spared a deal of exertion had we but known it was you. We have buried eighty stone of beef beneath the mews since we sighted you on Workhouse Lane. And our mother even now scrubbing down a bloodied meat block."

"Ah," he said. "So ye have even slain the fatted calf for the prodigal." He looked at Andrew. "Well, Andrew," he said, "have we a groom left on the place? The mare has been ridden steadily for four days."

"I will see to her myself, M'lord," Andrew said.

"And fetch my saddlebags into the Priory. I am carrying a sight draft against a London goldsmith for a thousand pounds. And a brace of pistols."

"Pistols?" I said. "And you wear a sword? And you claim a mount? In Reigate they will scarce permit us the liberty of a fowling piece. Bedfordshire must be kinder to royalists than Surrey, Henry."

He was smiling at me, but not in amusement. "A man learns to live with them," he said. "Shall we announce my arrival? Take our mother away from her ablution?"

His tone was mocking now, and his lip curled, and his nostrils pinched and white, and I wondered if just once I could refrain from quarreling with him within an hour of his arrival. "She will be in the kitchen," I said. "It will be shorter if we enter through the scullery."

"No apologies, brother," he said. "I have entered a deal of houses through the scullery since '49. I am a man has learned the vanity of pride. Pride in these times is a luxury to be afforded only by unlettered Anabaptists."

"So I am given to understand," I said. "Though it is a lesson I am still learning. But I was ever slower at my lessons than you."

They had worked a miracle in the kitchen. Miss Agnes was still at the dresser with basin and brush, but the meat block was scrubbed white, and the hearth raked clean, and the floor without trace of meat scraps, and my mother was sprinkling lilac water about as I came into the scullery doorway.

"There is no longer need, Mother," I said. "The rider was Henry."

"Henry?" she said. "Henry?" And then my brother brushed past me and was standing before her, one hand fumbling at the buttons to his cloak, a puddle of water forming beneath his muddied boots.

27

"I am glad to see you are in health, Mother," he said, and his voice may not have been gentle but at least it was no longer mocking.

"Henry," she said. "What brings you—"

"Business," he said. "What else on roads as foul as betwixt here and Guildford?"

"Guildford?" I said. "Do you come from Turvey by way of Guildford these days, Henry?"

"I had business at Guildford," he said briefly. He crossed the flagstones and laid his dripping cloak atop the meat block, along with his belt and the long, old-fashioned, Cavalier blade and scabbard he had inherited from my father. He did not look at us the while— not until, free of his accouterments, he strode to the hearth and turned and faced us, his feet wide apart, short and blond and stocky and as arrogant as a French rapier. "Ah," he said, "it is good to come home again. It is good to ride into the bosom of the family, over forty leagues of the foulest roads in Christendom, and be welcomed without stint or reservation. It fills a man's heart."

"You are welcome, Henry," my mother said quietly. "You need not question that."

He laughed. "Question it, Mother? Question it, when your joy is stamped on your very faces? I do not question it."

"Henry," I said sharply, "Henry, we do not require—"

His eyes drifted to me, and the curl was to his lip again. "Pray you, brother," he said, and his voice like silk, "pray you, do not interrupt a man when he is counting his blessings. The prodigal has returned, and they have slain the fatted calf for him, and I require but one more thing for my cup to run over. Which is for Miss Agnes there to face me full and favor me with one of her rare smiles."

At the dresser, Miss Agnes set down the basin and turned. But there was no smile on that thin, sharp, pious, disapproving face. "I meant no offense, My Lord Henry," she said. "I was but doing what I had been ordered. I was set to scour down—"

"There, now," Henry said. "And is her smile not radiant?"

"Henry," I said, "Henry, I will not abide—"

"Ah," he said. "My brother will not abide. And has the coxcomb then grown since we last set eyes on each other?"

"Aye," I said. "I have added an inch or so to my stature, Henry."

"Why, give me leave to congratulate you," he said, and then he lidded his eyes, and his smile faded, and his voice was no longer like a hot knife pressed to butter. "Nay," he said. "Nay. I am sorry. I did not come to Reigate this time to quarrel."

"No," I said dryly. "You came on business. As you did two years ago."

"John," he said softly, "it was an action I would I had opportunity to do over, for I am ashamed of it. But is it not past? Can we not forget it?"

"Why, easily," I said. "It was but a small matter of a son bringing a lawsuit against his own mother. A mere trifle and of no more importance than a touch of the French disease."

"The Priory," he said, "was part of the Peterborough estates."

"The Priory," I said, "was willed to my mother."

"There were extenuating circumstances. Had—"

"There were indeed. My Lord Monson had made you an offer for the Priory. True, it was not yours to sell, and true, it was but two thousand pounds for two hundred very fair acres—"

"That is scarce fair," he burst out. "You know it is not, John. The Committee for Sequestration had given me but three months to raise the fine against Turvey. And half the royalists in England were throwing land on the market that spring, and estates in the north were going for a shilling an acre, and not even the usurers in London willing to advance money on Turvey, and only Reigate—" He broke off and dropped his eyes. "I was wrong," he said. "I admit to it. It was the action of a scoundrel. But I was desperate, and I begged your forgiveness once—"

"Very well," I said, for he spoke the truth and these no times to be casting stones at a man's motives. For I might have acted the same way had Turvey been mine and I fresh from abroad with a price on my head and all I owned in the world to go on the auction block unless I fell to desperate measures. "Very well," I said. "You stand forgiven, and let us leave off quarreling. And what is it ye require of us this time?"

His head was down now, and he was kicking idly at a rough stone on the hearth. He was two years my elder, he was in his thirtieth year, but just now he looked like a street urchin who had been caught with his hand at the purse thong. Then he raised his head, and the light in the kitchen was bad and the distance to the hearth a pretty one. But I could yet make out the sweat on his forehead. "How much money can ye lay hands to, John?" he said.

I shrugged. "I know not. Perhaps a hundred pounds."

"A hundred?" he said. "No more? An the case were desperate, could ye not—"

I stared him through the gray light. "Why, Henry?"

His eyes held mine for the length of a pair of heartbeats. Then they wavered. "There have been plots discovered in the north. Silly schemes, spun in taverns by fools in their cups."

"This is no news," I said. "Mr. Secretary Thurloe discovers one such weekly, and the Protector issues a proclamation each Monday protesting that in his infinite goodness, mercy, and patience, he will not hang the ingrates but only relieve them of food for their bellies—"

"There have been plots discovered," he said. "And I stand accused."

"Accused?" I echoed. "Accused? *You* stand accused, Henry?"

"I do not blame them," he said. "They have little else left them, God knows, what with their land sold to meet their compositions, and laws passed against all the old pleasures, and nought to while away the time save only to sit in taverns and spin idle dreams. Of a sudden and universal rising which will bring Charles Stuart back—"

"And have you ridden from Turvey," I said, very softly, "only to confess that you have no more wit than to get drunk in a Bedford tavern and—"

"Nay," he said. "That was not the way of it. I have lain quiet since Worcester. It was a groom of mine. A fellow I horsewhipped a month since for insolence. He hath borne false witness against me, carried a tale to Colonel Butler—"

"A groom?" I said. "False witness? And can ye not confront a groom, then? Can ye not face him down with the truth?"

"You are no unbreeched boy, John," he said. "You know it is foolishness you are speaking."

And he had me there, I thought, he had me there. For it is as out of fashion these days for a man to be permitted the luxury of confronting his accuser as it is for him to be tried by a jury of his peers. Aye, I thought, you have me upon the hip there, Henry, for Colonel Butler is the law in Bedfordshire, and the bastards will not rest content until they have their hands on the last inch of royalist land. "So they have taken the fellow's word," I said. "And now there lies a further fine on Turvey."

"Six hundred pounds," he said. "Atop the seventeen hundred now due against the Worcester composition. And I can lay hands on no more than a thousand of it."

I looked a little longer into his pinched look. Then I turned a shoulder to him. "I am sorry, Henry," I said. "Truly. But if you have ridden forty leagues for anything save our sympathy, I fear you have reined your horse into the wrong stable and taken bed in the wrong inn."

"You could raise it," he said. "On the Priory."

"Why, yes. I could also suffer a conversion to Quakerism. Or slit my throat. Or sit in the Swan and spin plots against the Protector, with half those about me paid agents of John Thurloe."

"You could raise it," he repeated. "On the Priory." Only he was no longer speaking to me. For now he was looking full at my mother, standing at the dresser, with one hand lying white and frail as tissue against the block, and her eyes on Henry's, and no expression at all in her face. My mother's face is one which lends itself to quick and easy expression, for the flesh on the bone is scant and the skin drawn back tight to create hollowed shadows in her cheeks, and her lips are full and mobile, and her eyes large. But there was no expression on her face now. It is as if she had spent all her emotion another time, another place, I thought, and now no reserve left to draw on. It is as if somewhere in her past—perhaps on that day in '48 when My Lord Monson led his Roundhead dragoons to her door and carted off her hangings and plate and fine furniture for his own use; or on that day in '51, when Henry (in flight for France) lay hidden under the mews, the wound on his cheek still blood-crusted, while another Roundhead troop searched the Priory and cut down our fruit trees for firewood and slaughtered our last cattle and laid axes to paneling and windows; or on that day when she sat in a Guildford courtroom and heard her eldest son lay claim to lands deeded her —it was as if on all those other occasions she had spent freely of her emotions, drawing on her capital as well as her interest, and now, the capital exhausted, now, facing Henry, no further reserve of anger or terror or outrage or bewilderment or sorrow, no more water in the well, no more salted beef in the barrels or hams in

31

the smokehouse, no more preserves in the stillroom or dried fruits hanging from the kitchen rafters.

She stood there thus, and Henry's eyes on her. And he said again, softly, "You could raise it. On the Priory."

She made a small gesture, helpless and sad and unfinished, with one hand, the free one. But she did not say anything.

He leaned toward her, and his voice was like silk. But his eyes were not. His eyes were like a lawyer's eyes, with the witness in the box, and the last answer lying heavy in the silence, and the smell of perjury in the courtroom. "I have tried every other recourse," he said. "I swear I have. And in Guildford they will advance thirteen hundred on the Priory. And it is not for John to say. For the Priory is yours, Mother."

She looked at me. I have never seen a person drowning, but I think I know how their eyes must look. "He is my son, John," she said. "He is your brother and my son, and what say you?"

"Nought," I said. "For he is your son."

"I pray you, John, make me direct answer."

"Very well," I said, and if my voice was petulant, it was because I knew that no answer of mine would make any difference. For Henry was her son. "Very well. I think he has no right to ask it of you. And I think you are a fool if you listen to him."

"No right?" Henry burst out. "No right? Turvey hath been Mordaunt land since the Crusades—"

"If it had been in the family since Adam, ye still have no right. Reigate brings in scarce three hundred a year, and it can bear no mort—"

"Ye need have no fear on that score. I will see to it that they do not foreclose."

"And how will you, pray, if they take a mind to slap another composition on you within the twelvemonth?"

"I swear to you," he said, "I will have the money when it comes due. I will strap on pistol and mask and take to the highway afore I will let John Dove fore—"

He broke off. He broke off abruptly, though he was not interrupted. For he knew and I knew that he had committed a blunder. It was not in Henry's nature to blunder, but he had blundered there, and now it was I who leaned, with the witness in the box and the

32

answer lying in the silence of the courtroom and the smell of perjury like a smoldering taper in my nostrils.

"Who?" I said softly. "Who, Henry?"

He made me no answer.

"His name, brother," I said.

Still he did not answer, nor did he offer to meet my eye.

"Damn you, Henry," I said, "if you can come whining to us for our signature to a scrap of paper, you can favor us with an honest answer. Whose name did ye just drop?"

"John Dove's," he said sullenly.

"John Dove?" I repeated. "You would have us mortgage Reigate to John Dove, High Sheriff of Wiltshire and intimate of My Lord Monson? The John Dove whose strongbox already bulges with confiscated royalist lands, and if he cannot come by them for nothing, why, then, he acquires them by foreclosure. Though I fear his price for Reigate is heavier than is his wont. Thirteen hundred pounds for land that would fetch scarce four thousand." I swung about to face my mother. "Is he still your son?" I said.

"I do not understand you, John," she said. "I—"

"Do you not? Why, it is plain as the scar to his cheek. It takes no nose to smell a dead rat in the wainscoting."

"Come, John," Henry said, and his voice was steady again. "Come, ye credit them with overmuch deviousness. If they had a mind to Reigate, they would have seized it—"

"Why, yes, I credit them with deviousness," I said. "For they are devious men. And they have a mind to Reigate. But they have not seized it because I do not make it a habit to sit in the Swan and expound on my politics. And the Priory is my mother's, and my father, ere he had the rare good fortune to contract a fever, was Essex's General of the Ordnance. But put a mortgage in fat John Dove's hands and there will be a breach in the wall that Old Noll and all his saints can march through eight abreast." I broke off and turned a shoulder to him. "But he is in the right," I said. "It is you, Mother, must say him aye or nay."

She made a small, sad, uncertain gesture. "He is my son, John," she said. "As you are my son."

I looked at her another moment. Then I shrugged and turned away.

"I pray you understand, John," she said. "I cannot find it in my heart to see his lands forfeit. Were it you—"

"I understand," I said. "He is your son, and so we will mortgage Reigate to save Turvey," and I smiled at Henry, though I doubt there was much humor in the curl of my lip. "I trust," I said, "that you will make us welcome at Turvey as we have made you welcome at Reigate, brother."

"Why, yes," he said. "Whenever you choose to travel that way, John."

"We will choose. And before we see another spring. Mark me, brother, for I am a prophet."

He laughed lightly. "Forewarned is forearmed, John."

"Meanwhile," I said, "one favor of you, brother. I would borrow your mare. For I prefer riding to walking when I go up to London."

That brought a frown. "You are planning to go up to London?"

"I am. I intend to present myself at Goldsmiths' Hall in your place."

"Come," he said. "Come, John, there is no need—"

"There is need. Since London crawls with Thurloe agents. Since you are a marked man now. Since, as I have said, it is not my habit to idle in taverns and chatter empty politics."

"Nor is it mine," he said curtly. "Though I can count thrice within the hour that you have tried to give me the lie in that respect." He regarded me another moment through narrowed eyes and then shrugged. "Very well," he said. "If you prefer it thus."

"I prefer it thus."

He shrugged again. "It may be common sense at that. Now that I think on it." He smiled, and the smile could have been almost warm had it not been for the trifle of the eyes above it. "I suggest ye take lodging at the Belle Savage. On Ludgate Hill. You will find the sack there unwatered, and the beef pie not palpable mutton, and the linen clean."

"And the host, no doubt, a loyal Englishman."

And now he grinned. "Now that you mention it," he said, "I believe he hath been known to drink a toast to Charles Stuart."

⊰ *Three* ⊱

It was a fortnight later and mid-May before I set out for London. For Henry's business at Guildford required a week; and on his return I must obtain travel permits, since these were Commonwealth days and no man permitted to travel above five miles from home without written leave from the authorities. So all one afternoon I stood before thin-lipped, sad-eyed John Beauchamp, justice of the peace, arguing that a man with two thousand pounds of Commonwealth money in his saddlebags should be permitted to ride armed the score of miles to London. And by the time the pass was drawn, it was Saturday and the journey again postponed. For under the rule of the saints, no man in England traveled a foot abroad on the Sabbath save to attend divine service; I have known men who but went to fetch a midwife or lend a hand with a neighbor's fire and who were flogged for it.

I set out on a morning which would have conspired against even the dank, thin spirit of an Edinburgh Calvinist, with the sun coming up angrily and then looking down upon the earth and finding it good, and clouds like tufts of batting flung against one of my mother's blue coverlets, and the fragrance of double white violets in the Priory lane. It was a morning for the planting of maypoles in Earlswood Common, or for the begetting of a man's first-born, or for the breeching of a son, or for the overthrow of tyrannies, and I felt my heart in me as light as the lilt of an old song. For I was

35

starting off for London for the first time in half a decade, astride a blooded mare and with a sword to my side and pistols in my saddlebags and ten pounds in my purse.

It was the week of the annual cattle fair in Reigate, and when I rode into the village, the market place was already a tangle of herds of swine and cattle, and carts loaded high with grain, and red-faced countrymen in russet doublets and leather breeches and steeple hats with greasy brims and hobnailed shoes. In the innyard of the Red Lion, a dozen horses were already tethered, with Walsingham Heathfeild among them. He waved cheerily when he caught sight of me, and I waved back and stopped in the gateway.

"Ah," he said, his gray eyes narrowed with interest on the mare. " 'Tis a fine mount, Master John. She should fetch a good price."

"She is not mine to sell," I said. "She is Henry's mare."

"A pity. I am short on post horses, I would ha' ventured a bid myself. The rumor is true, then, that ye are for London this week."

"The village is small," I said. "And John Beauchamp's wife possessed of a most ingenious engine. A tongue fastened in the middle and loose at either end."

He smiled. Then his eyes sobered. "Looser than ye know. The talk is, you are carrying above two thousand pounds in those saddlebags. If so, I should ride with one hand to my sword, lad."

"I had so intended. Though a highwayman would have his troubles spending it, since all but ten pounds is in sight drafts against Edward Blackwell's running cash. A fact ye might publish at your ordinary this morning, Walsingham." I glanced at the horses tethered at his innyard rail. "You look to do well this year, an that be any test."

He spat. "Eight of the lot are badgers from beyond Betchworth, and closer fisted than a Belfast weaver. And four are down from London, and ye can lay the Priory against John Lyfe's dungheap they will go back with ten times what they fetch."

I looked again to the line of horses. Five hours yet to the opening of the fair, I thought, and already My Lord Protector's taxgatherers were descended on us like locusts for their one bushel of wheat in ten, their one cow in twenty. And that in a town which a decade ago mustered a militia rather than pay King Charles his sixty pounds ship money. "It is the price we pay for liberty," I said. "And ye had best erase that black look, friend malignant, else they will re-

36

turn home with more than you bargain for. If they have not yet a fine for surliness, they can quickly invent one."

He grinned. " 'Tis a look I reserve for a Mordaunt. Before them I am all smiles and bows," and then the grin faded and he looked at me as only a man can look who has shared with you lost causes and lost estates. "God speed you on your journey, John," he said.

"Why, thank you, Walsingham," I said, and felt a soft, quick rush of emotion, for Walsingham Heathfeild was my friend.

"And look to it," he said, "that ye keep a close mouth over your cup of sack. 'Tis said that one in three in London is a Thurloe man. And no wenching. The price for consorting with Southwark sluts is higher than a touch of the French pox these days."

"I will heed that advice, too," I said. "If for no other reason than that the Mordaunt estates cannot this year bear the outlay of another two shillings."

The Crossways is the main street in Reigate, and of an ordinary Monday morning it is a sleepy street in a sleepy village, with nought the full length of the street save a few swine rooting contentedly in the mud before New Market, and Nick Castlemaine emerging tousled and sleepy-eyed from the innyard of the White Hart with a bucket of mash to improve the public footing and lend interest to the eternal smells of dung and moldy hay. But this morning the street was a tangle of grunting swine and bawling cattle and cursing drovers and badgers. At New Market I shouldered rudely through a knot of men and beasts, collecting black looks as I passed. At Blatt's Barn was another crowd, Quakers this time with plain gray suits and black, steeple-crowned Dutch felts and sad, dour faces, gathered to hear Edward Hubbard preach on the iniquity of the times and the dark countenance of Almighty God. And at the Island, where the street is scarce a yard wide, the way was blocked solidly, with a herd of cattle choking one lane and a two-wheeled cart choking the other, and behind each a clot of pushing, cursing, sweating folk, and I must needs stand aside until the cart on one side and the cattle on the other exploded out this end like a ball out of a musket.

In Pudding Lane the going was easier; the Lane was as ruinous as always, with ruts knee-deep and the ditches unscoured and stinking, but the way was near empty of travelers. Indeed, the only hazard was the eternal dungheap before the lean-to abode of John

Lyfe, the town scavenger; skirting it, my fingers to my nose, I noted that it was above eye level, which meant that again this year Thomas Luck would lodge a complaint against John Lyfe in the morrow's court of piepowder and Lyfe would forfeit his annual ten shillings.

Then I was out of the village and onto the Dorking Road. Off to the right I could see the line of hills, their crowns hazy in the morning light, and below the hills the great stretch of open land which was the village commons. Looking across that fair expanse of land, I felt a brief flare of anger such as I had known back at the Red Lion, for it was scarce a twelvemonth since Lord Monson had sold all the timber on the town commons to London shipbuilders. But it was too fair a day for bitterness. Far to the south, the heather on Reigate Heath was in bloom, a purple cloud as soft and hazy as the edge of a feather; and to the north the copses of oak dotted the Downs a wet green; and everywhere you looked the wild flowers were in bloom. As I mounted Henry's mare, a magpie off in the gorse set up a scolding, and the other side of the ditch, a fat and impudent robin eyed me with eyes as sharp as broken glass. Sitting there on the mare, the sun so warm I knew I would be shedding my cloak within the hour, I felt the bitterness wash out of me in a soft rush, and I thought that even in the teeth of saints and tyranny and mouthing hypocrisy and affected, downcast gloom, a man must needs love this land of his, this England, if the month be May. So I took me one more look at Master pert and saucy Robin, and then I flicked the mare's reins. If the roads were no worse than I hoped, I would be the six miles to Dorking by noon, and from there to Southwark the road was chalk, and if I had no trouble with the watch at Leatherhead, I would be in London by nightfall.

The coach was a mile this side of Dorking. It was a light caroche, fitter for a cobbled London street than for Surrey clay, and it was most satisfactorily mired in a pothole the size of a garden fishpond. When I came upon it, its four horses were standing quiet, heads hanging, foam from lip to flank and buttocks still quivering from the recent touch of the whip; and behind the coach a thick-shouldered fellow, very pretty in crimson coat and fawn breeches, knee-deep in the mud, his eyes sadly on the rear wheels.

I was abreast the lead horse when the door was flung open and the passenger within showed herself. I had a fleeting impression of an oval face and red-gold curls beneath a great hood before the face was withdrawn. Then I drew rein before the open door and looked down at her.

"You, there," she said.

My first thought was to wonder how much the red of her nether lip owed to nature and how much to some London chemist. My second was that London chemist or no, I had only twice or thrice in my life laid eyes on a fairer face.

"You, there," she said again. "I am for Reigate and my coach mired."

There was some doubt about the color of her eyes, whether gray or green, but there was none about her voice. Her voice proclaimed her a great lady down from London, and I some servingman in his master's cast-off and mud-spattered buff suit and four-year-old hat, on his way to Dorking aboard his master's mare. I looked down into the interior of the coach, with her wedged into one corner and a great pile of luggage—portmanteaux and hatboxes and baskets of food—wedged in the other; and some humor in me made me choose to play out the role she had assigned me.

"Is't so?" I said.

"Have you no eyes in your head?" she snapped.

My eyes drifted to the back wheels. The hubs were out of sight in the mud. "Why, so it is," I said. "Had I taken the time to make a study on it, I little doubt I should have arrived at a similar conclusion."

"Well," she said, "think you you could leave off the staring and lend my coachman a hand?"

My eyes took rest on the patch aside her mouth. It was a tiny star, and very pretty beside the dimple. "Aye," I said. "If I had the stomach for mud to my thighs. And if I thought 'twould be to any purpose."

" 'Tis a light coach. I judge Robert to be something stouter in the beam than you, but on dry land he can lift it alone."

"Doubtless. But dry land is not Weald clay, my lady."

And now the red of her nether lip owed less, I wagered, to a 'pothecary's pot purchased for half a sovereign in the Strand than it did to the small, sharp teeth she set into it. "Look ye, fellow," she said, "an it be a matter of a shilling—"

39

"I find that a sore temptation," I said. "A shilling will pay my score at a London tavern this night, and a penny left over for bed and mount. But it would be vanity to put my back to those wheels. I would as soon set my will against quicksand."

"Damn," she said, under her breath.

"If you would have the kindness to specify what, I would doubtless agree, my lady."

"Damn your vile roads," she said.

I nodded gravely. "I can name you a score would echo that sentiment. Though we have a saying in these parts. What is worse for the rider is best for the abider."

"And damn you," she said, "for a thick-headed, obstinate, impudent country lout."

"And amen to that, too. Though I have the mother's sense to know that it would require planks and more men than two and fresher horses than yours to set you on your way again."

"And have ye the sense, too, to advise me what I should do, then?"

"Why, you might sit here till summer. The road is sometimes passable by mid-July."

I decided that her eyes were a gray, though a smoky one. "You are not only loutish," she said. "You are to boot one of the most insolent rogues I have had the ill grace to meet with this twelvemonth. I have a mind to order my man to give you a taste of the whip."

My eyes strayed to her coachman. He had by now come up out of the mud and was leaning against the left rear wheel, with his back to me and his eyes fastened on the indistinct line of sky off toward Dorking Town. "I would not advise it, my lady," I said quietly. "I have no great proficiency with this blade I wear, but I will still match it against a coach whip." I grinned down into her eyes, and I was finding it pleasant to repay her in the coin she had herself struck off. But I felt no anger. She had called me fellow and lout and had made me offer of a shilling, but looking down at her, I was only wondering if the form muffled in that cloak was as fair as the face above it. "You could also return to Dorking," I said. "You can obtain post horses of John Drury at the Chequers. The road is passable a-horseback."

"Well!" she said. "'Tis the first civil comment you have been guilty of this quarter hour. Now pray advise me further, young sir. How think you I should manage the mile back to Dorking?"

There was only a trace of a curl left in her lip now, but I did not miss the emphasis she gave the *sir*, and I dropped my eyes as insolently as her tone to the hem of her cloak. "I will hazard a guess," I said, "that you are made like the rest of us. With two good legs and feet soundly attached."

And now her lip lost the last trace of curl. "And now you are uncivil again, sir," she said, and no insolence left in the sir, neither. "I am but ill equipped for a walk. I am wearing these," and she lifted her skirts an inch and thrust toward me a foot shod in boots no more practical for walking a spring road than dancing slippers. "And this," she said, and undid the great silver button at her throat and parted the cloak for me to see the gown beneath, green taffeta and cut most immodestly low. "Now am I, sir?" she said, and her eyes wide and innocent and the clear and liquid gray of a willow pool at sundown, and her nether lip a pretty pout.

"So you are not," I said. "And were I a great lady and traveling down from London, I should have provided properly against the journey. I should have worn a good riding habit, high in the neck for warmth and Quaker-plain for the mud, and a safeguard over it, and stout riding boots, and splatterdashes with buckles. But then, I am no great lady. I have nought save a country fellow's common sense to guide me."

She shook her head. "I have newly revised that judgment. You are no country fellow. For all that your boots are too square in the toe, and your suit has seen better days, and your hat without feather or ribbon." She dropped her eyes to her hands resting in her lap. "I was advised," she said, her voice humble now and plaintive, "that it was but twenty miles to Reigate and the roads firm."

"By whom?" I said. "Some great traveler who this very week accomplished the journey from St. Paul's to the Southwark side of London Bridge?" I looked down at the crown of her hood, for her head was lowered now. "If you have nought save frills and frumperies in that portmanteau," I said, something more gently, "if you have no sensible habit or boots, then instruct your coachman to unhitch that left lead. He looks as if he had the spirit to carry you a mile. Leave the coachman to stand watch on your baggage. If you will, I will ride with you into Dorking."

41

"I have no saddle, neither. And I am at best an indifferent horse-woman."

I sighed, for it was yet eighteen miles to London, and the sun almost overhead, and it would be a slow mile to Dorking if I doubled the burden of Henry's mare. "Very well," I said, and cursed myself for a fool as I said it. "Very well. I am for Dorking. I will share my mount with you."

She lifted her head, and now her eyes were studying not my rough attire but the lineaments of my face. "I thank you for the offer," she said. "But we are strangers and this a lonely road," and her eyes fell again.

"As for that," I said, "I am John Mordaunt of Reigate, and you will come to no harm."

"Mordaunt," she said, and frowned. "Mordaunt. I have met a Mordaunt. A short, fair man with a great scar to his left cheek."

"That would be Henry. He is my brother."

"A notorious malignant," she said. "It is the gossip in London that he hath but recently been taken in another wicked plot against the government."

"So he has," I said.

She still studied my face. "You are not alike. He is short and fair. You are tall and darker."

"He favors my father, I, my mother."

"And tell me, John Mordaunt, do you favor your father's politics or your brother's?"

"My own," I said shortly. "If it hath bearing on the mile back to Dorking."

"Great bearing," she said. "I have been warned that malignants are ungodly men and not to be trusted by maids on lonely roads, and what are these politics which are your own, John Mordaunt?"

"To collect my few rents," I said, "and see to the comfort of my mother, and keep a close watch on my tongue when I meet with strangers, and now permit me to take my leave of you," and I touched my hat and straightened in the saddle and flicked the mare's reins.

"Nay," she called out. "I pray you, nay, sir."

If I drew rein, it was only to let the mare find surer footing. My back was straight in the saddle and my eyes firmly on the road, and I was thinking that she had called me fellow and lout, and had of-

42

fered me a shilling to wallow in the mud and set my back to the
wheel of her coach, and I had been amused. But now I was not
amused. Now, for all the patch to her cheek and the paint to her
lips, she had betrayed herself as one of your saints, and so I was resolved that if she were to accomplish the mile back to Dorking, it
would be through no fault of mine.

"Nay," she called out. "If I have given offense, but— Nay, sir,
have the goodness to draw rein an instant and look at me."

I did so. She was leaning far out the coach, and her cloak had
parted, and for all my anger, I must confess that the form below did
no shame to the face above.

"Look ye, sir," she said, "if I have in anything given offense, I protest I had no such intent."

"No offense," I said. " 'Tis merely that it is, as you observe, a
lonely road, and my brother one of your malignants, and that gown
sufficient to tempt John Calvin himself, and you wiser to walk the
mile to Dorking."

"I swear," she said, "I had no intent to impute ought save honor to
your character. Though surely you cannot hold caution against a
maid."

"No," I said. "Not caution."

"What, then? But tell me how I have given cause—"

"No cause," I said. "If you lack the stomach for a short walk, you
were wise to wait here for a parson to come along. It should be no
longer than a day or two, for Quakers abound in these parts."

"I think I prefer the company of a Mordaunt."

"As to that, you have but my word on it. For all you know, I may
be the devil himself in the guise of Prince Rupert."

"You have neither the years nor the face for that role. Your face is
an honest one, I think."

"Fair face can hide false heart. Did your tutor never give you
that to write in your copy book?"

But there was no longer heat in my words, and when she smiled
across five yards of rut and mire, I could not help but smile back.

"Come," she said. "An I can find it in my heart to swallow my
pride, surely you can find in yours a little charity."

"Very well," I said, and reined the mare about. "Very well, I shall
share my mount with you. But on one condition."

"And that?"

"That we have no more talk of politics."

"Ah," she said. "So that is where the saddle galls."

" 'Twould gall you in the same spot, were you for London with a fortune to put into the hands of the rogues at Goldsmiths' Hall."

"Ah," she said. "So you *are* a malignant."

"Not I. My brother. But they are some of them my pounds."

She held out her hands, and I dismounted and put my two hands to her waist and swung her up into the saddle. She looked down at me and smiled a demure smile. "You are somewhat free with your hands," she said. "For a gentleman."

"You have a child's waist," I said. "But you still weigh eight stone. And 'tis a pretty trick in this footing to swing you from boot to saddle." I clambered up behind her. "Henry has a groom with a way with animals. But even his horses require a hand to the reins."

She was smiling at me over her shoulder. "And the moral of that observation, sir?"

"I shall have to reach about you. I hope it will give you no offense."

"If it does," she said, "I shall feel free to speak to you of it," and then she looked to her coachman. "Robert," she said, and he turned and looked up at us with dull, black, puzzled eyes. "You are to stand guard on the coach," she said. "There will be someone along before sundown to fetch it back to Dorking. Do ye understand, Robert?"

"Aye, m'lady," he said, and ducked his head and touched his forelock.

"He is Irish," she said, "and not overbright. But loyal. Were no one to come for the coach before Friday a week, you would still find him standing exactly there."

" 'Tis a quality to be admired," I said. "Had I the choosing, I should prefer loyalty to wit." I permitted myself another long look at the line of her cheek against the line of the hood, and then I reached about her for the reins. She took that briefly into consideration and then settled back into the crook of my right arm, and we set off for Dorking.

In silence at first, for the footing was treacherous and I with my mind on guiding the mare across the road. And when the footing was surer, my tongue was still thick and my wits as foggy as her coachman's, for there was first the matter of the five years since I

44

had been within hailing distance of a pretty face, and there was second the matter of our separate persuasions. So it was she who broke the silence first.

"Art ever so silent?" she said.

"Aye," I said. "In the company of strangers. It is a habit the Mordaunts have acquired since Worcester."

"And are we yet strangers, then?"

"And in the company of pretty ladies. Just down from London and accustomed to the conversation of wittier men than I." I eased the mare around a pothole. "If ye have a mind for small talk, what would ye talk on that is not political?"

She glanced archly at me. "Shall we commence with your thoughts?"

"I think not. You might find them cause for offense."

She was still looking at me, her eyes demure and the start of a smile to her lips. "Let me be the judge of that."

"Why, then," I said, "I was thinking that it hath been five years since I was this distance from any woman save only our cook, who is most abominably fat, and my mother, who dresses like a London merchant's wife, and my aunt, who dresses the same and hath the look of piety to accompany it."

"I find the thought no great cause for offense," she said. "Though it might lead in that direction. And so I would think on something else, were I you."

"And so I was. For I was thinking on Mordaunt luck."

"And what of that, pray?"

"Why, it is the luck of a Mordaunt, that the first pretty face he hath laid eyes on in five years should belong to one of your persuasions."

Her eyes were no longer demure and she no more smiled. "That brings us about to politics again, does it not? And I have made you a bargain."

"I release you from it," I said shortly. "For I can think of nothing else to talk on."

"Very well," she said. "And what think you are my persuasions, Master Mordaunt?"

"But a quarter hour since, you delivered yourself of certain opinions on malignants. I would guess, then, that you are one of your Puritans."

45

"I suppose I am. If to believe in God make one a Puritan, why, then, I am one of your Puritans."

"It is no true test," I said. "King Charles himself believed in God, and his son after him. Though you may have been instructed to the contrary."

"And if not to countenance blasphemous oaths, nor ribald jests, nor drunkenness and adultery and fornication, nor all such pagan idleness as mummery and maypoles be Puritan, why, then, I am one of your Puritans."

"Nor are we so far apart there as you might think," I said. "Though my list might prove something shorter than yours."

"And if not to hold with bowing and scraping and suchlike popish idolatries and superstitions be Puritan, then I am one of your Puritans."

"I am no papist, neither," I said. "Though the present government would have it so, for I believe that a man should observe the common decencies of worship."

"And what are those, Master Mordaunt?"

"Why, that the fitting posture of a man before God were on his knees. And that a minister of God should look and speak the part, and not enter the pulpit in leather jerkin and hobnailed boots like some Northfield blacksmith fresh from his trade. And that having in one's possession a Book of Common Prayer should constitute no hanging matter."

"You do not hold with liberty of conscience, then?"

She did not look at me when she put that question. "I had expected we should come about to that ere we had done with this," I said.

"And you do not?"

"Why, aye," I said. "I hold with the concept most devoutly. 'Tis a noble one and worthy of such as the Protector. Liberty of conscience is the privilege granted a troop of Butler's dragoons to ride about London with their breeches down, wiping their arses on leaves torn from the Book of Common Prayer; it is also the privilege denied the rest of us to be joined in wedlock by any save some rude justice of the peace chosen for his art in rolling his eyes. Liberty of conscience is the right of a Quaker to run stark-naked through the public streets, and of unlettered Anabaptist weavers and Fifth Monarchy cobblers to interpret Scripture to the rest of us. Liberty of conscience is the forming of Committees for the Ejection of Scandalous and Insufficient Ministers, where canting pedlars and unwashed draymen can sit in judgment on their betters, and any man who dares say them nay labeled an Arminian rogue and relieved of his estates. Liberty of—"

And now she was looking at me, and full in the face. "I think we had best have done with this topic, sir," she said.

"Why, have it so. It was no topic of my choosing, and I fool for pursuing it. For I could be hanged for those sentiments."

"I shall not betray you," she said softly. "But I find the subject a dangerous one, and I think we should choose another."

"Agreed. And shall we talk of you, then?"

"And what of me? I am a dull subject at best."

"No puzzle is dull, my lady."

"La," she said. "Am I a puzzle?"

"I find you so. For you are the first saint I have met with to put patches to your cheek and paint to your lips."

She laughed. "Patching and painting are all the fashion this year. I have seen My Lady Lambert herself appear in St. Paul's with her face nigh hidden by stars and crescents and squares and circles, and I have watched her sit through a morning sermon in condemnation of the practice."

"Perhaps she hath more need than you to improve on nature."

"La," she said. "Were this London, I would swear you were a wit for that, sir."

"And the gown," I said. "Is it also in fashion? In London this year?"

She looked archly over a shoulder at me. " 'Tis overmodest. I have seen great ladies appear in public this season as naked to the waist as a whore being whipped behind the cart along Ludgate Street. There have been changes in London since you were last up, Master Mordaunt."

"So it would appear," I said, and then we fell silent again, and so we rode into Dorking Town. At the Chequers I dismounted and lifted her down.

"But give my name to John Drury," I said. "He is honest, he will charge you fair to fetch your coach and provide you post horse to Reigate. Provided only that you do not betray your politics to him."

"Tell me," she said, "are all the innkeepers in England king's men?"

47

"I would not know," I said shortly. "I have not been in all of England."

Another moment she studied me gravely, and then she smiled. "I thank you, John Mordaunt," she said. "And I am most sincerely sorry."

"For what?"

"For calling you lout and fellow."

"No need for sorrow there. For so I am."

My hands were still at her waist, and she was looking up into my face with those grave, gray eyes. "Nay," she said. "You are none of your London fops, all frizzled hair and perfume and simpering talk and mincing walk. But ye are none of your country fellows neither, all stink of stables and talk of crops." She dropped her eyes. "I am sorry, too, for the offer of a shilling."

"Do not be," I said. "For had it been to any purpose, I would doubtless have done your bidding and pocketed it and no shame."

"You jest with me."

"Do I?" I said.

"Do you not?"

"I will answer you thus," I said. "I am second son, and no fortune, and little prospect of one, for I doubt that my brother will have the kindness to die without male issue. Or, if he does, that the present government proposes to leave a foot of Peterborough land free for the bequeathing." I turned from her and swung into the saddle. "I do not jest," I said. "I am brother to a malignant. And as Henry recently put it, pride in these days is a luxury to be afforded only by an unlettered Anabaptist."

I sat there like that a moment, the silence between us, lounging a trifle in the saddle and the smile that was no smile to my lips, and the thought behind the smile that it was a pretty distance to London and the sun past its zenith, and yet the thought aside it that I was reluctant to bid her farewell, for she still looked up at me with those wide, grave, gray eyes. "I do not like your persuasions," she said then. "I find you bitter and you smell of sedition. But I like you, John Mordaunt."

"And I you," I said. "Though we have ridden an hour together and you have yet to tell me your name."

"It is Elizabeth Carey. My father is Thomas Carey of Sussex, and my uncle the Earl of Monmouth."

"Ah," I said, and I felt the sudden sickness at the pit of my stomach like a small, sharp blow. "So you are kin to My Lord Monson," I said.

"His grandniece. I am for there now."

"And to the Protector as well."

"A cousin. Though I do not know him overwell. He is a distant man, and much taken up with matters of state."

"So I have heard," I said shortly.

Now she was frowning up at me again. "And now I have given you offense a second time," she said.

I shook my head. "A man cannot take offense at an accident of birth. But it is still eighteen miles to London and the time past noon."

"Aye," she said, and her voice flat now. "It is."

"But one last word," I said. "Though it is meddling in what is no concern of mine. Were I a maid and for My Lord Monson's, I should remove the patch and paint, and I should don a gown cut somewhat higher in the throat. Otherwise, ye had best steel yourself for an hour's sermon on the wickedness of patching and painting and the evils of nakedness."

She flushed. "Tell me," she said softly, "do you find the patch offensive? Or the gown immodest?"

"Why, no. But I am brother to a malignant and doubtless ungodly."

"And so I shall pay your advice no heed," she said. "For I have sat through longer sermons nor an hour in my day." She laid a hand to the mare's flank; it was almost as if she had a mind to delay me a little longer. "Will you be in London long?"

"But long enough to lay two thousand pounds on the table at Goldsmiths' Hall. If I am in London by nightfall, I shall be returning on Thursday."

"Why, then, we may meet again. I shall be at Reigate a fortnight."

"Some doubt to that," I said dryly. "The Monsons and the Mordaunts are neighbors in name only."

She smiled. "So I have suspected this quarter hour. But I have been known to ride forth of a morning, an the day be fair and the saddle French."

"And I, too. But it is not my habit to ride on Monson land."

She dropped her hand then and stepped back. It was such a

motion as she might have made had I struck her, and I cursed myself for an obstinate fool, for she had spoken me fair and I had returned it with rudeness. "Well," she said, "God speed you up to London, John Mordaunt. And our paths may yet cross again someday."

"They may," I said, "if God be willing and fortune fair," and that was as close as I could bring myself to an apology, and then I pulled the mare about and touched a heel to her flank, and when, a stone's throw down High Street, I turned and looked back, she had disappeared into the innyard of the Chequers.

ᏒᏬ *Four* ᎠᏒ

It is not ten miles from Dorking to Kingston, and I did no dallying along the way but ate in the saddle the cold boiled beef and cheese and bread which Mary had provided against the journey. But at Leatherhead I was delayed by a silly fellow calling himself constable who spelled out my pass with lip and greasy forefinger and then asked me an infinity of questions about where I was from (though it was written plainly on the pass), and how much money in my purse, and where would I be lodging in London, and who was this John Beauchamp who gave me leave to ride with pistol and sword to the endangerment of honest men, and all such questions punctuated with much hemming and hawing and hawking and spitting, together with dire threats to relieve me of my arms, or to have me stocked for a hangdog vagrant, or to have me stripped naked and whipped through the town unless I erased the insolence from out my voice. So it was late afternoon before I sat my horse before a fair Kingston inn bearing the sign of a pawing black stallion. I sat there the space of a quarter hour, breathing my horse, the while I debated whether I should lodge here the night or push on for Wandsworth. If I stopped here, it would be past noon when I reached the Southwark side of London Bridge, for the next eleven miles would be crowded on the morrow with lines of pack horses staggering under herring and malt and grain and wool for the London market, and with farmers' wives herding cattle and pigs and geese into Southwark. But if I fell short of Wandsworth by sundown,

I would be lucky to reach London with my life, let alone my horse and coin. And so, Mordaunt luck being what it was, I prodded the mare into the innyard.

A boy of ten or eleven came out of the stables as I rode in. He had a face as sharp as a weasel's and eyes to match. He came across the yard, his eyes, bright as polished coal and wise as all of history, sitting in judgment on my horse and suit. I dismounted and passed him the reins.

"Rub her down well," I said, "and walk her twice about the innyard. And see to it that the measure of oats ye give her is a fair one."

"Aye," he said. He stood a-tiptoe and unstrapped my saddlebags. When he had freed them, he stood impudently before me with the strap lying across his open palm and the bags forming a kind of scale, and I remembered what Henry had once told me, how stable boys will sometimes weigh a stranger's saddlebags thus and if they weigh heavy, then the word passed that night to the first highwayman who will offer a share. Then the boy passed me the bags, and I grinned down at him.

"The weight is of two pistols," I said. "With plain butts and brass inlays. The pair would not fetch a sovereign in Bladder Lane, and if ye are in league with the brotherhood, do not waste hope on a down-at-heels fellow with no estate save a borrowed mare and a mountain of debts."

He looked up at me with eyes as round and innocent as those eyes would ever manage. "The brotherhood?" he said. "I know nought of any brotherhood."

"I am relieved to hear it," I said. "The face alone is sufficient burden for but one conscience."

The inn was as fair within as without, the oak beams swept of spider webs, a pleasant fire laid in the hearth, the landlord, behind the tap tucked into the back corner, in clean linen apron. I ducked across the room and dropped my saddlebags before him, a cheerful, red-faced man with an amazing belly and eyes as blue as cornflowers in bloom. "A bed for the night," I said. "If your prices be only half as outrageous as your inn is fair."

"A-horse or a-foot?" he said.

"A-horse. I gave her into the hands of a stable boy with a ten-year-old face and eyes as old as hell."

"A shilling for stable and bed," he said. "Two more for the ordinary."

I reached for my saddlebags. "There are other inns in Kingston. And I with two hours of daylight to search one out."

His hand dropped over mine. His eyes and lips and even his belly were laughing. "I would inquire first at the Blue Angel. The ordinary there is but twelvepence, and a bed under the stairs a penny. No coal for your room, and no taper to light ye to bed, but the spiders which drop in your mouth as ye eat and the company that will share your bed ignored in the reckoning."

"And what company might that be?"

"Small company. Nothing to crowd ye out o' covers. But ye will know on the morrow that ye have been visited. Art for London, friend?"

"Aye. On Goldsmith Hall business. And but ten pounds in my purse."

He no more smiled. "In that case," he said, "I have a small room far in the back for sixpence. With the first measure of oats for your horse free. The ordinary is yet two shillings, but ye will find no better this side of London."

And it was indeed cause for wondering, I thought, whether there was an innkeeper in all the land who was not a king's man. "And what for supper?" I said.

"Sack. A dish of hot salmon. Cold beef and fowl."

So it was noon the next day when, on the brow of the hill above Southwark, I pulled the mare off the highway and looked down upon London town. The city looked very fair from this distance, the red-tiled roofs glinting in the noonday sun, the leaded spires of the churches thrusting up past them, the great wall which squared London Within looking gray and solid and eternal, London Bridge looking from this distance like some toy built of child's blocks, and all along the Thames, from the Bridge to the sea, the ships, thousands of ships, so thick that the masts seemed a great forest into which some giant had come with a terrible drawknife to strip the trees of branches. I sat my horse and looked down upon that sight, the blood in me springing sudden and quick in thigh and throat, my breath thin, in my stomach the coil of excitement and anticipation and pride. For nowhere else on earth was such a city as this one, and no man on earth knew a feeling to equal the feeling of an Englishman who had just come within sight of it. It was a city you could smell for twenty miles if the wind were right, a city stinking of offal in laystalls and cesspools festering behind every abode and the contents of chamberpots flung from upper windows into the streets; of ditches filled to the lip with dead horses and dogs and rats, and of stagnant water steaming in unscoured kennels; of fish rotting in the harbor, and the guts of slaughtered beasts and fowls ground underfoot, and mutton ripening in the sun on butchers' stalls; and there were streets where, if a man did not hold a scented handkerchief to his nose, the noisomeness would nigh strangle him. It was a bawling, brawling city, a babel and bedlam of carters hurling curses at coachmen, of goodwives leaning out of upper casements to trade imprecations with drenched travelers below, of pedlars and stallkeepers hawking their wares and ballad makers the latest news, of orange girls hawking sweetmeats for a penny or themselves for a shilling, of hot-eyed fanatics hawking God. It was a city of a million people and half as many dogs and ten times as many rats, where the houses of great merchants flung their gabled roofs toward the church steeples, and where the miserable crept forth at midnight to tack lean-to hovels against garden walls; where in the Royal Exchange fair ladies threw away ten crowns on a pretty bauble, and among their coach wheels the street urchins scrabbled in the dust, sorting the very dung itself for something to put in their bellies. It was a city which could offer you an infinite variety of slow death, where one face in five bore the pits and ravages of smallpox; where a man who had not contracted the French disease was nine chances in ten a man who had never known woman; where of a hot summer day the crude red cross would of a sudden appear before a hovel off Thames Street, and within the month half the town fleeing the city with terror-stricken faces and the other half dropping in the streets where they stood, and on every church door the newest bill of mortality, and in the dusty summer dusk the sepulchral voices of the cartmen crying "Bring out your dead, bring out your dead." And if a man lacked stomach for a lingering death, why then the city could provide him with swifter passage out of this world, for here every man was law unto himself, and on Ludgate Hill coachmen knocked the brains out of carters for blocking the way, and in Holborn Roaring Boys stabbed clerks for hesitating in the stepping aside, and in every tavern a mere look could be followed by the flash of blades. It was a city of two hundred churches and more taverns and brothels than God Himself could count, with a gaol to every parish and a whipping post and stock and cage to every street corner; a city where cutthroats lurked in every crooked, narrow, unlighted alley and where cutpurses would relieve you of the very buttons to your coat while you idled in Lombard Street; a city where one woman in three was either great man's whore or poor man's doxy, and one child in seven bastard, and one husband in four cuckold; a city where half the inhabitants were lambs and culls and the other half hookers or whipjacks, pimps or shifters, charlatans or cozeners, footpads or cutthroats, so that if a man lived here but a twelvemonth, he would be convinced that half the human race lived by preying on the other half. It was a city where man had set all his wits to a study of practicing inhumanity to man; where debtors rotted in the dank cells of the Fleet Prison; where heads grinned down from the pikes atop Traitors' Gate on London Bridge; where the chains of felons on the gallows clanked in the soft breeze blowing across Tower Hill; where the sight of whore being whipped at the cart's tail down Cheapside or of men stocked in Poultry Lane, with their ears nailed to the wood behind them and their tongues bored through with hot irons and their foreheads branded, was so common that passers-by would scarce turn their heads to watch the sport. It was, in brief, a bawling, brawling, lusty, bawdy, blasphemous, filthy, pestilential, cozening, lawless, and godless city, and there were probably not ten men in the land would not have traded a year of life against a week's stay within its walls.

And I wonder, I thought, sitting my horse on the hill above the city, I wonder what that signifies about the nature of human nature.

But I was no philosopher, nor any time for the sport an I were, and so I nudged my mount back into the stream which flowed down the hill and along Bankside to London Bridge. I rode down the hill and along Bankside, past the mile of pestilential tenements which a Bishop of London had built out of the revenue from his brothels; past the Swan Theatre, the only theatre in Southwark left standing by the Roundheads, no flags flying this year from the crumbling tower, no crowds standing at the portals with sweaty pennies clutched in their hands; past the Bear Gardens, the walks and stone steps in disrepair now, the kennels long since torn down for firewood, the pit looking dusty and ruined and forgotten in the noonday sun.

And so I came to London Bridge.

There were Roundhead soldiers on the Bridge. Above the pack horses and carts and cattle and foot travelers that jostled and shouldered and sweated toward Traitors' Gate, I could see them all about, in cuirasses and iron caps, on their faces that frozen, expressionless, fanatic look of those Cromwellian pikemen who had stormed the walls at Drogheda singing hymns and then put three thousand huddled and disarmed royalists to the sword. So I dismounted at the Bridge, for a man a-foot and leading a horse was, in that press and snarl, less conspicuous than one mounted, and I was remembering the watch at Leatherhead.

The carriageway through Traitors' Gate paces forty yards from stone abutment to stone abutment, and when I set foot in the shadow of the arch, I was wedged between a pack horse to my right and a travel-stained youth to my left, with all his worldly possessions in a handkerchief, and five shillings next his skin, come up to London like Dick Whittington to seek his fortune. And yet, in the teeth of all that press, there was a pike suddenly slanting across my way and a foreign hand to my bridle and a pair of cold and civil eyes looking into mine from under an iron cap.

"I would see your pass," he said, and his voice as civil as his eyes.

"Why, surely," I said, "an you will hold the mare firmly. She is nervous in such a press as this." I fumbled at my belt and passed the paper to him. He scanned it carelessly, one hand still barring my path with the slanted pike.

"I think you will find it in order," I said.

"Aye," he said, and returned it to me. "And I must have your sword. And search your person and your saddlebags for other weapons."

"I have no other weapon on my person," I said. "Though ye will find a brace of pistols in the saddlebags. And leave to carry them, as ye would know an ye had given my pass any honest attention—"

"My orders," he said, "are to relieve all suspicious persons of any dangerous weapons."

"Who is your captain?"

"Captain Munke."

"Can he read? If the pass be writ fair and signed clearly? By a justice of the peace appointed by the present government?"

"He can read." His tone was still civil, but there was a suspicion in it now of sullenness.

"Take me to him, then."

He stared hard at me and then turned, and the press of people opened mysteriously before us and gave us passage, and I followed him through the great arch to the gatehouse.

It was a room a long-legged man could have traversed in three strides and as damp and shadowy and cheerless as one of your debtors' cells in the Fleet. It was furnished as befitted such a room, with two stools against one wall and a small, rude table in the center, on it a quill pen and an inkpot and a sand shaker. There was but one man in the room, seated on a stool behind the table, a man whose face had seen its share of sorties and sieges and forced marches but whose eyes were pleasant, a man dressed in the buff jerkin and breeches of a foot soldier, nought to mark him an officer save the white sash about his waist and the wide-brimmed hat and the cast of his mouth and the look of command in his eyes. I strode to the table and laid my pass before him. "I have a pass," I said, "signed by John Beauchamp, justice of the peace at Reigate."

He did not even look at it, only put a forefinger on it and pushed it an inch in my direction. "So you have," he said.

"It clearly gives me leave to travel armed."

Still he did not deign to look at it. "I ha' little doubt it does."

"If you will have the goodness to look at it, Captain, you will find that it states clearly that my business is honest."

"Nor do I doubt ye there," he said. "And if you will but step without that postern again, you will find the latest proclamation. It has been posted within the week, and if you will give it ten minutes of your attention, you will note that I have orders to seize the arms of any traveler entering the city who is not known to be above suspicion. For a fresh plot is suspected against the government."

I bent over him, my palms flat on the table. He did not raise his head, only kept his eyes on the scrap of paper lying between us. "Captain," I said, "my business is with Edward Blackwell. I am carrying next my skin two drafts against his running cash. Together they total twenty-three hundred pounds."

" 'Tis a pretty sum," he said.

"It is," I said. "And I have no stomach for traveling about the streets of the city with nought but my bare hands for protection."

"I can sympathize with your reluctance."

"Well, then, if you will but scratch your leave and identity to the bottom of that pass—"

Still he did not raise his head. "But still no bearing on my orders."

"Captain," I said, my voice strident now, "Captain, I am party to no plot. I am plain country squire come up to London—" I broke off, looking down at the crown of his hat, at the hand toying with the quill. "God damn it, Captain," I burst out. "God damn it," and then I broke off again, for now he did raise his head, and his eyes not so pleasant as I had first thought, and his fingers lying quiet now aside the feather.

I endured that look a long breath or two. Then I straightened and moved a hand helplessly. "Look ye, sir," I said, "were I engaged in that business, would I enter the city thus? In broad daylight, with my sword in naked sight and the butts of my pistols thrusting impudently from my saddlebags?"

" 'Tis a pretty argument," he said. "But it likewise does nought to the wording of my orders."

"In the name of God, Captain—" and then I again broke off, for his eyes were again on mine, and something about the line of his mouth to give me sudden pause. "Sure, Captain, you cannot expect a man to travel from Lombard Street to Ludgate Hill with his saddlebags stuffed with coin and not even a bludgeon to hand—"

"I remember nought in the proclamation to do with bludgeons."

For the space of another shallow breath or two his pleasant and amused eyes studied the color and disposition of mine. Then I shrugged out of my cloak and sword belt, and laid my sword before him. "You may instruct your man," I said, "to lessen the burden of my mare by the weight of two pistols. The money is intended for Goldsmiths' Hall. If I am relieved of it between Edward Blackwell's and its destination, I will lay you odds that John Thurloe himself will have your head for it."

"Now that," he said, "is the prettiest argument you have offered me yet."

"It is one you would have found in the pass an you had spared me the pains to read it."

"I have read a score of passes since daybreak. And none of their arguments to any purpose."

"And this argument?"

He pondered the prettiness of my argument. Then he reached for the quill. "The proclamation," he said, "clearly excepts any who are known to be honest. That would include any man fetching a fortune up to Goldsmiths' Hall. It is the only honest business you rogues have been known to engage in since Edgehill." He scratched something on my pass and sanded it. "I would offer you a word of advice," he said.

"Why, offer away, Captain."

His pleasant eyes watched me tuck the pass into my belt. "London has changed since last you laid eyes on it," he said, "what with young gallants as beribboned and simpering as any Cavalier, and the women patching and painting and appearing in public with naked breasts. But were I you, I should still set a watch on my tongue. We yet have laws about blasphemy. If I possessed a nicer conscience that I do, I should have fined you the value of your horse and set you in the stocks an afternoon to meditate on the meaning of the second commandment."

I looked down on him, smiling, liking on the sudden this pleasant-eyed man for all that he drew the pay of a captain in the Protector's service. "I thank you, Captain," I said, "for your generosity. And God for the bluntness of your conscience."

I turned then, breathing freer again with the signature of a Roundhead captain scratched on my pass. But at the door I turned back. "One question, Captain," I said. "Why did ye not have me stocked?"

"Were this six years ago, I little doubt I would have."

"If in '48, why not in '54, Captain?"

He did not answer me that. I looked across that cramped and ill-lit room to him, wondering how far I dared press him, not understanding myself why I should choose this man and this time to pursue such a matter. "Could it be, Captain," I said softly, "that a cause can pall in the space of six years?"

"I could also have you stocked," he said, "for asking impudent questions."

Very well, Captain, I thought, ye need not answer then, for the reason is writ plain on your face for any man with two good eyes in

59

his head to read. You were a boy of sixteen in '40 or '41, Captain Richard Munke, I thought, and you listened to all the talk of arbitrary tyranny, and then you buckled on your sword and helped rally the clerks and 'prentices at Edgehill and Turnbull Green and turned us back in the name of a cause that was still fresh and untarnished. And you lived through the bitter years of '42 and '43, I thought, the cause still bright but seemingly lost now, the same clerks and 'prentices fleeing London like rats deserting a burning barn, and through the triumphant years that followed, when you finally murdered a king and put a blunt and honest country squire in his place, the cause not so bright now but still serviceable. And now, I thought, you are in the midst of a lesson in what it is to be hoisted on your own petard. Now you sit here in your gatehouse, while parliaments are purged and then dissolved, and Councils of State make the laws and High Courts of Justice execute them, and your honest country squire made a Protector last year and, if rumor be true, crowned a king this, and your once bright cause looking at last like some cuirass left lying in the rain on some ruined and forgotten field.

Aye, Captain Richard Munke, I thought, I require no answer of you. Only I would know how many hundreds there are like you in the land, sitting down of a morning before their duties, with the doubts festering like boils in their breasts.

My business at Edward Blackwell's at the sign of the Unicorn in Lombard Street, and before the Committee for the Sequestration and Composition of Royalist Estates in Goldsmiths' Hall, required the afternoon. And so it was dusk when I rode out of Foster Lane into Cheapside.

Dusk is the quiet time in London. An hour earlier Fish Street Hill and Lombard Street had been a raucous brawl of coachmen and draymen and pedlars and stallkeepers, and the Cheap a broil of carts and great folks' coaches and fine ladies buying baubles and young gallants ogling fine ladies; and two hours from now the curfew would toll and the City would come awake again, with the cries of the watch drifting hollowly from two streets distant, and roisterers swaggering out of tavern and alehouse, and sudden laughter or drunkenness or mortal death coming from out behind the red lattices of the tipling houses, and gangs of 'prentices, escaped from their garrets by sheet or rope, setting out in search of some aged watchman to knock on the head or some unguarded shop window to break or some bawdyhouse to pull down. But now it was the quiet time, only the distant, sad cry of some cob with his last three gallons of water yet unsold breaking the silence, all the Cheap from the Stocks Market to St. Michael's deserted of coaches and carts, no line of watermen at the Conduit now, all the fine ladies gone home to dullard husbands and gallants gone off to supper, the last stallkeepers locking their stalls against the coming of night, the lanthorns of watchmen beginning to flicker, the Standard and the ruined cross in Cheapside looking ghostly and unreal in the gloom, and at the end of the Cheap St. Paul's steeple, looking like some shadowed ruin out of another, older time. As I rode down the Cheap and into Bladder Lane, the mare's hoofs sounded muffled and ghostly in the fine gravel, and in Paternoster Row they rang hollow on the cobbles, and I got out one of my pistols and cocked it, remembering suddenly that I had not looked to the priming since morning, hoping it would not miss fire if some footpad, desperate enough to be at his work early this night, were to emerge suddenly from some evil lane and seize my bridle and lay the point of his knife to my throat.

Once out of Paternoster Row and into Bowier Lane, and I breathed easier. For now Ludgate Hill was in sight, and Ludgate is lighted with stone lanthorns, and it is besides a street of fine taverns and inns and goldsmiths' and jewelers' shops and hence thick with watchmen. So just without the gate I pocketed the pistol and settled more comfortably into the saddle, looking for the sign of the Belle Savage.

I found it on the north side of the street and almost to the top of the hill. As I turned into the innyard, I was relieved to note that this was none of your mean London inns, cramped between a butcher's stall and a linen draper's shop, with an ordinary you could spit across, and a tap you could not turn about in without knocking your head against the lintel, and three rooms above-ground, none of them commodious enough to pull off boots or slide out of breeches save by sitting on the trundle cot that mine host called a bed. This was rather one of your great posting inns, with an innyard that would have accommodated a company of dragoons, and a stretch of gabled rooms flung along one side of the yard, and a massive stone stable facing them on the other.

The innyard was paved with flagstone, and I did not enter it by stealth. But no hostler came out of the stables to ask my pleasure, and sitting my horse waiting for one, I was on the sudden aware that great as the inn was, there were no coaches stacked against the stable walls nor any flicker of tapers to betray guests in any of that long line of rooms. I pondered that mystery a breath or two, and then I set fingers to lips and whistled.

The whistle brought a thick, hulking fellow out of the stable and across the courtyard. When he was to me, he ground the sleep out of his eyes with the backs of his fists and then peered up at me through the dusk. "Aye?" he said. His voice was as full of sleep as his eyes.

"I have a horse," I said, "that requires a stall for the night. This is an inn, is it not?"

"Aye," he said. "But there are no rooms to be had."

"I see no coaches in your yard," I said. "And I hear no stir of other horses in yon stable."

"I know nought of that," he said. "I only know what my master hath commanded me. There are no rooms to be had here this night, and ye had best try the Dog."

"If 'tis all one with you, sirrah," I said, "I prefer to hear that story from mine host's mouth." I dismounted and thrust the reins into his unwilling hand. "If I am not returned within the quarter hour," I said, "ye may assume that ye are free to lighten her burden by the weight of one saddle."

There was no sign of life in the ordinary neither. The ordinary was as large as the great hall at the Priory, and this a posting inn within strolling distance of the city gate; and at this time of day, the room should have been crowded with travel-stained squires eating at the two great oaken tables in the center of the room, and with lusty gallants waxing drunk and quarrelsome at the smaller tables against the one wall, and in the private rooms off two sides of the ordinary, rich lords or merchants or politicians dining discreetly behind drawn curtains with this week's mistress. But instead there was only the long, bare, deserted room, and all the curtains save one at the private rooms drawn back to betray the empty tables within, and the only sound of life at all the low murmur of voices coming from behind that one drawn curtain, and standing there in the arch, I smelled something on the sudden that did not sit as delicately as crushed rose petals in my nostrils.

Then there was life. It came out of the kitchen, a man with a meat pie smoking in his two hands and a bemused expression on his face that changed to another when he saw me standing across the way. One of the waiters, I guessed, for he was a slight man with the stoop of a clerk, and hair the color of wheat stubble left lying over the winter, and a face even he could not recall from one time he looked into the glass to the next, and nervous eyes that would not stay on mine as I crossed the ordinary.

"Is your master about?" I said.

"I am the host," he said. "And if that damned fellow of mine is snoring already—"

Why, aye, I thought, it fits as neatly as a deal box fashioned by some master joiner, for you look like no innkeeper I have ever clapped eyes on, and this inn more strangely conducted than some I have known. "If ye refer to a certain hulk that passes for hostler," I said, "he was awake the last I saw him. He was standing in the center of your yard holding my horse."

"And did he not report that I had no room?"

"He did. But I had a humor to hear the story from your lips."

"And now you have heard it," he said.

"None?" I said. "No pallet under a stair? No yard or two in garret or stable?"

"My life on it," he said. "Not a spare inch. I would suggest ye inquire at the Dog—"

"You must do a great traffic in foot travelers," I said. "For I noted no coaches in your yard and heard no horses in your stable."

"Aye." His eyes flicked from my face to that drawn curtain to my face again. "Aye, a very great traffic, and—"

"And have these foot travelers come from no parts distant enough to spur an appetite? For I see none of them waiting at your ordinary to taste of that beef pie."

"'Tis no beef. 'Tis palpable mutton, and intended for a private party in the Rose—"

"Very well," I said. "So you have no rooms. Would you have another of those mutton pies that smell strangely like beef?"

His eyes darted again to the curtained room. "None," he said. "But if your humor is for beef pie, I would suggest the Hawk and Pheasant. Their ordinary is but two shillings instead of four—"

"Four? My brother assured me your ordinary was but two."

"Your brother, sir?"

"The Earl of Peterborough."

"The Earl of Peterborough, sir?" His eyes were not so nervous on the sudden. "Then you would be—Charles, is it?"

"John," I said.

"Why, that may be a light of a different taper," he said. "If you will have the patience to wait until I have delivered this pie, sir, I will discuss with you further this matter of a room."

He crossed the ordinary and disappeared behind the drawn curtain. Then he appeared again, and behind him a man wearing a plain, black, satin suit and a black hat with brim so wide it shaded his face to the tip of his nose. "So you are John Mordaunt?" this new one said.

"If I am not," I said, "I have been cozened these twenty-eight years."

"I am Sir Richard Willis. And I should have known you. You and your brother are very like."

"Others have remarked the resemblance," I said. "Though it takes a sharp eye, since he is three inches shorter than I, and his complexion fair where mine is dark, and his eyes blue. Not to mention an indifferent matter of his face being bearded and mine clean, and a memento of Worcester—"

He smiled. "I see you are acquainted with the Earl."

"I am told it is the fashion among brothers."

"You are also a wit." He raised a hand and thrust back his hat, and for the first time I looked fairly into his eyes, heavy-lidded and sleepy-looking in a round face. "I hope you will not take offense, Master Mordaunt, were one to question what brings you up to London."

"I do not take offense easily," I said. "Else I should have done so long since. Though I find it a curious inn where a man must submit to an interrogation as thorough as if he were standing before John Thurloe himself, and that over so small a matter as a bed for the night. I am here on Goldsmith Hall business."

"Ah," he said. "So we have one more has struck up an acquaintance with Squeezing Hall, have we?"

"A most cordial one. The introduction cost me two thousand pounds."

His gaze drifted to the face of mine host behind me. "I think he is honest, Mr. Doyle," he said, and then he was smiling sleepily at me again. "Mr. Doyle will provide you with a light to your room," he said. "If you have a mind to sup here below, you are welcome to join a small gathering in the Rose on your return. It would be an honor to share with you a meat pie and a bottle of canary."

"The honor would be mine, Sir Richard," I said. "But I fear you would find me indifferent company. I have been a morning in the saddle, and have squandered the afternoon amongst a certain party of thieves in Foster Lane. Another time, perhaps."

He bowed slightly. "At the least, permit me to stand you to a bottle. And to provide you with a certain paper, newly out of France, which should interest one fresh from Goldsmiths' Hall."

I returned him a bow as good as he gave. "You are too kind, Sir Richard."

He studied me another moment through those sleepy eyes. Then he touched the brim of his hat. "Your servant, sir," he said, and then turned on his heel, and I swung about to face mine host.

Only it was not mine host, for Mr. Doyle's place had been usurped by a pair of black eyes, and a face the color and texture of cherries a week this side of the ripening, and lips somewhat moister and redder than that. Fifteen years old, I thought, if the face can be fairly judged by the light of that candle, and ripe for breeding, if smock and apron do not give the lie to the form behind it.

"Why, how now?" I said.

She curtsied. "I am Betty, sir. My father bade me light you to your chamber."

And there, I thought, give me leave to doubt you, wench, for no sop-faced Mr. Doyle spawned those eyes, and if your mother is indeed honest and mine host not possessed of a fine set of horns, why here lies a mystery for the wisdom of the ages to ponder on. "I doubt," I said, "that a man could ask for a fairer link bearer. Now could he?"

"You were better judge o' that nor I, sir."

She curtsied again and then led me abovestairs and into a commodious chamber overlooking the innyard, a room well furnished with a great valanced and curtained bed, and a chest set with pewter pitcher and bowl, and a wardrobe, and a gilt chair. She set the candle on the chest and laid flint and steel beside it, and then drew the curtains to the bed and set out chamber pot and turned down the bedcovers, while I watched her busy hands and counted back through the years to the last time I had known a pretty wench or even bussed one.

Then she faced me over the small, uncertain light from the candle. "I think you will find the bed soft," she said. "And the linen fresh."

"I believe it," I said. "For I can smell the lavender from here."

"Have ye a mind for supper in your room?"

I shook my head. "I shall go below for that."

"I could warm the bed for you," she said. "Though we are unprepared for guests this night, and it would take an hour to heat the stones."

"The weather is scarce that inclement," I said. "But you might relieve me of these boots. And provide me with a pair of my host's slippers."

I sat on the edge of the bed and watched the top of her pretty head as she tugged off the boots and then straightened. Her face was flushed, and I had lived five years without a woman, and she looked most exceeding pretty in the candlelight. "Shall I take them below, sir?" she said. "I can clean them for you against the morrow."

"It would not go unappreciated," I said. "You may score a threepence for the task, for they are uncommonly muddy." I held her eyes a little, and she flushed again before she dropped them. "'Twould be worth another small sum," I said, "if you could supply me with some information, Betty. For I would know whether it is common for this inn to stand empty of coaches in your yard and guests in your chambers."

Her eyes clouded. "Not common, sir."

"Then, why tonight? What business is it goes forward below?"

"I do not know, sir."

"Come," I said. "You have served that small gathering below, you have surely overheard a word or two."

"Truly, sir," she said, "I know nothing. I have fetched them but two bottles of wine, and both times they broke off talking."

Very well, I thought, I shall not press you, wench, for I think I have hit on the answer without you. And you may pray God, John Mordaunt, I thought, that the government chooses other than this night for its discovery.

"Have I your leave to go now, sir?" she said.

I nodded. "Though I could wish that ere we part, you could spare a lonely traveler one of your kisses."

And now the cloudiness went out of those black eyes, and she was smiling down at me. "That, sir," she said, "is one commodity but rarely sold at the Belle Savage."

"Why, the rarer the article, the worthier the purchase. How rarely sold?"

"Never, as yet. Though should someone happen along who is willing to pay the reckoning—"

"What reckoning? But name it. If it be a gold sovereign, it is still short of your worth."

"More nor a sovereign, sir. Though the article would not fetch that price in any stall in the 'Change."

"What price, girl?"

"A plain gold band to my left hand. And the space of a quarter hour squandered before one of your justices of the peace."

I threw back my head and laughed, and then something in those eyes, some look of seriousness or innocence or hurt, made me break off and rise from the bed and put the tips of two fingers to her cheek. "I think," I said softly, "that there is some man in this land whose fortune is more to be envied than that of the greatest lord."

"I would not know that," she said. "I am but a poor innkeeper's daughter. But the coin my husband pockets, though it be but a silver sixpence, will, an God be willing, come to his hand unclipped."

"I hope that God will prove willing," I said. "Truly. And now you may light me below again, Betty."

When I returned below, the voices in the Rose were no longer a murmur; as I crossed the ordinary and sat down at one of the small tables along the wall, I heard the flat, hollow sound of an open palm slapped down on oak, and a raised voice arguing that the scheme were madness, that they little doubted but what they were already betrayed, that within the month they should all be paying their fees

67

to Gregory the Hangman, and another voice, lower than the first but still insistent and fierce and clear, replying that this time they could not fail, that three hundred men were already sworn and the city sure to rise. Then my host was advancing on me from the kitchen with a bottle pressed under an armpit and a pie smoking in his hands.

"And would this also be your palpable mutton?" I said.

He smiled. "Beef. And the bottle is with the compliments of Sir Richard." He pulled a paper from his belt and laid it before me. "Sir Richard asked that I show you this. He would have you study it as you sup."

I looked down at the paper. I know not what I was expecting, some new ballad on the Rump or the Protector, I suppose, some scurvy verse with false rhymes and halting meter lately scribbled in some garret in Fleet Street and sold surreptitiously from out a bookstall in St. Paul's. That is what I expected, I suppose, as I dropped my eyes to that paper, and then the words leaped out at me, first the ending (for that was black letter), GIVEN AT PARIS, THE 3RD OF MAY, 1654, and then the signature, CHARLES REX, and then the greeting (also black letter), CHARLES THE SECOND, BY THE GRACE OF GOD KING OF ENGLAND, SCOTLAND, FRANCE, AND IRELAND, DEFENDER OF THE FAITH, TO ALL OUR GOOD AND LOVING SUBJECTS, and then the proclamation itself, my eyes not following it word upon word, like an old, blind, halt man crossing a street, but in great leaps and bounds, like a cat crossing a field newly burned and still smoking: *"Whereas it is apparent to all rational and unbiased men . . . that a certain mechanic fellow, by name Oliver Cromwell, hath by most wicked and accursed ways and means, against all laws both divine and human . . . most tyrannically and traitorously usurped the supreme power over our said kingdoms, to the enslaving and ruining the persons and estates of the good people our free subjects therein, after he had most inhumanely and barbarously butchered our dear father, of sacred memory, his just and lawful sovereign; these are therefore in our name to give free leave and liberty to any man whomsoever . . . by pistol, sword, or poison . . . to destroy the life of the said Oliver Cromwell, wherein they will do an act acceptable to God and good men, by cutting so detestable a villain from the face of the earth. . . . And we do by these presents . . . promise, as a re-*

ward for his services, to give to him and his heirs forever 500 £ per annum, free land . . . and also the honours of knighthood. . . . And because we know, that great numbers are involved in the same guilt with the said Oliver, more through his crafty, ensnaring devices, than their own malicious or wilful inclinations; we do therefore freely pardon and forgive all and every man whatsoever, for all and everything by them done and committed against our person, crown, and dignity . . . provided that they renounce and forsake their rebellious courses. . . ."

I sat there stone-still, no need now for answers to innyards empty of coaches and ordinaries bare of diners. For you have indeed wandered into the heart of a plot, John Mordaunt, I thought—and none of your nightly tavern plots neither, no hare-brained scheme hit upon between supper and bawdyhouse, but rather one subtly and carefully laid in Paris, the instrument drawn up by Edward Hyde himself. And now, I thought, in taverns and private houses in York and Shrewsbury and London, there will be small gatherings of men more desperate than most, heads together in the light from uncertain tapers, voices murmuring of when the Protector walks forth and when he returns, of what armor he wears under his coat and how many guard him and of what honesty, of which officers in the city are loyal and which sullen, of what gates to seize and what places in town were best for leaping upon a convenient stall or scaffold and crying out that tyranny lay murdered and Charles Stuart restored and freedom in the land again.

And thinking that, I felt the blood suddenly cold in me and the breath shallow. For I also knew that this business was as surely doomed as all the others that had been hatched since Worcester. The business doomed and the plotters damned, I thought, and within the month another twenty men drawn on hurdles to Tyburn, and another five hundred victims of the Protector's clemency, relieved of estates rather than lives, or transported to the plantations. Aye, Mr. Doyle, I thought, I would lay odds that Mr. Secretary Thurloe is even now at some desk in Whitehall, with this document before him and the guards at all the city gates doubled. And you should have sought out another inn when the advice was offered you, John Mordaunt, I thought, for the odor of treason was not as plain here as the smell of tobacco smoke, but it was enough, it would serve. Only too late now, I thought; venture out that door now and you will have a length of steel between your ribs ere you can cross the innyard.

And so I did nothing at all save look up at my host with the pretense of a smile on my lips.

"My dreams would be pleasant were such a business as this to come off," I said.

"You will find a warm welcome in the Rose, sir."

I shook my head. "One plot hath already cost me two thousand. The only estate left me is my life. It is a poor thing, I know, but of some sentimental value to me."

"This business might recover an estate for you."

His eyes were not nervous now, only shrewd and searching. Behind him, Betty emerged from the kitchen and disappeared into the Rose. I bent an inch or two into his expression.

"Have you heard of Worcester, Mr. Doyle?" I said. "My brother was at Worcester. It was a fair army that crossed the border that August of '51, twenty thousand Scots veterans with Leslie to lead them. But within the week that brave army was routed by a force half its size, and that an army composed of clerks and tailors who were nigh dead on their feet from fever and starvation and so hoarse they could scarce warble their hymns as they breached the wall and fell to the slaughter." I dropped my eyes out of his. "That is what my brother has told me about Worcester, Mr. Doyle," I said. "And I do not think that three hundred men with a hundred rusty swords and not half as many pistols between them can succeed where twenty thousand failed."

"The times have changed. In '51 the people had but a taste of tyranny. They have since burned their tongues on the broth."

"Aye," I said. "And in the same three years, Mr. Thurloe has developed a nose for rebellion. He can smell treason from here to Edinburgh, and that against the wind."

"We have not been discovered yet."

"Have you not? Art sure you have not? For I have heard that John Thurloe finds pleasure in the sport of cat-and-mouse." I moved an impatient hand. "Were all your conspirators lured in as I was, Mr. Doyle? After a scant five minutes of indifferent questioning? Are these your plotters, Mr. Doyle?"

He did not answer me that, only continued to stare stubbornly at me. I endured that look briefly and then turned a shoulder to him. "I wish you well in this business," I said. "But I want no hand in it."

"Why, as to that," he said, "an you are not friend, you are enemy, Master Mordaunt."

And now I no longer smiled. "Have it so," I said softly. "But before you go further forward in this, Mr. Doyle, give your enemy leave to inform you that there were Roundhead soldiers on London Bridge this morning. And a new proclamation posted without the gatehouse."

"There are always soldiers on the Bridge. And as to proclamations, we have proclamations thrice weekly this year."

"Also a certain Captain Munke," I said, "who let it drop—"

I was given no opportunity to relate what Captain Munke had dropped. For in that instant there was a sudden cry and the sounds of a scuffle in the Rose, and then the curtain was flung aside and Betty appeared, her smock askew and her hands thrust out before her, and following her out a swarthy, hook-nosed face in which the teeth gleamed white in what, I suppose, it were possible to call a smile. The two were frozen like that an instant, and then the face developed a hand that grasped the wench by an elbow and whirled her about so that her back was to the wall, and now the face was a back that towered above her, one hand still to her arm and the other to the wall so that her path to the kitchen was barred.

"I put a question to ye, wench," the back said, and his voice like that gleam of white teeth. "I shall put it to ye a second time. Do ye find my breath stinking?"

"No, sir," she said. "Oh, no, sir, 'tis sweet—"

"My face offensive? Pocked, perchance? Scurvy?"

" 'Tis smooth as silk, sir—"

"My hair, perhaps. Is my hair greasy? Crawling with vermin?" "No, no, 'tis—"

"Why, then, 'tis my manners. Ye find my manners boorish, is that it?"

During that inquisition Mr. Doyle simply stood in his tracks and watched. But now he drew a sudden breath and then stepped forward. "Mr. Brodrick," he said.

The back developed a face again, a face that managed to look over a shoulder without the body turning or the right hand taking leave of the wall. "Aye, Mr. Doyle?" he said.

"Mr. Brodrick," my host said, "she is no tavern wench. She is my daughter, sir, and scarce turned fifteen."

"Fifteen?" the face said. "Why, 'tis an eternity. I have known queans of eleven were brought to bed of their first bastards. Wouldst have her carry her maidenhead to her grave, man? Hast no one told you 'tis a jewel that shrinks in value with age?"

"She is none of your tavern wenches, Mr. Brodrick."

"I do not have a humor tonight for one of your tavern wenches, Mr. Doyle."

Mr. Doyle drew another breath or two, while Brodrick smiled across the ordinary at him and silence pressed in around us and death paused in the passing to glance aside at this scene. Then, "You are in your cups, Mr. Brodrick," Doyle said quietly. "And I must ask you to take your hands off my daughter, sir."

The face still smiled. "An I do, 'twill be to introduce your guts to a foot of steel."

Doyle advanced a pace. "I am none of your swordsmen," he said. "And were you falling down drunk, I little doubt you could still run me through at will. But if your humor this night is rape, you must first commit murder."

And now it was I who spoke. It was none of my affair, this business of the virginity of a tavern wench, and I was thinking that there would be soldiers down on us were murder committed here this night. But I also found that I had taken a small dislike to Mr. Brodrick. Indeed, I found everything about Mr. Brodrick uncommonly offensive—the white teeth in that long, bony, swarthy face, the great hook to his nose, his beribboned and befeathered hat, the love knots tied to the ends of his two braids, the expanse of shirt showing between short-waisted doublet and breeches, the petticoat breeches with thrice the number of points required at the knees, the stirrup hose that bagged down over his garters, the boots with three-inch heels. You are one of your Roaring Boys, Mr. Brodrick, I thought, and you sleep till ten and then squander two hours tying those ribbons to knee and waist and wrist and braided hair, and you game till dusk, when it is time to get drunk, and the rest of your waking hours you alternate between wenching and quarreling, provided only that the quarrel be with some clerk who cannot tell hilt of sword from point. This is none of my affair, I thought, but I find myself with an aversion to you, Mr. Brodrick, and so I found my voice and made it my business.

"Brodrick, is it?" I said. "Pray take your hands from the girl, Mr. Brodrick."

He did so. He did so as suddenly as if I had put pistol to his head in the asking, and Mr. Doyle turned to stare at me, and Sir Richard's face appeared at the curtain of the Rose, and Brodrick dropped one hand from the girl and the other from the wall and turned. He stared briefly and then halved the distance between us, and now his eyes were traveling insolently over my face and suit and boots. "And what scurvy plowman have we here?" he said.

"No plowman," I said. "My name is as good as yours, Mr. Brodrick."

"Is it so? And what your interest in the wench, sirrah? Art her brother, plowman?"

"Not her brother. And address me as something other than plowman. Has no one told you that wit ceases to be wit on repetition?"

"Her suitor, then? For on my word, you are dressed the part."

"Not her suitor, neither."

"Why, then, ye have a mind to the wench yourself."

"Nor that neither, Mr. Brodrick."

"And now I have run clean out of motives," he said. "Unless it be simply that long nose of yours."

"I have little choice there, Mr. Brodrick. Since it is the nose God saw fit to provide me with."

"And me He provided with a passion against them. Indeed, when confronted with one, I can scarce refrain from pulling it. Indeed, I find myself seized with such a humor now."

"Mr. Brodrick," I said, "I only asked you civilly to take your hands from one who clearly does not welcome your attentions, and do not crowd me into a quarrel. If ye do, this inn will be entertaining Roundhead soldiers within the hour."

"Or if not a nose pulling," he said, "a baptism may test whether your courage comes but halfway to matching your insolence."

"Mr. Brodrick," I said, and then broke off. For now he was advancing on me, and then he was standing over me, all white teeth and glaring eyes, and a hand going to the bottle at my elbow, and the crash as the neck of the bottle splintered on the edge of the ta-

73

ble, and then the wine running off the brim of my hat onto my up-turned face.

I sat quiet until the bottle was emptied. Then I removed my hat and looked at my landlord. "I would trouble you for that apron, Mr. Doyle," I said.

He aroused himself from his trance, and his hands darted to his apron strings. I sopped off my face and clothing and tossed the cloth aside. "I regret ye saw fit to do that, Mr. Brodrick," I said. "For I sought no quarrel with you."

"But I seek one with you. Though if ye still lack the stomach to undress that blade, I can provide a whipping instead of a death."

I got to my feet then and crossed the ordinary to Sir Richard. "I would advise you, Sir Richard," I said, "to clear your persons of any such papers as the one you recently conveyed to me. It would appear we will soon be entertaining Roundhead soldiers here."

"Nay," he said. "Nay, this is madness," and he stepped past me. "Look ye, Brodrick," he said, "this is no time for such business. Call the man out tomorrow if ye have a sudden thirst for blood—"

"I have a thirst for blood tonight," Brodrick said.

"And I do not. God damn it, man, we do not—"

"Step out of my path, Sir Richard."

"I will not. There is a larger stake here—"

"'Sblood," Brodrick said. "Must I provide two of you exits out of this world?"

And now Sir Richard stepped aside, and I turned to Betty, still with her back to the wall and her two hands pressed to the wood behind her. "Will you hold my coat, girl?" I said.

"He will kill you, sir," she whispered. "He hath murdered four—"

"Do not all of us owe God a death, lass? Come, hold my coat."

"Aye," she whispered, and I shrugged out of coat and sword belt and then faced Brodrick. His coat was off and his rapier naked in his hand, and I hefted my own blade, accustoming my hand to the unfamiliar feel of it, for it had been two years since I had crossed swords with a man and then only in sport. Then I looked to the floor of the ordinary. It had been freshly swept and sanded, no bones or greasy scraps of meat or spat-out fruit skins to slip on, and I kicked off my host's slippers.

"It takes you a deal of time to prepare for a bloodletting, plowman," Brodrick said.

"When a man has but a quarter hour to live," I said, "surely ye cannot begrudge him the savoring of it, Mr. Brodrick."

I advanced to meet him then, noting as I did so how his eyes fell to the floor before him, there to inscribe an imaginary circle and within it a triangle. And is it possible, I thought, that there is left in England a man who uses the Spanish style of fence? Nay, I thought, the geometrical style hath not killed a man these twenty years, and this some trick newly learned in a Holborn academy. Then I touched my blade to his, waiting as Nicholas Armitage had taught me to wait for my opponent to make the first pass. Only Brodrick waited too, and so I feinted, noting how his lips tightened as he met my move, remembering how Nicholas had used to tell me that tight lips meant tight grasp. "I can only hope, Mr. Brodrick," I said, "that your skill with that toy is not half as scurvy as both your manners and that clown costume you wear are offensive."

"You will find it sufficient to dispatch a plowman," he said, and lunged.

It was an indifferent thrust, his point unsteady and his grasp tighter than skill or prudence dictated, the thrust itself that one called a *pasada*, very deadly fifty years ago but now no more effective than a fool's mate attempted against an opponent who has had ten lessons at chess. A *pasada*, I thought, a *pasada* is in the Spanish style, and again I remembered Nicholas Armitage, my father's master of the horse—Nicholas, who had been pupil of the great Vincentio Saviolo and who had given me ten lessons in the Carranza style of fence and then told me that the system was very geometrical, hence pretty on the pages of a book, but that you fell back on the Italian style when you had a mind to kill a man. "You might venture next on a *pasada simple*, Mr. Brodrick," I said. "If you have progressed as far in your lessons."

"I have progressed as far," he said, and thrust again, his foot moving an exact thirty inches but the execution otherwise as scurvy as before, his point undisciplined and his grasp so tight it was miracle he could manage his wrist at all.

"And the *pasada doble*?" I said. "Has the rook who cheats you a crown for what he calls a lesson shown you the *pasada doble* yet?"

He tried that as well, while I smiled down into his eyes and could have come in over his sword and killed him but did not.

"The first principle of fence, Mr. Brodrick," I said, "is a steady

75

point. The second is to recover from your thrust within a quarter hour."

"What art thou?" he said. "Art some damned fencing master?"

"Why, no. Though I could have given you a lesson at this, and that before I was twelve."

"Give it me, then," he panted. "Cease prating and give it me."

"As you wish. Though let us make it Italian. Do you know the *stocata*? The *stocata* begins thus, the point steady as ye straighten your arm, then the blade falling away as ye come in," and I completed the pass, though slowly enough for him to follow it. "And shall we make this second pass faster?" I said and did so, and this time I must flick my own point aside to avoid spitting him. And now I was weary of this and I stepped back.

"In God's name, Mr. Brodrick," I said, "what fool hath given ye lessons? Some clerk who spelled out Gerard Thibault's *Académie* and practiced his strokes before a glass and then set himself up in some two-shilling school at the Grey Friars?"

He did not answer me, only stood there with the rage and bafflement in his eyes.

"What lessons did he cheat you for?" I said. "Six or seven, before you touched him the first time and then sallied forth to try your skill against carriers and coachmen?"

He did not answer me that, neither.

"Sir Richard," I said, "wilt instruct this coxcomb to put up his weapon? I have played at this five minutes now, and I can count you six times I could have run him through."

"Sheath your blade, Brodrick," Sir Richard said.

"Why, aye," Brodrick said. "Aye, I will sheath it," and he swaggered a step toward me, his blade careless in his hand. And then, out of the corner of my eye, I saw the lunge, and this time all the skill I could muster needed to parry the thrust.

I looked down into his eyes. I think he never doubted that that thrust would be the death of me, and I watched the look of murder in his eyes fade to amazement as he realized that even with my guard down and my eyes elsewhere he had still not spitted me.

"Why, very well, Mr. Brodrick," I said. "Very well, we shall pursue the lesson. Only now it will cost you somewhat dearer."

I offered him no banter now. I was silent now as I drove him

76

back across the ordinary with all the strokes Nicholas Armitage had taught me, determined now to kill him but taking my time at it, for I first wanted to see fear in his eyes. By the time I had driven him to the far end of the room and back, I had shredded his shirt from armpit to breech top. But still no fear in his eyes, and so, with his back to the wall and the rage still pulsing in my throat, I resolved that I would pin him to the wall and so have done with this. Only I paused first to draw breath, and in that instant he made a final desperate lunge, and as I warded it, my hand remembered a trick Nicholas had taught me, very useful against a tight grip, and I completed my parry, my blade beginning the upward arc, the flat pressing firmly against his, and then the quick wrench, and his weapon flying out of his hand and clattering against the tap, and he now flatted against the wall and his hands down and his palms pressing the wood behind him and his head flung back and my point just beneath his chin.

And still no fear in his eyes. Hatred and to spare but no fear, and I thought, You are a brave man, Mr. Brodrick. You are scum, I thought, but you are no coward.

"But move one muscle the breadth of a hair, Mr. Brodrick," I said, "and you will find yourself spitted to that wall like a beef stuck on a butcher's hook. But take too sturdy a breath and the assembled company shall have a look at the color of your blood."

He did not move a hair's breadth or take any breath at all.

"You are vermin, Mr. Brodrick," I said. "And it is my policy to crush vermin 'twixt finger and thumbnail. And all that stays my hand is the balancing of the satisfaction it would give me against the misery of a visit to Newgate."

I held my point to his throat another moment, while I looked into smoldering eyes and thought, If you ever meet with this man again, John Mordaunt, ye had best see to it that the reunion is face to face. Then I stepped away. "He will offer you no further harm, Betty," I said. "If he does, if he but brushes against a sleeve or comes close enough to give ye scent of his breath, call out. You will find me a light sleeper." I turned to Sir Richard. "If this coxcomb be fair sample of your plotters, Sir Richard," I said, "I doubt I shall be laying out any considerable sum this month against a new suit."

"A new suit?" he said.

77

"Why, aye. To be wearing when we greet Charles Stuart on his return from his travels. For I would guess that Oliver hath still a little while to draw breath."

He offered me no reply to that, and I looked briefly to the ring of faces behind him. Six of them I counted, and I touched a finger to where my hat brim would have been had I still been covered.

"I bid you good night, gentlemen," I said, and turned on my heel.

⑃ *Five* ⑆

I am, as I told Betty, a light sleeper. But I had risen this morning
at dawn, and Mr. Doyle's bed was soft and my conscience easy.
And so my slumber this night was like falling softly into a pleasant
pit.

I came up out of that warm, dark, furred slumber to the sound
of rapping on my door and someone pronouncing my name in a
voice a little above a whisper but not much. "Aye," I said. "Aye,"
and threw back the covers and groped my way to the door and
found the bolt.

She was standing just without the door, behind the light from a
candle guttering in an earthenware holder. She was still in smock
and apron, but her hair fell loose about her shoulders. "Why, Betty,"
I said, "what is it, girl? Is it that damned—"

"Nay," she said. "Nay, sir," and brushed past me. Then she faced
me again, her back to the door and her hair in pretty disorder and
her eyes wide behind that uncertain flame.

"What, then?" I said, though I hoped I knew. For I must confess to
a weakness for hair which falls in soft waves down a pretty back,
and she was woman grown for all her child's face, and I was after
all human. "What is it, girl?" I said softly.

"Soldiers, sir."

I was still drunk with sleep. "Soldiers? What soldiers, Betty?"

"Roundhead soldiers, sir. They are betrayed below, and the soldiers have burst in and seized my father and the others, and they

79

are about to search the inn. I heard their captain give the order."

I rested a hand over hers. "I am sorry to hear it," I said. "Though I expected little else to come of this business."

She dropped her eyes to my hand resting on hers, and I considered the glint of the flame on her black and careless hair, and then I put a finger under her chin and lifted her eyes back into mine.

"Come," I said. "Be not too downcast, lass. I doubt this is any life-and-death matter for any save Sir Richard. Your father may spend a threemonth in Newgate and pay a pretty fine. But it is common knowledge the Protector hath no stomach for hanging."

There was a look in her eyes which I could not read in that dancing light. "Did you not come to me for help?" I said.

"No, sir," she said. "To warn you. About the soldiers."

"To warn me? But what have Roundhead soldiers to do with me? If they search the inn, they shall find me abed and snoring. Which is one act I can hit on that is no hanging matter these days." I smiled down at her. "I thank you for coming, lass. But I think I have little to fear from Roundhead soldiers."

She did not return my smile. "Their captain gave the order to search the inn," she said, "and bring before him any other rats they might fright from their nests."

I think the smile stayed to my lips. "Their captain said that? You heard him say that, Betty?"

She nodded. And aye, I thought, aye, it is how a Roundhead captain would put it, and suddenly the last cobweb of sleep was swept from out my brain, and I knew that I stood to be accused of a hand in this. If you were lying here at the point of death, I thought, you would stand to be accused, John Mordaunt, for all the present government needs to hang you by these days is the breath of suspicion. For John Thurloe is a thorough man, I thought; it is said that one in three in this land is engaged in selling him intelligence, it is said that let a royalist but break wind in the privacy of his chamber and there will be news of it in Thurloe's hand as fast as favorable wind or galloping courier can fetch it there. And so, I thought, you are rat caught in a trap, John Mordaunt, and not even a taste of cheese to make the broken back the easier to bear.

I stood there, my fingers still at Betty's chin, cursing Henry, who had bid me search out this inn, cursing all silly and desperate plotters everywhere, cursing John Thurloe's agents, cursing myself for lacking the mother's wit to search out another inn when I caught the whiff of treason in this one. But cursing tanned few hides, and so I made my way to the casement and moved aside the drape and peered down into the innyard, hoping, I suppose, that I might still drop to the yard below and make my way to the stable and so, by some miracle, escape.

The hope was, of course, vanity. There were flaring links at the innyard gate and a figure in cuirass and iron cap at the stable door. I turned back to the girl. "Ludgate Street is full of soldiers," I said. "And they have set a guard on the stable. Have you a back stair leading to your cellar?"

"No," she said. "There is but the one stair."

"A garret, then?"

" 'Tis but a small, bare room, and no place to hide if they find it out."

Which was probably as well, I thought; if they found me skulking in cellar or garret, it would be as clear an admission of guilt as any confession. "You had best leave me, girl," I said. "They will be here shortly, and I would not have them find you with me."

"Will they accuse you, then?"

"Aye," I said. "They will accuse me."

"And nought you can do?"

"Why, yes," I said. "I can contract the plague within the next quarter hour. Or I can snuff out this candle and be abed and snoring when they break in. Which will not spare me a pilgrimage to Newgate, though it might provide me grounds for protesting my innocence when I am brought before them at the Old Bailey. And wouldst leave me now, wench?"

Only she would not. Only she yet stood there, her breath delicate in the silence, and when she spoke, her voice was as delicate. "There is one thing might put them off," she said.

"Is there? And what is that?"

"An they were to find you in bed with me," she said.

Her meaning did not reach me for a moment. Then it did, and I stared across the chamber to where she stood in the shadow. "That were desperate ruse, indeed," I said. "Dost know what they could do to you if they found us thus?"

"They could not hang you for it. This I know."

"But do you know what they could do to you?"

"I know."

"And you would still make me the offer?"

"Freely."

"Betty," I said softly, "Betty, come ye here to me."

She came out of the shadows to me, and her head was held proudly, and whatever it was in her eyes was neither shame nor fear. I put my two palms to either side of her face and bent and planted a kiss on her lips. "What is it o'clock?" I said.

"Nigh midnight."

"Then it is but six hours since first you laid eyes on me. And yet for my sake you are willing to risk a whipping at the tail of the cart from Newgate to Cheapside."

"An you can risk your life for me, my lord, I can risk a bloodied back for you."

I turned her about and smacked her heartily on the backside. "I never met Mordaunt yet was worth the spoiling of a pretty back," I said. "And so get thee hence from here, wench."

She still would not do as I bade her, and so I must put a hand to the small of her back and push her across the chamber. At the door, I drew the bolt as quietly as I could, and opened the door as carefully, and stepped into the hall. I heard Mr. Doyle's voice below and the sounds of boots starting up the stairs, and I ducked back into the chamber.

"Quick," I whispered. "They are on the stairs now. Get thee into another chamber, girl—"

The command was addressed to thin air, for she was not standing at the door. She was in the middle of the chamber, and her apron lay at her feet and her hands were fumbling with her smock. "In God's name," I whispered, "what are ye about, girl?"

"I am preparing for bed, my lord. Ye had best bolt the door again."

"Look ye," I whispered, "I cannot permit—" and then she was stepping out of smock and petticoats and standing afore me in bodice and shift. "Betty," I said, "Betty, I will not abide—" and then she had stepped out of shift as well, and I could not read her eyes in that light but I doubted there was any shame in them.

"Betty," I said helplessly. "Oh, Betty, must I be taken off to Newgate with you on my conscience—"

"You must out of those drawers and half shirt, my lord," she said. "An you are half clothed when they burst in, they will know it is a ruse—"

"They will know it anyway," I said. But I did as she bade me, and when I walked naked toward her, there was shame in my eyes, for search party or no search party, she was woman grown and I human. "They will know it anyway," I repeated. "And all you stand to gain by this is to be called whore when they call me traitor."

"What matter," she said, "if in our consciences we know them both to be false?"

"Matter enough. An hour ago I might have ridden in the cart to Tyburn as a man should. But how think you I shall manage the ride now? With you on my conscience—"

"I am hoping there will be no such ride. An there be not, 'twill be worth any small whipping they may give me."

"Nay," I said. "If I escape the rope, you shall escape the whip. For I shall marry you ere I permit—"

She shook her head. "Do not promise me that. I am only an inn-keeper's daughter, my lord, and do not—"

"Innkeeper's daughter or no, ye are better bargain than many a great lady in this land, and a second son could do worse."

She turned from me then and snuffed the candle, and her hand found mine in the darkness.

We lay in the bed, my arms close about her, my face in her hair. I was listening for the sounds without, for the tramp of boot and the crash of musket stock against the barred door and the sharp command to open in the name of the Commonwealth. But I could hear no sounds.

"My father has taken them to the far end of the inn, my lord," she said.

"I am not my lord. I am second son and plain John Mordaunt."

"To me you are my lord." She stirred in my arms. "It will be half an hour before they come to this chamber."

"I am glad it is no more," I said. "For I discover that I am only human, Betty."

Her breast was against my breast, her thigh against my thigh. "And I am sorry, my lord," she said. "For I am human, too. And I find, My Lord Mordaunt, that I am grown weary of waiting for a husband."

And may God forgive you, John Mordaunt, I thought. And may

God in His infinite wisdom and mercy forgive you, for certain it is that you will not soon forgive yourself.

I know not what o'clock the search party came to our part of the inn, for there are occasions when a man is not as accurate a judge of time as a clock. But I do know that it seemed a matter of some indifference when I finally heard them enter the chamber next to mine, for the bed was warm, and the girl was imprisoned within my arms, and her breath was as slow and her heart as quiet as mine, and in that drowsy contentment I listened to Mr. Doyle's voice raised in protest, and to another, sharp with command, laid aside it, and to furniture being moved.

"Art asleep, lass?" I whispered.

She stirred a trifle. "Nay."

"Then mark me, for they shall be demanding entrance soon, and they shall not let me out of their sight once I have unbarred that door. Dost know where your father stores his coin?"

"In a great chest in his chamber. Why, my lord?"

"He hath a purse of mine containing ten pounds. If they permit you out of this room for but ten minutes, you are to get it."

"I shall," she said. "But how convey it to you—"

"It is not for me. It is for you."

"Nay," she said. "Nay, my lord, I am none of your whores, I do not—"

"I know you are not. But you will be called one shortly. And taken off to Bridewell for it. And when you are, you are to be wearing that coin next your skin. For you shall have need of it to fee your whipper. For a pound or two he will spare your back as much as he dare."

In the chamber next I heard a crash as someone overturned a chest. And their captain was not speaking metaphorically, I thought, when he gave the order to frighten rats from their nests. Though little profit in that, I thought, since rats can neither fee a gaoler nor compound for an estate.

"And what of your needs, my lord?" she said. "If they take you to Newgate, you must fee keepers and turnkeys and forfeit garnish to understrappers. Else they will commit you to the common hold. And load you with enough bolts and shackles to cripple you."

"Do not fret yourself on my needs," I said.

"But I shall, my lord."

"Why, then," I said, "if they provide you opportunity, pay someone a pound to post to Reigate and search out my brother Henry at the Priory and tell him I have been seized."

"And if they provide me no opportunity?"

"Then do not worry your pretty head about it. I can endure the common hold so long as I know your needs are supplied."

They were without my chamber now. I let the sharp command to open echo in the chamber while I pressed lips one last time to each of her closed eyes.

"Even if the end of this is a fee to Gregory the Hangman," I whispered, "I shall mount the scaffold with one sweet memory, lass."

This time it was a musket stock that commanded me to open, and I called out for them to cease and groped my way across the room and drew the bolt. I would have opened the door as well, but before I could find the latch, the door was swinging in and I was stepping back from it.

The light they held was this time no candle but a flaring link, and in it three figures. One was Mr. Doyle, looking not merely terrified, looking horror-stricken, as though the rope were already about his neck and the cart in motion. The second could have been that same soldier who this morning had slanted a pike across my path. And the third was a man with a grave, firm mouth and pleasant eyes whose acquaintance I had made something earlier this day.

He advanced on me as slowly and steadily as doom, while I stepped back one step and then another. "Ah," he said softly. "So it is you."

"Aye," I said. "And to what do I owe this visit, Captain Munke? Was my pass after all not in complete order?"

"It may not have been."

"And in what, then, did it lack?"

"It may have neglected to state that your business in the city was treason."

"Treason?" I said. "What treason, Captain? Is it treason now to sl—"

He was not listening to me. He was rather staring beyond me, and I followed his look, and Betty was sitting up in the bed, with the bedclothes clutched to her chin.

"So," he said. "I have interrupted something other than slumber, have I?"

"I get up to London but infrequently, Captain," I said, and moved a careless and knowing hand. "And would ye hold it against a man for taking advantage of the opportunities of the city when he comes up to it but twice a decade?"

"Why, no, Mr. Mordaunt," he said. "Though it would seem to me that for most men, simple treason would do to fill the space of one day. I am, I confess, but a simple soldier, but to my mind it is only the glutton who must further season his day with wenching."

"That is twice ye have spoken of treason, Captain," I said. "And twice ye have spoken in riddles."

"Doubtless," he said. "And what of fornication, Mr. Mordaunt? Ye are pretty at arguments, sir, and the time but half after midnight. Come, shall we sport a little with fornication?"

I did not answer him that.

"What?" he cried. "Not one argument? No protest before heaven that reality is no reality, and appearances are deceiving, and my eyes betray me, and the girl is not there in that bed?"

"She is in the bed, Captain."

"And no explanation for it? Why, then, mayhap I can offer one," and he strode to the bed and tore the bedclothes from her grasp. For a moment she huddled before him, both arms crossed over her naked breasts. Then she dropped her arms, and her head came up proudly, while behind the Captain Mr. Doyle took one step toward her and then stopped as suddenly, and on his face a look of black murder, though whether it was intended for me or the Captain I could not tell.

As for the Captain, he merely stood there, slumped a little, looking down at her in a brown study. "Now here is sport," he said softly. "Here is rare sport indeed." He swung back on me. "Bid your whore cover her nakedness," he said, and his voice was absolutely flat.

"Captain," I said, "I do not know why you burst in on me thus. But I doubt it was for the purpose of abusing a wench who has done no harm."

"No harm?" he cried. "No harm? Art wedded to the girl, then?"

"You know I am not, Captain."

86

"And is lechery no harm? Doth not rank, hot, foul fornication stink in the nostrils of God and decent men? Is Babylonian whoredom no sin, sir?"

"I cannot claim as intimate an acquaintance with God as some," I said. "But I cannot think that He would give a man an itch only for the purpose of forbidding him to scratch it. I cannot believe that He will make a man miserable only for the taking of a little pleasure out of the way."

"Aye," he said. "'Tis a sentiment I should have expected from such as you. Treason and fornication and now blasphemy, and I find the sentiment worthy of Charles Stuart himself." He stood now with his feet apart and his head down, and he was looking across a distance of only six feet but it could have been as many leagues to judge by his expression. "Wilt do as I command ye?" he said. "Wilt cease the silly prating and bid your strumpet cover the proof of her bitchery?"

"Do as he bids you, Betty," I said, and watched her come forth from the bed and stand proud and unashamed before the lot of us, while in the doorway the Captain's man drew a tongue over his lips, and Mr. Doyle looked on his daughter and planned someone's death, and I thought that a second son could indeed do worse than this girl.

"And while we are on it," Munke said, "I would advise you to follow suit, Mr. Mordaunt. Though it is a matter of indifference to me, since I would as lief herd ye to Newgate as ye are."

"And might I be spared a reason for this journey, Captain? Or are reasons gone out of fashion these days?"

"Why, the reason is insolence, Mr. Mordaunt. And if that will not suffice, we can add high treason and fornication. And should that be still short of the mark, we can always compound impudent blasphemy. Ye have precisely five minutes to don your clothes, Mr. Mordaunt."

"My boots are in the kitchen, Captain."

"A pity. Since it means that on your walk through Old Bailey, ye will have nought but boot hose between you and the cobbles."

"Could I not dispatch the girl—"

"The girl stays under my eye. I would put some questions to her before I have her escorted to Bridewell."

I pulled on my breeches. "Captain," I said, "can you not let the girl go? Sin she may have, but her sins have done neither you nor your government harm. If you have a single drop of kindness in your veins, sir, leave the girl's judgment to heaven."

"A pretty sermon," he said. "A pity to waste it on a strumpet."

"She is no strumpet," I burst out. "She was maid but half an hour ago, and what she did, she did at my importunity. Indeed—"

"You lie," he said flatly. "You lie in your teeth. An I ever saw harlotry in a face before, 'twas in hers but five minutes since."

"Captain," I said, "forget the girl and I will make an honest woman of her. If I have to arrange for the ceremony in a Newgate cell—"

"You have but two minutes left of the five I permitted you," he said. "And boot hose yet to accomplish."

"Captain," I said, "it would be worth ten pounds to me if you could forget you found the girl in my bed."

He stared at me from across two paces.

"Ten pounds, Captain. And something on top of it for your man."

And now no stare but a soft, disarming smile, and then he was advancing on me. When he was to me, he smiled another while into my eyes, long enough for me to note that his eyes were a shallow blue. "There is some small risk to me an my memory prove faulty in this quarter," he said softly. "Offer me twenty pounds, Mr. Mordaunt."

And aye, I thought, this is the extent of their godliness, and I was trying to remember why, twelve hours since, I had liked this man, and I could not recall the reason. "I cannot put my hands on the sum immediately," I said. "You would have to dispatch a man to Reigate to search out my broth—"

"But it is agreed? Twenty pounds?"

"Aye," I said. "It is agreed."

"She must have been rare sport indeed," he said, and then, suddenly and without warning, he struck me straight across the mouth.

"The next bribe ye offer," he said, "offer it to God."

I ran a tongue over my lips. "I would repay you that kindness with a word of advice, Captain," I said, and my voice, I think, as soft as his. "Which is that you devote an extra quarter hour to your prayers this night. Pray that the charges against me are sturdy ones. For if they are not, I propose to seek ye out and kill you. As God is my witness, if they do not hang me for treason, they shall for murder."

"Will they so?" he said. "Why, then, here is something to refresh your memory should it prove short," and he struck me again.

I shook my head to clear it. "My word on it, Captain," I said. "My memory will not prove short. If I rot in Newgate twenty years, it will not."

"I trust it will not," he said. "If you escape the rope you so richly deserve, Mr. Mordaunt, I shall myself find some pleasure in exacting the death you owe hell. And now get you below, you and your harlot and yon whey-faced landlord there."

Munke had posted guards below, one at the front, one in the kitchen passageway, and six were penned between. Five of them huddled together in the exact center of the ordinary, on their faces expressions of stunned and amazed despair. It was as if they were Sodomites and the heavens had just opened fire and brimstone upon them, or as if they were cattle waiting in the pens and some terrible foreknowledge allowed them. But Brodrick's face wore no such look. Brodrick was sitting at one of the great center tables, with his elbow propped on the oak and his chin cupped in his palm and stamped on his face that same black and sullen arrogance I think he had been born with. As I emerged from the passageway, his eyes flicked from me to Betty behind me, and he grinned a knowing grin, and I thought, You are a brave man, Brodrick.

Either that, I thought, *or you have less to fear than some of us.*

The two thoughts entered my mind as one, and I broke stride. Even sitting, he managed somehow to swagger, and Aye, I thought, it fits. It fits as neatly as my lady's glove, I thought, for wenching and gaming and drink and that pretty costume can drain a man's estate, and Mr. John Thurloe has no great niceness of conscience about using whatever tool comes conveniently to hand. And if you would know what Judas betrayed you this night, Sir Richard, I thought, why, search out this man's pockets for silver.

Munke brushed past me. "Is this the man, Mr. Brodrick?" he said.

Brodrick did not bother to cast me another look. "The very one," he said.

"Look closely at him," Munke said. "It is no small crime ye charge him with, and I would have you sure and certain."

And now Brodrick did favor me with a glance. "There are hang-dog visages a man does not readily forget, Captain. And his one of them."

I leaned against the tap and tried to engage his eyes and could not. "What man am I, Brodrick?" I said.

Still he would not look at me, only smiled into Munke's eyes and moved a hand languidly. "Did I not say the rogue would feign innocence?" he said.

"An you can bear false witness behind my back," I said, "you can offer it to my face. What man am I, Brodrick?"

"Why, the man who at half after seven this evening engaged me in conversation. On that exact spot ye now stand on."

For one foolish moment I knew an impulse to hurl myself across the space between us and seize him by the throat, and would have had I been certain I could have choked the life from him before the guard could break my head with the butt end of his pike. "What conversation?" I said.

"Why, a conversation on the subject of assassination."

"The particulars. Cite me the particulars."

He shrugged. "An you wish. The story you told was of being straight out of France. Straight from Charles Stuart's pretended court, and with a document you urged me to read."

And now I did shorten the distance between us and then pulled up short and glared down at him. "I should not have stayed my hand," I said. "I should have done God and myself the service of dispatching you when the opportunity presented itself." I faced Munke again. "Is this the story that is to hang me?"

"Why, I imagine it might serve," he said pleasantly. "Though a better one may come to light ere we have done with this."

I laughed shortly. "There are no less than three in this room can give this rogue the lie as well as I. Sir Richard for one." I looked across the ordinary to Willis. "Sir Richard, wilt tell the Captain the truth of this?"

My demand settled to the sanded flagstone between us and festered a little in the silence. Then Willis shrugged. "I know the truth of nothing, sir. Save only that I knew of no plot until the Captain burst in on us."

"Sir Richard," I said, "you at least know—"

But I was speaking to the man's back, and I swung about. "Mr. Doyle," I said. "Mr. Doyle can tell you this rogue lies in his teeth."

But no help from that quarter neither. Nought from that quarter save only the flat look of murder, and even as I moved my hands into that expression, I knew that supplication would be to no purpose. "Mr. Doyle," I said, "I confess to having wronged you, but—"

"Wronged me, sir?" he said. "How ha' ye wronged me, pray?"

"Your daughter. I have taken advantage of your daughter—"

"My daughter? What daughter? I have no daughter, sir."

"Mr. Doyle," I said, "you know before God that this villain lies. And though Scripture admonishes us to exact an eye for an eye, it doth not demand a life for a maidenhead."

He made no reply to that, only smiled a small and terrible smile, and I swung back to Munke. "Betty, then," I said. "Betty can—"

Munke's smile was almost gentle. "Come sir," he said. "Is the innocence you protest reduced to one prong? And that the word of your own quean?"

"No. But give me a week, I can produce a dozen will swear I have not only not been to France recently but have not—"

"Why, as to France, I would imagine that were irrelevant. And as to the week, I do not have a week." He turned a curt and final shoulder to me. "Eight of you are for Newgate," he said. "And there are ten of us. So make no foolish moves, gentlemen; give me no excuse to pistol one of you." He touched a finger to his hat. "I trust we understand each other," he said, and then nodded to the guard in the passageway.

The guard saluted him. "What of the wench, Captain?"

"Ah. The wench." Munke looked at Betty. "If I put some questions to you, girl, wilt answer them truthfully?"

She nodded.

"Then tell me what went on here this night."

She told him what she knew, while he studied her face and thought his thoughts. "And that was all the reason for your wickedness?" he said, when she had done. "To put us off because you thought this man innocent of treason?"

She looked steadily at him. "Not all," she said, and her voice as steady as her eyes but soft, too. "Not all, I think."

"What else? Was it as he said? That he importuned ye?"

91

"I do not know the meaning of that word, sir."

"Why, he besieged you with pretty arguments. He made you offer of marriage, perhaps."

She shook her head. "I am but an innkeeper's daughter, sir. And he a fine gentleman."

"He offered you compensation, then. A crown mayhap—"

"I am an innkeeper's daughter. But I am no whore, Captain." She raised her head in a gesture brief and proud and sad. " 'Twas not he who urged me. 'Twas I who urged him."

He stared at her. "And now you give me little choice, girl."

"You said I was to speak truth, sir."

"And so you are. And I must order you to Bridewell for it. If your reason was nought but concupiscence, you must be punished, girl."

"I suppose I must. Though I know not that word, neither."

"It means naked lust. It means a wicked and willful itch that must be whipped out of you."

She dropped her head. "An it must, it must. Though that not my reason."

"Not that, neither? What was it, then?"

"He drew his sword for me. I have been all my life called tavern wench, and he risked his life for me."

"And for that small act," he said softly, "you would forfeit him your virtue? For that bit of trash you stand ready to bear his bastard?"

"I do not think I shall mind. For what he offered was no trash, sir."

He placed two fingers beneath her chin and raised her eyes into his. "There are occasions," he said softly, "when I doubt the truth of Genesis. And if that be blasphemy, let them make the most of it." He dropped his hand, and now his voice belonged again to a captain of foot in the service of the Protector. "I think we may safely forget the girl," he said.

He was immediately behind me when we reached the entrance, and I broke stride and turned. "I am grateful to you, Captain," I said.

"Are you so?" he said. "Then have the goodness to spare me any expression of it. For it is my settled opinion that you are a scoundrel, and what I did, I did not do for you."

"I know you did not. Nonetheless, I think my memory may prove short after all."

"If you do not face about, I shall take some pains to refresh it for you."

But I only smiled on him. "Newgate or no Newgate," I said, "I do not think I would willingly change places with you, Captain. For there may be some estates which are even less to be preferred than hanging."

"You speak in riddles," he said. "For I am content with my estate."

"Are you, Captain?"

"Aye. And so I would have you expound your meaning."

"I should," I said, "were it not also a hanging matter, Captain." I still smiled pleasantly on him. "Am I still to walk bootless to Newgate?"

He thought on that briefly, his eyes hard. Then he flung an order over his shoulder. "You, wench," he said, "fetch this rogue his boots."

❧ Six ❧

We were seized on Friday, the twentieth of May, and all that week London was a-talk about the latest plot and Mr. Secretary Thurloe was busy at his arrests. By the following Friday a sennight, Thurloe had laid over five hundred by the heels, and the prisons full, and the naves of churches and the cellars of taverns converted to a foreign use. It was a good week for keepers, and the smiths in London waxed fat on charges for ironing or striking off or easement, and the prisoners in Newgate or Marshalsea were stone drunk for a week on garnish.

But we were the first to be seized, and there was room and to spare for us in Newgate that night.

There is a ritual if you would join the congregation at Newgate. It consists of baptism and instruction and confirmation, and the manner of my baptism was thus.

It stands, Newgate Prison, just at the juncture where Holborn Street becomes Newgate Street. If you are one of the casual free in the city, it is no prison but one of the city gates, adorned with great Tuscan pilasters, with the statues of Justice and Fortitude and Prudence, of Liberty and Peace and Security and Plenty set in the niches between them. The statues are smoky and begrimed, and behind the gate the prison is a line of blackened stone flung for half an acre along both sides of Newgate Street; and if you pass through the gate of an early morning or again at dusk, you may hear the curses of the women in the female felons' ward, for the grate to their ward opens into Newgate Street. But if you are free, there is only that, or the press of a distorted face against the grate, or the thrust and stretch of clawed and begging hand through it, to warn you that the statues represent the bitter humor of the designer of the gate, and that this pile of ruined stone is no true human edifice but a half acre carved out of the heart of Hell itself.

But we were to learn it. We were to learn, and well, why it is that the statue of Justice above that gate holds no scales in her left hand but only a raised and naked sword in her right.

It was half after two when we set out from the Belle Savage, with Roundhead soldiers before us and Roundhead soldiers behind us, the light from their links glinting bright and deadly and evil on their slanted pike heads and dull and evil on the cobbles at our feet. The city was quiet as a forgotten grave; in Lower Old Bailey Street, where the timbered and gabled houses of the prosperous define the street, the heavy boots of our escort echoed hollow as doom in the silence; and at the top of the street, the Sessions Hall, its bail dock emptied now of misery and despair, loomed ill defined and foreboding in the gloom that shifted and swirled like fog about the small, bright flare of the links. And then, just as we came abreast of the Sessions Hall, a cloud scuttled before a west wind, and the moon sifted through the edges of it, and the bail dock reminded you on the sudden of a graveyard on All Hallows Eve, and behind the dock the stately and balconied Sessions Hall looked like some ruin out of an older time.

And it is an omen, I thought, the look of the Sessions Hall in light which Lucifer would love. It is an omen, for I have heard tales of Newgate Prison.

There is, hard by the gate and over against the keeper's apartments, a room called by prisoners in Newgate the Lodge. It is a room almost bare of furniture, nought save a stone floor underfoot, and a bench against one wall, and hung all about the room on great hooks the bolts and shackles, the manacles and leg irons. The room was empty when we were herded into it, and the eight of us stood miserably in its center, blinking in the sharp light of the links. Behind us, Munke came into the doorway and lounged against the jamb and called out for the keeper.

His call echoed against the stone and settled to the floor and died. Then the iron-studded door facing me opened, and a man appeared in it, and then the room was not empty. And that, I know, is a curious statement for a man not gone clean out of his wits to make, for nine of us were crowded into that room. But that was my first thought when this man came into that door, that one moment the room was empty and the next it was not. It was as if the nine of us were mere men and the devil had come suddenly among us. And if not Lucifer himself, then some devil's spawn, begotten at the stroke of twelve on some blasphemous altar, with the witch moaning and writhing in ecstasy beneath him, and the moonlight filtering through the clouds like frozen metal seen through gauze, and the congregation chanting the Black Mass at the exact instant of conception.

It was not merely that he was ugly, though he was, God knows, that. He was a hunchback; his right shoulder was pulled cruelly up behind his ear, and hip and flank and backbone were as awry as if he had sometime been put to the rack. Above that thick and twisted body, his great head bobbed crookedly toward his shoulder like an ill-balanced boulder, and below it, his legs were a child's legs, the feet as tiny as a woman's, the shanks frail and shrunken as if by age or disease, and he walked with a kind of painful sidle, one foot jerking forward half a pace, the body twisting about for balance, then the other foot dragged up to meet the first one. It was a forward movement that resembled the advance of some mutilated crab or some great beetle with but half his legs left him.

But it was no twisted body or painful walk that made me feel what I felt when this man appeared in that doorway. For I have seen my share of the mutilated or the ill-favored and I have not recoiled. I have seen men whom the wrathful forefinger of God or the malignancy of witches has touched; I have seen them twisted in leg or back, or blotched of skin, or rotted by plague or gaol fever, or marred by the pox. And I have seen them when the hand of man has had done with them. I have seen them come down from the pillory with ears cropped angrily to the skull and tongues bored through with heated irons and cheeks branded and noses slit from nostril to bridge. Or I have seen them come blinking up into the light from out a prison cell, with ribs showing blue-veined through the taut and scaly skin and hair and beards matted and caked with filth and crawling with vermin. I have seen all that, and I have not felt the touch of cold at my heart as if it had been subtly touched by frozen metal.

But I felt thus now, and that over as simple a matter as a smile.

It was a smile as crooked as his back. He stood with his great head lowered and his eyes upward turned, and the eyes rested briefly on each of us in turn, and the smile hung crooked on lips as meaty as butchered pork, and it was a smile I could not read. It is not, I thought, the smile of a man who has risen content from his supper, nor yet the smile of a man tickled by the latest bawdy jest, nor yet again the smile of a man who means to kill you. Then the eyes rested on me, long enough to appraise the value to within a farthing of the buttons to my coat, and I thought, No great cause for panic, John Mordaunt. For the man is but counting his fees, I thought, and the smile that of some shopkeeper on Paternoster Row, with the day's trading done and the week's profits scattered before him.

Except, I thought, that this man deals in souls, and I am still not overfond of that smile.

Then the eyes took their leave of me and drifted to Munke, and the smile changed subtly in deference to authority.

"Yes, Major?" he said, and his voice as sweet as one of your Quakers fetched before a local justice.

"Captain," Munke said, and his voice told me that he had no great liking for this man neither. "Plain Captain Munke, and I would see the keeper."

"I am deputy keeper. Richard Dicke, an I can be of service, Captain."

"You can. You can do as I bid you and fetch me the keeper."

"'Tis somewhat advanced o' the clock, sir, and Mr. Johnson abed—"

"Rouse him out, then. For this is Commonwealth business, and I have instructions to charge the keeper himself—"

"Ah. Commonwealth business, is it?" Dicke swung about to look at us again. "The lot o' them, Captain?"

"The lot of them."

"And a desperate crew of rogues they are. I have not set eyes on a more cunning parcel of gallows bait this twelvemonth."

"Look ye, Mr. Dicke," Munke said, "'tis half after two in the

97

morning, and I no time for your idle prating, and would ye therefore do me the great good courtesy of fetching me your keeper?"

"Why, no need to rouse out Mr. Johnson for such a trifling matter as this. Let me but fetch a smith—"

"I did not ask for a smith. I asked for the keeper, and that thrice." Munke glared across five paces to Dicke, and Dicke's eyes retreated. "These fees are for your master's pocket, Mr. Dicke," Munke said, and his voice suddenly soft as a striking snake's.

Dicke's hand moved briefly in protest. "Nay, sir, ye misread my motives."

"Do I so?" Munke said. "I have heard tales of you, Mr. Dicke. And if I had not, I can read greed in a hangdog face as well as the next man, and do I so, sirrah?" He paused long enough for Dicke to wet lower lip. "Perchance," he said softly, "ye have a mind to feel iron about your ankles too, Mr. Dicke."

And now I was certain that Dicke's was a smile I did not like. Had I just then put a rule to those lips, I doubt they would have been found to move the thickness of a muscle, and his eyes were lidded, and his head still modestly bent. And yet his smile now conveyed another message. Now it said that if Richard Munke had his own best interests at heart, it were well if he never showed up here in another capacity than guard. That smile stayed on Dicke's lips long enough to provide Munke with fair and ample warning. Then he ducked his head and lurched through the yawn of iron-studded door behind him.

He was gone an unconscionable while. He was gone half an hour, while Munke glowered at us from the entrance; while Sir Richard Willis fidgeted with the purse at his belt, and next him Mr. Doyle rested despairing eyes on the table of fees posted on the wall; while Brodrick favored us with his arrogant smile; while beyond Brodrick the four I did not know huddled together as if for warmth. One of the four was a thick, bearded man with blunt, honest lips and shoulders that pronounced him army. The second was blond and five years my junior, with an eye as arrogant as Brodrick's but a weak, slack mouth. The third was pallid of complexion and watery of eye and thin in shoulder and chest, some village schoolmaster if ever I saw one. The fourth owned a ragged, washed-out beard and a knobby forehead and hot, fanatic eyes and the gray Quaker garb to go with them. For a little I wondered if among those four was one

98

honest man with the courage to give Brodrick the lie. Then I gave up that sport and bethought me instead on the penalties for high treason and the fate of penniless men in Newgate. For innocence bought no bread in Newgate Gaol. For there would be smith to fee if I did not want enough iron hung about waist and ankle to cripple me; and turnkey to fee if I would have a candle to light my misery in the condemned hold; and, once I had begged or stolen coin enough to admit me to the Common Felons' Side, garnish to pay the thieves there if I did not want the very clothes torn from my back; and thereafter fees to the understrappers for daily bread and water and a board to sleep on and permission to use the house of office. And so, I thought, pray God, John Mordaunt, that even now some groom is beating a horse toward Reigate and Henry. For if he is not, you are dead of starvation or gaol fever ere ever they can fetch you before John Thurloe for questioning or Chief Justice Rolle for trial.

But such thoughts feed no keeper, and so I fell to a contemplation of Mr. Brodrick's Adam's apple, a spot my sword point had rested on once and would again if ever the two of us escaped this place. That sport I found more pleasant but shorter-lived, for just as I fell to it, the iron-studded door vomited forth four rogues male and one rogue female. In the van was a slight man in slippers and night-cap. Behind him came a hulking brute in a smith's apron and two hangdog vermin carrying great rings of keys. Bringing up the rear was something that passed for woman, an enormously fat creature with a face that had first seen light of day in a Southwark bawdy-house, and had been weaned in an alley off Lower Thames Street, and schooled in Bridewell, and the education completed in some thieves' den in Alsatia.

The man in the van advanced on Munke. The smith and the turn-keys took up stations behind us. The woman waddled two paces into the room and stopped short and fell to a study of the fish that had swum into her net this night.

The man in the nightcap stopped before Munke. "Captain Munke, is it?" he said. His voice was womanish, and he owned a small lisp. "My deputy hath it that your business is too urgent for his ears."

"You are the keeper, then?"

"I am told so. 'Twas my understanding six months since, when I laid out three thousand pounds for the post."

"And I think you speak truth," Munke said. "You have the scurvy look of a keeper, now I examine your face from this distance."

"Is this your urgent business, Captain? Did you rouse me from bed but for the pleasure it affords you in insulting me?"

"My business is to charge you with the safekeeping of these eight."

Johnson threw us a single careless glance. "And for these I have been denied half a night's sleep? For *these*, sir?"

"They be eight desperate men, Mr. Johnson, and my—"

"These? These desperate? 'Sblood, I have had them committed for but the breaking of a curfew that were more desperate than these lambs."

"They be eight desperate men," Munke said stubbornly. "And my instructions to charge you face to face with their close keeping. If anything goes amiss, you are answerable for it, sir."

"Why, no warning could be fairer than that," Johnson said softly. "And I thank you for it. Though why my deputy could not have committed—"

"I will tell you why, Mr. Johnson. Because men have taken of late to disappearing from this place, that is why."

" 'Tis Hadley ye have reference to, I suppose," Johnson said. "For I have heard nought save Hadley these six weeks now." His face assumed an aggrieved look, the look of a man unjustly accused. " 'Tis common knowledge this Hadley had devised a trick to make ankles and wrists swell—"

"Aye. And secreted a key on his person would open any lock in the city."

"Is it so?" Johnson said. "That I had not heard, Captain."

"Though the key looked like no key. Indeed, it looked uncommonly like a heavy store of gold sovereigns."

For a second time that night a smile warned Munke that if he ever found his way into Newgate, his comfort were an uncertain matter. "I take it," Johnson said softly, "that your meaning is to cast some doubts on my honesty, sir."

"My meaning," Munke said wearily, "is to deliver you instructions from Whitehall. Which are that these men are to be present when Mr. Thurloe calls for them. If they are not, some turnkey may be the richer by fifty pounds, but you are the poorer by one head, Mr. Johnson."

"They shall be here," Johnson said, and his voice sulky now, and on his lips a delicate pout.

Munke nodded curtly. "I am relieved to hear it. These be uncertain times, sir, and not every man you meet owns a conscience for his duties." His eyes swept the room once more, and then he turned on his heel and left us to the tender mercies of Mr. Johnson, keeper of Newgate Gaol, and a hulking smith, and two hangdog turnkeys, and a tun of guts that went by the name of woman.

There was a brief silence in decent observance of the Captain's passing. The woman broke it, in a voice that seemed to come from out a well. "Now yon goes a bilious cur, Mr. Johnson," she said. "An I had any skill at physic and he in my care, I would prescribe a strong purge against that humor."

"I could wish, Doll," Johnson said, "that he were in your care."

"Oh, you may lay to it, I could cure him. I ha' cured worse in my time." She chuckled in memory of other times and other cures, and then her eyes, nigh hidden by folds of flesh, set to roving about the room. "Come," she said. "No need for gloom, gentlemen. Mark me, there be worse lodgings than Newgate, and what say ye to a drink all around afore the smith sets to his business?" Her eyes came to rest on me, and fragile, rosebud lips above an infinity of chins shaped themselves into a coy smile. "You ha' the look o' a worthy gentleman," she said. "Indeed"—and she cast down her eyes, and doubtless would have blushed too, had she not lost that art at the age of nine—"you put me in mind of another, a humble servant o' mine until they carted him off to Tyburn."

"I thank you for that opinion, ma'am," I said.

"A proper young gentleman," she said. "And shall we say a drink all around? For the good o' the house?"

"You may say so," I said. "But I lack the coin to pay for it."

"Why, it can be scored, sir. None of us greedy here, and no need to pay on the nail. Shall we say a pint o' mulled sack for the smith and turnkeys, and a bottle of French white for Mr. Johnson here?"

I considered the matter of mulled sack and French white, for I knew what a refusal brooked, I could feel already the irons, heavy enough to cripple me and fitted so as to chafe ankle and wrist. Then I shook my head. "I have no funds, ma'am. Nor any prospects."

"A pot of ale? A pint all around would not separate you from a crown."

"I do not have a crown. I do not have a farthing, ma'am."

She no more smiled. "Your coat. 'Tis most damnably out o' the fashion and the cuffs frayed. But it might fetch—"

"I think," I said, and my voice stubborn now, for the die had been cast, "I think I have some further need of the coat. 'Twill serve me better against the chill of the condemned hold, I am sure, than your watered wine."

She shook her head sadly. "Now that I think on it, you do not put me in mind of another young gentleman. My recollection has it that he was fairer than you, and broader in the shoulders, and straighter in the back."

"I am sorry to hear you say so," I said. "For I little doubt that he was as handsome as you are fair."

I but cast pearls before swine there. "Also," she said, "there is a cast to your mouth I do not like on the sudden."

"Others have remarked the same fault," I said.

"A certain obstinate cast o' the mouth, a shifty look to the eyes. A desperate rogue or I am no good judge of character, and the smith a fool to settle a grain less than fifty pounds on you."

"He can double that, and 'twill not put a sixpence in my pocket. There is no blood to be squeezed out of a turnip, ma'am."

But her eyes had now wearied of me. "Is it the same scurvy tale all around?" she cried. "Are the lot of you but beggardly culls without the price of a pint of stout in your pockets? An 'tis so, God spare me your plotters, send me instead an honest highwayman."

Willis stepped forward a pace. "I will stand a drink all around," he said.

"What?" she said. "And is there one proper gentleman among us? Shall we say claret, sir?"

"A flask of brandy for me. For the others, what they will."

"My soul on it," she said, "a *very* proper gentleman. I should ha' guessed by the cut o' the coat, and I will serve ye anon, sir." She curtsied ponderously and then waddled out the door, and Willis stepped close to Johnson.

"Mr. Johnson," he said.

Johnson's eyes were fixed speculatively on me. "You may set to work on that one, smith," he said. "I should say fifty pounds on that one, and his wrists well cuffed."

"Mr. Johnson," Willis said again.

"As for the others"—and Johnson's eyes, still speculative, drifted about the room—" 'tis a matter for your discretion."

"Mr. Johnson," Willis said, "I would have a word with you, sir."

Johnson's eyes finally admitted to Willis's existence. "Why, that is small enough request," he said softly.

"I mean in private, sir."

"Why, now," Johnson said, still softly and sweetly, "now 'tis no more a small request. For I have my instructions, sir."

Willis tapped the purse at his belt with one knowing finger. "I have something here might make the request more trifling, Mr. Johnson."

Johnson smiled. "Now, now," he said. "Dost think to bribe me, sir?"

"Why, no. I only thought that were we to step without that door, you should find it more to your interest than mine to hear me out."

"And so I might," Johnson said, "were it not that you are committed on suspicion of high treason, and my instructions plain."

And now Sir Richard smiled, a smile full of knowledge of this world, and weary. "Come," he said. "I am none of your gentry from out Newcastle, and this my first journey down to London." He tapped the purse again. "I have ten pounds on my person. And I can lay hands to another ten ere the clock on St. Paul's comes full circle. And what say ye to that, sir?"

"Why, you are more fortunate than some I could name," Johnson said.

"It has been six years since I last campaigned," Willis said. "And my bones unused to beds as hard as some you might provide me with. And what do ye further say to that?"

"I have a fondness for a soft bed myself," Johnson said.

"In short, sir, I have no humor for a stone bed in Limbo this night. Nor for fifty pounds of iron about ankle and wrist."

Johnson's hands came up and out in a gesture of sweet reasonableness. "You heard my instructions, I believe."

"I have heard little else the past half hour. I find myself grown infinitely weary of your instructions, sir." And now in Willis' voice was no further pretense of soft and patient reasonableness. "This is but a poor game for this hour, sir," he said. "And I would have your fee for other accommodations than the condemned hold."

"An you were common felon, the fee is plainly posted. For admission to the Common Felons' Side, four shillings sixpence plus garnish—"

"I have no mind for the Common Side, neither. I would guess that the oak boards in the Common Side are only a trifle softer than the stones in the condemned hold, and the scum that calls itself human there little to be preferred to the vermin that goes by name of rat in Limbo."

"Why, then, admission to the Masters' Side is thir—"

"Nor for the Masters' Side. I can find company more to my liking in a Southwark stew than is to be found on the Masters' Side, and the stench only half so noisome."

"Then what have ye a mind for, sir?"

"A private chamber."

"Ah," Johnson said.

"Also, a flock bed and clean sheets to it."

"Ah," Johnson said.

"Also, a diet something more palatable than your charity meat and moldy bread and water piped in from Newgate Street and tasting of dead dogs."

"Ah," Johnson said.

"I assume that in my case your fee for admission to the Pressyard will be a trifle higher than the usual ten pounds. Since you are burdened with certain instructions."

"Why, yes," Johnson said. "A trifle. I would say a trifle, yes."

"How much higher, Mr. Johnson?"

"Why, fifty pounds higher, I should say."

There was a silence while Johnson smiled sweetly and reasonably into Willis's eyes, and Willis turned a trifle pale. Then Willis returned that smile with an uncertain one of his own. " 'Tis somewhat advanced of the evening for jests," he said.

"I do not jest," Johnson said. "Believe me, sir, I do not jest."

"Mr. Johnson," Willis said, "you do not deal with some unlettered country boor. I have been sufficiently tutored to be able to spell out a table of fees, all established and posted by order of parliament—"

"Ah," Johnson said. "But those are fees for common felons. Your offense is high treason. The price for high treason comes somewhat higher."

"Somewhat?" Willis cried. "Somewhat? 'Sblood, fifty pounds can purchase an escape from this abomination ye call a gaol."

"Oh, no," Johnson said. "No, I think not, sir. Not when the offense is a Commonwealth matter."

A little longer Willis glared into that reasonable smile. Then his shoulders sagged, and one hand went uncertainly to his forehead. "It is a handsome sum," he said. "I am not in the habit of carrying fifty pounds on my person. I must have a sennight to come by it."

Johnson shrugged. "Why, then, shall we discuss this in a sennight?"

"Mr. Johnson," Willis said, "'tis an exorbitant sum. I doubt even the Protector could pay down such a sum on the nail. But for lack of it I am to be loaded with an infinity of iron and tumbled into the condemned hold, is that it?"

Johnson shrugged again. "Would you say I had any choice, sir?"

"Mr. Johnson," Willis said, and his voice desperate now, and the sweat definite on forehead and lip, "Mr. Johnson, there is gaol fever in your condemned hold. The hold stinks of it, sir, and I am but six months away from one bout with fever."

"Come," Johnson said. "There is gaol fever in the Pressyard as well. An ye have a gaol, ye also have gaol fever, though the disposing of it is in God's hands." He smiled gently. "For a small sum ye can purchase from the turnkeys a nosegay will guard you against it."

"In God's name, Mr. Johnson," Willis said, "I am a dead man if—" and then he broke off, and now whatever was in his voice was no longer supplication. "Look you, sir," he said, "I am not without friends—"

"Ah," Johnson said. "I am sure you are not, sir."

"They are not without influence at Whitehall—"

"Ah," Johnson said. "I am sure they are not."

"So mark me. If I spend a single hour in your condemned hold, you have not heard the last of this, I promise you."

"Ah," Johnson said. "I am sure I have not."

"You may ah me until Michaelmas next," Willis said, "and it will not settle any score. Throw me into the condemned hold and ye shall do other than bleat like a damned sheep, or my name not Sir Richard Willis."

"Ah," Johnson said. "So you are Sir Richard Willis, are you?"

"Aye. You have heard of me, then?"

"Why, no. But I shall endeavor to remember the name." Johnson bowed slightly and then abruptly swung away. " 'Tis my opinion, smith," he said, "that this one is a most impudent, recalcitrant, and dangerous rogue, and I think it only discretion to weight him as heavily as that one there."

"Aye, sir," the smith said. "I have the iron for it to hand, sir."

"He is also for Limbo with the rest of these lambs. An he offer ye a sum to lighten his iron or accommodate him elsewhere, ye are to decline it."

"Aye, sir."

"If any of you disregard my instructions," Johnson said, "I shall have your ears for it. And a slice of nose for good measure. And do ye understand me?" He waited a moment and then bowed, very slightly, and touched a finger to the lace of his nightcap, though to whom the courtesy was directed, whether to any one of us or to all, it was impossible to tell. "I bid ye good evening, gentlemen," he said. "May your dreams be not too unpleasant."

ᚷᚪ *Seven* ᚦ᚜

Such was the manner of my baptism into Newgate Gaol. And the manner of my instruction, first in the condemned hold and later in the Common Felons' Side, was thus.

This is the condemned hold. An underground cell just across the way from the Common Felons' Side, at the far end of a corridor lighted by tapers thrust into the stone and smelling of sweating granite and lingering rot and the misery that lies just this side the grave. An underground cavern, with a hatch and ladder for entrance, and a sewer splitting the cell in twain with fetid water standing in it from out the kennel in Newgate Street, and hooks and chains fixed into wall and floor for the soothing of those guests who go clean out of their wits with terror.

This also is the condemned hold. A stone cell twenty paces square which four times a year (that is, after quarter sessions) will entertain a score of riotous rogues tumbled headlong through the hatch to spend their last night on earth before they ride at dawn to Tyburn; and an inhabitant of the Common Side on these nights will hear the sounds from the hold which mark the passage from night and revelry to dawn and death: first, the declamatory paragraphs as some cutthroat practices his gallows speech; then the laughter as the St. Giles cup is passed from hand to hand; then the soft screams or giggles of the women admitted by the turnkeys from out Phoenix Court, come to help celebrate the passage from this world, and the grunts or groans of pleasure as coiner or murderer commits his final sin on this earth; then the ceasing of all sound save the drunken snore or the sleep-heavy mutter; then, toward morning, out of the silence the sudden sob and the voice raised in awful and repentant prayer, *May God have mercy on my soul may God have mercy on my sinful soul may God have mercy oh sweet Christ Jesus have mercy* . . .

This also is the condemned hold. A cramped and noisome pit which is a most miraculous tamer of desperate men, a most persuasive extractor of fees from stubborn ones; a cold, damp, pestilential corner of hell which in the space of a pair of nights can make a man remember resources he had forgotten he had, usurious Jews he can borrow from, friends whose estates are at his command. A week in the condemned hold and a man will prove willing to give keeper or turnkey his entire estate for exit from it. And if he prove more stubborn than most, there is always another week to do the work, this time strapped on his back to the floor, with the hatch secured, and the darkness pressing in on him like a pillow, and the lice marching to the attack, and the rats brushing across his lips.

For this finally is the condemned hold. A stone hold which, when the hatch is secured, is emptied of everything save a thick darkness, and the rustle and squeak of rats, and the crackle of smaller vermin underfoot, and the stench of the open sewer, and behind these the flat, musty smell of that which can strike terror to any heart —the smell of gaol fever. For gaol fever can bring death as quickly as ever the plague can, and it is always with you in the hold, and it can bring the sweat out on a man even when it is cold enough for thin ice to form on the water lying in the open sewer.

Such is the condemned hold, with good reason called Limbo by the inhabitants of Newgate; and at four in the morning the eight of us were prodded from the Lodge to the hold, one of the turnkeys in the lead, and just behind him Brodrick, swaggering in irons not ten pounds in weight (for he had had a sovereign about him to fee the smith for easement), and in front of me the one with knobby forehead and sober, godly garb, his irons equal in weight to mine (for he had not had a sovereign), and behind me Sir Richard cursing and sobbing under his breath, and as for me, what with wrists cuffed and iron dragging from each ankle, the distance from Lodge to hold seeming somewhat prettier than it is. At the hatch, before the door which leads into the Common Side, one of the cutthroats not yet drunk enough to be snoring caught sight of our heads through the grate and set up a cry of "Garnish, lads, garnish," and a score of voices joined in the cry. Then the turnkey threw open the hatch, and in the Common Side the shouts changed to curses as the scum there learned we were intended for the hold instead, and I was at the hatch and looking down the ladder into the darkness below, and the stench of stagnant water and urine and offal and wet fur and three centuries of sweating stone rose up out of the darkness to greet me, and I gagged against my will, and at my elbow Sir Richard sobbed once again, and this time it was not under his breath.

The turnkey set foot to the ladder and descended, the candle he carried guttering in the draft as he went down. He stood there at the foot of the ladder, the candle held head-high, his face in that light looking sharp and greedy and white, like something God had fashioned with faulty tools out of the flesh of a mushroom. Behind him I could make out the shattered glint of candlelight on the water standing in the open sewer, and in one far corner of the hold the coming and going again of bright, tiny, beady eyes.

"Come, lads," the turnkey called out. "Down the ladder wi' ye, and who among ye to first call this 'ome?"

No one of us set foot to the ladder.

"None?" the turnkey called out. "Must the smith tumble ye in, then?"

I was to one side of the hatch and Brodrick to the other, and the smith set hand to Brodrick's shoulder, and Brodrick shrugged out from under it. "Nay," he said. "Nay, give me leave, sirrah." He stooped and grasped leg irons in his right hand and started down the ladder. He paused in the descent and looked at me, on his lips a smile as cold as ditch frost of a February morn and as triumphant as though this were Tyburn and he come to watch me hang.

It was the smile, I think, that did it.

It was a smile which said that my irons were five times the weight of his, and once I set foot to the ladder, they would drag me scrabbling and tumbling eight feet to the stone below. It was a smile which said that such a fall could break a man's arm or leg, and that a man who lay a night or two in the hold with a broken bone was a dead man indeed. It was the smile of a frilled and simpering monkey who earlier this day had intended to run me through when my guard was down and who later had spoken the barefaced lie which had brought me to this pass. And standing there I felt the throb of rage in my throat, and lying aside it the fear that were I tumbled down this hatch, I might never live to know the satisfaction of again resting sword point just below this thin, arrogant, mocking smile and this time pressing home. And so I did not wait for the smith to put hand to my shoulder. Instead I stooped and grasped my irons awkwardly in my two cuffed hands and then waited, crouched like that, until Brodrick's head was a foot below the hatch level.

Then I straightened and leaped straight on him.

I would have seen his face. Had this been my final moment in this life and one last request granted me, I would have seen Brodrick's face when, still looking up at me with that triumphant and mocking smile, I came hurtling down on him, my ankle chains slipping from my grasp almost as soon as I cleared the hatch, the turnkey below leaping backward when he saw my intent and the candle flying from his hand and clattering across the stone, and the sudden rush of darkness as though God had thundered let there not be light and instantly there was no light, and Brodrick's scream as one of my swinging leg irons met flesh and bone, and the sharp blow as we struck the floor together, he writhing soundlessly beneath me, and then, in that velvet darkness, me scrabbling with cuffed hands for his throat, the thick, muted, animal sobs lodged in my throat behind clamped teeth, and somewhere a long way off, as though it came from across a distant field, the smith crying out as he scrambled down the ladder, and one unknown hand in my hair and another to my collar as they hauled me off him, the rage still thick in my throat, the darkness now flecked with spots of red from the blood behind my eyes.

Then there was light again. Above us someone thrust one of the tapers from out the corridor wall through the hatch, and I saw that it had taken both smith and turnkey to drag me off Brodrick, and both panting from the effort. Brodrick lay at the foot of the ladder, as quietly as if he were laid out for his shroud, and I thought, Well, you have murthered him, John Mordaunt, and it is certain they will hang you now. But the thought brought with it no new rush of despair, the thought brought only a curious relief that it was over and done with now and one score, at least, settled before I died, no need now, once the hatch was secured, for me to search him out in the dark or for him to search me out, no cause for one or the other of us to start up out of the uneasy sleep and the two hands at the throat and the whispering in the ear until all threshing ceased.

"Mad," the turnkey panted in my ear. "Clean gone out o' 'is wits, this 'un be. And canst 'old 'im, Robert? Whilst I look to t'other 'un?"

"Aye," the smith said grimly and tightened his grasp on my collar.

The turnkey loosed his hold on my hair and ran to Brodrick and stooped over him. "Dead?" the smith said. "Be 'e dead, Jonathan?"

"Nay," the turnkey said. "A cracked rib mayhap and a broken pate. But 'e will live to 'ang yet, this 'un will." He came to his feet and turned, his head lowered and his face in the shadow, for the only light was still from the hatch above. "Mad, that 'un," he said, and took a single cautious step toward me. "Meant to kill 'im, 'e did. Wits flown away clean as any bird's, 'is be."

"Nay," I said, and tried to take a step backward and could not, for the smith pressed against my body. "Nay, I—"

"Meant to cheat Gregory o' 'is 'anging fee, 'e did," the turnkey said, "and we must be at taming that 'un, Robert. And art ready, man?"

I felt the smith's body part from mine and move to one side. "Ready when thou art, Jonathan," he said, and the turnkey moved one more cautious step toward me, and I thrust my cuffed hands out before me. "Nay," I said. "Look ye, he had done me grave wrong, and I am not mad, turnk—" and that was all, for in that instant the smith yanked hard at my collar and the turnkey leaped across the space between us.

It did not take them long. They were experienced at this, and skillful, and it took them but a little while. There was the sudden stopping of breath and the wrench of knuckles against neck bone when the smith yanked at my collar, and the brief feeling of flying as his heave pulled me across an ingeniously braced leg, and the sharp blow between my shoulder blades as I struck the floor with the turnkey atop me. There was the pain in my wrists, so sharp I must needs set teeth and lip against it, when the smith, the turnkey still atop me, dragged me across the stone by the chains to my wrists. There was the brief fumbling while they secured hands and feet to the great iron staples driven into the floor and wedged the iron bars across thigh and chest. Then there was but the breath coming painfully back into my throat, and somewhere above me the panting of the turnkey, and the dull throb in my wrists, and straight above me, like a small, bright, deadly sun in my eyes, the flaring torch held through the hatch.

"That should tame the whoreson," the turnkey said. The breath was still thin in him. "And if it do not, why, then, fasting will, eh, Robert?" He chuckled. "Oh, I 'ave seen 'em beg," he said. "I 'ave seen 'em worse nor this 'un whimper for a few drops o' stinking ditch water." He stepped over my body. "You above," he called. "Let us secure the rest o' the lot."

I watched the first foot feel for the top rung of the ladder. At the bottom of the ladder someone groaned, and I thought, It is Brodrick on his journey back into this world. Above me another foot appeared while I thought, In another quarter hour he will have recovered his senses and that is how long you have to live, John Mordaunt. If I have read his character aright, I thought, he will do me the kindness of fair warning—the hand clapped over my mouth, the identity hissed into my ear—and then one hand to my mouth and the other to my throat and only the small and indifferent rattle of my chains to betray the deed. I lay there and dwelt on that certainty while the last of them accomplished the climb down the ladder and the turnkey walked into the light falling from the hatch and there faced us.

"Mark me," he said. "An one among ye should put 'and to 'is throat and provide 'im exit out o' this world, 'twere all one wi' me. 'E is a most desperate knave and penniless, and I bear 'im no great love. But afore one o' ye dwell overlong on the temptation, there is a trifling matter o' the interest Mr. Thurloe takes in 'im. Should 'e depart this world for natural causes, should gaol fever strike 'im down or a diet o' ditch water and stale bread prove not sufficient nourishment, why, that were God's will. But should 'is exit be from other causes, 'tis one among ye will take 'is place at the staples. When yon black 'un regains 'is senses, 'twould be an act o' friendship to convey 'im that message."

He faced about and climbed the ladder and disappeared through the hatch. The hatch clattered to, and the darkness dropped in on me, as soft as any feather bolster and as treacherous as swamp ground, and with the darkness came despair.

❈ ❈ ❈

112

I have no very firm notion of how long I lay stapled to the floor of the condemned hold, with the stink of the sewer to my right hand and the darkness pressing in on me. In the beginning I had the murmur of voices across the hold to keep me company, and Brodrick's groans as he recovered his senses, and his whisper when he joined the others, and another's laid passionately aside his when someone tried to dissuade him, I suppose, from murthering me. Later there was the snore or the restless mutter or the small clank of a chain when someone stirred in his sleep. And something later than that I fell into a fitful and troubled sleep.

Thrice I started up out of the softness of that sleep and then drifted back into it. The first time I came awake to the cramps in shoulder and thigh, and I stirred as best I could for the easing of them. The second time I started awake to a squeak in my ear and the brush of wet fur against a cheek and the whisper of small feet on the stone when I set my chains to clanking. The third time I came back from out a pleasant dream; I was in a cool, dim forest, and it was May and the path soft with moss underfoot, and a clear, frost-cold pool bubbling up from between the gnarled roots of a great oak, and I on my stomach and my face within an inch of the water when I awoke; and then there was the darkness, and a dry tongue on cracked lips, and the thought, The fever is in me. The fever is in me, I thought, and even if Henry is already spurring sweated post horse along some moonlit road, he will arrive only to bury me.

The fourth time I came awake, it was to a hand laid stealthily against my cheek.

I came full awake but I did not cry out. I do not think I was afraid. I came full awake and the hand was to my cheek and I thought, So the deed is to be executed after all. He has lain across the hold, I thought, kept awake by a hatred that will not give him rest or ease, and he has laid that hatred against the turnkey's warning, and the hatred has weighed heavy in the balance. But the thought was weary and indifferent; it was almost as if I contemplated another death than mine, and that someone known only casually and certainly not loved. And atop that thought was the more urgent thought of water, for the fever truly raged in me now. So I lay quietly and waited for the hand to search out my throat and thought on water—on water bubbling up from out some frosty spring in some dim forest; on water let down over the grate at a ha'penny the drop; on water lying close and stinking in the nearby ditch; on any water that would wet cracked lips and cool parched throat.

I lay there and waited for the hand to close on my throat and thought on water and said, softly, "Brodrick," and did not recognize my own voice.

The hand paused in its journey along my cheek.

"An it be you, Brodrick," I said. "I would remind you that once tonight I could have run you through and did not. For this it would seem that you owe me one small courtesy."

The hand lay quietly to my cheek and did not give me answer.

"I do not cry you mercy," I said. "For I am a dead man already. Gaol fever or a Tyburn rope or fingers to my throat, it is all one. But I would ask that you do what you have to do as quickly as you can."

Still the hand refused me the courtesy of an answer.

"If you dispatch me quickly," I said, "I promise you I will not cry out. I may thresh about near the end, but I will not cry out."

"Nay," the hand said. "Nay, I intend thee no harm," and it was not Brodrick's voice. It was a deep voice and one, I would guess, that was capable of great volume. But just now it was small as any child's and tender as any woman's. "I intend thee no harm," the voice said, "and thee cried out in thy sleep."

"Did I so?" I said. "I little doubt it, for the fever is in me. And if your whim be for playing at Samaritan, I would give all I have in this world for a taste of water."

The hand came to rest on my forehead. "There is only the water in the ditch."

"If it be wet, I would trade my place in the next world for a dozen drops of it."

The hand left me, then returned to lay a dripping cloth to my lips. The cloth had been wetted in water from out the ditch; the source of that water was a kennel in Newgate Street, and it had been scented by every cur and horse and chamber pot 'twixt here and Houndsditch, and flavored by all the secret filth and garbage of a busied street but lately washed down in the rain. It was a drink that was a foulness to the taste and an abomination to the nose, but

114

I do not think that I have tasted more than twice or thrice in my lifetime a more delicate beverage.

I sucked the cloth dry. Then I turned my head, for the cloth was harsh against my lips. "I do not know your voice," I said.

"Is it of great consequence? Was it for ignorance of my name that thee cried out in thy sleep?"

"From the 'theeing' and the 'thouing,' I would guess you are the large one in the sober Quaker garb."

"Aye. And my name Somerset Fox."

"Why, I thank you, Somerset Fox. If God be merciful and I more fortunate than I deserve, I shall shortly intercede for you in the next world."

"In that voice?" he said dryly. "Dost expect to persuade the Creator in that same voice?"

I had not thought I had betrayed myself. "I am sorry," I said. "Quaker or no, you alone among them have done me a Christian kindness, and I am sorry, Somerset Fox."

"Do not be," he said softly. "For most in the land feel even as thee. We are not understood, my people, and not loved overmuch."

And there, I thought, you are in the wrong, Somerset Fox, for loved you may not be but understood you are. You talk of peace and brotherly love, you people, I thought, but you also run stark-naked through the streets crying out for the destruction of Sodom and Gomorrah. Your preachers wander up and down our highways and byways, I thought, with their score of wives and concubines in attendance, preaching to those among us of little learning and less wit that they are the risen Christ, and you call this the Word of God and not blasphemy. You refuse to uncover even in the presence of a king, for you acknowledge no master but Almighty God; and you will not swear civil obedience nor even so much as take an oath in a court of law, for there is no law but His law and all oaths blasphemous. But the weavers amongst ye interpreting a Scripture they cannot even read, these are not blasphemous, and aye, you are not loved, you people. But understood you are, and reason and sufficient for your being harried by both Cromwell and by Charles afore him.

Fox might have been a reader of minds. "There be the mad among us," he said. "Aye. But were I the Creator and a choice be-

115

tween our poor witless ones and some among thee who call themselves godly, I think I should know which to call Christian."

Well, I thought, you have wisdom with you there, God knows. "And I also," I said. "And I also, Somerset Fox. For I was thirsty and ye gave me drink; I was in prison and ye came unto me."

"And inasmuch as ye did it unto one of these my brethren," he said softly, "even these least, ye did it unto me."

I turned my face away from him, for the hand to my forehead was suddenly more than I could bear. "Your hand is heavy to my forehead, Somerset Fox," I said.

"So soon? But a pair of hours since the fever struck, and pains in thy head so soon?"

"Nay. It is shame that made the weight."

"Why, do not feel so. If thee be Presbyterian, thee must feel thus toward us. For they have taught it thee."

"I am Church of England," I said. "We are not loved overmuch in the land neither these days," and in that moment I knew despair. For a time I had known courage, I had known a fine and careless bravery in the teeth of death. But I knew no courage now. Now I felt the manhood seep out of me like spoiled cider in a faulty barrel, and what prompted it, I think, was not the hardness of my couch, nor the fever raging in me, nor yet the sharp cramps in shoulder and neck; what prompted it, I think, was the softness of Fox's voice.

I turned my face away from the knowledge of him sitting there beside me, though it pained me to do so. "How long for it to do its work, the gaol fever?" I said. "How long, Somerset Fox?"

"'Tis no certainty thee have the gaol fever. It may be but dampness—"

"How long? A day? Two days?"

"I have seen them has withstood it three," he said. "I have even known one or two has survived it." He put his hand to my face again, then tapped my forehead a single sharp tap. "Hast no pain in the head? Truly?"

"None. A lightness. But no pain."

"Thee did not retch up the water, neither." He was wrapped in thought a little. "Until they throw us down the bread, it will be little more than guessing. But I do not think it is gaol fever. An bread will lie quiet on thy stomach, it is sure and certain thee do not."

"Why, then," I said, "I may live to hang after all, may I not?" The bitterness of that hovered between us a moment, and then it did not. "There is a giddiness in my head like to too much strong drink," I said. "I think I would sleep again now. And were you to stretch out beside me, I do not think I should cry out again."

"Why, gladly," he said. "An thee would have it so."

"I would have it so," I said. "Aye, I would have it so, Somerset Fox." I pressed my face against the comfort of his hand, and now my bed was not so hard, nor the fever so angry in me, nor death so fearful after all. Indeed, falling lightly down into oblivion, it was almost as if I were not in Newgate but in mine own bed in mine own chamber and my senses reeling from a night of merriment. "Wilt do me one more Christian turn, Somerset Fox?" I said.

"An it be in my power, friend."

"An I should march the full distance to death in my sleep, wilt waken me? For I have sins to repent of, and I would have you pray with me. We are not of the same persuasions, you and I, but I think God might lend you His ear, Somerset Fox."

"Thee will not die in thy sleep," he said. "But I shall pray for thee nonetheless."

When I awoke again, the fever was gone out of me.

I came awake, and the fever was departed, and I was clear-headed and ravenously hungry. For a moment, opening my eyes into the darkness, I was not certain that all that had happened to me had not been some dream. The stink of the sewer was still to my right hand, and my hands were still stretched out above my head (though the cramps in shoulder and neck were gone and I could feel no cuffs to my wrists), but for a little I was not dead certain.

"Fox," I whispered. "Somerset Fox."

"Aye," he replied, and it was no dream after all.

"I do not think I have the fever," I said.

"Why, no. It broke in the night."

"I have no fever," I said. "And I own a most monstrous and healthy gnawing in my gut."

"I have a taste of bread for thee," he said. His hand felt out my lips. "'Tis but a mouthful," he said, his voice apologetic, "but even that hard to come by. They were like wolves when it was thrown over the grate. I must needs knock heads together to get thee a single bite."

I chewed on the dry bread, and thought on water to help me in the swallowing of it, and then thought on the flavor and fragrance of the water in the sewer and managed without. "Thou'rt a strange Quaker," I said. "I am told you subscribe to the doctrine of turning the other cheek, you people. Yet you join a conspiracy to relieve the Protector of his life, and you knock heads together to purchase a stranger a bite of bread."

"I am no saint," he said. "I am but a poor weak human."

Amen, I thought. "Wouldst answer me one more question?" I said.

"An I have the wit for it."

"I stood falsely accused. Yet you stood by and said nothing. I had done you no wrong, why did ye not speak out for me? Is it not commanded that thou shalt not bear false witness?"

"A Quaker? Think thee they would ha' heeded the word of a Quaker?"

"Ah," I said. "That was the reason of it, was it?"

He fell silent a moment. And then, "I do not know," he said. "Truly. Mayhap it was the girl. She was not fifteen, and it was a grave wickedness thee committed."

Now it was I who fell silent, and my thoughts not pleasant. "One thing I have noted of ye godly ones," I said. "Ye read Scripture morn and night, and is not the tale of the woman taken in adultery in your version of the Book? Did not Christ say, 'He that is without sin among you, let him first cast a stone at her'?" I turned my face from him. "I would ha' married the wench," I said bitterly.

"Would thee have? Thou'rt not lying to me?"

"No," I said. "No, I am not lying to you. I do not think I am."

He sighed. "Canst forgive me, then?" he said softly. "I am no saint, and canst forgive me?"

"Nay," I said, "nay, ye are saint enough for my choosing, Somerset Fox," and I knew a desire to put out a hand to him. "I have swallowed a mouthful of bread," I said, "and my stomach has not rebelled, and I do not have the gaol fever, Somerset Fox."

"Why, no," he said. "By God's grace thee do not."

"Have I slept long?"

"The clock around, I think."

"And have you watched over me the entire while?"

"Why, no. I slept a little."

"It would appear that ye own a most intimate knowledge of gaols."

"I ha' spent a third of my life in them. Scarce ten among us has not."

"Canst tell me this, then? Do they intend me to lie here an eternity?"

"Why, no. They should ha' returned ere now, your Mr. Johnson or Mr. Dicke. Come to bargain with us further over fees, now the hold hath tamed us a little." He paused, and it was pitch-black in the hold, but I somehow knew that he had cocked his head. "Ah," he said. "I think I was in the right of it there."

He was indeed. I was looking straight above me into the darkness, and there was a square of light on the sudden and a foot feeling for the top rung of the ladder. It was the feeble light of a lanthorn, no more, but even so it was more than my eyes could bear, and I closed them against it. When I opened them again, I saw that Lucifer had returned in the person of Mr. Richard Dicke, and his lieutenant the smith just behind him.

Dicke advanced on me in that twisted, jerky, crablike shuffle of his. "Why, how now?" he said. "Art returned to your senses yet, duck?"

I looked steadily up at him, though the lanthorn he held pained my eyes. "I was never parted from them," I said.

"Were you not? 'Tis not the tale I heard." He set the lanthorn down and moved somewhere above me while the smith knelt at my feet. "No," Dicke said, " 'tis not the tale I heard. But no one at Bedlam hath departed his wits neither, to hear his version."

I looked up into Fox's face. He was crouched beside me, his great, homely, knobby face worn with its quarrel against sleep, and he shook his head slightly, and I held my peace. Dicke finished with whatever he was about at my cuffs and stood up. "There, now," he said. "Is it better now, duck?"

"I could answer ye to more purpose," I said, "an I knew what ye were talking about."

"Why, thou'rt free," he cried.

There was a question in Fox's eyes. "He speaks truth," he said. "Canst move thy arms?"

119

"Why, no," I said, "since I cannot even feel them."

"Then I must needs move them for thee, friend."

There was that in his voice which asked me my forgiveness, and I gave it him with a small smile. "Why, move them then," I said.

He moved out of my sight. I felt nothing for a moment. Then I screamed.

"What?" Dicke said. "Art a trifle cramped, duck?"

" 'Tis the only way I know," Fox said.

"Why, then," I said, through my teeth, "if that be the way of it, move it again, Somerset Fox."

I set my teeth to my lower lip, and he moved my hand again, and my teeth went through my lip as though it were cheese, and I screamed again.

"Nay," Fox said. "Nay, then, we must try another course." He set to massaging my right shoulder, and now I did not cry out. I felt the blood leap into finger and wrist, but it was not more than I could bear, and I did not cry out. "Now," Fox said. "Canst move the arm now?"

"I think so," I said. "For I can feel my fingers," and I flexed my fingers and then moved the arm an inch, and Fox said "Ah," and set to work on my other shoulder.

"The feet, now," he said. "Canst draw them up?"

I put my mind to the nothingness below my thighs, and tried to do as he bade me, and could not. "I cannot, Somerset Fox," I said.

"Then I must do that for thee as well, friend."

"But a moment," I said. "But allow me a breath or two to set myself."

"Nay," he said. " 'Tis never bad in the legs until thee set weight to them." His face went away, and I felt the slow pressure in knee and thigh, and he was in the right of it, it was not so bad in the legs.

"And now to walking," Fox said, and slid a hand under me and helped me to sit up.

"When I am to my feet," I said. "Ye said when I am to my feet. Will it be bad again when I am to my feet? Like the shoulders?"

"Bad enough," he said grimly. "Dost want a minute?"

"No. Let us get on with it."

He lifted me up by main force, and I could feel no legs under me, and I laughed aloud. "You were in the wrong there," I said. "For I

120

feel nothing, and someone hath stolen my feet away while I slept."

"Think hard on thy right foot and walk a small step," he said.

This time the pain was slow in the visit, no sudden blinding stab but a slow roll, and I let go in the knees. "Let me down," I said through my teeth. "Let me down, for I would not scream again."

"Nay," he said. "Walk, man."

"I cannot. As God is my witness, I have no feet and my thighs afire and I cannot."

"Aye, thee can. I ha' seen them has spent thrice the hours thou hast in the staples, and aye, thee can."

I tried again. This time the pain was no slow roll but a stab as sharp as a knife laid to my manhood, and the fog rolled in upon me and then fell away again.

"Ah," I said. "Ah."

"There," Fox said. "That is the worst of it. Another now."

I took another step. The hot, steady throb in my thighs was like some great heartbeat.

"Canst stand alone now?"

"I can try."

He let go of my armpit. I swayed against the sick weakness in me, but I stayed on my feet. And so I shall walk again, shall I, I thought, and I tried a step on my own and did not topple over. "Why, I shall walk again, Somerset Fox," I said. "I shall walk again," and I took another step, and now I realized that no weight was dragging at my ankles. And they are most consummately kind, these gaolers, I thought, most amazingly and Christianly humane, for they have struck off my irons without ever the payment of a six-pence fee, and in the same instant I thought, *Henry.*

Henry, I thought, it is Henry arrived from Reigate. But thirty hours since a groom set out from the Belle Savage, I thought, and they must neither of them have spared whip or spur then. He must have flung himself cursing into the saddle the very instant word arrived, and he must have galloped out of town without a pass or a by-your-leave, and a fresh horse begged from John Drury at Dorking and another commanded at pistol point in Kingston, and on the moonlit road out of Kingston his eyes aglare from lack of sleep, and his third horse laboring and foam-flecked and staggering when they came into Southwark, and on London Bridge one piece of gold parted with in lieu of any pass, and Dicke here the richer by another when Henry burst in on him and demanded entrance to the prison and the striking off of my irons.

Aye, I thought, Henry, and it was kindly of you, brother. My apologies, brother, I thought, for I have harbored doubts about you, I have known moments when I could not have sworn how thick the blood was between us. I came slowly about (it will be a day or so afore I am again steady on my feet or comfortable about the shoulders, I thought as I did so), and Dicke was just to my elbow, the fawning smile pasted to his crooked, meaty lips. "Is it better now, duck?" he said. "Canst cross a hold and climb a ladder, think you?"

I looked at him. "I have a visitor, have I not?"

"Why, yes. Awaiting you in the gigger room. And dost have the gift? Art one o' your thieving gypsies with second sight?"

I looked beyond him to Fox. "If it be my brother come from Reigate," I said, "as I have reason to think it is, you shall not be lying in this place long, Somerset Fox. If it take my brother's estates to do it, I shall fee you into the Common Side within the hour." I looked back to Dicke. "Wilt show me the way now, Mr. Dicke?"

As I crossed the hold, I saw the shadows of the rest of them off in the corner, some sprawled out on the stone, some standing. Then one of the shadows separated itself from the others and advanced on us, his walk as crablike as Dicke's, the iron balls to his ankles clumping and scraping on the stone, and when the shadow came into the lanthorn light, I saw it was Sir Richard Willis.

"Mr. Dicke," he said, "I have spent a night and a day in this hell ye call a hold. Am I to spend a Sabbath here as well?"

"Why, I do not know, sir," Dicke said. "Hast discovered fifty pounds on your person since last we parted?"

"You know I have not."

"Why, then, God can hear a man's prayers as plainly from one place as another, can He not?"

"Mr. Dicke," Willis said, "I must confess to a small lie. My entire estate is to my belt." And now Willis moved full into the light, and there was sweat on his face and a pinched, desperate look in his eyes. "It would be worth two pounds to me, were I to gain admission to the Common Side, sir."

"I ha' little doubt it would. I ha' heard them offer twice that."

"Two pounds. Eight times the sum demanded of one of your common felons. And a thistle crown to the smith there for the easing of these irons. What say ye, Mr. Dicke?"

Dicke wetted his lower lip. "I must speak wi' Mr. Johnson—"

"Surely no need to rouse Mr. Johnson on a matter as trifling as this. Two pounds, sir, and no need for the matter to stray beyond the three of us, eh?"

Dicke's eyes faded away from Willis's. "Mr. Johnson hath given me firm instructions, sir."

Willis shrugged. "Very well, an ye are determined to split the fee. But will ye perform one small act of charity this week, Mr. Dicke? Will ye call Mr. Johnson's attention to the fact that in two hours the Sabbath is upon us?"

"Why, aye. Provided Mr. Johnson be not too drunk to hear me or too sleepy to follow that argument."

Willis shrugged again, and the shrug said one thing but the eyes said another. There was an elaborate and careless indifference in the shrug, but it was not indifference I read in the eyes. "The offer stands but to midnight," he said. "If I must rot here over the Sabbath, ye get no more nor five shillings six out of me."

"Why, then, I shall be the poorer by two pounds, shall I not?" Dicke smiled into Sir Richard's glare, and there was greed in his eyes and regret in his voice. "But should I neglect to speak o' this to Mr. Johnson, I should be the poorer by two ears. 'Twould be a poor trade, I think."

He turned back to me. "An ye will follow me, sir," he said, and started up the ladder, and I after him. The first rungs I found a small problem, and so I paused near the top and looked behind me. Below me, Sir Richard glared up at us, his expression amazed and angry and baffled and frightened. Just behind him stood Fox, and there was no anger on that great, ugly, knobby face, nor any fear neither. There was only a slow, calm smile, and I smiled softly back at him and then climbed through the hatch.

But it was not Henry's face I found pressed to the bars when I followed Dicke past the hoots and jeers of the scum in the Common Side cells and up a pair of stairs and into the gigger room. It was not Henry but Betty, and her eyes troubled as she studied my approach.

"Why, Betty," I said. "Why, child, I had not expected—"

"Oh, my lord," she said. "Oh, John, what ha' they done wi' ye?"

It was the first time she had ever called me John, and I put my hand over hers and smiled into her eyes. "Nought of any consequence," I said. "But a small stiffness in the joints. It will pass." I could feel her hand trembling under mine. "And what of you, child? Have they—"

She shook her head. Then her eyes drifted behind me, to Mr. Dicke, I suppose. "I have brought your purse. I should have come sooner, my lord—"

"Nay," I said. "Call me John. As ye did just now."

She thought on that a moment. " 'Twould not be seemly, my lord."

"Aye, it would."

"John, then." Her voice was uncertain but it was a little proud, too, and she managed a small smile and then was serious again. "It is something lighter than it was," she said. "I gave Daniel a sovereign to set out for Reigate. And they demanded a shilling afore they would admit me here—"

"Nay," I said. "I require no accounting of thee, child." I thrust a hand through the bars. "Pass me the purse."

She fumbled in her bodice and brought forth the purse. "Mr. Dicke," I called out over my shoulder. "Wilt be good enough to join us, Mr. Dicke?"

I heard his shuffle behind me and then his breath in my ear. "Aye?" His voice was thick as honey, and I swallowed ere I faced about.

"Mr. Dicke," I said, "would ye do me the courtesy of searching out your Mr. Johnson?"

But he only stood there with his great head hanging crooked over one shoulder and his eyes fixed on the purse and his tongue wetting his meaty lower lip.

"Aye," I said. "It is a purse, sir, and I would have a word with the keeper."

"Ah," he said. "And that a word about a fee, sir?"

"Mayhap."

He ducked his head. "Ye be out o' irons, sir, and 'tis late, and I fear I cannot leave ye unattended."

"I shall accompany ye, then."

"No need. 'Tis a business we might settle between ourselves, sir."

I stared into his eyes. "That is not the tale ye gave Mr. Willis."

124

"That was Mr. Willis. Mr. Willis is Mr. Willis and you are you. There is a small difference or two."

"Is there so? And what might this difference be? A smith within earshot perchance?"

His eyes shifted—no more nor a hair, but enough. " 'Tis truth Jonathan be not overbright. And he hath been known to babble in his cups."

And you are a rogue, Mr. Dicke, I thought. Oh, you are a consummate rogue, Mr. Dicke. "And what else might have bearing?" I said.

"Another small difference, I think. Though I cannot be certain of it, and ye may prove me in the wrong." His eyes fell again to the purse. "What might it be worth to ye, admission to the Common Side?"

"Nay," I said. "Shall we put the boot on the other foot? For that was the question I was about to ask you."

I could not read his eyes, for they stayed fixed on the purse. But I could read his thoughts, and that as easily as if his mind were a book and open to the proper page and the letters writ large; I could see only an edge of his lowered face, but I could follow his thoughts as he had a try at guessing whether the purse bulged with double gold crowns or only copper ha'pennies. " 'Tis some risk I run," he said. "For I have had my orders, sir." He raised his eyes into mine. "Mr. Willis made me offer of two pounds."

"There is a small difference between Mr. Willis and me. It lies in the size of our purses. Shall we say a quarter of that, Mr. Dicke?"

It might have been pain I read in his eyes. "Nay," he said. "Nay, it would scarce pay me—"

"There is another difference between Mr. Willis and me," I said. "The floor of the condemned hold is a deal softer against my back than his." I turned back to Betty. "I have offered Mr. Dicke twice the posted fee for admission to the Common Side," I said. "But there is some risk in this business, and Mr. Dicke is a fearful man. And so you can have your small store of shillings and pennies back again, child."

"Nay," Dicke said. "Nay, let us not be overhasty—"

I looked over my shoulder. "I am not hasty, Mr. Dicke. Only poorer than ye guessed."

He wetted his lower lip again. "Ten shillings, then," he said, "an that be all the store—"

"Not all. I can find another ten for the release of Mr. Fox. True, it is an outlay will leave me not a shilling for garnish—"

He nodded gloomily. "Agreed," he said.

I smiled civilly on him. Then I emptied the purse into my hand. I gave him one sovereign and one half crown. I did not look into his eyes as I did so; I did not have to to know what expression he would wear when he realized he had been cozened. I thrust another few shillings into my breeches pocket, store against the garnish I would be forced to pay out once I was among the scum on the Common Side. I put the remaining coins back into the purse and thrust it through the bars.

"You are to take this, child," I said. "It is scarce five pounds, but—"

She shook her head. "Nay, my lord—"

"John," I said.

"Nay, John, I ha' no need—"

"Aye, you do. Against your journey north."

"My journey? I intend no journey."

"But you do. And that within the month, I would guess." She was looking strangely at me, and I shook my head. "They have not addled my wits," I said softly. "But they will examine us within the week and try us within the month. And if it be the cart for us, you are to go north to Turvey and seek out my brother Henry. You are to tell him that you bear his nephew in your belly, and that it was his brother's dying wish—"

She caught her breath and her eyes widened.

"Nay," I said gently. "Nay, there be worse deaths than hanging, and you are not to cry, child."

"My father?" she said. "My father as well?"

"I do not know. It is certain they will find us guilty, for the Protector will see to it that the Court has its instructions. But whether it will come to hanging I do not know."

"But you think it will," she said. "You think it will."

"I do not know. Truly I do not." I pressed the purse into her hand. "If it comes to the cart, promise me you will go north, girl."

She closed her eyes and nodded.

I laid my hand to her cheek. "Come," I said. "No man worth spill-

126

ing tears on, child, least of all me. And let us have a smile now."

She put a hand to mine and then assayed a smile. I looked down at her and thought, Aye, a younger son could indeed do worse. "If they do not hang me," I said, "I shall search you out at Turvey. For I do not think I would have our son called bastard." A little longer I let her hand rest on mine. Then I faced about. "You may show me to the Common Side now, Mr. Dicke," I said. "On the way, perhaps you can answer me one last question."

"If I can," he said.

"A little ago you implied there was a further difference between Mr. Willis and myself. But you did not enlarge upon it. Woulds't do so now?"

"Why, the difference is fear, sir." He smiled up into my eyes, and there was cunning and greed and roguery in that smile. "Mr. Willis offered two pounds for a release ten shillings would ha' purchased him. Give Mr. Willis another hour, I think he might offer three."

"And you think I would not have?"

"Why, I do not know. But I saw you spend twice twelve hours in the staples and then get up and walk. You screamed out, but you got to your feet and walked. I do not think Mr. Willis would ha' accomplished his feet, sir."

I grinned. "Mr. Dicke," I said, "you are a scoundrel."

He ducked his head. "Aye."

"Possibly," I said, "you are the most consummate scoundrel I have ever laid these two eyes on."

"Why, as to that, you may meet my equal, sir. An your stay here a protracted one." His head fell toward his shoulder, and he looked sidewise up into my eyes. "This difference between you and Mr. Willis. Why do ye ask?"

"Nought," I said. " 'Tis but that I thought it might be yet another one."

"And what one?"

"Innocence," I said.

There were a round dozen of as precious a set of branded cheeks and slit noses and cropped ears as a man could wish for in the Common Side when Fox and I were ushered into it. They were all in the great center cell, for it was an hour yet to the Sabbath and Doll's Black Dog still serving; and they faced about as one when we en-

127

tered—all, that is, save one ferret-faced rogue who was engaged in making water against a far wall and another who sat within a foot of him, his back to the wall, and looked drunkenly on. We stood there, our backs to the clang of the door and their eyes fixed on us. Then one of them bawled out for a Tom Walker, and the reply that came back up the taproom stairs sounded like the bellow of a hurt bull floating across a distant field, and then another appeared on the stairs.

I have seen men as large in my time, but no more than twice or thrice. When the ring of grinning faces parted and he came across the cell to us, I guessed he would weigh eighteen stone on an honest scale and would tower two heads above me. He wore a shirt open to the waist and scurvy breeches and scuffed and dirtied boots, and he walked with arms loose to his sides and hands turned out; with that ring of bearded, mutilated, pocked, grinning faces behind him, and the mat of black hair to his chest, and that walk, he put you in mind of some bear come upright in the pit and the dogs just loosed on him. Then he had planted himself before us, feet apart and a grin on his face, and I leaned back against the bars and fixed my eyes on the scar to his right cheek. It was a scar as fresh as this week Wednesday, and beneath his stubble of beard it looked like a long, fine, delicate brush stroke, and I wondered how he had come by it, in what brawl or drunken taproom argument, and whether the one responsible for it was now out of here with a broken back or crushed ribs.

"Chummage, Tom," one of the scum behind him said. "Chummage, as God is my witness, and me wi' a raging thirst."

He grinned down at us. "Doll," he roared. "Damn ye, Doll, ye damned pocky tub o' guts—"

Doll's fat, sweated face appeared on the stair. "Aye, Tom Walker?" she panted. "What art bawling about now, like a calf has lost a mother's tit?"

"Drink," he said. "Nigh dead I be from a parched throat—"

"Ye ha' run up a week's score a'ready," she said. "And ye do not wheedle me out o' one more pint, Tom Walker. An ye were gasping your last for want of drink and my immortal soul at stake—"

"Why, open your eyes, woman," Walker said. "Is the fat so thick ye cannot see through it to what hath joined us?"

She looked at us and recognition dawned. "And be these your

128

chummage, Tom? These?" She made a mouth and spat on the stairs. "'Steeth, these two have not a pair o' ha'pence to rub one against the other."

"They had best," Walker said. He looked from one to the other of us. "Welcome to the Common Side o' Newgate Gaol," he said.

Our backs were to the bars, and my shoulder was touching Fox's. I wanted to turn my head and look at him but did not. "I thank you," I said.

Walker threw back his head and roared with laughter. "He thanks me," he gasped. "God love me, he thanks me, and hath he not breeding, this one?" He broke off laughing as abruptly as he had given voice to it. "Hast a shilling to go wi' the breeding?" he said. "Hast chummage, m'lord coxcomb?"

"Chummage?"

"Aye. Chummage. Ye ha' heard o' the custom?"

"An it is garnish ye mean, I have heard of the custom."

"Why, ye are a fine gentleman and have breeding. And so 'tis garnish to you. But I am out o' a Southwark stew, and so 'tis chummage to me." He snapped his fingers; in the brief quiet it sounded as loud as a pistol shot. "A shilling. Hast a shilling?"

"Aye."

"And the one wi' ye. Hath he a pair to go wi' it?"

"Is this also the custom? One shilling from one man, two from another?"

"'Tis my custom. I ha' little fondness for your damned saints, and 'tis my custom."

"He does not have two shillings," I said. "He does not have so much as a tradesman's token about him."

"I hope 'tis truth you speak," he said. "For 'twould be sport to strip the bastard and prance him through a gauntlet. 'Twould pleasure me to rosy the arse o' one o' his breed."

"I shall pay his garnish," I said, "if you will settle on a single shilling from each of us."

He shook his head. "One shilling from some, two from others. 'Tis a custom o' mine."

"Then strip the both of us. For ye get no garnish from me."

"Look ye, m'lord coxcomb," he said. "I could snap ye in two with one hand. I could but break wind small and bend ye like a sapling in a gale."

129

"Little doubt. For certain it is ye are a deal of wind and all of it stinking." I lowered my head. "There are two of us. And wouldst prove ye are aught else? Wouldst have a go at us, whatever your name is?"

"Walker," he said. "Tom Walker, as ye shall ha' cause to remember."

And now Fox's hand was to my arm. "Nay," he said. "Nay, he is understrapper here, and a baker's dozen of them to but two of us—"

I shook his hand loose. "I think he will have need of them, this scum." I looked at Walker and spat. "Come. Come, sirrah, and have at us."

And now his grin was the grin of a man who had joined in a dozen tavern brawls and discovered joy in every one, and his head was lowered and his hands loose to his sides, and I crouched and waited for him, seeing behind him the ring of amused, bearded, verminous faces, hoping as he advanced one step and then another that Fox would have time, ere he could crush my ribs or snap an arm, to get behind him.

He took a third step and then froze. For another face, another voice had appeared on the tap stairs.

It was a pallid, girlish face, the nose and lips thin and delicate, the eyes dark and long-lashed, the voice as girlish as the face, and Walker froze and then turned to face it. "Tom Walker," the face said. "And what art brawling about now, Tom Walker?"

"Why, nought, Nick," Walker said, and I wondered, in the presence of such a one as this, at the sudden surliness in his voice. "Nought but a coxcomb wi' breeding and one o' your damned godly ones and a small difference over chummage."

The face came the rest of the way up the stairs, and the faces parted for it, and something that was all ribbons and lace and a mincing walk like some dancing master's came toward us. "Is it the truth Tom speaks?" he said. "Have ye not a shilling?"

"I have one. One for me and one for my friend here. But not two for my friend, as this whoreson claims is the custom."

" 'Tis a custom I also hold with. I have no more love than Tom here for their damned cant. And art one of them? For ye are not dressed—"

"No, I am not."

"Yet ye call this one friend?"

130

"Aye, I call him friend. I have spent a day and a night in the staples in the condemned hold, and he gave me water and fought for a bite of bread for me and saw me through a bout with the fever, and aye, I call him friend."

He was smiling at me, a smile I did not find to my liking though I could not tell you why. "Ye have spirit," he said. "I have seen Tom break a man's back, and the quarrel over less than a shilling. What art committed for?"

"Treason."

He raised his eyebrows. "A king's man, are ye?"

"So John Thurloe would have it."

"And this one ye call friend? What his offense?"

"The same."

"Come, now. A king's man dressed in that garb?"

"Garb or no, he was seized for plotting the Protector's life."

"Why, then," he said, and swung daintily about to face Walker again, "why, then, this is a different tale, is it not, Tom?"

There was a scowl on Walker's face to balance the smile on the other. "Now, look'ee, Nick," he said, "'tis twice in as many days ye ha' cheated—"

"Why, twice or ten times twice, 'tis all one, is it not?"

Walker did not give him reply.

"Is it not, Tom?" Nick said again.

Walker's eyes gave sullen ground. "A shilling apiece, then—"

"Why, no. Not a farthing. Not a groat. For we have an agreement, have we not?"

"An that be what ye choose to call it."

"Why, aye, I choose to call it so. Do ye not choose to call it so, Tom?" He lounged there, his smiling face, upturned to Walker's, slim and womanish and pale; and Walker, half again his height and thrice his bulk, glared down at him, on his face an expression as old as time and as savage as original sin. And yet, watching these two, I did not know which of these, smile or scowl, I would prefer to face down. "Do you not choose to call it so, Tom?" Nick said again.

This time Walker's eyes refused to break. "Now look'ee, Nick—"

"I put ye a question," Nick said. "I would have a reply. And I would deem it a courtesy were you to heed your voice in the answering of it."

If it was volume this other referred to, then Walker was in no humor for courtesy. "No," he said. "No, I do not choose to call it so. I hold it no agreement when—"

"Art raising your voice to me?" Nick said. "Hast forgotten your instructions so soon, Tom?"

"Look'ee, Nick," Walker said, "but move that devil's hand o' yours a hair, but twitch a finger, and I swear—"

And now it seemed to be Nick who broke. One moment he was lounging there, almost as if there were a wall or a post to his shoulder, and smiling up into Walker's glare, and then the next he seemed to wilt. "Ye disappoint me, Tom," he said. "I had thought your memory longer—"

And then his right hand disappeared.

It is no hyperbole I speak; it is the plain, unvarnished truth. One instant the pale, delicate-fingered hand was there, a little before him, the white lace of his fine shirt framing the wrist below the dark line of the coat, and the next instant it was not—or if it was, it was no clearer than the blur of a hummingbird of a summer morning and your head turned. Then the hand was back, the knife in it long as a plumed quill and a deal sharper, the point laid lightly and precisely to the right of the line already to Walker's cheek, and Walker seemingly paralyzed in the very act of reaching out for him, his hands a foot from his hips and his body bent and his fingers curled like claws, and I now knowing how the scar had come recently to Walker's cheek.

"Shall we be at repeating our catechism, Tom?" Nick said, and his voice so low you must needs strain to hear it.

Still Walker glared down at him. "Draw blood again," he said through his teeth, "and I swear I shall murder you, Nick."

Nick moved the knife quickly, a single inch along the cheekbone, and the knife point bit, and the blood welled. "Let us to our lesson for the day," he said. "What is my name, man?"

"Nick. Nick Swiftsure." Walker's voice was thick, his words as blurred as if he spoke through a mouthful of porridge.

"Why, good, Tom, good." The knife moved another inch. "And what my humor in voices, Tom?"

"Ye cannot abide a loud voice."

"And what is our agreement?"

"No chummage from a king's man. Double chummage from your saint, but none from a king's man."

132

"And do ye choose to call this an agreement?"

"Aye. Aye, I choose to call it so."

"Why, good, Tom." Nick stepped suddenly and daintily back from him. "Very good indeed, Tom," he said, "and am I not a fine tutor?"

Walker's hand went to his cheek and then came away, and he stared down at his bloody fingers. "I warned ye, Nick," he said. "I warned ye fair. I shall be avenged for this. An I must search ye out in hell—"

"Why, Tom," Nick said, "wouldst still be at your lessons? And me in a humor to declare a recess for the day?"

"Jest," Walker said. "Jest. But do not fall asleep, Nick."

Nick smiled at him, a quick, cheerful smile. "I sleep like a nervous cat, Tom." Then his eyes dismissed Walker and he turned carelessly to us. "Wilt join me in the Black Dog, gentlemen?" he said. He wiped the soiled blade lovingly on his sleeve, his head down the while, his shoulder turned indifferently to Walker. "I would hear the news of the latest plot," he said. "Wilt join me, then, in a bottle of Doll's very bad wine?"

I looked from Walker to him and back again. "I have a pair of shillings in my breeches," I said. "I would stand drinks all around, if I were permitted to do so without an argument with that toy of yours."

He looked at me quickly and smiled the smile I did not like. "Why, no need. Is there, Tom?"

He put the question carelessly, over his shoulder, his back turned indifferently to Walker, and Walker but stood there, the look of black murder stamped on his face, his body crouched as if to spring, the blood dripping off his chin. "Is there need, Tom?" Nick repeated, and I wondered that Walker did not choose this instant to spring and break a neck with one buffet aside the head.

But he only said, "No. No need," thickly.

"For we have an agreement, have we not, Tom?" Nick said cheerfully.

"Aye," Walker said. "Aye. An agreement."

"Agreement or no," I said, "it is the custom, and I would stand drinks all around."

He shrugged. " 'Tis your pair o' shillings, friend."

I dug into my breeches and put the coins into Walker's hand.

Then I looked again to Nick. "If I am to stand you a drink as well," I said, "you will have to help me off with a boot first."

Again he threw me that quick, sidewise look. This time I found his smile somewhat more to my liking. "I shall stand for the drinks," he said, "an ye will do me the kindness of joining me."

"Aye," I said. "Aye, we will join you."

ʅɑ *Eight* ᴆʒ

I lay a sennight in the Common Side before I was fetched before John Thurloe for examination. I lay a sennight among the vermin and the rats, the cutpurses and the cutthroats, the fat, rich, acrid stench of the buckets that served us for house of office and the subtler smells of sweated bodies and fouled clothing and sour breaths; enduring the braggart tales and the bawdy, swinish jests; occupying my days in drinking with Nick Swiftsure, in discussing politics and religion with Somerset Fox, in searching out lice in arm-pit or crotch; looking on whenever the great door would swing to and another poor devil admitted and Tom Walker roaring up the tap stairs to extract his garnish; looking on one afternoon when a light-fingered one among us (a boy of no more nor fourteen) re-lieved another of sixpence and was rewarded with six inches of steel between his shoulder blades; looking on another night (until I must needs turn away in disgust) when a crown passed into a turnkey's hands and two women from the Debtors' Side, born shameless or brought to it by confinement, accommodated a score of my com-panions at sixpence a rutting. I lay a sennight in the Common Side while my small store of coins grew smaller—threepence to Walker thrice a week for a cupful of the swill made of broken meats from the taverns and bread seized for short weight in the market and water, all boiled together in a delicacy somewhat thinner than paste and as tasteless as untanned leather; another penny to Walker for a

135

fistful of the moldy bread that was our diet on alternate days of the week; a shilling a day to Doll against my reckoning in the tap; another penny to a turnkey each night for the privilege of staying in the great center cell rather than being turned into the small and infinitely filthier cells to either side of this one.

I lay a sennight in the Common Side and watched my coins disappear and heard no word from Henry and wondered what mishap had occurred. Sometimes, in the small of the night, lying amidst the vermin and the drunken snores, I would think on the time when I would be penniless, and my name, one among five hundred, forgotten among John Thurloe's papers, and my fate to lie forever in this place. Sometimes, in the small of the night, I would think on that and despair.

By the end of the week more than eighty of us were crowded into a cell intended for thirty, and of these, threescore had been taken in the plot. By that time Brodrick and Willis and Doyle, the innkeeper, had joined us, along with a John Gerard and a Thomas Henshaw and a Peter Vowel and fifty nameless ones, and the cell was so crowded that come night, some of us could not find space on the floor to stretch out but must sleep sitting up, our backs to the wall and our feet drawn up and our chins sunk on our chests.

They came first for Somerset Fox.

They came on a Monday just at noon, eight stern-eyed, cold-lipped soldiers, and marched him away. They returned him four hours later, and eight or ten of us crowded about him, all of us asking questions at once about how he had fared at their hands. He made no reply, only shouldered his way through us and made for the far wall and sat down and buried his face in his hands.

We followed him. I crouched down before him. "Fox," I said softly. "Somerset Fox."

He made me no reply, and he would not lift his head. They have not racked him, I thought, else he would have betrayed it in his walk. "What did they do to you?" I said softly. "What, Somerset Fox?"

Again he made no reply.

"Have they relieved you of your tongue, then?"

"Pray thee, leave me be," he said, into his hands. "Pray thee, depart, and leave me in peace."

I stood up and looked at Sir Richard and shrugged a trifling shrug. He remarked the shrug and then dropped his eyes. "Look ye, Fox," he said, and his voice was not rude, but neither was it soft, "look ye, we would but know how they dealt with ye."

"Why, they asked me a deal of questions," Fox said.

The look to Willis's face was quiet and musing and puzzled. "And what else? What rude handling from your guards? What threats of racking—"

"Nought else. Nought but a deal of questions."

Willis drew a small breath. "Why, an that be the sum of it, we have little to fear, have we? An we but choose a story and cling to it—"

And now Fox did raise his head, and his garb may have been Quaker but his eyes were not. "Ye think that is the sum of it, do ye?" he said, and it did not escape me that his pronouns were on the sudden not Quaker, neither.

Nor did it escape Willis. He stood there, his stance as idle as a masterless servingman's standing before a pillar at St. Paul's and the day yet young; but the lapse did not escape him neither, for I noted the look that flitted across his face. "And what is the sum of it, then? If they do not propose to rack the truth out of us—"

"Why, no," Fox said. "No, they will not rack ye. Doth a man go in search of a cow he hath already milked?"

"I am none of your wits, friend Fox," Willis said. "I am a plain man, and I would have a plain answer from you."

"Would ye so? Why, then I shall supply you." Fox's eyes made a brief circle of the ring of faces before him. Then he was to his feet, and the look in his face one you might have seen on a battlefield, with the sun setting on the lost cause and the last man left it ringed about. "They shall not rack the truth out of ye because they already own it. They can name ye names and places and times, and is that answer plain enough?"

Willis shrugged. "They can doubtless hazard a shrewd guess."

Fox laughed. "A shrewd guess? I tell thee I stood before Thurloe and heard him name thee and me and Gerald and Brodrick and Vowel and a dozen more, and he itemed which of us was to do for the Protector, and who to fall on the Meuse, and who to seize horses in Smithfield. Name of God, they can even name thee the tavern scores for each meeting, and who took his leave for a visit to the house of office and how long his stay."

137

And now Willis's stance was not so negligent. "They cannot," he said. "There were not a dozen of us at the center of this—"

"I tell thee they can."

"I will not believe it. Unless" —and Willis leaned—"unless— How didst answer their questions, friend Fox?"

Fox shook his head. "Nay. Ye do not put this off onto me."

"How?" Willis repeated. "How, damn ye?"

Fox's eyes did not waver. "I betrayed no one. I but confessed my part—"

There was, on the sudden, a silence you could have counted to ten in, only the murmur of voices coming up the tap stairs to our backs and the sound of Willis's shallow breathing. Then Willis said "Ah-h-h," the sound long and drawn out, the sound he might have made had the steel just entered his back, and his hand went uncertainly to his face, as if he had just brushed into a spider's web on some dark garden path. And then, "Ye confessed? And ye call this no betrayal?"

"I betrayed no one," Fox said stubbornly. "We were already betrayed—"

"So they made ye no threats? They must have made ye promises, then. What promises? How many pieces of silver didst agree upon, friend Judas?"

"They promised me I would not hang," Fox said.

Willis laughed, and the laugh dropped between them as short and sharp and bitter as glass hurled against stone. "And ye believed the bastards?"

"They took an oath on it. If I confessed, I would not hang."

Willis laughed that laugh again. "And why shall they not? Dost have land they have set their hearts on, M'lord Fox? Hast laid up a fortune with the goldsmiths? 'Sblood, think ye they propose to settle accounts for but those miserable clothes to your back?"

Fox shook his head. "But I ha' one thing they want. I own the health to endure a sea voyage. And the strength to chop sugar at the end of it."

"Transportation," Willis whispered. "They mean to transport us."

"Some of us."

"Why, may God have mercy on your soul, then. For myself, I prefer the quickness of a rope," and now he turned a shoulder to

Fox, and a little longer the faces behind him still ringed Fox about, and then they did not, and only Fox and myself left in that corner, Fox still with his back to the wall and his eyes circling a ring of enemies who were no longer there.

"Fox," I said.

His eyes drifted back into mine. "Thee had best join the rest o' them," he said. "An confession be betrayal, then I ha' betrayed thee as well."

"But one question first. Ye say they named ye names. Did they name my name, Somerset Fox?" I waited decently and reasonably in the silence, and then I put a hand to his arm. "Come," I said. "Though you accused me falsely, you stand forgiven for it, and I would but know—"

"They named me thy name," he said. "Aye. And I swore that thee stood falsely accused."

"Why, I thank you."

"Do ye so?" His eyes fell heavily to the stone at his feet. "They named me one further price for my life. If it come to a trial, I am to testify against thee."

I stood in the silence between us and tasted the bitterness. "And you agreed," I said, and it was no question.

A little longer he stood thus. Then he brought his head up, and his eyes were wide and wild, and I felt his arm trembling under my hand. "It is the traitor's death I cannot abide," he whispered, and he may have been speaking to me and he may not have. "Canst understand it is only that? Were it but over quickly. But 'tis the cutting down while ye are still alive, and the quartering—"

"Nay," I said. "Nay, Somerset Fox," and I tightened my grasp on his arm.

"And do ye thank me now?" he said.

"'Tis a high price they exact for a life, these saints," I said bitterly. "Even the price of perjury. And aye, I thank you. For is it you, then, demands forgiveness?"

They came for Brodrick and the youth they called Gerard the next morning, and for me that afternoon. They marched me out the prison into a May sunlight that struck me sharp as a blow in the face and into air that did not stink of urine and excrement and foul breaths and sweating stone and dead rats, air that even here in Newgate Street smelled like a spring breeze drifting across wet, growing fields into the open casement of a death chamber.

I was examined at Guildhall, in a large, fair chamber provided with a polished table littered with papers and inkpots and quills and sand shakers, and enough chairs to provide all the Council of State with their ease. There was but one man in the chamber when I was ushered into it. He was busy at the papers before him, and he did not raise his head when my name was given him, only ordered the captain of my guard, in a dry, distant, indifferent voice, to inform My Lord that I had been fetched and to look to the witnesses against me. I stood there, just within the door, breathing against the small, dry scratch of his quill, thinking, Is this, then, John Thurloe? For he looked like no man who had risen to Secretary of State under Oliver Cromwell. He was bent over his papers, and so I could see only the top of his head and his right hand, the ink-stained, grubby fingers curled childlike about the quill. But that was sufficient to tell me that I would not have cast him in the role of the third or fourth most powerful man in the kingdom, that rather I should have guessed him some small, hurried, fearful clerk in some haberdasher's shop in the Cheap. He was uncovered, and he wore an unkempt scratch wig of no certain color, and his coat was a severe brown save where it was spotted by greasy food and splashed wine, and the lace to his shirt front was grimed from too long in the wearing, and no need for him to raise his head for me to know that the skin to his face would be dry and scaly and that he would wear the soft, thick look of the small-framed man who has gone slowly to fat at jowl and wrist and paunch. And is this, then, John Thurloe, I thought.

I stood there just within the door, with the May sunlight falling quietly into the room, and the scratch of the quill small and dry in the silence, and this John Thurloe, this five-shilling clerk, oblivious to my presence, or playing at it. Then he laid his quill precisely aside his papers and raised his head.

"Yes," he said. His voice was as dry as the skin to his face and as neutral as his eyes or wig. "John Mordaunt, is it?"

I nodded.

"Yes," he said. "Mordaunt." He looked at me as he might have looked at a flounder of uncertain age and quality lying on the block in Fishmarket Street and his dinner yet half a morning off. Then his eyes dropped to a sheath of papers before him. "Ye know whereof ye stand accused?"

"Falsely," I said.

He did not raise his eyes from the paper. " 'Twas not the question I put you."

"I know whereof I stand accused. The accusation is false."

Now he raised his head. "In four years," he said, "they have fetched an infinity of you malignants afore me. I have yet to clap eyes to one was not falsely accused."

"I stand falsely accused," I said stubbornly. "I am party to no plot. I was but a chance guest in the inn—"

He cut short my protest with a wave of his hand. "Your quality?"

"Gentleman."

He fastened dry, distant, speculative eyes on my coat and hat and boots. "Are ye so, now?"

"I am son to one Earl of Peterborough," I said, "and brother to another. My paternal grandfather was Henry, fourth Lord Mordaunt, and my maternal grandfather Lord William Howard, Lord High Admiral—"

"Content," he said. "Your means of support?"

"A gentleman's."

Now his eyes were not so dry and indifferent. "Do I find you impudent?"

I shrugged. "I have no such intent."

"Nonetheless, I find ye so. Indeed, ye are as surly and recalcitrant a cur as I have laid eyes on this twelvemonth. I shall put you the question again, and as plainly. What visible means of support?"

"I abide with my mother. We live on what little has been left us."

"And your meaning there?"

I shrugged again. "The times are scarce propitious for one of my brother's persuasions."

"Your brother's?" he said dryly.

"My brother's. I hold no persuasions. I have little head for politics."

"And religion? What of religion, Mr. Mordaunt?"

"I do not follow your meaning."

"Why, my meaning is papacy. Art a papist, Mr. Mordaunt? As was your grandfather afore ye?"

141

His reference was to the fourth Lord Mordaunt and the Gunpowder Plot. "Yours is a long memory," I said. "Is it long enough to remind you that I also had a father? Is Edinburgh Calvinism papacy, Mr. Thurloe?"

"Nay," he said. "Softly, softly. No cause for heat."

"No cause? Is it Whitehall policy this season to hang a man for the crimes of his grandfather? Is that no cause for heat?"

Now he was smiling. "An I so chose," he said, "I could find that speech treasonable. An I so chose. You are no papist, then? Ye cling to none of the old superstitions? Ye practice none of the old secret rites—"

"Why, yes. I yet address my Maker on my knees. I find childhood habits easy to come by but hard to part with."

"Nought else? No Book of Common Prayer secreted—"

So that was it, I thought; so they have used this week to advantage. I wondered how thorough their search of the Priory had been this time, what casements broken or walls mutilated, what trees axed and crops trampled, what outbuildings burned, what insults endured by my mother or our servants. "I had thought," I said, "that our discussion concerned papacy, not the established church—"

"The established church?" he said. "Come, are Reigate roads so bad that ye have not heard that England no more has bishops? Or that the Book of Common Prayer has been burned at the hands of the common hangman these four years? Or that possession of it is a grave offense against the dignity of God and the peace and safety of this king—"

"It was a childhood gift," I said angrily. "It was given me by my tutor—"

Again he interrupted me with that curt movement of hand, and then the door across the chamber opened and another entered. He tarried there a trifle, his face obscured by his sweeping hat brim, a stranger dressed in a blue and silver suit, and rich boots, and rings to his fingers that would have purchased freedom for half the rogues in Newgate. Then he advanced on us, and the light fell on his face, and he was no more a stranger. It had been two years since I had last laid eyes on him, and the times gone, it would appear, when those in power must announce their saintliness by the drabness of their clothing. But in fifty times two years I would not have forgotten this face, for it was one the Mordaunts had cause to remember. I watched his advance across the chamber, my heart thick in me, noting that his fifty years had had their way with him for his face was sallow and the flesh sunk away from the bone; noting as well that the old familiar mark was still to his left cheek, a mark no Vandyke or mustache could ever hide, the mark the size of a child's hand and very near the same shape, with the heel printed just below the eye and the fingers reaching out toward the lips, the malignancy grown visibly grosser and more angrily mottled these two years. And is the putrefaction in your blood having its way with you, I thought with satisfaction, and then I was thinking, And did I not warn you, brother? Oh, they are devious rogues, I thought, and was I not a prophet now, Henry?

He crossed the chamber and acknowledged Mr. Thurloe's "A fair good morrow, My Lord" with a perfunctory nod, and then sank into a chair. His eyes narrowed when they drifted to me, for I yet stood in the shadow near the door. "Is this the one, My Lord?" Thurloe said.

"The very one," he said. "Hath he not the look of a malignant, now?"

"Aye," Thurloe said. "And the manners to boot."

I inclined my head slightly. "I note ye are still in health, My Lord Monson," I said.

The shaft went home; the beringed right hand, still the slave of habit, came up to cover the sign of God's disfavor. I smiled my satisfaction. "I see ye had a speedy trip down from Reigate," I said. "News travels faster than I had thought over our spring roads. Did you flog your horses the entire way, My Lord?"

"You have lost none of your insolence these two years, I see."

I smiled still. "I trust not. I only pray I have the wit to accompany it."

Now he also smiled and as politely as I. "Mayhap we can find the means to correct both faults."

I read that smile below that blotched and mottled affliction and felt within me the sudden and foolish marriage of anger and recklessness. "Why, as to that," I said, "I had a father once used to preach that affliction was a sign of God's favor, sent to test a man in His grace. I can believe it, My Lord, and would ye know why? Because it is the one reason I can hit on why the Almighty, for all

143

His infinite patience, hath endured your existence these fifty years."

The smile stayed to his lips. There was on the sudden blood in his face, and his eyes told me that were I more convenient, he would have struck me for that. But the smile stayed to his lips. "And blasphemous," he said softly. "Insolent and blasphemous. Wilt be so good as to make a note of that blasphemy, Mr. Thurloe?"

Standing there, looking bitterly into his eyes, I thought briefly on the subject of hypocrisy. He had been in his youth notoriously dissolute, had My Lord Monson; he had, as a page at Charles's court, been frequently a scandal. But now, in the serenity of his age, he could speak glibly of blasphemy. "Aye," I said. "Make a note of it, Mr. Thurloe. And is it not a pity ye cannot hang a man twice or thrice?"

Thurloe was already bent over the paper before him. He looked up sharply. "Hang you?" he said. "We do not mean to hang you. The Protector in his patience and mercy hath sworn that few of you will hang, provided only that ye freely confess your part in this."

"Why, gladly," I said. "If you will but spell out what offense it is I have committed. For on my life I can recall none."

His smile was quiet and his eyes patient. "Come," he said. "It is but a quarter hour since you admitted to a knowledge of a bloody and inhuman plot to murder the Protector, and raise horrid rebellion and insurrection in the land. A plot to restore Charles Stuart to a throne and this nation to tyranny. A plot to endanger the peace and freedom of this kingdom and the prosperity and contentment of her subjects."

"I have been told there was a plot," I said. "I confess to it. But—"

He waved me quiet. "You confess to a knowledge of this plot. And is it, then, the part of a loyal subject to keep such knowledge secret? If you had not raised a hand or stirred a foot in the execution, did not the knowledge alone make you traitor?" He sank back in his chair and intertwined his fingers in the fashion of the old childhood game of here is the church and here is the steeple, and he dropped his head and rested his chin on his two forefingers. "You have hanged yourself with one confession," he said. "Now save yourself with another. Confess your part in this."

I stood silent before him now. Without the chamber, the afternoon sun was midway between noon and sunset, and one casement of that chamber was directly behind Thurloe, and against that bright light I could only guess now at the patient and clerkly eyes, the dry and quiet smile. In that silence and that light we waited a small eternity, and then he sighed.

"We are patient men, John Mordaunt," he said. "But men nonetheless. And there can be an end to patience. The land must be provided with examples, and your neck will fit a noose as prettily as the next one's." He allowed that dry and certain threat to lie between us while I looked into the light, and tried to read the patient, persuasive smile which I knew was to his lips, and could not. "Come," he said. "Who lured you into this? John Wiseman, fresh out of France with a proclamation from Charles Stuart—"

"I know no John Wiseman," I said.

"Then it was John Gerard, and your part—"

"Nor no John Gerard, neither."

"And what of a Somerset Fox? Dost deny knowledge of a Quaker named Fox?"

"I know Fox. He befriended me in your condemned hold. But afore that I knew him not."

"Did you not?" he said softly. He ceased the game with his fingers, and his right hand dropped to the table, and one unwashed finger set to toying with the papers before him. "I have his sworn statement afore me," he said. "Also the statement of one Alan Brodrick, who says ye approached—"

"Brodrick is forsworn. As well ye know."

"Why, no," he said. "No, I do not know. For their statements lie before me, and they have taken their oaths on it," and now he came forward in his chair, and I could read his face again, and his eyes were no more patient. " 'Tis not the whole of the evidence against you," he said. "Though we can hang you on this alone an we so choose." He permitted that to fester a little in the shadows that lay between us. Then he looked to My Lord Monson.

My Lord was sprawled out in his chair, his legs thrust straight out before him, his head sunk on his chest, one beringed hand cupped over the fault to his cheek, the skin about his jowls looking sallow and slack. Had his eyes been closed, he might have been some ancient country squire asleep of a winter evening before his fire. But his eyes were not closed.

"What would you of me?" I said.

His lips, I think, did not move the thickness of a piece of parchment. But I still caught, there or in his eyes, the small, quick, triumphant smile. "But honest answers to honest questions," he said.

"I have given them you. I have said that I stand falsely accused, and that is an honest answer. I have said that I know not any John Wiseman nor John Gerard, and that is an honest answer." I spread my hands. "But those are not the answers you would have of me."

"Why, no," he said. "No, they are not."

"And so I must ask what it is I am to confess to. For as God is my witness, I do not know, My Lord."

"Why, very well," he said. "Very well, we shall supply you," and he dropped his hand from his cheek and came upright in his chair. "Item," he said. "You were visited this month by your brother, a notorious malignant and but newly taken in another horrid plot. Within a fortnight, you are for London, armed to the teeth with pistols and sword. Agreed?"

"No," I said. "I but came up to London to pay the fine against my brother's estates. As for pistols and sword, you know as well as I that the roads are thick with high—"

He waved a hand. "Oh, you had your reasons. You rogues are ever well supplied with reasons." He came about in his chair and again his hand strayed to his cheek. "Item. You begin your journey by talking an hour with an innkeeper, a certain Walsingham Heathfeild, another known malignant. Agreed?"

"I but passed the time of day with him. And it was no hour, nor anything like—"

"I can produce three witnesses will swear it was at least an hour. Conducted in the middle of his innyard where no one could overhear, and your voices kept to a whisper." He smiled again, that brief, slack, triumphant smile. "Item. On the Dorking Road you rescued a certain lady, my niece, from a bout with a pothole. At which time you expressed certain treasonable opinions on the subject of liberty of conscience. Agreed?"

And so she had betrayed me too, I thought, and I knew on the sudden not despair alone but a thick and reckless rage as well. It was no more than I should have expected, but I nonetheless felt the swell of rage in me, while he reclined indolently before me and surveyed me through lidded and triumphant eyes.

"Agreed?" he said. "Or have ye the impudence to deny—"

"No," I said. "For you have the lady's word on it, have you not? And is she not as honorable as the rest of her ilk?"

Yet he smiled. "I think I shall vote to hang you yet, John Mordaunt," he said. "Though you confess your part in this and name us enough names to fill a ledger, I think I shall. For I have endured your impudence these five years and more, and I find I have a belly full of it." He played with the devil's mark to his cheek while his smile tried to wipe out my glare. "Item," he said. " 'Tis an easy day's ride from Reigate to London. Yet you must squander two days on the journey. Agreed?"

"True," I said. "For I was born with but a portion of my wits, and I must spill time on strange ladies mired in potholes."

"And are ye not grateful? Did she not provide you convenient excuse to put up the night at Kingston? Under the roof of another known malignant?"

And in God's name, I thought, how fine a net can they spin? "Is it also noted in your report," I said, "that I made water against a hedge just without Leatherhead?"

"We could have mentioned it, had we thought it pertinent."

"I am relieved to hear it. I had almost thought that your agents were proving slovenly."

He slid down in his chair and stretched out his legs. "Item. You arrived at London Bridge at high noon. Where you argue an hour for permission to enter the city armed. Agreed?"

"Also with two thousand pounds on my person. And no wish to fight off London cutthroats with my bare hands—"

"What?" he cried. "At high noon? And the distance from Edward Blackwell's to Goldsmiths' Hall scarce a quarter mile? Dost think us children, John Mordaunt?"

"No," I said wearily. "I know not what you are, My Lord, but well I know you are not children."

"And once free of Goldsmiths' Hall, you must make straight for the Belle Savage. A score of inns between the Cheap and Ludgate Hill, but none will do save the Belle Savage," and now his eyes opened full, and I read what was to be read there and thought that if by miracle I did escape hanging, I should someday repay My Lord Monson kindness for kindness, courtesy for courtesy. Then I looked to Thurloe.

147

"Dost stand convinced, John Mordaunt," he said, "that the evidence is sufficient to pronounce you guilty in any court in the land?"

"What need for confession, then?"

He shrugged. "A sign of repentance. Repentance is the price we exact for mercy."

"If that be the sum of it, I confess. But name me any plot since Worcester, I confess to it freely."

"Nay," he said. "Softly. 'Tis not the whole and entire sum of it."

"I had thought it would not be," I said dryly. "And what is the whole and entire sum of it, then?"

"Why, names. We must have names—"

"And there a small rub," I said. "For I have not strayed from out Surrey these five years. But if you will name one or two names—"

There was the small, damp slap as his flattened palm struck the board. "Do we find you insolent yet?" he said.

"I cannot tell until I hear from you the full price for this poor life of mine." I leaned against the door behind me and quarreled with a hand that would have come up to brush at the sweat, cold and sick, to my forehead. "You would have names. And what other fee, Mr. Thurloe? Transportation, mayhap—"

"Have no fear on that score. You are gentleman born. And so a small fine perhaps—"

"What is small for one man is impossible for another. How small a fine, Mr. Thurloe?"

"I cannot say. 'Tis a matter for the Committee for Sequestration—"

"Of which My Lord Monson there is a member," I said. "And so I can say, for I am a prophet these days. Shall we hazard a guess that the fine will come to a third of the value of Reigate Priory? And the Priory already mortgaged and so no usurer in England rash enough to advance a further sum against it, hence my mother forced to purchase her son's life by selling to the first buyer who chances along. Which buyer will be My Lord Monson." I swung about into that feigned sprawl, that small, slack smile, those lidded eyes. "And am I not a pretty prophet, My Lord?" I said.

He shrugged. "If ye purchase the pint, ye must settle the tally. And so one more time. Were ye or were ye not party to this plot? Aye or nay?"

"You leave me little choice in the answer."

He nodded his satisfaction. "And who was it lured you into it?

148

Willis? Gerard? This Islington schoolmaster, this Peter Vowel?"

I shook my head. "None of those." And now I must put my mind to fighting a weakness in my knees. For I was resolved to defy him and in the defying to burn my bridges behind me; and yet no man can look death level and deliberate in the face and not feel the brush of fear, and if this be cowardice, why, then, call me coward. "There was a tall, black fellow dressed in a clown's costume—"

"Brodrick," he said.

"Why, so I think he called himself."

"And who else? Who in Reigate—"

"I know not his name. But I can describe him a little. He was near your height, My Lord, and an ancient, with a beard gray as yours. And he had a curious mark to his face. The shape of a child's hand, and just here to his cheek."

And now the sudden and awful silence. It was the silence you will meet with when someone has given the lie, and the assembled company falls deathly quiet, and nought to break that quiet save quick, sharp, shallow breathing and glare meeting glare across the board and the memory like an echo of the raw scrape of boot against stone as two men have lurched to their feet and one has made the other gift of the flat slap across the mouth. There was that silence while I watched the blood mount into his face and the mark to his cheek so angrily mottled you could follow his pulse in it, and me with the sweat cold and sick on forehead and palm and the emptiness in my chest and the weakness in my thighs, for I knew now that there would be no further retraction and no hope of retreat.

Then Monson broke the silence, his voice thick, for the blood was in his throat, too. "Very well," he said. "Very well if you would have it so."

"I would have it so. For I will see you rot, My Lord, ere you get Reigate Priory through any fault of mine."

"I shall not rot," he said. "But you shall. Oh, you shall beg twice or thrice for the quickness of a rope ere I have done with you. And wouldst do me the kindness of giving that bell rope a small twitch, Mr. Thurloe?"

Thurloe looked at him and then pulled at the rope, and the door across the way opened and the guard stepped through. "Fetch me Captain Munke," Monson said. "And his man with him."

We waited, eyes meeting eyes and parrying and retreating. Then

149

the door opened again and Captain Munke was with us. "Dost know this man, Captain?" Monson said.

Munke glanced once at his man, just at his shoulder, and once, shrewdly and bitterly, at me. "Aye, My Lord. He would be one I seized at the Belle Savage."

"And what the circumstances when you seized him, Captain?"

Again Munke looked at me, and something passed between us, though I could put no name to it. "Why, he was abed, My Lord."

"And was he alone and snoring?"

"That I could not testify to, My Lord. For we beat on his door five minutes afore he unbarred it. And so when I first laid eyes on him, he was to his feet—"

I could not see Monson's face, for it was turned from me. But I could see Munke's, and his eyes looked wide and level and innocent down into Monson's, and I wondered what he was about. For he bore me little love, and yet this was no very sure tack for but a captain of foot. And was it for the sake of the wench, I thought. Would he go so far to spare a wench a whipping?

"Ha' ye a faulty memory, Captain?" Monson said. "Or a short one? And the length of a sennight too great a strain on it?"

Munke shook his head. "I had not thought so, My Lord."

"Why, then, your humor is a jesting one this day."

"Why, no, My Lord. I have been as serious as Job the entire day."

"Then I shall put the question more plainly. When you burst into this rogue's chamber that night, did you not find him bedded down with his whore—"

Munke's eyes opened a trifle wider. "Why, no, My Lord. Sure there was a wench in his chamber, come to fetch away his boots for cleaning—"

"Stark-naked, Captain? And with the door barred?" And now Monson looked to Munke's man. "You. You were with the Captain the night this whoreson was seized. Was there not a wench in his bed when ye burst into his chamber?"

The man's eyes flicked to Munke, and he drew tongue over lower lip.

"Afore ye answer," Monson said, "I would remind you of the penalties for perjury. They are at the very least the loss of a tongue. Now did ye not, a sennight since, burst into this cur's chamber and find him aboard a wench?"

150

The soldier licked lip again, while his eyes tried to choose between loyalty and fear. "No, M'lord," he said. "For 'twas as the Captain said, he was at the door—"

And now Monson was to his feet. "Dost quibble wi' me, sirrah? Dost ha' the gall to bandy words wi' me? Was there not a slut in this man's bed that night?"

The man's eyes took their leave of Munke's back. "Aye, M'lord," he said.

"And the girl naked?"

"As the day she was born, M'lord," the man said miserably.

Monson looked again to Munke. "Has your memory proved less faulty on the sudden, Captain?"

"Why, no," Munke said. "No, I think it has not."

"Mayhap we shall take steps to amend it. Mayhap ye have a mind to be ridden backwards out of your regiment."

Munke's lips were white now, but his voice was still even. "Ye may threaten me the afternoon, My Lord," he said. "But it is still written that thou shalt not bear false witness. And it is the truth I speak, that I saw this man in bed with no woman. And threats or no threats, I have no further stomach for the games we play these days."

"Games? What games, sirrah?"

"If a man have something ye covet," Munke said evenly, "and if ye cannot find him guilty of one thing, why, then, find him guilty of another."

A little longer Monson tried to stare him down. Then he swung back on me, and the eyes above the mottled cheek were hot with righteousness or anger or greed. "You have heard this man's testimony," he said. "And wouldst hear God's law as well as man's? 'For this is the will of God, even your sanctification, that ye shall abstain from fornication: That every one of you should know how to possess his vessel in sanctification and honour; Not in the lust of concupiscence, even as the Gentiles which know not God.' That would be Thessalonians Four."

"Is it not also written," I said, "that no man shall defraud his brother? And in the same place?"

"What?" he cried. "And can the devil quote Scripture to his purpose?"

"Cannot you answer that better than I, My Lord?"

He glared a moment longer. Then he drew a slow breath and smiled. "Mayhap you do not know the penalty for fornication," he said. "For the law is recent and roads vile this past winter. The penalty is loss of a right hand."

I stared at him. "I have seen naked greed in my time," I said. "But never the match of yours. And my answer is yet the same. Separate me member by member an ye will; it will mean I am that much lighter in the hanging. But ye shall not have the Priory."

"There is another law. An a man be palpably guilty of high treason but obstinate in the confessing of it, the state may employ pressing—"

"There is still a third law. If a man does not confess, his estates cannot be confiscate to the crown. And one death is but a little harder than another. So pile stone on stone until I am the thickness of parchment—"

"Very well," he said. "An this is how you would have it, we shall endeavor to oblige you." He looked again to Thurloe. "This one is for the condemned hold until his trial," he said. "And no privileges. If he be as rich as Midas and his entire estate offered for relief, he is to be denied. And the rogue turnkey who says me nay to that shall hang aside him."

She was standing just without Guildhall when we came out into the late afternoon sun. Her back was to us, her eyes on a vehement and most blasphemous quarrel between an ancient drayman going north on Milk Street and a diminutive coachman going south. She turned when we came down the steps and cast a glance at me, and then she advanced on the sergeant of my guard. "I would speak with your prisoner, Sergeant," she said. " 'Twould be worth a shilling to you."

My sergeant was a thick fellow with a black forelock splitting a low, broad forehead and flat, black, sullen eyes. He shook his head. "Not for a sovereign, milady. M'lord hath forbid—"

"I am niece to My Lord Monson," she said sweetly. "And cousin to the Protector. And I would have a word with your prisoner."

"An ye were Lady Cromwell herself, I could not oblige—"

She cocked her head and looked up at him from under the brim of her hood. "Is it your habit, Sergeant," she said, and her voice still soft and sweet, "to accost gentlewomen on the public street with improper invitations?"

He stared down at her, sullen and amazed. "I do not understand—"

"I had not expected to hear such bawdry this side the Thames docks," she said. "And so I fear I must step within Guildhall and report your manners. Mayhap a turn in the stocks—"

And now he did understand. "I swear I cannot," he said desperately. "My Lord Monson hath promised me a flogging—"

"A flogging or a turn in the stocks," she said sweetly. "A difficult choice. I am glad it is none of mine."

And now I broke in. "In God's name," I said, "let the man be. He is but doing as he hath been commanded."

She looked at me, gravely and innocently. "Why, aye. But I would have a word with you, Master Mordaunt. I ask but to withdraw with him to the shadow of yon wall, Sergeant."

The sergeant threw me a glance miserable and desperate. "An he should take to his heels, I shall rot in Newgate—"

"Pshaw. With his hands cuffed thus? And eight sturdy men with you to set up the hue and cry? And as for my uncle, there shall be candles lit ere he emerges from Guildhall this day."

Ten paces from my guard I set my back against the stone and looked briefly down into her face. Then I looked up at the spires of St. Mary Magdalen across the way. "And what should we discuss this time?" I said. "The fairness of the day?"

"If you will," she said quietly. "Is it a fair day, John Mordaunt?"

"I do not recall having seen a fairer. Not in my entire twenty-eight years." I kept my eyes firmly on the church spire and the blue, blue, cloudless sky beyond. "And that exhausts that topic, doth it not? And so shall we choose another? And shall it be philosophy? We were discussing liberty of conscience when last we parted, I think."

"I fear we have had sufficient of that topic," she said softly.

"Why, aye to that. Since it hath served to help hang me."

She was, I knew, still staring at me, though I refused to lower my eyes from the church spire. "I little wonder," she said. "If you were fool enough to express to them the opinions you expressed to me."

And now I did look down into her face. "Have we not had sufficient of this silliness?" I said. "I expressed them no opinions. But my opinions were reported to them."

Her eyes, grave and gray and innocent as childhood, did not waver out of mine. "And you think I played the reporter," she said, and it was no question.

I shrugged. "It is a lonely place, the Dorking Road. I remember none within earshot of the two of us. Or if a third, it was God. And I cannot believe that My Lord Monson is on speaking terms with Him."

"And if I had betrayed you, why should I now be standing here?"

"The saintly mind is a mysterious thing. I do not pretend to understand it."

Still her eyes held mine. "I did not betray you, John Mordaunt." She marked my movement as if to turn away from her and put a hand to my wrist. "I mentioned our meeting to my uncle. I confess I did. I also mentioned in passing the topic we discussed. But I told him no more."

I looked into her eyes, level and frank, and I remembered how My Lord Monson had put that question. He had indeed not enlarged on the seditious nature of my opinions, only charged me with them. And oh, they are devious rogues, I thought. "It is no great matter," I said. "They had other pretexts than this one. And if they had not, they would have invented some."

"But you believe me? That I did not betray you?"

"I believe you. And is it of great importance to you, then?"

"It is. Of great importance." She studied me a long moment, gravely and calmly, no foolish simpering or blushing or coy fluttering of lashes but steadily, as one man might consider another. "And they mean to hang you?" she said. "And you hold my uncle responsible?"

It was a silly question, and I refused to dignify it by replying.

"Why, then," she said, "I shall speak to him in your behalf."

I smiled. "You are like to find him gone deaf on the sudden."

"Then I shall but speak the louder."

"It is a stone-deaf kind of deafness. An infirmity brought on by heat in the blood and a vapor rising into the brain. *Radix maleorum cupiditas est.*"

"And what is it my uncle is greedy for?"

"Two hundred acres of land and forest called Reigate Priory."

"Why, then, give it him."

I shook my head. "I have a disease as well. It is called stubbornness."

"Do you prefer to die?" she burst out. "Over but a scrap of land—"

"I am not your Earl of Bedford," I said quietly. "I am plain John Mordaunt, and the Priory all my mother possesses in this world. And aye, I prefer to die."

"I shall go higher then," she said. "If I must plead your case before the Protector himself—"

"Doth it mean that much to you?" I said. "The life of a poor stranger you shared a mount with for one hour on a lonely Surrey road?"

And now she did flush, very prettily, though her eyes remained firm. "I have a passion against injustice," she said.

I smiled. "If that be the sum of it, there will be a God's plenty left after I am but a memory."

"Pray do not speak thus. You must not despair, John Mordaunt."

"I do not despair," I said. "We all of us owe God a death. If I discharge mine early, I shall not have to fear it later."

"Nay," she said. "They have not hanged you yet."

I looked a little longer into her eyes, quietly, not smiling now, no more banter about death now, for the time had passed for further pretense between us. I looked down into her eyes, thinking that were this other circumstances, it would be no great task for a man to fall in love with this one. But these were these circumstances, and there was nought that any niece of My Lord Monson's could do against hate that had festered for five years and greed that had fattened for longer than that. There was nought she could do, and I looked beyond her to my guard.

"It is fondness and vanity, this discussion," I said. "And if we do not shortly bring it to a close, I fear my sergeant will have a falling-down fit."

So for a second time I was marched off to Newgate, and made free gift of fifty pounds of iron, and tumbled into the condemned hold. And I cannot say whether it was a day or a week before the trap above me opened and the candle guttered down the ladder, and Mr. Richard Dicke once more sidled crablike across the stone to me.

"Thou'rt to follow me," he said.

Since they had tumbled me in here, nothing had passed my lips save ditch water, and I had not washed or changed clothing in two weeks and my person crawled with vermin. But for all that, I did not think on food or decent linen. I was beyond hunger now, and there was a great tiredness in my bones and a greater indifference to whatever fate held in store for me, and my only humor was to know the time.

"What day of the week is it?" I said.

He blinked down at me, his mouth pulled crookedly out of shape in what might have passed with some for a smile if they were generous enough. " 'Tis just turned Friday," he said.

"A pair of days? Have I sat here but a pair of days?" I closed my eyes against the light of the candle. "And what o' the clock, Mr. Dicke?"

"Nigh two i' the morning."

"And do they hang men afore daybreak now?"

"In God's name," he burst out, "wilt cease the silly questions and climb to your feet and follow me, man?"

There was fear in his voice, and I wondered at it. "I have known some would run to meet death," I said. "But I not one of them, Mr. Dicke. And if I were, I doubt I could manage in these irons."

"Aye," he muttered. "I had most forgot." He stooped and set the candle down, and now I saw that he carried in his free hand a maul and that he had thrust a smith's long chisel into his belt. "I ha' no skill at smithing," he said. "But where there is no wine, beer must do, eh?" He knelt, and he was in the right of it, he was indeed poor excuse for smith, and my wrists and ankles throbbing before he was done. Then he was standing before me again, the crooked, fawning smile returned to his lips, his meaty lips looking as soft and blurred as a reflection in some rippled stream, one small blob of spit at the corner of his mouth glinting pale as water in moonlight. "Wilt follow me now?" he said.

I got to my feet and faced him. It was two in the morning, and they neither heard nor hanged a man at two in the morning. But they could rack a man at two in the morning, or part him from a right arm, or press a confession out of him, and standing there and swaying against the weakness in knee and thigh, I toyed with the

156

temptation to resist, to leap upon Mr. Dicke and attempt escape. Then I looked at the thick set of shoulders above the hump and decided against it; in my present condition I could not have overpowered a twelve-year-old boy, not if he had attained his proper growth.

There was sweat to my face when I achieved the top of the ladder, and I paused there to renew spent breath. Then I set out after Dicke's candle. It led me past the grated door into the Common Side, and down a turn of sweating and deserted corridor, and up one brief set of stairs and down another, and through two great doors. I waited just at Dicke's shoulder while he turned a key in that last lock, and the door swung open, and the candle went out in the rush of cold, fresh air, and I stepped through the door and

I was without Newgate Gaol.

I was without Newgate Gaol and the air so fresh it stung my lungs and throat, like the air you will drink in when you step without a warm and wood-smoked room into the iron-cold of a January midnight. I was without Newgate Gaol, and above me an infinity of stars, and amongst them a moon, sliver-thin as the print of a boot heel in wet sand. I was without Newgate Gaol, and in the light of that moon Mr. Dicke, an arm's length distant, was only an ill-formed shadow, and nought else to tell me he was yet with me save the linger of the flat, greasy, tallow smell from the extinguished candle. I was without Newgate Gaol and my only guard a hunchback with a walk like a crippled crab's; and I was weak from hunger and my thighs and knees protested the movement of a foot, but I yet knew that if I took to my heels, I could be half across the city before he could accomplish the boundary of Phoenix Court.

He might have been some devil with a gift for reading thoughts. "Thou'rt free to," he said.

"Free?" I said. "Free to? I am free to what?"

"To take to your heels."

"Free?" I repeated, my voice flat with amazement. "I am free? I have been ordered free?"

"Not ordered," he said, and I could read the smile in his voice, crooked as his back and fawning as a whipped cur's and formless as the blob that would be affixed to the edge of his meaty lower lip. "I would not say ordered," he said. "I would say purchased."

157

I closed the distance between us and put a hand to his shoulder and thrust my face to within a foot of his. "Purchased? Someone hath bribed you? Who, man?"

He shook his head. "I would say purchased. And I do not know his name."

"His appearance, then? What his appearance?" though I thought I knew. For it had cost a pretty sum, this business; if it had cost a farthing less than a hundred pounds, Mr. Dicke was a greater fool than I took him for, and not four people on earth would have purchased my life for that sum, and one of them without the youth or strength to travel or the skill to bring this off, and the second an innkeeper's daughter with not two pounds in her entire estate, and the third a brother. And so Henry had come after all, I thought. So word had reached him after all, and he had somehow obtained leave to travel, and he had taken lodging in some inn nearby and purchased information of me from this turnkey or that one, and then, one midnight, he had sauntered into a tavern just without Phoenix Court and dropped into a place across from Mr. Richard Dicke and made him offer of a bottle of bastard stand and stand about. . . .

I tightened my grasp on Dicke's shoulder. His breath stunk of cheap wine turned sour in the gut and meat held prisoner a fortnight between blackened teeth. "What his appearance?" I repeated. "A short man with a fair complexion and a great scar just here—"

He shook his head again. " 'Twas one of the turnkeys," he said.

And aye, I thought, that would be Henry's way. He was ever better at his letters than I and quicker witted, and he would have matched them deviousness for deviousness. But whence had he come by the money? Some friend in Reigate, Walsingham Heathfeild, perchance? Another piece of Turvey sold? Some Jew in the 'Change, the sum to be doubled on return in ninety days?

My hand still made free with Dicke's shoulder. He sidled out from under it. "But follow me across the court," he said, "ye shall find food waiting ye. And clothes suitable for travel."

"Travel?" I said. "Where am I to travel, Mr. Dicke?"

"North," he said.

❦ *Nine* ❧

Which is all they would tell me. Dicke led me to a small tailor shop just without Phoenix Court, where I was admitted by a small, thin, bent man with a skin that had not known sun since birth and eyes as affrighted as if I were a Roundhead officer and here on other business than I was. Here they provided me with a pail of water to rid me of some of the stink of prison, and the first meat and drink fit for a human that I had tasted in God alone knew when, and the leather jerkin and canvas breeches and coarse stockings and heavy shoes of a groom. They provided me, too, with a forged pass which, come daybreak, should get me without the city walls. And they said I was to travel north. There would be a price on my head come morning, they said, and search parties in all the port towns and about Reigate, and I was to travel north.

It took me almost six weeks to reach Turvey.

Turvey lies sixty English miles north of London and six northeast of Bedford Town, and I circled wide around Bedford as I had circled around the other villages on the way, following the south bank of the River Ouse to the ford which provides poachers from out Triploe Heath and mischievous small boys entrance to Peterborough land. I splashed through the ford and entered the woodland where once I had hunted and fished and dreamed boyhood dreams on other July afternoons, the wood smaller now than I had remembered it, the stumps here and there betraying the sale of Peterborough timber to London shipbuilders these past years. Then

159

I was crossing fields thick with ripening grain, the land lying beneath the fat, hot, lusty afternoon sun like some sprawled, spent peasant wench, and then I was through the orchard and within sight of the manor.

Beyond the orchard Turvey is open garden and shrubbed lawn and nought else. And so, stopping at the edge of the orchard, I knew for a moment, in throat and belly and knee, the quick alertness like small, bright panic, for I had lived six weeks now with a price on my head and this the first I had emerged from cover in broad daylight. But there seemed small need for fear. Out on the grounds there was no sign of life anywhere, no hostlers about the stables, no serving wenches at the kitchen entrance, no travelers on the distant Bedford Road, and the manor itself, sitting solid and medieval and seemingly eternal beneath the afternoon sun, looking like some town laid siege to and surrendered, and all the inhabitants fled, and the invading army marched on to other conquests. I stood there briefly on the edge of the orchard, searching the grounds out foot by foot. Then I stepped forth into the open.

The stables at Turvey are stone below and timber above, the stone almost white when the afternoon sun is shining without mercy from out a cloudless July sky; and when I strode into the cool shadows of the stable, the sun stayed in my eyes a little, so that within was nought but an indistinct blur of empty stalls and rude, sad ladders leading to the lofts. Standing there just within the great carriageway, amid the sweet, heavy smells of aging manure and oiled leather and drying, fragrant hay, with the sun yet in my eyes and the deserted grounds without still in my memory, I knew the feeling again, like some ill-defined stab of terror, of Turvey deserted, master and man packed up and gone elsewhere, and I some traveler on his way from nowhere to nowhere, pausing for a brief and dreamlike moment in some silent and forgotten void before setting out on his lonely and bitter way again. And then the sun was out of my eyes, and I caught the movement in one of the further stalls, and a figure was coming up the line of hard-packed dirt and trampled straw toward me.

The figure was Andrew.

I knew first the brief amazement, *Andrew, what doth Andrew at Turvey?* and then I read his walk and knew the sharper surprise, *It is Andrew and he doth not know me.* For there was an alert suspicion, a surly hostility, in his walk, his head forward and his hands before and away from him and his shoulders hunched like some country wrestler stepped out of the crowd to answer the challenge of a traveling professional, and I thought, *It is Andrew, who has known me forever, who dandled me on his knee and watched me take my first steps, and now he knows me not*. And then I remembered that I had been six weeks on the road, and my only bed in all that time copse or haymow, and my face covered with a matted beard, and my dress the ripped and travel-stained clothing of some runaway groom.

He halted twenty feet from me, his great hands still alert to his sides, the forelock hanging down across the low, broad forehead in the way I remembered, the dark, sullen distrust written plain on lip and brow. "Aye?" he said.

I was about to step forward and make myself known to him, and then some whim prompted me to play-act awhile. "Methought," I said, and raised a hand to brush at my beard while I tried to recall just how a stable hand should speak, "methought— I am a stable hand without employment. And I ha' eaten nothing these three days save berries and one rabbit I snared—"

"There be no work hereabouts for runaways," he said. "And nought to pay ye wages wi' an there were."

"I am no runaway. And I would require no wages. But food for my belly and a corner in yon loft to keep off the rain at night. And I ha' a hand wi' horses. My master—"

He took another slow step toward me. "I think ye be no stable hand," he said. "Ye be dressed for it, but ye play the part badly, and ye trespass on Peterborough land."

"An I lie to you, may God strike—"

"The gate to Turvey lies a mile distant," he said. "A man can accomplish it in a quarter hour an he proceed at a fast trot."

"In God's name, I cry you mercy. But let me ha' a word wi' your master—"

" 'Twould be to the same purpose. But wasted wind." He stepped suddenly into the stall to his left hand and emerged with a horse whip. "Come, fellow. Off wi' ye, now."

And now I had no further humor for this, for I had never in my life heard ugliness in Andrew's voice and I did not like the sound of it. "Nay," I said softly. "Nay. No need for that, Andrew."

161

There was for the nonce the same ugliness in his face, and then, slowly, there was not. "Who be ye?" he said. "Ye know my name, and ye pretend to the part o' a groom though ye be none, and who be ye?"

"My clothing hath undergone some change since last I saw you," I said. "And my face. But hath my voice changed as well, Andrew?"

He stood rooted there another long moment, with the whip in his right hand and the black forelock lying across his forehead and his eyes beneath the thick brows changing from distrust to bewilderment to disbelief. Then his fingers let loose their hold on the whip stock. "You," he said. "Mother o' mercy, is it you?"

"Aye," I said. " 'Tis me, Andrew."

I know not how he managed the twenty feet to me. One instant he was four paces distant and the next I was swept into his arms in an embrace that threatened my ribs, and when I pushed myself away and looked down into his face, the tears stood unashamed on his cheeks. "You," he said. " 'Tis you, and ye be alive and not taken, and—" He stepped back, his hands on my shoulders, his eyes searching out my face. "Name o' God," he said, and his voice softer than I had ever before heard it, "name o' God, what ha' the bastards done to ye, Master John?"

I shrugged. "They have their small sports," I said, and then the thought was with me again, *What doth Andrew at Turvey?* "And is Turvey deserted save for you?" I said.

"They are all at the Bedford Fair," he said.

"My brother amongst them?"

"Nay. Ye will find him at the manor."

"And what o' you, Andrew?"

"I ha' small interest in fairs these days, Master John."

"That was not my meaning. What do ye at Turvey? And who is it minds my mother at Reigate?"

And now he was not smiling, and in his eyes the same look he had worn as he came out that stall with the whip. "Ye ha' not heard?" he said.

I knew again the small, bright stab of panic in throat and heart. "Heard? What is it I have not heard, Andrew?"

"Nay," he said. "Nay, ye would not have. They ha'—" And then he broke off and his eyes drifted beyond me, and I turned, and Henry was standing in the carriageway.

162

He was framed in the light from without so that I could not see the face he wore but only the dark outline of arm and shoulder and beard. And the riding crop. He was tapping the crop impatiently against his right knee, and so I had no need to read his face. For there was, in the small, nervous tap of crop on leg, enough to tell me that were my face thrust into his and the light something better, the expression he wore would not have bid me welcome.

"This fellow," he said. "Art acquainted with him, Andrew?"

"Why, aye, M'lord," Andrew said. "And do ye not—" and then he read the glance I threw him and broke off. "He is a stable hand in need o' employment, M'lord," he said. "He lays claim to a gift wi' horses."

The crop tapped the knee lightly, once and then twice. "Doth he now? And what other gifts hath he? Since all the horses they have left us are three, and those fit only for a plow?"

"I can plow as well, M'lord," I said. "And lend a hand come harvest—"

"We have small use for such gifts, neither."

"I would ask no wages, M'lord. But a bit o' food for my belly and six feet o' straw in yon loft—"

This time the riding crop tapped the knee but once. In the silence that lay between us, the sound was as flat as that of a musket ball striking into a soft board. And then: "Ye trespass," he said, and his voice flatter than the sound of crop against leg and more sullen than the silence. " 'Tis Peterborough land ye stand on, and ye trespass. Ye have half an hour—"

"I pray you, M'lord—"

"—to take to your heels and get free and clear of my land. An ye fail to do so by the space of a single minute, I shall have the law on you as a poacher—"

"Nay," I said. "Nay. Softly, softly."

And now the crop was pressed quiet and hard against the flat of his leg. "Do I find ye insolent, fellow?" he said softly. "Do I find ye surly, dog? Hast a mind to a cheek laid open with this crop?"

"Why, no, M'lord," I said, and my voice as soft as his. "But if ye can spare me a moment's patience, I would remind you of a promise you made me once."

"Promise? Promise? To my certain knowledge I have ne'er laid eyes—"

"I own to other gifts, M'lord. Amongst them a small talent for prophecy. And did I not say I would be at Turvey before another spring? And did not you promise to bid me welcome?"

He gave a small start, and then he stood stock-still, frozen in that small, intent lean, the tip of the crop pressed so hard to the leg that I could follow, against the bright, hard light behind him, the brief, black bend to its stock. "You," he said. "So 'tis you."

" 'Tis me, brother, and am I not a pretty prophet?"

He yet stood as still as if he had looked on the forbidden way behind him and been turned to salt, like Lot's wife. The silence was as thick as batting between us. And then, "Ye still have half an hour to be free o' my land."

"Nay," I said. "Have we not carried the jest far enough, Henry?"

"You think I jest, do you?"

"Why, I can hope so. Since I have spent six weeks hiding out in copse and hayloft, and have been nipped in the heels by every village cur 'twixt here and Chipping Barnet, and have lived since June like one of your damned 'gyptians, nought in my belly save berries and ditch weeds and poached—"

"I jest, you think." He took another step toward me. "Search parties still make free with Turvey gates one day in three, and not a stranger steps foot across the border but what is close questioned by someone in Berry's command, and every peasant 'twixt here and Bristol dreams o' nights of the fifty pounds on your head, and you think I jest."

He stood close enough now for me to read his face, and I did so, and there was fear in his eyes, and he did not jest. "Why, what to fear, Henry," I said, "when my own brother knew me not?"

"They own sharper eyes nor us," he said sullenly.

I brought my hands, palms up, before me. "They told me to come north," I said. "I had thought they meant Turvey."

He looked at me with eyes, above the beard and the long, vivid scar, as pale blue as sapphire polished by some master at gems. " 'Tis a mile to Turvey gates," he said. "And half an hour not over-much time to accomplish the distance. An I were you, I would squander no more of it."

I stared down at him, but not in anger. Not yet in anger. There had ever been the differences between us, but this was yet my brother who with cold eyes and nervous riding crop bade me depart his land. And yet for the nonce I knew not anger but only a blank amazement, a bafflement as thick as the fog that will lie heavy and sullen over a marsh of a fall evening. "They instructed me to travel north," I repeated. "If it were not your intent that I should come to Turvey, why was I instructed to travel north, Henry?"

He stared blankly at me. "Intent? Ye speak in riddles, brother."

"Dicke," I said. " 'Twas Dicke told me—the hunchback with a walk— But no, you would not know him. 'Twas doubtless some turnkey—" I reached out and grasped his shoulder, so suddenly and roughly that his hands started up as if to defend himself. "Was it not you purchased my escape?" I cried.

For a little there was still the blankness in his eyes, and then there was not, and he stepped out from under my hand. "Aha," he said softly. "So there lies the direction of the wind?"

"Answer me. Was it not you? Did you not receive my message? Was it not you laid out the necessary hundred pounds—"

"I received your message," he said. "Aye. But as to your freedom"—he looked at me, a long, dark, sullen look, and then he looked to the ground at his feet, and when he spoke, the same dark sullenness was in his voice—"what was I to have purchased the commodity with? The two pounds six I had in pocket when ye departed Reigate? And how was I to come to you—"

"If not you, then who?"

He shrugged. "I would not know. Count over your friends with a hundred pounds readily to hand and warmth enough for you to lay it out on so poor a cause."

I laughed shortly. "I can do that and not use a pair of fingers."

He shrugged again. "Why, then, count over your enemies."

I looked across the brief distance to him, the look steady but not yet in anger, though my lips may have worn a curl. For a long moment he returned me look for look, his lips so tight pressed the blood was clean out of them, in his eyes no shame that I could read of brother turning away brother and for no cause I could hit on save only that they had bled out of him, drop by drop, all sense of courage and honor and family. We stood thus while without the stables a meadow lark sounded a single brief and lilting trill and then as suddenly ceased, and the thick and sullen silence the only thing between us again. Then I turned a shoulder to him.

"Very well an you would have it so," I said. "Brother."

"Aye, I would have it so," he said hotly. "And are ye not content with the grief you have visited on us? Must you see to it that the last scrap of Peterborough land goes into their pockets afore you can sleep dreamless?"

I was about to say that it was he who now spoke in riddles, and then Andrew stirred somewhere behind me, and *Andrew*, I thought, *what doth Andrew at Turvey?* and in that instant no need to put that question.

"The Priory," I said. "They have seized on the Priory."

He made me no reply. He had no need to.

"But they cannot," I cried. "The Priory was my mother's—"

"Oh, they hit on the way of it," he said. "First a troop quartered on us a sennight to frighten off the servants and waste the provisions. Then axes laid to window and paneling, and stable and outbuilding burned on pretext of smoking you out, and kitchen garden trampled, and orchard chopped for firewood. Then, when we still would not stir, orders down from London to deliver you up within three days on pain of forfeit—"

"Whose orders? Monson's?"

"Aye. And Thurloe's."

Monson, I thought, and now I did know anger. For five years I had walked lightly and spoken softly and greeted them fair and thought mine own thoughts while ill-bred jackals had lowered breeches and emptied bowels on this land of mine, and in all those five years I had known the bitterness but not the anger. Five years, I thought, and my reward for circumspection false arrest; my reward insolence and abuse at the hands of one of their captains, very brave when he had men at his back and an opponent naked of weapons; my reward Newgate's condemned hold and a hanging intended in the bargain had not some unknown friend . . .

"Monson," I said aloud, and the rage in my throat so thick it was like trying to breathe through blood. And *Monson*, I thought, and *Some unknown friend*, and *Why, then, count over your enemies, Henry had said,* the remark idly made and idly taken. *Monson*, I thought, and Aye, it fits snugger than your Italian boot hose—the hundred pounds slyly offered and slyly received; my instructions to journey north while Monson quartered troops on the Priory and directed search parties and no fear of discovering me until his purpose accomplished; then word sent tardily to Bedfordshire to search me out here, since, if I came foolishly to Turvey, there were yet two thousand acres of fair Bedford land and forest for the taking. And oh, ye did well, My Lord, I thought, ye purchased Reigate at lower rate than even you dared hope.

A little longer I stared into the dim, cool light within the stable, into the distance between brother and brother. "So he hath his hands on Reigate," I said. "Well, he had best enjoy it whilst he can. For my word on it, he shall live to regret it."

"Do not speak silly, John," Henry said.

"I speak not silly. An there be justice in heaven or luck on earth, I speak not silly." I turned abruptly and strode to the carriageway and looked out across the grounds. Beyond the manor I could see the road to Bedford Town, winding up the slow hill, empty of ought save sun and shadow and the dust of a late summer afternoon. "No search parties for Turvey this day, I think," I said.

"No," he said. "They will all be at the fair today." And then, "I am sorry, John. Truly. I would offer you refuge if I dared."

My back was to him but I did not face about. It was the first time he had spoken me fair but I did not face about. "Why, do not be," I said. "For the fault is none of yours. And I think it best I leave as I came. By the ford."

"Aye," he said, and then the silence again, and then, "If ye will hide out at the ford, I will send Andrew to you at dusk. With a napkin of food and what small sum of money I can lay hands to."

And now I did turn to him. The crop was now idle in his hand, and beyond him Andrew still stood, thick and stolid and the forelock hanging down over his forehead and the dull, quiet, puzzled hurt in his eyes. "Why, that were Christian of you, brother," I said.

I intended no irony. But I think he took it thus, for his eyes would not rest comfortable on mine. "I would do more," he said, "if I dared."

"I would not ask more. He shall not have Turvey too, and that because of me."

"Whence shall you go, John?"

I shrugged, though it was but a brave pretense, for I knew not where to turn to find one hand that was not turned against me, and I felt empty and sick within. "Where'er my nose leads me," I said.

"And where that, think you?"

I shrugged again and then smiled. I doubt there was little humor in it. "To smell out rebellion," I said. "If there be rebellion left in the land, and my luck hold, and I escape swinging before I can find it."

Andrew came to the ford at the thick end of dusk, bringing bread still warm from the oven and soggy with butter, and cold beef, and a bite of cheese, and a jug of milk. He watched me while I crouched before him and attacked the food.

"Mary is at Turvey, too," I said. "There is no bread like Mary's in all the land. And she remembered how I like bread buttered."

I thought while I ate that I should save a bit of food against the morrow. But my hunger was stronger than my will and I did not. In the thick of the dusk, with the moon as thin as a sliver and the color of a new-minted shilling just below the treetops and Andrew a shadow against the darker shadow of the river to his back, I swallowed the last of the bread and washed it down with milk and sighed my contentment and then rose to face him.

" 'Tis the first full stomach I have known this summer," I said.

"I have a purse for ye," he said. "And a knife to wear next your skin." He passed them to me, and I weighed the purse in my palm " 'Tis but four pounds," he said.

" 'Tis sufficient. 'Twill see me a mile or two, Andrew."

"I ha' seven more," he said. "Less a sixpence or two."

We stood no more than an arm's length apart. But in that light, with his back to the sighing, slow-moving darkness of the river, he was faceless, and I wished that the day were younger or the moon fuller, for I would have seen his face just now. And is this all the sum you have laid by in all your years with the Mordaunts, I thought; is this the total of your reward, Andrew? "I have no wish to part you from it, Andrew," I said softly.

"And cannot I own the wish to gi' it ye? Can ye not allow a man his affection for ye?"

"I know what affection you bear me, Andrew. I do not require your small savings to prove it me."

I had put my hand to his shoulder. Beneath my hand, he shrugged a small, impatient shrug. "I shall keep it, then. 'Twill be there when ye ha' need of it."

"And what intend ye by that?"

"I mean to join you on your travels."

"Andrew," I said. "Oh, Andrew, Andrew," but even as I said it, I felt within me the swell of affection for him and with it the quick, small rush of relief. "Nay," I said. "Nay, I cannot allow it, Andrew," but even while the words were passing my lips I was thinking, If there be one man in all of England I would choose to share danger with, that man, I think, were Andrew. " 'Twould be madness, man," I said. " 'Twould profit neither of us. Two together would make discovery twice as easy."

" 'Twould also be two to show them fight."

My hand was still to his shoulder, and I thrust my face to within an inch of his. "Look ye, Andrew," I said, and my voice a kind of soft, "I mean to get myself hanged. If I have any luck at it, two or three of the bastards will pay in advance for the pleasure it affords them, but I propose to smell out rebellion and get myself hanged for the joining."

"And ha' they no rope will fit my neck as nicely as yours?"

Another breath or two we stood thus, in the darkness, in the almost silence of the clearing, while behind him the river drifted another foot closer to wherever it was going and above us the cold sliver of moon parted ways with the treetops. Then I dropped my hand and turned from him.

"Very well, if you would have it so, Andrew."

"I would have it so."

I stepped around him and walked to the edge of the river. The sliver of moon overhead cast so little light I could not even make out the surface of the river. But I no more minded the darkness as I had. "We had best be on our way," I said. "Though I confess I know not where."

"An it be rebellion we seek, I should go west, I think. If there be a king's man left in the land, ye are like to find him west in Wales or south in Cornwall. And my name is known in Caernarvon."

I pondered that suggestion a breath or two and could hit on none better. "Well, then," I said, "we shall go west, Andrew."

Rebellion was, as Andrew said, west, about Chester and Shrewsbury, where in the alehouses the unvanquished yet touched glasses over bowls of water in silent and secret homage to a king across the

169

water, and where, come nightfall, Roundhead soldiers still walked the streets with circumspection. Or rebellion was in the hills and caves of Wales, where the Protector's taxgatherers were not always made to feel welcome. But between Bedford and Chester lay parliament country, with bristling garrisons at Coventry and Birmingham, and the great highway across the Midlands patrolled, and constables alerted for strangers. And so we traveled north, into Leicester and Nottinghamshire, before we faced into the setting sun.

We were in the north country now, where even the king's highway into Nottingham Town did not know repair from one progress to another and was so narrow in places that a wide-shouldered man would brush the thickets to either side as he passed; where the byways were but narrow footpaths, with ruts to above a man's knees and potholes the size of ponds and so ill ditched that a sudden summer rain could find a man a-swim within a quarter hour; where the hamlets lay at great distances one from the other and then were only a rude smithy and a mean alehouse and two or three wretched hovels; where the lords of the great estates had known their fair share of sequestration and were still sullen at heart, and the common folk had not forgotten how to touch forelock and address their betters with respect. We were in the north country now, and so we breathed easier and traveled more boldly, sleeping by night and pushing on by day.

Too boldly. Just above Melton Mowbray we took leave of the road into Nottingham Town and struck out west toward Loughborough. The way was little more than a winding footpath, and a morning's walk out of Melton Mowbray we swung around a sharp bend and came face to face with a man a-horseback, pistoled and cuirassed and sashed. A Roundhead officer if ever I saw one, and no chance for us to duck back and dive into the thickets to left or right, for he was within spitting distance as we rounded the bend and his hand was already to his pistol. So nothing for it but to pretend a brave show, and I glanced at Andrew and then lowered my eyes and made for him.

I ducked my head and touched forelock as I came up to him. His eyes remained fixed on us until we were abreast the horse, and he did not speak until I made as if to pass him.

"Ho, thou," he said then. He was lounging a trifle in the saddle, looking down on me, and I had little liking for the way his hand

170

rested on his pistol. "I think I have lost my way," he said. "Am I right, then, for Oakham?"

I nodded. "Ye will find Melton Mowbray straight ahead a pair of leagues. Oakham lies ten miles below it."

And now methought I could read suspicion in his eyes. "And where to, fellow?" he said, and his voice too casual, his seat in the saddle too indolent, his hand to his pistol too careless. "And what your errand?"

I glanced again at Andrew. He had taken root just at the horse's nose. "To Loughborough, sir," I said. "To purchase a bullock. For my master, the squire."

"The squire? And hath this squire a name?"

I had put my foot in it, and I cursed myself for the slowness of my wits. For if he were native to these parts, I had laid my own snare and then set foot in it. Then I thought of the knife beneath my shirt, wondering whether I could have it to his throat before he could free and cock that pistol.

"Come," he said, and his seat not quite so indolent now, his hand to the pistol not quite so careless. "Which squire? Henley or Adams?"

I had no choice but to grasp at the straw he held out. "Why, Squire Henley, sir."

He smiled a small, quick smile. "Henley, is it? And would this Squire Henley have provided ye with pass to travel?"

"Pass?" I said. "My master said nought of any pass. He hath sent me to Loughborough four times this twelvemonth—"

And now he provided me with answer as to which could appear faster, knife or cocked pistol, for one instant I was looking up into careless eyes and the next I was looking straight into the barrel of his pistol, the bore not four inches from the bridge of my nose and the eyes beyond the pistol no longer pretending nor the lips no longer smiling.

There is a fascination in looking straight into the barrel of a pistol. Rooted there, I was thinking that we were two to his one, and I would have thrown Andrew a look to tell him so. But instead I could only stand there, mouth agape, staring foolishly beyond the pistol into the cold amusement in a pair of pale gray eyes.

"Come," he said. "Who be ye, and what your business in these parts?"

"Nay," I said. "Nay, I swear we be honest—" and then, out of the corner of my eye, I caught the small movement from Andrew and thought, Pray God he hath read our necessity, and I brought my hand up to hold the trooper's attention and then threw myself sideways just as Andrew struck the horse a blow across the nose, and my right hand was to his wrist when the horse plunged and reared, and I twisted once, and the pistol flew out of his hand, and then he was on his back in the road and I astride him and my knife delicately to his throat, while behind me Andrew braced himself and spoke once to the horse, sharply, and then again, more softly.

He looked up at me. There was amazement in his eyes but no great fear. "I have a pass," I said. " 'Tis this. And do ye find it valid, then?"

"So I was in the right of it," he said. "Ye are no plowhand."

I grinned down into his eyes. "I have heard that curiosity is a killer of cats," I said. "But I think suspicion an even more dangerous toy. Had yours not hindered us from passing, you might still have been breathing this same hour tomorrow."

His eyes were a pale gray and level and still without trace of fear or fret. "If ye intend to slit my throat," he said pleasantly, "I promise you, you will be swinging for it within the month. If I fail to report back to my garrison by nightfall, they shall be searching me out by sunup, and the hue and cry out for ye by tomorrow high noon."

"And if I do not," I said, as pleasantly as he, "it will be out as soon as you can spur horse into Melton Mowbray."

"Granted. But ye might yet escape a hanging."

"I have had some practice these weeks in that sport," I said.

"Dispatch me and have done with it, then," he said. "I have said my prayers but this morning, and I think I am in a state of grace, and be about the work, then. For I have no intent to whine for mercy."

His eyes were still steady and without trace of fear, and he still smiled faintly. And I had never before killed a man.

"Come," he said. "Art not sufficiently a rogue to slit a man's throat and be on your way and your conscience clean of the memory within the hour?"

I had never before killed a man, and this was a brave man who looked up into the death in my eyes and did not flinch, and on the sudden the taste in my mouth was like to overripe mutton. "Andrew," I said, "I cannot do it. 'Twould be in cold blood and I cannot."

Andrew was standing just at my shoulder; the shadow he cast fell straight across the trooper's face. "Why, do not, then," he said.

"What, then? If we set him free, there will be troops beating the country for us by nightfall."

"Not an we lengthen his journey. He wears a stout belt and a sash, doth he not? Were it I, I should relieve him of his boots and hobble him—"

I chuckled. If we hang for this, I thought, it will be worth the price, the picture I got of a man set loose in that condition. "Why, Andrew," I said, "thou'rt inspired this morning. Get his pistol out of the dust there and level it on him while I set to work."

I worked busily a little. Then I helped him to his feet, and there was something other in his eyes now than amusement. "A pleasant walk back to Melton Mowbray," I said. "'Tis but seven miles. You should be within hailing distance by tomorrow high noon." He yet looked hard at me, his eyes gray but not as pale as I had thought. "And do you find my face curious?" I said.

"No," he said softly. "'Tis simply that I would know it again, if I have the luck to come face to face with you another day."

"I can hope that the possibility were a doubtful one."

"Aye, you can hope so."

"Come," I said. "It cannot be as bad as that. Give a man an afternoon, sure he can master the skill of walking hobbled."

"I promise you," he said, "it were better you had slit my throat."

I smiled on him, very pleasantly. Then I faced him about. "Our gratitude for the loan of your mount," I said. "We had not thought to be riding into Loughborough."

At the next bend in the path, I reined in the horse and looked back. He was still standing as we had left him, a child with his first step facing him. Sitting there, the thought came to me that I had indeed smelled out rebellion now, that now I was committed. Then the trooper took a first step and stumbled and fell. He lay quiet a little and then rolled over and spat out dust. Then with his heels he pushed himself to a tree aside the path and set his back to it and got thus to his feet, and I thought, It may be more than a pair of miles before he masters the art. Then I faced about and prodded the horse and once more headed west.

Rebellion was west. From the beginning it had smoldered, like some coal charred without but still treacherous within, in the far reaches of the kingdom. But in this year of suspected plots and baseless accusations and groundless arrests, of country squires offered crowns and cobblers made bishops in all but name and packed juries and arbitrary justice arbitrarily executed, rebellion had spread like some slow malignancy out of York into Cheshire and Salop and Wiltshire, out of Cornwall and Devon into Hants and Sussex.

Rebellion was west. You met with it in the surly replies of country folk of whom you inquired directions, for a man aboard a horse was nine times out of ten a parliament man and suspect. You met with it in the small, out-of-the-way inns, where five or six would gather together of an evening in some dim corner, their heads close and their voices kept low and their eyes heavy with distrust as you entered. You met with it in the guarded talk of innkeepers, talk of garrisons strengthened in Shrewsbury, of curfews strictly enforced, of arbitrary searches for arms and arbitrary arrests. You met with it of a summer afternoon, when the dust in the distance would warn you of another Roundhead regiment riding west; or of a summer evening with just at dusk the hollow sound of galloping hoofs and the lone courier sliding by, with next his skin the scrawled letter dated defiantly *Salop. 20 August. VI Charles II.* And were you west as far as Caernarvon, you might meet with it in the thick of early morning, with the small boat battling the surf in the darkness and the next day a new face in one of your coastal inns, the beard lately trimmed by a French barber and the clothing a trifle richer (though more frayed) than a shopkeeper's but no more conspicuous, and the eyes quietly alert.

Rebellion was west, and it required no great keenness of scent to smell it out, and we smelled it out, Andrew and I, in the north of Salop of an evening early in September.

There was, on the road between Chester and Shrewsbury, one of your tiny crossroads inns, two rooms above and an ordinary below commodious enough to entertain a single table. There was a landlord with fine, red veins in thin-skinned cheeks that betrayed the

174

Scot in him and eyes sullen with suspicion as we entered. And there was a single guest at the ordinary table, a slight man with a black beard and a hat that had come off some Parisian shelf within the fortnight and before him a bottle of wine which he sipped as if he had another twenty years to live and his chances thin of ever purchasing a second. There were these two, and the landlord's guarded reply when we inquired him out about lodgings, and then the stranger rose negligently from the table. He kept his head a little down as he approached the tap, and his right hand rested lightly on the small sword to his side.

"Ye be strangers in these parts," he said. "Down from Chester mayhap."

I did not like his eyes. They were of a color to match his beard, and they were uncommonly restless, and I did not like them. "Not down from Chester," I said.

His eyes drifted to the sober clothing Andrew and I had purchased in Loughborough. "From the south," he murmured. "Two shopkeepers if the clothing be any test."

I leaned an elbow on the tap. "You have hazarded two guesses in as many minutes," I said. "Neither of them shrewd. And I do not find your manners amusing. I have been in the saddle since daybreak, and I have no whim for being close questioned like some penniless vagrant brought before one of your crossroads bailiffs."

He shrugged. "If ye would put up at the Unicorn, it is the price exacted for being stranger to Salop."

"It is a price I do not propose to pay. And so how far to Shrewsbury?"

His eyes rested speculatively on a point just below my chin. "A short ten miles," he said. "Though the road not recommended beyond sundown. Should you manage the distance with your life, you might sound out the Rose and Crown. It is much frequented by officers from the Castle and Anabaptist tradesmen, and you are like to find the talk at ordinary more to your understanding than mine."

I looked at his hand, resting on the basket hilt of his small sword, and then I looked at the cold smile, and then I thrust my face close enough to his to smell his breath. "I think," I said, "that were I you, I should have done with the sport of guessing. Ye clearly lack the knack of it."

"La, now," he said pleasantly. "And dost seek a quarrel with me?"

175

"Aye. An that be the price of your leaving me in peace."

For the first time his eyes met mine, and he smiled suddenly. "But I none with you. I would rather share with you that bottle of wine."

I looked into his smile and liked him enough better on the sudden to return it. "On one condition," I said. "That ye cease prying into what concerns you not."

His smile broadened. "Agreed. I am Sir Joseph Wagstaff."

"My pleasure, Sir Joseph."

"Am I to drink with a man whose name I do not know?"

I had returned his smile. But I still mistrusted those eyes. "My equals call me John," I said, and for the nonce it was all the satisfaction I would allow him.

For the nonce, though later I was to provide him with more. We had the two of us honest faces, he told us over that bottle of wine, and so he would hazard a third guess, which was that we were disaffected toward the present government; if that were as wide of the mark as his others, why, then, his life was in our hands. He was recently out of France, he told us, and he carried a commission from Charles Stuart to raise troops and nurture rebellion in the land. England was ripe for a rising, he said, you could smell it in the air this fall, and already two hundred in Cheshire alone had pledged themselves to this action. And then he leaned across the table, his lips dead serious now and his eyes no more restless. "And what say ye to that?" he said. "Whate'er your names be?"

I had heard tales of Thurloe agents sounding out the unsuspecting with some such trick as this and then clapping them to. But when you go in search of rebellion, I thought, you must hazard your throw of the dice somewhere, sometime. "Why, I say," I replied, "that I would have a look at this commission you claim to carry."

He produced it. It was as he said, a commission issued by Charles Rex to one Joseph Wagstaff to raise foot and horse in the west of England, and I raised my eyes from it and drew a slow breath, resolved now to take the plunge. "John Mordaunt," I said. "Once of Reigate in Surrey, late of Newgate Gaol. And this Andrew Harris."

"Mordaunt," he murmured. "Have I not heard this name?"

"You may have. My brother is the Earl of Peterborough and a strong supporter of the Commonwealth." I smiled grimly at my own jest. "Two thousand a year strong. Since Worcester."

176

He shook his head. "It was your name I heard, and recently. You are fresh out of Newgate, say you?"

I nodded. "On charge of high treason."

"Then you would be one of those taken with Gerard. The one who escaped Newgate in May."

"I am."

"I was sulking about London in June. I witnessed the execution of Gerard. And of poor Peter Vowel." His hand fell to toying with the wine glass before him. "So you have a price published on your head. And I can score me one guess was close enough to the mark."

"Two," I said. "For you have hit on our business in these parts."

"Have I so? And what would that be?"

"The charges they brought against me were false," I said. "The next time I am taken, the charges will not be false."

He was happy to hear it, he said; clearly we were two good men, cautious and close-mouthed as well as heated in the cause, and His Majesty had need of such. I replied that if a man with a price on his head and no estate left him could prove of use, I would do what I could for the king's cause. He said that if I did, I should not go unrewarded. I answered that the only reward I sought was the return of two hundred acres of land rightfully mine and the pleasure it would someday afford me of placing a sword point nicely to the throats of two rogues I could name. "And let us drink to that," he said, and called out for another bottle of wine, and over that he told us of rebellion seething and bubbling in the land: of the Sealed Knot, a committee of lords and gentry in England, sworn to secrecy, loyalty, sedition, and the restoration of the king; of the fanatic sects who were disaffected of late with the Protector's religious policies; of the army unpaid since spring and grown sullen this September, and of mutiny but a month since in the navy; of the muttering where'er you went, complaints of taxes too burdensome and officials too officious and churchmen too pious and laws too strict. "And so," he said, his eyes bright as buttons in the light of the candle, "we must find you a part in this business, must we not?"

"But name me what I can do," I said.

"For the present, you can be counted a pair more swords in Salop. Art totally without fortune?"

"We have a few shillings between us," I said. "And a sturdy horse.

177

A present from a Roundhead officer who was overcome one summer afternoon with generosity."

"If you are to fight, you must also eat. Canst write a fair hand?"

"I am no clerk. But it can be read, I think."

"You will find a Sir Thomas Harris two miles from here. They call his estate Boreatton. I think Sir Thomas hath a sudden need for a secretary."

"If he hath an equal need for a gardener, we shall seek him out on the morrow."

He nodded and then raised his glass. The wine in it glinted rich and dark as blood. "To His Majesty Charles the Second," he said.

I touched my glass to his. "To liberty and justice," I said.

ᵭᵭ *Ten* ᵭᵭ

Boreatton lies seven miles north of Shrewsbury, nigh a thousand acres of rolling pasture and fair woods. The master of Boreatton, Sir Thomas Harris, was one you could hear, if he were out of doors and the wind right, from any point on his land, for Sir Thomas never whispered when he could speak aloud and never spoke aloud when he could roar. He was so engaged when we rode down the drive between manor and stable and so came upon him; he stood feet apart and heavy head forward, with before him a wide-eyed stable boy and beside him a slighter man who looked on amused. Then he looked around into the slow clop of our horse's hoofs on the gravel, the cords to his neck bulging, his face red to the hairline with hard drinking and hard fighting and hearty eating and the humor he was presently in.

"God's arse," he said. "What the de'il ha' we here, Ralph?"

The one beside him owned the cleanest blue eyes I have ever seen. "Two of your godly, by the looks, Sir Thomas," he said. "Come to seize on Boreatton and clap ye in the stocks for the evil of your ways."

I looked down at the two of them. "Not so," I said. "We are come to inquire you out about employment."

"Employment?" Sir Thomas roared. "What employment? The setting up of a haberdashery for Quakers on my land?"

"The clothes," I said stiffly, "were what we had the coin to purchase in Loughborough. We have found them serviceable enough

179

for travel and sober enough to pass through Leicester towns without drawing attention."

"Ha' ye so, now? Well, gi' me leave to inform you that they draw attention in Salop these days. They draw attention here at Boreatton, damn me if they do not."

I shrugged. "I have already spent the sixpence. 'Tis pity I cannot unspend it."

"And so ye seek employment. What employment, sirrah?"

I swallowed my temper. "I have been told you stand in need of a secretary. Now that I have laid eyes on you, I can well believe it."

"What? Canst write, then?"

"Aye," I said. "My name."

"Now here is impudence, damn me if it is not. And I ha' a mind to whip the pair o' you off the place." He looked at his companion. "Art of the same mind as I, Ralph?"

The one he called Ralph looked up at us with those clean blue eyes out of a face as fair and well formed as any I could remember. He shook his head slightly. "None of your godly," he murmured. "I know not what knavery they represent, but they are no psalm singers. Were it for me to say, I should invite them to dismount, for I think they may have a tale to tell us."

I nodded politely at him. "Have I your permission, sir?" I said to Sir Thomas.

For a little his face was knotted in thought; thick as an oak he was, and near as thick in the wits I should guess. Then he growled me a surly leave, and I clambered down off the horse and Andrew after me. The fair one studied us across ten feet of raked gravel. "You seek employment at Boreatton," he said, and his voice as fair as his face. "As secretary, though you cannot write."

I smiled. "I spoke in jest. Though I am no clerk, I grant you."

"And what else can you do?"

"Fight," I said.

His frown was quickly come and as quickly gone. "We be peaceable men in these parts," he said mildly.

"Are you so? 'Twas not what Sir Joseph Wagstaff gave me to understand."

"Sir Joseph sent you?"

I nodded. "I am called John Mordaunt. I carry a price on my head. Since May. The charge was high treason."

"And what hath this to do with us?"

"I have a score to settle with our Protector. And hopes that certain gentlemen in these parts might join me in the settling of it. If I have been misled, we had best pack up and seek satisfaction elsewhere."

"Nay. Softly, sir, softly." He looked at Sir Thomas. "Think you they look honest? If Sir Joseph Wagstaff—"

"Wagstaff," Sir Thomas growled, and spat in the dust at his feet. "Wagstaff is a fool. Wagstaff would sound out Oliver himself if he could approach within speaking distance. Aye, and put him in command of the business in the bargain and that within the month. A pox on Sir Joseph Wagstaff."

"Agreed. But I think he hath hit on an honest one here."

"An impudent one. And I cannot abide impudence. Damn me if I can."

"You bark loud, Sir Thomas," I said. "Do you bite as sharp, I wonder?"

He glared at me, his mouth working, the cords to his neck knotted, the crimson seeping toward his hairline. "Hast a mind to test me?" he said thickly. "Hast guts to match that waspish tongue o' yours while the light is yet proper?"

"Why, no," I answered sweetly. "Damn me but I do not, Sir Thomas."

Again the smile flitted across the fair one's face while Sir Thomas's mouth worked. "Dost mark that, Ralph?" he roared. "Impudence. An I am to join with this pup in this business, I shall wet my blade on his guts afore the week be out."

I grinned at him. "I should rather call a truce, Sir Thomas. I have no quarrel with you. Have we anger to spare, let us put it out to common use. It were better spent on Protectors and scurvy Rump Parliaments than on each other."

"He speaks you wisdom there, Sir Thomas," the fair one said.

Sir Thomas still glared. "I cannot abide a waspish tongue. Damn my eyes but I cannot."

"Nor I a bilious rudeness," I said. "If you will call a halt to the one, I shall to the other."

He dropped his eyes out of mine. "Ye had best prove honest. Damn my guts but ye had best."

"We shall prove honest."

The fair one glanced at Andrew. "What of your companion? Is he dumb?"

I shook my head. "But not given to wasting words, neither."

"A commendable trait. There are scores in the kingdom could profit by it." He fixed his eyes on Andrew. "And what skills bring ye to Boreatton?"

"I have been my whole life a gardener," Andrew said. "And I can care for a horse. And drag pike as far as the next. I was at Worcester with Master John's brother."

The fair one smiled on Andrew and then stepped forward and extended me a hand. "I am Ralph Kynaston of Rusnant," he said. "We may be seeing a deal of one another afore spring."

I returned his smile, and this time my heart was in it. Sir Thomas was a man you could abide if the cause were bright enough. But this one with the frank blue eyes and the fair, firm mouth was one I would have found it hard to dislike even were our politics across the way. "If it be daily," I said, "I shall have no complaints on that score, Ralph Kynaston."

It was a season of discontent. All that fall and winter riders galloped through October dust or labored through November mud or braved the iron of December, carrying in false boot sole or coat lining the letters in cipher—"The business goeth so well forward in Plymouth that Mr. Dunham hopes for a full eight per cent return on the moneys let out. Word from Mr. S. hath it that Mr. Cross's imports will be aboard ship next month, though he finds the duties stiff at Dover and prefers Sandwich." And all that fall and winter heads were together in malignant taverns and alehouses, murmuring of ways and means, of hopes and doubts. By November disaffected fanatics were also deep in the plot, and by Christmas London gunsmiths were busy with a flurry of orders, and throughout the kingdom horses were on the sudden high-priced and hard to come by.

They were also busy at Whitehall. In November the letters we received out of London spoke gloomily of great preparations going forward against us: of the Tower guard doubled and the City chains looked to and cannon planted before Whitehall; of the Protector speaking before his latest parliament of a very full discovery of a Cavalier design on the government; of arrests of gunsmiths in London and of the interception of cartloads of arms. And of Roundhead troops dispatched to York or Yeovil or Chester.

The last were a piece of intelligence we had already guessed. For with the first frost they sent to Shrewsbury one Colonel Humphrey Mackworth, four and forty years old, one-time officer in Cromwell's own Ironside regiment, ten years governor of Shrewsbury, twice member of Commonwealth parliaments, and presently member of the Council of State. Mackworth was lean in the body and long in the nose and thin in the lip and pious of eye, and he rode into Salop with thirty-seven troopers at his back, sent down to strengthen the garrison at Shrewsbury Castle.

Within the week he was at Boreatton with six of his men. They sat their horses without the manor while Mackworth's sergeant bawled out for Sir Thomas to show himself. In the midafternoon of an early winter day, with the light thin as dusk and the scuttling clouds overhead smelling of first snow, Mackworth looked down at the pair of us.

"I would have a word with Sir Thomas Harris," he said. His voice was a proper one for the singing of psalms and the quoting of tags of Scripture; it had just the proper twang for it.

"Why, speak it, then," Sir Thomas said.

Mackworth considered him with eyes saddened by the presence of a sinner lacking in grace standing afore him. "Art Harris?" he said.

"What game is this, Mackworth?" Sir Thomas said. "We were spawned, you and I, not five miles apart, and what game is this?"

Mackworth had been all his grown life a professional soldier, and he sat his horse like one; but he had the look otherwise of some fanatic weaver, some one of your Fifth Monarchy Men with the spirit descended on him, just climbed into the pulpit at the Cross in Cheapside. "I put ye a question," he said. "I would hear a civil answer to it."

"Aye, I am Harris. Ye well know I am, Mackworth. 'Sblood—"

"I shall have no blasphemy here," Mackworth said sharply. "I shall not abide blasphemy, Sir Thomas."

Sir Thomas glared up at him, his feet an ell apart, his hands clasped behind his back, his head forward. And there shall be spleen, I thought, there shall be roaring, and one sword less a month hence if they choose to cart him off to Shrewsbury Gaol. "Ye are on my land, Mackworth," Sir Thomas said. "And uninvited. Ye shall abide what I choose ye shall abide."

"Dost propose to defy me, then?"

Sir Thomas's mouth worked, and the cords to his neck swelled. "What is your business wi' me, Mackworth?"

Mackworth gazed down at him, his eyes sad and abstracted, a sad, godly man engaged in doing his duty to God and state. "Yesterday I made the acquaintance of one Bishop. A small, gray man. A rogue by inclination, a carter by trade. Would ye know such an one, Sir Thomas?"

"I have lacked of late some o' your advantages, Mackworth," Sir Thomas said. "I have not sat in parliament since Praise-God Barebones lent his name to one. I do not count carters and cobblers among those I drink with."

The shaft struck home; had Mackworth had sufficient blood in that lean body, he might have flushed. " 'We have made a covenant with death, and with hell are we at agreement,' " he intoned. " 'When the overflowing scourge shall pass through, it will not come unto us, for we have made lies our refuge, and under falsehood have we hid ourselves.' "

"Ye quote Scripture prettily," Sir Thomas said. "Ye have just the proper snivel and twang for it. And ha' ye the stomach, too, to give me the lie? Straight out, like a man?"

Mackworth smiled thinly. "And what of one John Skinner? Ha' ye heard that name? A gunsmith near Tower Hill?"

"Nor him, neither."

"Why, then," Mackworth said, still smiling, "ye will have no wish to lay claim to as delicate a brace of pistols as I have laid eyes on this twelvemonth. The box sent down by John Skinner of Tower Hill, with instructions it was to be delivered by Bishop into your hands." And now he no more smiled and his eyes no longer sad, for he was Moses come down to destroy the Golden Calf, he was Daniel passing judgment on Belshazzar, he was Jeremiah come to Babylon. "Ye find Scripture not to your humor," he said. "Hast a mind to hear law instead? 'Hereby all persons who have been sequestered for delinquency, or borne arms against the parliament, are disabled to buy, use, or keep in their houses or elsewhere, any arms whatsoever, offensive or defensive, on pain of loss thereof, and to be

184

treated in such manner as the Lord Protector and his Council shall direct.' "

Sir Thomas heard him out, though it was touch and go. "Hast a warrant for me, Mackworth?" he said. "If ye have, produce it. If ye have not, get ye off my land."

"I have a warrant," Mackworth said. "But look behind me for it."

Sir Thomas looked to the six troopers to Mackworth's back, while I watched his face and thought that there would be more nor one sword missing this month in Salop were Mackworth to clap him to. He was born bilious, I thought, and he lives with the taste of spleen in his throat, but he is known honest, and others are in this business through his persuasion. And so I cleared my throat and stepped forward. "Sir Humphrey," I said. "If you will give me leave, I can explain that brace of pistols."

He had, I think, noted me, but only as you might note a pillar to the porch a man stood on, or a tree he leaned against. But now he bent his attention full on me, and I doubt I would have called his eyes friendly. "And who might ye be?" he said.

"Richard Parr, sir."

"I do not know you. What do you at Boreatton?"

"I am employed as secretary to Sir Thomas. And tutor to his son."

"Tutor?" He thought on that a little. "And what teach ye the boy? Theology, mayhap?"

"A scrap or two, though the boy is yet tender—"

"Ah. And what theology? Hath it a Babylonian spice to it? Doth it taste of Romish sauces?"

"I am no papist, Sir Humphrey."

"Armenian, then. You have an Armenian face, I think. Do you read morning prayer prettily, sirrah? Dost bow and scrape at all the proper points?"

I swallowed my temper; there was more at stake here than pride, and if Sir Thomas had not the discipline to spit soft and swallow bitter, then I must. "I am newly out of Christ's College, Cambridge," I said.

"Are ye so?" he said dryly. "And have they read ye the law at Cambridge? 'Hereby all persons are disabled from entertaining in their houses, either as chaplains, schoolmasters, or as private tutors, any sequestered clergyman, schoolmaster, or university scholar; no

185

person ejected for delinquency or scandal is to be permitted to teach a school, or to preach—' "

"I am out of Christ's College, Cambridge," I repeated. "And my theology Presbyterian. And I cannot see what bearing—"

"Bearing?" he cried. "I shall inform ye what bearing. Ye are at Boreatton, that is what bearing. Ye are tutor in the household of a known malignant, that is what bearing. If your theology were sound, you could not tolerate Boreatton a fortnight, that is what bearing."

"I did not inquire out Sir Thomas's politics," I said. "And ye are free to put out inquiries to the Committee for the Examination of Ministers. Or to Christ's College—"

"I shall. Never fear, I shall." He stared gloomily down at me. "And what this tale of yours concerning pistols?"

"They were intended as a gift," I said, and paused, for I had almost said Christmas gift, I had almost forgot that Christmas was one more heathen practice the fanatics had put down. "I had heard Sir Thomas express a desire—"

"What?" he said. "Of the cloth, and ye choose pistols for a gift, and the recipient a known malignant? Hast no better tale than that to tell?"

" 'Behold, thou desirest truth in the inward parts,' " I said. " 'And in the hidden part thou shalt make me to know wisdom.' And if that be not apt, Sir Humphrey, what say ye to this? 'My goodness extendeth not to thee, but to the saints, that are in the earth, and to the excellent, in whom is all my delight.' "

He looked sadly down upon me. "Why, I say," he said, "that I can hope that the Committee found your persuasions as clean as your choice of Scriptural passages, Richard Parr. Though if Harris there hath chosen one of us for chaplain, it is the first honest act he hath been guilty of since Edgehill." And now he looked at Sir Thomas, and the look plainly said that a fish might escape his net one day but not forever. "Do not think me a fool, Sir Thomas," he said quietly. "There is sedition in the land, the west country stinks of it, and do not write me off as a fool."

We watched them depart Boreatton. "Mackworth," Sir Thomas muttered, and cursed. "They give us Mackworth to deal with. The smell of treason must be strong about Whitehall this month if they sent down Mackworth."

I watched the troop swing into the road to Shrewsbury. "I do not think that tale of mine put him off," I said.

"Put him off? Put Mackworth off? He is a damned leech, Mackworth."

"And no fool," I said. "And his surrender too easy. I think it wise were visitors to stay clear of Boreatton this month, Sir Thomas."

"You do not have a month," he said gloomily. "That tale of yours will hang you within a fortnight."

"A little longer, I think. One fortnight for Mackworth to find out that Richard Parr is indeed out of Christ's College and his theology sound. Another to discover that Parr is vicar of the Chapel of St. Lawrence in Reigate and not tutor in Salop." I grinned at him. "Give us a pair of fortnights, it may be Mackworth who finds himself laid by the heels."

He did not return my grin. "If we accomplish that," he said, " 'twill be more nor ever Sir John Grenville or Rupert before us could manage."

Sir Thomas was in the right of it on one count: Mackworth was indeed a leech. Thrice within the month he appeared at Boreatton with his contingent of troopers, on pretext of searching out stable or cellar for arms, or my quarters for surplice or prayer book. He set a watch on us, too; one such skulker we smoked out one afternoon and near frighted to death with threats of hanging. And commonly the servants we dispatched into Shrewsbury reported that they were close followed.

For a month Mackworth was but a minor nuisance, a small thorn caught beneath the skin but not yet festered. Then word came of a rendezvous at Bromsgrove at which Sir Thomas's presence was urgently required. And now Mackworth was more than a small nuisance. For Bromsgrove lies forty miles south of Shrewsbury, and so we must absent ourselves from Boreatton a pair of days. And in 1654 absence from your place of abode was suspect. Absence provided the saints an excuse for fetching you before a justice for close questioning. For a month we at Boreatton had smiled bland innocence before the world. Now we could only hope that the game had scored in our favor, that Mackworth would not choose this week to pay us another visit.

We departed Boreatton at midnight, meeting Ralph Kynaston

and Sir George Booth from Cheshire at Boreatton Park. At noon the next day we rode into Bromsgrove and inquired out the Sign of the Cock. By nightfall near a score of us were crowded into an ordinary not fit to accommodate ten, a score of quiet, determined, desperate men who had ridden in from all points of the compass and from as far distant as seventy miles. Four of us from Salop and Cheshire were there; and Sir Joseph Wagstaff and Hugh Grove and John Penruddock had come up from Wiltshire; and a dozen were in from about Bristol, including one I had last seen in London, a man with a round face and sleepy eyes, a man who started when he recognized me and then smiled and touched his hat brim.

I returned the courtesy. "I see you are in health, Sir Richard," I said. "No gaol fever after all."

"No," he said. "By the grace of God, I escaped that."

"And the rope, too," I said dryly.

He was no more smiling. "Aye," he said. "And that, too."

"I am told that Mr. Gerard did not fare as well."

"Gerard was a fool," he said. "And Vowel, too. They must refuse to plead. They must bluster before the court of the illegality—"

"But you," I said. "You were no such fool, eh?"

"We were explained equally the consequences of such a course," he said stiffly. "If we pled, the worst we had to fear was five years at chopping sugar, the best a stiff fine and banishment from London. I deem it no loss of honor—"

"I do not recall that I imputed any such to you." I turned a shoulder to him. "I think," I said, "that services are about to begin."

"Gentlemen," Sir Joseph Wagstaff was saying at the ordinary table, and the babel in the room faded to a murmur. "From Charles the Second, by the grace of God King of England, I bring you greetings," he said, and looked about the quiet, crowded room. "The date hath been chosen," he said, and bent into the now dead silence. And then, "Two months from hence, if it be God's will, and this land shall no more know tyranny," he said.

He had watched out plots before, he told us in the next hour, but none with so fair a chance of success as this one. He could count you ten meetings throughout the kingdom this night, all attended by men as resolved as we. There would be risings throughout the kingdom, he said, and the Duke of York was to lead five thousand insurgents in Kent and Surrey, and Charles himself was to land at

Hull at the head of ten thousand French troops. As for our part in this business, he and Penruddock would recruit forces at Salisbury and then fall on Major Butler's garrison at Marlborough. "And you, Sir Thomas," he said, and looked across the ordinary to where Sir Thomas Harris leaned against the tap. "From you we must have Shrewsbury Castle."

"Mackworth is commanding the Castle," Sir Thomas said. "With thirty-seven Roundhead regulars and fifty Shrewsbury volunteers."

"We must have Shrewsbury Castle," Wagstaff repeated.

"I have but two hundred pledged," Sir Thomas said. "And we lack cannon or scaling ladders. And Mackworth hath planted four six-pounders on those—"

"We must have the Castle," Wagstaff said. "Who commands Shrewsbury Castle commands the road to Caernarvon, and we have hopes of five thousand Irish—" He broke off and bit his underlip, while a murmur grew in the room and then quieted. And now, at the ordinary table, John Penruddock was frowning into that quiet. "Irish?" he said. "Did ye say Irish, sir?"

"Aye," Wagstaff said and bit his underlip again.

"We have been told nothing of Irish troops," Penruddock said. He was a man with a broad, blunt face and honest gray eyes, and just now his heavy jaw was set and his eyes harder than was their wont. "I do not like the sound of Irish," he said.

Wagstaff shrugged. "What would you, Penruddock? Think you two thousand Englishmen can bring this off without help?"

"I do not like it," Penruddock repeated. "And I think there are others here that do not, neither. Ten thousand French from the east, five thousand Irish from the west. Is it Charles Stuart's intent to bring back Rome—"

"Do ye prefer the rule of the saints?"

"Aye," Penruddock said quietly. "I find this government as insufferable as any here. But whate'er we can lay to Oliver, he hath at least lit us no fires in Smithfield."

Wagstaff looked about the room. "Are others here of a like mind?"

"I am." This was Sir George Booth from Cheshire. He was seated beside Penruddock, and he was not so sturdy as Penruddock nor his jaw so thick, but otherwise, in complexion and cast of eye and color of hair, they could have been brothers. "I have lost estates to the rogues at Whitehall," he said, "and I have suffered the in-

189

solence of their officials, and I have fretted under their laws. But I yet would not exchange government by saints for government by priests."

"And the rest of you?" Wagstaff said softly.

There was a scattering of ayes in the room, but there was a louder chorus of nays. There were, I suspect, one or two secret papists in that gathering, but I do not think these were all the reason. Rather, it was the times. For if Rome was past, Independency was now. I doubt there were six in that room over thirty, and the burning of the heretics in Smithfield was something that had happened before Elizabeth. But sequestration and pious hypocrisy and High Courts of Justice and the insolence of jackals were something they suffered daily. And under Rome a man at least dared jest again, or tumble a wench, or walk forth in his fields of a Sabbath afternoon.

"It would appear," Wagstaff said, "that ye stand outnumbered in your sentiments, Mr. Penruddock." He looked again about the room. "Fear not," he said. "We shall not have papacy in England. Toleration for tender consciences, yes. But you have Charles Stuart's solemn word—"

"His word?" Booth said dryly. "Charles Stuart's word? With fifteen thousand papist soldiers overrunning the land—" and then the silence in the room silenced him, and he fell to a gloomy contemplation of the nails to his right hand, while Wagstaff looked again to Sir Thomas.

"And shall we return, then," he said, "to the problem of Shrewsbury Castle?"

It was young Ralph Kynaston who solved it. Sir Thomas was right, he said, without cannons or mines or scaling ladders, the Castle was impregnable. But he remembered from his schooldays the tale of Troy and the wooden horse, and perhaps . . . Tuesday was market day in Shrewsbury Town, he said, and provisions brought into the Castle on Tuesday afternoons, and if five or six of us could enter disguised as peasant women and secret ourselves within the walls until midnight . . .

And so a month later we lay, Andrew and I, atop a modest hill overlooking Shrewsbury. It was the supper hour, and behind the Castle the town looked almost uninhabited—the town's three stone bridges deserted now of foot travelers and farm carts; the market place, marked by the great stone market cross, emptied of all save litter and deserted stalls. In the thin, cheerless, winter light, the walls of the town looked ruined and unrepaired and sad, as indeed they were, for Shrewsbury had been seven years King Charles's town and it had seen its share of civil war.

But the walls to the Castle were not unrepaired; breached they had been twice or thrice, but they stood firm and rebuilt again. There was just now a last trickle of business at the gates, a farm cart departing, a slim young officer standing just without the gates, engaged in thoughtful contemplation of the north wall. But in another half hour dusk would settle thick upon the road below, and they would close and bar the Castle gates, and Andrew and I would pull coat collars up and hats down against the night air, settling down for the long watch from seven to midnight. And if we did not bring word to Sir Thomas that our design were betrayed, they would assemble at Boreatton in three hours, two hundred men with pistols primed, and pockets heavy with balls molded from Sir Thomas's lead roof tiles, and hopes at pitch. And in five hours they would be a quarter mile distant, waiting in the darkness for the Castle gates to swing open and the torch to flare in Ralph Kynaston's hand, signal that the guards were surprised and the garrison still asleep and the Castle sprawled as helpless before us as some captive wench taken in some barbarous and distant storming.

If all went well, I thought. We had lain here the afternoon, and so far no suspicious activity below. In midafternoon, Ralph Kynaston and five companions, dressed as farm women, had straggled through the gates with scarce a second careless glance from the guards. And since then no hint of betrayal, no looking to the cannon that gaped on the deserted walls, no watch doubled at the gates—nothing, unless it were this officer studying the north walls, to cause us uneasiness.

"I would give a crown," I said, "to know what that one hath on his mind."

"Why, supper, Master John."

"He is owner of a monstrous appetite, then. For he shows more than a passing interest in the stones to those walls." Then the officer sauntered back through the gates, and I looked at Andrew. He lay beside me, his expression stolid and comfortable. "I do not like it," I said.

" 'Tis a nervous time, the hour before your first battle. It could not be quieter below."

"Too quiet. Were I baiting a trap, I should do it just so, my cannon commanding every approach but the proper one, and no watch on those ramparts." The wind was to our backs, and I pulled up my cloak collar against it. "And I could like this wind better were it in our faces. There shall be no moon before midnight. And in another half hour, we shall have nought but our ears to tell us of any action there below."

"I think," he said, "that all the action down there this night will be snoring."

Five hours later and I was prepared to grant him that. The moon, but a yard above the horizon, was as yet of small use, but there were enough stars so that if you knew where to look, you could see the Castle below, a bulking shadow squatting in the lighter shadow of midnight. By now the wind had shifted to the north, and I could hear crosswind the muffled, hollow cry of the watch, "Twelve o' the clock and all-l-l's well-l-l." If they had been alerted, I thought, they would surely have betrayed it by now—by the stir of armed men gathering in the courtyard, by the sound of cannon being moved to that north rampart.

And then I heard it, a single thin clank of metal on metal, the sound small and distant and uncertain as to direction. "Listen," I whispered. "Heard ye that, Andrew?"

"Aye."

"From the Castle, think you?"

"On our right hand, I think. From the road."

"Then damn Harris for his thick wits," I hissed. "Hath he not the mother's sense to respect that wind? Was it not agreed they were to walk their mounts the last half mile and maintain a good six feet between—"

"There is no sound of alarm below," he said.

I strained my ears for a sound from the Castle. But with that crosswind I could make out nothing. And then the link flared. The link flared, and in the light of it I saw the Castle gates already gaping, and in the distance I heard the single shout and then the sudden drum of two hundred horses spurred to a charge, and I leaped to my feet with "For King Charles" on my lips and took a

192

single step, and then Andrew's hand was hard on my shoulder and pulling me up short.

"The ramparts," he said, and no whisper this. "The ramparts. Sweet Mother of Jesus, look to the ramparts."

I did so. There was but one flare at the gates, but one link was all that was required to see what was to be seen. Which was betrayal. Which was the death of our hopes once again. Which was sudden murder for some of those two hundred and summary execution for others. Which was all four of Mackworth's cannon somehow moved between full dark and midnight without light or sound, four cannon all facing north, all facing straight down the road into the sound of those drumming hoofs. And even as I drew breath to scream out betrayal, I saw the glow of the match and heard the roar, like the end of time, like the clap of judgment, and in the darkness fifty yards down that road the mortal screams of hurt horses and hurt men as four charges of grape smashed into two hundred massed and galloping horses, and Andrew saying, almost as if he were at prayer, "Sweet Jesus Christ, oh, sweet Jesus Christ, oh, sweet Jesus," and I sobbing, "The bastards, the bastards, the bastards," while more links flared at the gates and Mackworth sallied out of the Castle at the head of his troop, riding forth to the glory of God, and the further honor of the Protector and Colonel Humphrey Mackworth, and the perpetuation of English liberties without king or lord or bishop. . . .

⊰ᴑ *Eleven* ᴆ⊱

For a little I was clean mad; and then, as suddenly, I was not. I stood atop that hill and watched, coldly and dispassionately, while four or five of Mackworth's men saw to the dead and wounded and the rest took off in hot pursuit of the fleeing. And if we had had the shrewdness to place half our men on this hill, I thought, we could even now sweep down on that road and take the Castle in the teeth of those eight or ten still planted on the ramparts. And just once, I thought bitterly, I wish there were one king's man in this land could match foresight with hindsight.

"I think," I said, "that there is nothing further we can do here. And so I think we are for Wiltshire, Andrew." And then, quite calmly, "I would be near Salisbury before another sundown," I said.

It was too dark to see Andrew's face. But I had no need to. It required but small imagination to guess at his stare. "Salisbury?" he said. "By sundown? 'Tis an impossibility—"

"If Nick Swiftsure could post from London to York in thirty hours," I said, "we can try for half that distance in eighteen."

"That were on summer roads," he said. "And a full moon on his side. And he yet killed four mounts. And his still the most famous ride—"

"We will kill four too, if that be required. For Penruddock marches on Salisbury in another sundown. And if there is a trap

194

laid for him, I would warn him. And if there is none, I would have a hand in the business."

We were not in Wiltshire in eighteen hours, but we were in something over twenty, though heaven alone (or hell) knows how we managed it. We did so in part by galloping our horses in reckless abandon over that iron-frozen and evil Bristol road by the light of a slice of moon and a few cold stars; by paying avaricious rogues at Ludlow and Chepstow thrice their wonted fee for fresh horses, and by taking others at pistol point at Marlborough; by galloping through Bristol in broad daylight, which was scarce prudent, and by boldly inquiring out John Penruddock's place of abode of the watch in Chippingham, which was less prudent yet. And so, by ten of the clock on the following night, we had found out Compton Chamberlain and had turned our staggering mounts into Penruddock's grounds.

There were horses tethered before Penruddock's manor. We burst without knocking into a room where half a dozen men were seated around a table. On my entrance Penruddock rose from the bench with a hand to the pistol thrust into his belt. "Friend," I said thickly. "I am friend, Penruddock—"

"Mordaunt," he said.

"Aye. Ridden from Shrewsbury since midnight last," and I swayed there in the doorway and then recovered. "Come to warn you of betrayal," I said, and swayed again and would have fallen had he not risen quickly and put a hand to my arm. "Four rounds of grape hitting two hundred bunched horses," I said, "and Christ knows how many dead—" His face blurred before me, and I shook my head to clear it. "He moved four cannon on those ramparts in the dark," I said. "By witchcraft, I think, for God knows I lay atop that hill and heard no sound—" and then his face blurred again, and shaking my head cured nothing, and I reached for something to steady myself only nothing was there, and then I pitched forward in a dead faint.

I floated back into this world with the feel of water on my face, and the taste of brandy on my lips, and Penruddock's blunt and honest face straight above me.

"What?" I said, and struggled to sit up. "Is it morning already—"

"It is not yet midnight," he said. "And do ye lie quiet, man."

I remembered then. And I was no longer in a room below but in a bed. "Penruddock," I said. "You must not attempt Salisbury. They baited—"

"Nay," he said gently. "Your man told me of it before we led him off to bed. And we do not propose to. Not this night." He cocked his head, listening for something, and then I heard it as well, the drum of hoofs on the approach below. "That would be Wagstaff," he said. "Come with intelligence from Salisbury." He looked down on me, his eyes soft as any woman's. "Sleep, man," he said. "For ye ha' earned it."

But I would not. I sat up and threw back the covers and stepped forth from the bed, in the teeth of aching bones and sore muscles. "No," I said. "For I would hear this intelligence."

He put out a hand to steady me. "Thou'rt not made of iron, man."

I smiled at him. "Why, no. But I have something in me to equal it."

"And what would that be?"

"Hate," I said.

When we returned below, Wagstaff stood framed in the open door, his beard gray with dust, his eyes red-rimmed for want of sleep, to his hat and on his coat sleeve the white ribbons they had chosen for colors here in Salisbury. "I think we are betrayed, gentlemen," he said, and stepped a step into the room. "Butler hath seized seven in Bristol, the Wyndhams among them. And a troop rode into Salisbury just at dusk."

"The Wyndhams taken?" someone said. "Both of them?"

"Their Major Butler is a thorough man," Wagstaff said dryly. "Their major shall be a colonel ere the winter is out. I confidently predict it." His eyes fell on me. "Why, Mordaunt," he said, "what do ye—"

"They baited us a trap at Shrewsbury," I said. "I do not think there are as many king's men in Salop tonight as there were last."

There was again the drum of hoofs without. "That would be Richard," Wagstaff said. "Come to tell us something further of that troop. What of Sir Thomas? Taken, think you?"

"Dead, more likely. If I know him, he would have been in the very front—" and then I broke off. For behind Wagstaff a new face was now framed in the doorway, this one also grimed with dust and hungry for sleep but clean rather than bearded and ten years younger than Wagstaff's. "The troop is here for but a pair of days," the face said. "They are for Bristol day after tomorrow to reinforce Butler—" and then he ceased speaking, for I had now clawed my way to my feet, and my hand was groping at my side for the sword that was not there, and his eyes had shifted to me, and in them the recognition slowly dawned. . . .

We faced each other for what seemed a full minute, eyes firmly fixed on eyes, while the amazement in his faded to amusement. I found my voice first. "Sir Joseph," I said. "This man. Would he be one of us?"

"Why, aye," Wagstaff said. "It is Richard—"

"For how long?"

"A pair of months here in Salisbury. Afore that—"

"A pair of months," I said bitterly. "A pair of months should be time to post a letter as far distant as Shrewsbury, should it not?"

"Look ye, Mordaunt," Wagstaff said, "I have lost sleep these last days, and if you will but plot more firmly your present drift—"

"My drift?" I cried. "Why, this drift, Sir Joseph. God knows how many lie dead without the gates of Shrewsbury Castle, that is what drift." I stepped out from the table, my hands busied with the buttons to my coat. "You wear a sword, Sir Joseph," I said. "Would ye be good enough to lend it me? While these gentlemen move this table but a little aside—"

Wagstaff looked once more, fleetingly, to the face in the doorway. "Have twenty hours in a saddle scrambled your wits, Mordaunt?" he said.

I looked bitterly into his eyes. "You are a fool, Wagstaff," I said quietly. "Sir Thomas was a man of no quick wit. But even he was wont to say that could you get within speaking distance, you would recruit Oliver himself for this business." I tossed my coat to the table behind me. "Your sword, Sir Joseph," I said.

"No. Not until I have heard some cause—"

"I have no skill at physic, Wagstaff. But any man short of blind can see that this one hath a jaundiced look about the eyes. Not a surgeon in the land but what would prescribe a bloodletting—"

"This is an ill time for wit, Mordaunt. If ye have reason to think Richard is not honest—"

I laughed. "Honest? 'Twas this one arrested me last May. I know not what name he goes by here. But in London he was Richard Munke, Captain—"

"He is still Richard Munke. Though he is no longer captain."

In the doorway Munke was smiling. I stared at Wagstaff. "You knew?"

"He was cashiered out of his regiment in July."

I looked at Munke. He nodded. " 'Tis the truth he speaks, Mordaunt," he said. "Though if those blows I once made you gift of still sting, you can demand satisfaction. I should recommend the morning, however. The light will be better then. And we might both profit from a short sleep."

"If you speak truth," I said, "they sting something less than they did a quarter hour ago. For what offense—"

"Why, you, I think. Or a tavern wench."

I looked him in the eye and knew that he spoke truth. You could lay some things to Richard Munke's door, I thought, but informing would not be one of them. Informing would scarce be in character. "Monson," I said. "Monson."

He smiled. "It would appear that we share an enemy, Mordaunt."

"I am sorry," I said. "I am sorry to have caused—"

"Why, do not be. For I am not." He looked again to Wagstaff. "There is a sergeant in that troop with a fondness for strong ale and a weakness for conversation. The troop is for Bristol." He turned and looked to the others there assembled. "The justices for the assizes will arrive on Sunday. The court will open on Monday. It would appear, gentlemen, that we may have at Salisbury after all."

Had it not been for Wagstaff, I doubt we would have assembled at Clarendon Park that Monday morning. Or had we had word from elsewhere in the kingdom, it is certain we would have dispersed, resigned to enduring this Commonwealth for yet another set of years. For elsewhere in England that week, the schemes entered into with such high resolve were to end everywhere in ruin—a comic ruin if you were not in the middle of it, for it was the story of men very forward in the king's business so long as they had to pay none of the price; of men who saw danger at a distance with great courage but who looked on it less resolutely when it faced them from a yard away.

But this was Wiltshire and Sir Joseph Wagstaff was Sir Joseph Wagstaff, and he argued down the arguments that week. He was prepared to grant that Thurloe had made a partial discovery of the plot, and that a trap might await us in Salisbury. And he stood to lose more than some of us, for Thurloe had posted a price on his head. But he for one was prepared to pay that tally; a man could endure worse fates than loss of life, and he had pledged Charles Stuart his word that he would proclaim him king in Sarum's market place. We could slink home like whipped curs, but he was resolved to attempt one Roundhead city if he had to do so singlehanded. Aye, and recruit there and march west to engage Butler in the bargain, for there was heart elsewhere in the kingdom, on this he would take his oath. But show a dram of spirit, he said, and we would have a thousand at our backs within a single day, for the land was ripe for rebellion.

He shamed us out of our irresolution, did Sir Joseph; and so four days later, at three in the morning, a hundred of us gathered at Clarendon Park. The morning was chill and blustery, and we sat our horses an hour, hats down and collars up, waiting for the pledged horse from Hampshire. By four, it was clear that we were deserted in that quarter, and there were dark mutterings among us that this was an ill omen to open the business on, that Salisbury had been a parliament town from the beginning and it were fondness to hope for any recruits from there, that Butler would be on us from the west and Lambert from out London before nightfall and the lot of us dancing on air within the month. Before we ever wheeled about to the Blandford Road, there were a handful of desertions among us, men who feared Butler's horse at forty miles more than they feared Wagstaff's or Penruddock's scorn at a yard.

Hugh Grove was awaiting us at the Blandford Road with eighty more horse from Blandford. By now dawn, bleak and cheerless, was upon us, and a mile down the road we could see the spire of Salisbury Cathedral, thin as a dagger and black as weathered lead against the thin, gray, winter sky. We sat there above the unwalled, sleeping town while Grove and Wagstaff and Penruddock exchanged a few whispered words. Then we touched heels to mounts and cantered the mile into Salisbury.

There was no trap. The streets of the city were deserted, and we splashed our way to the market place—three rivers empty into Salisbury, and the streets have always six inches of water in them, summer and winter, very curious. At the market place we received our assignments: some of us to guard the inns, some to commandeer horses, Wagstaff and his party to seize the justices and the high sheriff. Me Penruddock dispatched with ten men to break open the gaol and recruit its prisoners.

I found the gaol hard by the cathedral. It was a place in great decay, for like the cathedral its foundations stood under water and the pilings unlooked to these ten years. One of my detail fired off a musket and another beat on the door with a pike butt before we finally brought forth, out of the damp and secret gloom within, a sharp and pallid face, a pair of pale and nervous eyes.

I sat my horse and looked down upon him. "I would have your keys, sirrah," I said.

He blinked up at me out of the despairing morning light. He had no keys, he said; they were in the possession of Mr. Freeland, the keeper.

"Why, then," I said, "rouse me out this Mr. Freeland."

He replied that Mr. Freeland did not abide at the gaol, that he also kept the Green Parrot, an inn five minutes distant if you proceeded hence at a dogtrot. I bade him assume that dogtrot. "And, sirrah," I said softly, "do not think to raise an alarm. Unless you would be breathing an hour hence through a slit gullet. And do we clearly understand one another?"

The one he fetched back looked like no Roundhead keeper of gaols. He was a tallish man, with a walk that betrayed a familiarity with the sea, a man whose eyes and lips would have been friendlier were this not half after six in the morning and he newly aroused from a warm bed. He stood before me, in his own hair and uncovered, breeches and coat and boots drawn on hastily over nightclothes, a great ring of keys dangling in his right hand, his eyes wide but not frighted. "I would know the meaning of this, sir," he said.

"Is it not evident? I would have the keys to this place."

" 'Tis not yet seven in the morning," he said. "And the assizes—"

"I do not represent your chief justice, Mr. Freeland."

"Ah," he said. "I had thought you might not. And by what authority—"

"God's," I said. "And Charles Stuart's. And these." I waved to my men. "And none other, Mr. Freeland," I said softly. "And hast a mind to contest me, then?"

He grinned and tossed me the keys. "Not I, sir. And much good may they do you."

"And what your meaning there, Mr. Freeland?"

He grinned impudently up at me. "Why, only this," he said cheerfully. "Dost hope to overturn the Commonwealth cart with six starved and ragged debtors, and four or five pocky whores, and a dozen sturdy beggars who had as lief hear the devil as a drum and who fear the report of a caliver worse nor a struck fowl? 'Sblood, sir, ye had better unload the gibbets and press the dead bodies; they would drag pike as willingly and stand up to cannon more sternly."

I grinned into his grin. "I think you talk like no saint, Mr. Freeland," I said.

" 'Steeth, I hope I do not, sir."

"I would also guess that ye bear this government but small love."

"Ye may be in the right there, too. Though ye will find me a cautious man, and ready to endure this one until a better shows itself."

"And if I could show you hope of one such, sir? For were you to find yourself an hour hence in the market place, you might lay eyes on an army somewhat braver than the one you describe."

He laughed. "Name of Christ, I can hope so."

I dangled the keys speculatively before him. "Could you be trusted, I wonder, to report there at the head of these charges of yours?"

He laid a hand to his stomach. "Do not ask it of me, sir. I plainly lack the belly for playing at Sir John Falstaff."

"They are as bad as that?"

He nodded. "As bad as that. Oh, they will talk brave when you offer them rebellion in 'change for a gallows. But you will find them nimble in the heels when it comes to fighting."

I tossed him the keys. "Nonetheless, release them."

He caught the keys neatly. " 'Tis you wear the sword here," he said. "But I will not herd them back for you. An you pistol me, I will not. I can face a rope, but not jeers. 'Tis too bloody early i' the morning."

There were sly, derisive grins and a guffaw or two when I herded my recruits back to the market place. Except from Penruddock and Munke. They sat their horses a little apart from the hundred or more who ringed the scaffold the town had built this week against the assizes, and the two of them only stared, open-mouthed, as I came up.

"Name of God," Penruddock said. "What call ye these, Mordaunt?"

"Recruits, John," I said cheerfully. "A round two dozen, and stoutly loyal to a man. And Mr. Freeland here to lead them."

He stared at my parcel of rogues, his look amazed and bitter. "Christ have mercy on Charles Stuart, then," he said. "For certain it is he can count on none here below."

I grinned. "I think they may serve our purpose. They can be counted on when we march against Butler."

"Butler!" Munke said. "You mean to oppose these scarecrows to Butler's horse and foot? God's grace, but persuade them to hold a square long enough to soil breeches and you will have accomplished a miracle to match the resurrection of Lazarus. 'Tis plain you know little about Roundhead cavalry, man."

"Why, no," I said. "But I know couriers. And if we can march them five miles, they will be three hundred when the word comes to Butler." I looked over the assembled heads to the scaffold. There were three nooses dangling from the pole that ran lengthwise of it, and three necks already in them. "What diversion have we yonder?" I said.

"Sport," Penruddock said. "Or what passes for it with Wagstaff."

"The two in the robes. Those would be your justices. And who the fat one?"

"John Dove," Penruddock said. "Lord High Sheriff of Wiltshire."

"Dove?" I said. "That tub o' guts is John Dove?" I wheeled my horse about. "I think I would watch this sport," I said, and forced my way through the crowd to the platform, with Penruddock and Munke following in my wake.

At the platform, Wagstaff sat his horse carelessly and looked up at Dove. There was a pleasant smile behind his beard. But there was no smile to Dove's fleshy lips. He was ringed about by three men, two with clubbed pikes, the third holding the other end of the rope flung over the pole. He stood, this John Dove, moon-faced and fat of lip and fatter of gut, and looked down at Wagstaff, his hands secured behind him and the noose comfortable about his neck and his eyes glazed and the sweat to forehead and lip. Wagstaff said something to him as I pushed through the throng, and Dove shook his head slightly. Behind him, one of his guards looked a query to Wagstaff, on his face a grin something broader than Wagstaff wore. Then I was to the scaffold and looking up at this John Dove, this Salisbury brewer turned regicide, this fat-gutted collector of royalist estates who had come at long last to grace a scaffold with hat crooked on his head and lips and forehead pale as the morning light and a deal damper.

"I shall pronounce you the words again," Wagstaff was saying, and his voice pleasant as his smile. "Clearly and slowly, as before. And I would have you repeat them even as I. 'I, John Dove . . .'"

"I, John Dove," Dove repeated, though you must strain to hear him.

"Come, man," Wagstaff said. "You own more voice than that. Reach into that brewer's gut for it, for I would have you heard as far distant as yon cathedral spire."

"I, John Dove," Dove said again, and then he shook his head. "I cannot, sir," he whispered. "On my word—"

"Why, aye, you can." And now the pistol was in Wagstaff's hand. There were upwards of a hundred men behind them, but you could hear no sound at all in that crowd, not even breathing, and against that silence the snick as Wagstaff cocked the pistol lay flat and thin on the winter air. "Aye, you can," Wagstaff said again.

Dove only shook his head.

The pistol shot was not flat. It was sharp and very loud in that silence, and Dove's hat was lying a yard distant on the sudden, and Wagstaff was leaning carelessly over his pommel, watching the smoke drift idly up from the barrel. "The next time, friend Dove," he said, " 'twill be two inches lower." He rammed home powder and wad and ball and raised the pistol again. "I, John Dove," he said.

Dove opened his mouth, but no sound issued forth. Wagstaff nodded pleasantly to the one at Dove's left hand. "Wouldst play centurion to this Christ, John?" he said. "Wouldst teach this tallow-gut some respect?"

The man grinned. "Why, cheerfully, sir," he said and stepped back and clubbed his pike. It sounded very like a flat board striking into a pillow when he swung it into Dove's side, and Dove gasped and doubled over and then jerked upright again at the command of the twitched rope behind him.

"Hast found your voice yet, friend Dove?" Wagstaff said.

Dove's lips were pressed tight and gray against the pain. "Aye," he said, and this time he had. And something else, I thought. The sweat stood out on lip and forehead, and his eyes were glazed. But for all that he had reached deep into that belly and found something else. "Aye," he said again, and then, "No."

Wagstaff smiled softly at him. "No what, friend Dove?"

"No, I shall not proclaim this Charles Stuart of yours king."

Wagstaff shifted weight in his saddle. "I think my ears play tricks on me," he said. "It may be the cast of the wind this morning. But I do not think I heard ye aright. I could swear—"

"Ye heard aright."

Wagstaff threw back his head and laughed. "What?" he said. "Hast found something other than a voice? Hast found courage, too?"

"Call it what ye will," Dove said. "But I say I shall not. And so hang me and ha' done—"

"Why, I propose to," Wagstaff said. " 'Tis a large part of my intentions this day. But mark me, Dove, and My Lord High Justice Rolle there, and you, Nicholas. Dangle you shall, but whether you cling to life ten minutes or the day rests on you. For you shall, afore you depart us, proclaim a king of England. If I must string you up and chop you down forty times, you shall. And so let us to our catechism once more, friend Dove."

Dove only looked at him. Wagstaff returned the look, long enough for a papist to mutter a Pater Noster. Then he nodded to the one who stood just behind Dove. "Hoist this blubber," he said.

"No."

The voice was Penruddock's, and the command sharp, and Wagstaff turned his head. "Why, John," he said, "I had not thought—"

"There hath been sufficient of this foolery," Penruddock said. "And now I would have you release these men."

"Nay," Wagstaff said. "I pray you do not ask this of me, John."

"I do not," Penruddock said. "I command it, rather."

"I had not known a colonel outranked a major general," Wagstaff said. "But if he do, what squeamishness is this, pray tell?"

"Call it what you will. But I am no Turk, and this no Christian act."

Wagstaff stared at him. "Christian act?" he said, his voice amazed. "Name of God, is it Christians we deal with here? That blubber-gut sat in judgment on King Charles himself, and think you there would be Christian acts were the boot on t'other foot? Damn me, but I propose to use them as they would use me were I under their hand."

"And I say you shall not, Sir Joseph."

Wagstaff wheeled his horse about. "Now, mark me, John—"

"Nay," Penruddock said. "You mark me. Know you how many we have recruited here this morning? Seventeen. Seventeen in all Sarum Town, and I lay you it will be the same tale retold at Blandford and Yeovil and Exeter. And if the end of this is to be a Devon gaol for the lot of us, how many shall pay for the hanging of these three, think you?"

"Now, by God," Wagstaff said, and his voice soft and wondering, "now, by God, I think you are afraid, Penruddock."

"It may be I am."

"Now, by God. You had a father distinguished himself at Edgehill. And I had not thought to see the day his son would turn craven."

For a long moment, stare met stare, bitter and quiet. And then, "I could call you out for that," Penruddock said quietly.

"Why, do so."

And now Munke spurred his horse between the two. "Cease this, the two of you," he said sharply. He looked at Wagstaff. "He is in the right of it, Sir Joseph," he said. "It lacks reason to hang these three. For Rolle there is an honest man—"

"Honest?" Wagstaff cried. "Lord High Justice under this Hinchingbrooke squire, this Huntington fanatic who calls himself Protector, and you call—"

"Rolle hath defied the Protector a dozen times. If we have left one scrap or tag of law in the land, it is Rolle you can score it to. And Nicholas—"

"And Dove?" Wagstaff said fiercely. "What of John Dove, my ex-captain of Roundhead foot? You have had ten years' practice, can you read me an apology—"

Munke flushed and bit his lip. Behind him you could hear the sudden murmurs, for enough of us in that crowd had added to Dove's store of coin or enriched his holdings by this or that corner of land. But when Munke answered, his voice was still reasonable. "I grant you Dove is a very rogue," he said, "and hanging his desert.

But look to him. Would you have two or three of us hang in repayment for such an one as this? Do you pay out a pound for a ha'penny loaf, then?"

A little longer Wagstaff's eyes defied Munke's. "It hath ceased to amaze me, Munke," he said, "that a company of clerks and shoemakers and tinkers could turn us back at Edgehill. It doth no more amaze me, I swear it does not." And now his voice rose, bitter and outraged. "Do as ye would with them," he said. "Treat them as brothers if ye will, with kiss and embrace, before ye bid them go in peace. For I am schooled in patience, I can wait another ten years to see one such bastard paid in the coin he hath earned." And now he dropped his eyes and turned his back on us. "But mark me, friend Munke," he said. "If Penruddock is right, if the end of this is a Devon gaol, then tell me a month hence whether justice be fondness and mercy politic."

We were to remember those words. Penruddock and Grove and thirty-three others were to recall them in the spring, when they mounted scaffolds at Exeter and Chard; and more were to remember them something sooner than spring, I among them. Even now, sitting our horses there in the despairing morning light, they cast a brief pall upon us before Penruddock looked to Munke, a question in his eyes, and Munke shrugged. "Were it I," he said, "I should release these two. For they have not earned this treatment. As for Dove, I should truss him to a horse and fetch him with us as hostage for an honester man. It may be one rogue in the land shall serve a single honest turn before he dies."

ᕵᑏ *Twelve* ᑏᕵ

It was now well into the morning; and there in the market place, with our spirits something dampened by Penruddock's prophecy, we held a council of war. By nightfall, Munke guessed, word of this would have come to both London and Bristol, and Desborough would be marching west out of London and Butler east out of Bristol to intercept us at Yeovil, and we caught like a soft-shelled walnut between iron prongs. And so some of us argued that we should disperse, each of us to go our separate ways, the lucky among us to reach Plymouth and so catch a bark for abroad, the unlucky to make our terms with God or the devil. But Penruddock urged us to cling together; let us make for Cornwall, he said; if we drove hard, we might yet beat Butler to Yeovil and then only the small garrison at Exeter between us and the Cornish coast; and if Butler beat us, then two hundred of us, made resolute by desperation, might yet break through his force. And now Wagstaff ceased his sulking and turned on us fiercely. And did we call ourselves English, he asked, hotly and profanely. God's wounds, had five years under the rule of tinkers and cobblers brought us to this pass? Had we any cause for despair save John Penruddock's gloom? Had one among us received sure and certain word that the rest of the land was not up and that Charles and ten thousand French did not lie off Sandwich? Time enough to run like field mice before a brush fire; let us first make certain the fire was lighted. And if we did not, if we slunk home now like beaten curs, let us think as we did so on the tale we should tell children and children's children of the part we played this day for king and country.

He persuaded us once again to his persuasions, did Wagstaff. And so at high noon we started south to Blandford in search of recruits instead of taking the Exeter Road straight west.

We reached Blandford at dusk, our horses spent from stumbling over twenty-six miles of frozen road, my convicts all melted away and with them seven Salisbury recruits who had thought better of this ere they were five miles from home, the rest of us chilled to the bone and nigh famished. We assembled at the village square to hear John Freeland proclaim King Charles, and the true Protestant religion, and the liberty of the subject, and the privilege of parliament, an act of temerity for which he would hang a threemonth hence. In the teeth of the landlord's protests, we quartered in the town's only inn and supped thin and then sent out parties to recruit. At midnight the last of these reported back.

There were no recruits from about Blandford. Blandford was not parliament country, Hugh Grove could swear it was not, but there was not one recruit from about Blandford.

Penruddock heard Grove out, face in hands, while beside him Munke sat stony-faced and Wagstaff gnawed his lower lip. I sat across from Penruddock, and I watched the tremor of his finger tips against his cheek, and I could have wept. Then he raised his face into the light of the tallow guttering between us, the lace to his throat grimed from the day's ride, a spot of mud at the corner of his lip, the long curls of his periwig wind-blown and matted.

"Why, I thank you, Hugh Grove," he said softly.

"'Tis not parliament country," Grove said. "I swear it is not, John."

"Devon is no parliament country, neither. But we shall find no more recruits near Exeter, I think."

And he was right, I thought, for I was remembering, briefly and bitterly, the faces we had seen on the Blandford Road this day, stolid and indifferent faces which would appear in the doorways of yeomen's cottages to watch us pass; or the faces of townspeople when we entered the village, faces distant and distrustful, faces that remembered five years ago and a nation torn by civil strife, faces fearful only that we would quarter on them. And remembering, I struck the board before me. "In God's name," I cried, "is there no other man in England does not fret under this abomination they call a Commonwealth?"

Penruddock smiled wearily. "Were we a fair company and fresh from some great success," he said, "they would have thronged the road to cheer themselves purple in the face. Some of us shall live to see that day."

"But some of us shall not," I said bitterly.

"Why, no. You must break eggs to make an omelet. And art afraid, then?"

"No," I said, too quickly, and then, "Aye. I do not know, John Penruddock. If I am, it is not of death."

"What, then?"

"That I shall hang ere I have struck a blow in repayment."

"We may accommodate you there," he said grimly. "If we can hold them together another pair of days." He looked at Grove. "Would there be a way west except the Exeter Road, Hugh? To the south, say—"

Grove shook his head. " 'Tis no seasonable time of the year to be at swimming fords."

Wagstaff laughed shortly. "And Butler blocking our way at Yeovil by sunup tomorrow. And us with not five horses we can prick to a charge."

Penruddock looked at him, his eyes hard. "Have you another alternative, Sir Joseph?"

"Aye," Wagstaff said. "We can disperse."

"There are near two hundred of us. How many of that number, think you, can accomplish Cornwall if they have no one to lead them?"

Wagstaff shrugged. "How many an we attempt Butler's regulars?"

"I know not," Penruddock said wearily. "But this I do know. There are some assembled here because of me. And I shall not cut and run from them now. If I can help them to safety, I shall. If I cannot, I shall hang beside them."

"Why, I shall not desert you," Wagstaff said. " 'Tis simply that I think it silly to entertain hope when a man is engaged in the act of suicide." He smiled mildly into Penruddock's eyes, and then he cast a glance, swift and sly, in my direction, and then he dropped his eyes. And looking across the table at him, I knew that he lied in

209

his teeth. For all that his eyes were lidded and his smile soft, it was plainly written on his face that this one lied, that come tomorrow or the day after our ranks would be thinned by at least the number of one. And reading that, I rose abruptly from the bench and left that room.

Forty or fifty of us were quartered in the inn stables, and I found Andrew there and shook him awake. "Is it morn already?" he asked thickly.

"It yet lacks seven hours," I said. "But I would speak with you, Andrew. Come walk into the courtyard with me."

He stumbled to his feet and followed me out into the courtyard. It was a fair winter night out there, with a moon white as windswept ice riding the edges of the clouds, and the stars, in the clean winter air, looking cold and distant as all eternity. "I would have from you a kindness, Andrew," I said. "I would have you return to Turvey."

"I can try," he said. "And what message—"

"No message."

"What the purpose, then?"

"The easing of my conscience."

I could read his stare, not in the thin light there in the shadow of the innyard gate, but in his voice. "I do not—"

"They brought in no recruits this night," I said. "Five parties scouring as far distant as ten miles, and not a recruit. And it will be the same tale tomorrow at Sherborne. This cause is lost, Andrew. And I would rest easier if I knew you were back home with Henry."

"And you? What o' you, Master John?"

"I shall stay a little," I said. "I watched John Penruddock tonight, and I could have wept, and I shall stay a little." I turned my back on him. "This were never cause of yours. You have ever had little head and less heart for politics, and what you did was out of love for me."

He was silent a long moment, nought to betray his presence behind me save his long, slow breathing. And then, "So I am to desert you," he said. "And what say I to My Lord Henry? Think you he will bid me welcome?"

"If he does not, go elsewhere. Those hands of yours have a skill, sell them elsewhere."

"And where would that be, Master John?"

"I know not," I said savagely. "But sure you can find some place—"

"I ha' already found a place."

And now I did turn on him. "Look ye," I said, "I shall certain hang, Andrew. And cannot you get it through your thick head that you will hang with me?"

" 'Twas scarce a year ago," he said, softly and stolidly, "that I told you my neck would fit a noose as nicely as yours. Though I doubt it will come to that."

"It will come to that. God damn it, man, they would hang me thrice over an—"

"But not I. I do not think the Protector will spend his entire wrath on but a Surrey gardener."

He was shrewd there, I thought, though hanging or chopping sugar, it was all one, a devil's choice. "Damn you, Andrew," I said, "wilt do as I command you?"

" 'Tis a command, then?"

I drew a slow breath. "I cannot command you," I said. "But I ask it of you. If you love me, man—"

"An it be no command," he said, "then I think I must refuse, Master John."

I peered through the thin darkness to him and read the shadow of his stubbornness and cursed. It was soft, the curse, but it had my heart in it. "Why?" I said. "Name of God, what profit for any if the both of us—"

"What profit," he said, "to cling wi' Penruddock, an the cause be lost? I think my reasons as firm as yours, John Mordaunt."

It was the first time in my life I had ever heard Andrew so familiar. "Is there anywhere on earth a man as stubborn as a Cornishman?" I said. "And is there in all Cornwall five men to equal you in the trait?"

" 'Twas God made me so, Master John. Score to Him the fault."

"Stubborn," I said. "And a fool in the bargain." And then I must smile. "But wouldst know something? I am glad. If you do hang, it will be because of me, and so God help me for feeling thus. But in my heart I am yet glad."

"They ha' not hanged us yet, Master John," he said. "And may not. Not an ye cling a bit longer to the name o' Parr."

211

We did not ride into Sherborne on Tuesday. We did not reach it until Wednesday night, for the way straight north was impassable and so we must travel south to Dorchester first. In Dorchester, we again proclaimed Charles Stuart and then broke open another gaol, more for petulance than profit, for the six we garnered here would not last ten miles. We also parted ways with wheezing John Dove, for in another twenty miles he would have killed a horse under him and we had better use for our mounts. Then we rode north, twenty miles cross-country through the bleak forests and icy streams about Frampton, for so certain were we that Butler would be waiting for us at Crewkerne or Yeovil that we did not even send scouts ahead to make certain.

Sherborne offered us for quarters two inns, and a smith to look to our mounts. We had not been at Sherborne an hour before a rider thundered up from out of the west and flung himself into the inn, crying out in the name of the Commonwealth for a fresh horse, and then stopped short in the doorway to the ordinary, the cry stuck fast in his throat and his mouth dropping open and his eyes fixed wide and startled on Penruddock's grin.

"Colonel Penruddock at your service," Penruddock said cheerfully. "And wouldst join us, Sergeant? It would be Sergeant, would it not?"

The man opened his mouth to speak and closed it again and then recovered himself. "Ensign," he said.

"My apologies," Penruddock murmured. "Wouldst sit, then?"

The man's eyes, shrewd and blue in the broad, fair English face, moved from one to the other of us. "I thank you," he said, and his voice was rueful but no longer afraid, "I thank you, but I am in some haste—"

"Aye," Penruddock said. "For a horse. I fear me Sherborne is most desperate short o' fresh horses tonight. A goodly supply o' spent ones, but none fresh." He wiped fingers on his coat and belched delicately. "Most excellent boiled beef," he said. "And I think I failed to catch your name, Ensign."

"Sound cause," the man said, "since I did not offer it ye, Colonel. 'Tis Lane, sir."

"And Major Butler. Did you leave him in health, Ensign Lane?"

Again the man's eyes, shrewd and unafraid, drifted from one of

212

our faces to the other. "I am attached to Colonel Copplestone's company, Colonel. And that all the information the fortunes of war require of me, I think."

"Copplestone? I think I do not know this Copplestone. And your ride from Bristol, Ensign. Was it not a hungry one?"

Lane grinned. He looked boyish when he did so, standing there in the ordinary door, shoulders broad and English in the buff coat, eyes blue and amused and honest in a face sweated and grimed from hard riding. "Come, Colonel," he murmured.

And now Penruddock no more smiled. "I invited you to sit," he said. "Now I command it. Just there an you will."

The Ensign yet smiled when he dropped across the table from Penruddock. "If I am prisoner, Colonel," he said, "I would remind you—"

"Ensign Lane," Penruddock said, "this is no game we play. We are desperate men, and pray do not put our desperation to the test. We were speaking, I think, of your ride from Bristol. That would have taken you through Crewkerne, would it not?"

"It would if I had ridden from Bristol, Colonel."

"And did you not?"

Lane but looked at him. Penruddock waited a moment and then drew his pistol and laid it gently and sadly on the board before him. "What age ha' ye, Ensign?" he said softly.

"Five and twenty."

"A brave age. But foolish on occasion. I beg of you, do not make it necessary to deny you the experience of six and twenty."

"On my word, I think you mean that, Colonel."

"I am a desperate man. I never meant anything more."

"Offer me violence and it shall be remembered, sir. When we have closed the net on you."

"There will many things be remembered," Penruddock said wearily. "This not the greatest among them. And so let us return to our mutton. Did you or did you not ride from Bristol?"

Lane but looked at him, his face young and set and full of foolish honor. "You had best resort to that pistol, sir. For you get no further information out of me."

"Pistol? Have I said ought of pistol?" Penruddock looked to Wagstaff, leaning against the wall behind us. "A pair of days ago, Sir Joseph," he said, and his voice as calm and cold as if he were captain of a ship and this a mutineer before him, "your humor was all for a hanging. Art of a similar mind tonight?"

"Why, greatly, John."

"Then search me out a length of rope."

And now Lane's face was gray-white and his eyes amazed. "You cannot be serious, Colonel."

"Think you I am not?"

"I am officer," Lane said. "And gentle born. And there are rules—"

"I am desperate," Penruddock said. "And desperation makes its own rules, Ensign. As you may learn if you ever achieve thirty."

"By God, you shall pay for this, Colonel."

"You rode from whence, Ensign?"

A little longer Lane's eyes resisted Penruddock's. Then they surrendered. "Exeter," he said sullenly.

"And what your destination?"

"Newbury. With a dispatch for Major Butler."

"Newbury!" Penruddock said. "What doth Butler—" and then he broke off. For Newbury was thirty miles north. If Butler were at Newbury, he had not marched south to Crewkerne after all but straight east from Bristol, a strange maneuver if you wished to engage rebels riding west. "Butler lies at Newbury?" Penruddock said.

"He hath effected a junction there with Desborough."

"And what this message you bear?"

"Nought ye do not know a'ready. But that a small part of your forces marched yesterday by Frampton."

And now it was no more a mystery, this march of Butler's. A small part of our forces, Lane said, which meant that our number had come to Butler greatly exaggerated. Which meant that Butler feared to engage us with but four hundred men, that he must join Desborough before he would try us in the field. And so there were, on the sudden, smiles in the ordinary of Sherborne's King's Arms, the first smiles we had been guilty of these two days, for we now knew that the road clean to Cornwall was empty save for Copplestone's garrison at Exeter.

Penruddock bent his smile on Ensign Lane. "And your Colonel Copplestone bawling for reinforcements," he said. "Is it not so, sir?"

He required no answer there; it was written on the Ensign's face.

"How many in the Exeter garrison, Ensign?"

Lane's eyes, heavy and sullen, fell out of Penruddock's. "Four hundred reformados. And as many militia."

Penruddock chuckled. "If we quarter that, we may come to the truth."

"Try Exeter, then, Colonel. Have a go at the gates and then doubt me. And have I leave to retire to my quarters now?"

"With parole an ye wish."

Lane shook his head. "Guards an ye please, Colonel."

He rose and sauntered to the door. He looked once aside, idly, when Munke fell in beside him. He turned at the door. "Tell me, Colonel," he said, "was that indeed but a contingent yesterday? Or the whole of this rising?" He looked across the ordinary to Penruddock, and then he was grinning that boyish grin once more. "Now, by God," he said softly. "Now, by God. Not two hundred of you up, and your horses so weary 'tis very miracle each time they put one foot in front of the other, and you would think we had just sighted a second Armada. Not two hundred of you, and half of those so strange to their nags they must ride sidesaddle for the galls, and Butler ordered to join Desborough afore they dare face you in the field, and all of Somerset in a blind panic, and Copplestone a-tremble behind Exeter walls, and by God." And now, still grinning, "See well to the guards you choose this night," he said. "Pick honest men, Colonel. And wakeful, sir, wakeful. For it would scarce do, would it, were I to come to Exeter afore ye?"

We slept sounder that night and awoke more cheerfully. There was in Sherborne a guide who promised to lead us to a footpath a mile beyond Honiton that would bring us around Exeter to Bradninch. That was a day's ride, and north to Taunton and South Molton was another, and if we accomplished South Molton, we could breathe easier. For beyond South Molton a two days' ride lay the Cornish coast, and friends who would open their doors to fleeing rebels, and rocky hills to hide us out, and smugglers who could get us abroad. And so we were some of us smiling when we assembled at dawn the next morning.

Ensign Lane was smiling as well. He stood in the stable door and grinned impudently up at us through the thin, cold, Devon sunshine. "Luck, gentlemen," he called out. "And may the devil ride wi' ye this day."

Wagstaff glowered down at him. "You are most damnably cheerful this morning, sir."

"Why, aye. For is it not a fair morning for rebellion?"

Wagstaff studied him a little, teeth caught over lower lip, face a brown study. Then he wheeled about. There were faces missing from among us, and he seemed to be trying to put memory to them. Then he took his place at the head of the column with Penruddock.

Two miles out of Sherborne and the column halted. From our place in the rear, Munke and I could see Wagstaff, leaning in the saddle, speaking vehemently to Penruddock. "We should ha' hanged the pup out of hand," he was saying when we came up. He swung about in the saddle. "What guards put ye on Lane last night, Captain?" he said to Munke.

"August Greenwood the first watch. Hugh Edwards the second."

"Are they present this morning?"

"I spoke to Edwards at muster. Greenwood—" He broke off and turned to look behind us. "I have not seen Greenwood this morning."

"No," Wagstaff said. "Nor shall you, I warrant." He cursed, briefly and bitterly, and then fell again to gnawing at his nether lip. "Greenwood," he said. "And would ye not know the bastard would hit on a tailor for his business? I should ha'—"

"I think Greenwood honest," Munke said. "But if he hath committed any fault—"

"Fault?" Wagstaff cried. "No fault. If ye are not free to bring a message yourself, bribe another to do it for you. But count that no fault. There shall be a visitation to greet us at Honiton, but count that no fault."

"Nay," Munke said. "He may yet be among us, Sir Joseph."

But he was not. We waited in the raw, thin, winter sun of a Devon morning while word ran through the column. We waited, Wagstaff worrying his lower lip raw, Penruddock looking tired and sick and defeated, until the word returned. And then Wagstaff was no more at work on a bloodied lip. His face was quiet on the sudden and impassive and his eyes steady. "I have had my fill of this rebellion, Colonel," he said, and his voice as flat as his eyes.

"I had expected you had," Penruddock said. "I have waited a pair of days to hear you admit to it."

"And you have not?"

Penruddock looked wearily to the column behind him. "I shall not desert them now. If I can see them through, I shall. If I cannot, I shall bear with them what they have to bear."

"My felicitations on your steadfastness, Colonel."

"And mine on your discretion."

"You impute it, I gather, a loss of honor." He waited for a reply and got none, and then he shrugged. "They are not thirty of them of consequence. Husbandmen and small tradesmen and carpenters and suchlike."

"I pray you leave us now, Sir Joseph."

Wagstaff touched finger to hat. "Bear me no ill will," he said, "an it be God's intent that we should chance to meet again, John Penruddock." He circled about us and parted from the road. We watched him, making his lone way south across the gray, frozen Devon heath, until he was but small in the distance.

But he was wrong, was Wagstaff. No troops awaited us at Honiton, and we were through Bradninch before sundown. We lay that night in the fields south of Collompton, our bellies growling our hunger, our cloaks too thin against the sting of the frost, our eyes open to the cold, clean, bitter dark. We were on the road again at dawn, a third of us afoot now, not ten of the rest still astride a horse that did not limp, the country hilly and the road bitter and our pace so slow it took us the morning to go the fifteen miles to Taunton and the afternoon to come within sight of South Molton, our progress marked by abandoned pikes and muskets and clothing, the impedimenta of a routed army.

On a hill a musket shot from South Molton, we paused for the fourth time within the hour and looked behind us. "Sixty, I would say," Munke said. "And I would give five years of my life for horses as fresh as those."

"Reformados," Penruddock said. "And their captain panting for a promotion." He looked about him. The country just here was open fields, burned over only last fall and not cover enough to hide out a hare. "Should we attempt a stand, Captain?"

Munke shook his head. "They are near dead from weariness, sir, and the fight gone out of them. And if we could find a baker's dozen could hold a square long enough to get the smell of a charging horse, we have not that many pikes. And those are Roundhead regulars we deal with, Colonel."

"We cannot fight," Penruddock said, "and we are too spent to flee. It would seem we have little choice left us."

Munke looked west to the village below. "There would be cover in those cottages."

"If they be reformados, they are not like to ride into a trap as obvious as that, Captain."

"Perhaps we can make it something more subtle," Munke said.

We straggled into South Molton not an hour ahead of our pursuit. In the village street Munke gave us our instructions. Thirty of us would herd our horses on through the village; these were to proceed to the crest of yon mild hill, close enough to be seen but far enough distant not to provide the enemy with too plain a view. The rest of us would lie in ambuscade behind these cottage walls. And if the Roundhead captain back there took the bait . . . Munke looked around at the faces of yeomen and tailors and cordwainers and bakers and small gentry ringing him about, men some of them who had never yet touched match to powder save in drill—or, if they had, the musket or fowling piece aimed at nothing more solemn than a partridge or a deer. "If they are wearing iron under those red coats," he said, "shoot for their horses. If they are not, shoot for your man. And mark me. Not a shot to betray us until they have swallowed the bait. I want them just here before we greet them. One nervous finger among us and we shall all be stretching string a month hence. Remember that when you feel the sweat break from too stern a waiting."

From behind the windows of the cottages, we watched them ride to the edge of the village, the entire troop in the scarlet coats which had once been the uniform of Cromwell's Ironsides and were now general in the army, their captain in the van very gallant and brave and eager, the faces behind him beneath the leather caps only a little travel-worn and as eager as their leader's. They drew rein just without the village, their captain looking ahead to the hill, then looking one by one to the line of quiet cottages before him. At the other end of the village, it would be just now that one of our men would open a cottage door and a village woman would walk slowly across the road. Then two troopers dismounted and walked to the first cottage and, carbines at ready, kicked open the door. Munke had anticipated that, and I turned my head and looked at him, thinking just then of all the mistakes we had made since '42 and all the mistakes they had not made, admiring this Roundhead captain his experience, thinking that he was not three generations removed from common freemen but more able in the field than some generals I could name you, thinking that there may have been more reason than fanaticism for the stone wall we had met at Edgehill, for Rupert's rout at Naseby, for the fiasco which was Worcester.

The two men came out of the cottage and spoke briefly to their captain and remounted. The captain raised a hand, and beside me Munke let out a long, slow breath. "Now God be wi' us," he muttered, "for I think—"

And then the single shot.

I am given to understand that at the trials of John Penruddock and Hugh Grove, both Captain Unton Croke and Ensign Lane testified under oath that we fired on them that day from the doors and windows of the cottages in South Molton. If they did so, they lied, for but a single shot was fired. A single shot coming from straight across the way—some hand a-tremble on the key, I suppose, as it wound the snaphance of a long pistol—and the young Roundhead captain reining up short, and behind him the red coats scarce breaking gait as they wheeled, and beside me Munke speaking aloud the first curse I had ever known him guilty of, and on the face of the young officer the sudden smile.

They drew up just without the village. One of their number detached himself and rode toward us, the handkerchief fluttering from his bayonet; when he came nearer, I recognized Ensign Lane, his smile as broad as when I had last seen it and not a whit less impudent. Beside me, Munke looked to Penruddock. "They would parley, Colonel," he said.

Penruddock's fingers were already busied with the once-white scarf to his throat. I have but twice or thrice in my lifetime seen a man's eyes as sick.

So once again Ensign Lane faced Penruddock across a table, this time in a yeoman's cottage in the west of England, with the boot on the other foot and the Ensign's blue eyes less rueful than when we had last met. "That were a merry chase you gave us, Colonel," he said. "I had not thought to see you slip by us at Honiton. Had ye had fresh horses—"

"I had thought," Penruddock said, "that we were met here for a parley. If the purpose be instead to hear crowing, I can wait until dawn, sir." His eyes moved from Lane to the Corporal, one Rogers, who stood just at the Ensign's right shoulder. "What terms are you instructed to offer, Ensign?"

"Free quarter. And a speedy trial. And quick justice."

Penruddock smiled wearily. "We could have obtained that by but crying out yon window for it. An that be the sum, I fear you must smoke us out."

Lane shrugged. "If we do, I promise you not one among ye will leave this place alive. An it is your wish to make this a small Drogheda—"

"You are young, sir," Penruddock said. "And so your lack of wit, I hope, mainly a fault of your years. Know you the country west of here? I have heard that much of it is heavy wooded. And the rest most entertainingly hilly and rocky, with caves can hide a man out a twelvemonth, and inhabitants who yet favor a king's man. And know you further what time o' day it is, Ensign? Nigh five of the clock and dark within—"

Lane laughed. "We are already a ring about this village, Colonel, and you so many fish in a net—"

"With sixty men?" Penruddock said dryly. "That is a net with fair large holes in it, I think. Give me a single night, I will lay you even there will not be forty of us left here—"

"Well, then," Lane said impatiently, "what terms would you have of us?"

"Free quarter," Penruddock said calmly. "And leave to march forth from here with all our arms and the honors of war. And a convoy to our several homes. And every man of us to have our lives, liberties, and estates, and never be further questioned by any power whatsoever."

Lane laughed shortly. "You are mad, Colonel. This were no war, it were rank rebellion, and you are stark mad."

Penruddock looked mildly at me. "Wouldst serve as messenger, John?" he said quietly. "Captain Croke holds as hostage one Thomas Hunt and one Henry Clarke. Tell him we offer in ex-

220

change a certain Ensign Lane and a Corporal Rogers. Tell him further that we most respectfully decline his terms, since we find death as easy in South Molton as in Exeter or Bristol."

"Nay," Lane said. "A moment, Colonel."

Penruddock looked at him, eyebrows raised a trifle, the smile to his lips faint. "Aye, Ensign?" he said, and the dry amusement in his voice told me that he read what I read on Lane's face: that this man was five and twenty and but an ensign and ambitious; that were this day to bring him the promotion he hoped for, he had best effect our speedy surrender as he had been instructed. "Aye, Ensign?" Penruddock repeated.

"I cannot permit you the arms," Lane protested. "You know I cannot—"

Penruddock moved a hand. "I doubt we shall have further use for them. I might grant that small concession."

"And we must have your solemn oath," Lane said, "never again, by word or deed, to move against the present government."

"I cannot speak for others," Penruddock said. "But for myself, I think I should be prepared for this." He moved a hand. "And as to the rest?"

Lane was silent a little. Then, "Agreed," he said.

"In writing. I would have this in writing. You and the Corporal to sign the articles in your captain's name."

"An you can provide paper and ink, Colonel. Otherwise—"

"Not a man among you does not carry his pocket Scripture," Penruddock said. "The flyleaf will do, I think, and no blasphemy intended."

We waited for Corporal Rogers to go in search of quill and ink and paper. In the fading light of a winter dusk, we scrawled out our articles on the flyleaf of a soldier's pocket Gospel. We watched Lane sign them in his captain's name. In the road without, the lot of us faced Captain Unton Croke and twenty of his men, the light not yet so thin that I could not make out Captain Croke's face. He owned fewer years than I, and command still sat heavy and solemn on him, and he sat his horse before us, his smile thin and faintly triumphant, his eyes already confident of the majority that would fall to him for this day's work. "Your sword, Colonel," he said.

Penruddock passed him up his walking sword. Croke looked to Lane.

221

"We cannot accommodate half of these at Exeter," he said. "They must some of them be marched to Taunton or Ilchester—"

"Nay," Penruddock said. "Nay, Captain. The articles are clear—"

"Articles?" Croke said. "This were rebellion, sir, not war, and what articles, pray, save free quarter?"

Penruddock repeated the articles, his voice trembling a trifle. "I had Ensign Lane's solemn oath—"

Croke was staring at Lane. "You promised this, Ensign? This?"

Lane shrugged. "I thought it speedier and something less bloody than smoking them out."

"You promised them this madness?" Croke swung about to Penruddock. "An there be promises broken this day, Colonel, they are not mine. For I gave my Ensign no such freedom—"

"I should ha' expected no more than this," Penruddock said. "If I had but borne in mind whom I dealt with, I should have expected no more nor this." He looked at Lane. "When ye hear of honor next," he said, "pray think on your word forsworn this day, sir."

For a little Lane's eyes were heavy with something other than impudence. Then he straightened and was smiling again. "You told me once," he said softly, "that desperation makes its own rules. Did you not say so, Colonel?"

"Aye."

"Why, so doth victory, then," Lane said. "So doth victory, sir."

ℑ *Thirteen* ℜ

I am Presbyterian enough to stand convinced that fortune is the working out of the will of God. And yet I have on occasion wonered at the wisdom of the Creator, for sometimes His ways are mysterious indeed. That were blasphemy, I know, and yet there it is, make of it what you will. A Hampden falls in his first battle; a Cromwell walks through twenty unscathed. The Wagstaffs of this world cut and run and so escape into France; the Penruddocks die for lesser offenses. In the streets of a village in the west of England of a winter morning, a Roundhead captain nods thus and not so, a trooper stands here and not yonder, a half-pike is slanted this way and not that, and one John Mordaunt alias Richard Parr marched with sixty others south to Exeter and not west to Taunton.

And thereby hangs my tale. For once again I had lent my hand to a cause that failed; and once again I was not to pay the full, dear, bitter price for it. But for the happenstance of this nod, that slanted pike, I should have stood my trial with men whose offenses were no greater than mine; and later, I would have climbed the scaffold with John Penruddock and a score of others, come to lay my head on the block for the amusement of a crowd gathered to break the monotony of their day, to watch this afternoon's sport, to witness the fate of traitors.

But that morning I was among the sixty who marched south to Exeter. It had turned bitter cold in the night, and a thin snow had fallen, and we arrived at Exeter with fingers and toes numb and

223

bodies nigh fainting for want of a mouthful of bread or a sip of water. We lay in the Exeter Gaol a pair of days while the rumors filtered in to us that we were to be tried not by any High Court of Justice but by jury—though by Monday it was also known that Butler was searching out "sound and honest men" to serve on that jury. We lay over the Sabbath in an indolence of despair; but on Monday John Penruddock (more to be quarreling with the melancholy in him, I think, than out of any hope that we should have justice) busied himself with drawing up our defense. If we faced a High Court of Justice, he said, we must deny the legality of the court. And if we were tried by jury, we must claim the right to challenge thirty-five jurors without cause, and we must demand a copy of the indictment before our trial, and upon the reading of the indictment we must say, "We conceive the indictment not sufficient in law, and therefore we desire council." There was other stuff in Penruddock's articles, in legal language too thick for my wits, but that was the gist.

But for forty of us, those instructions were superfluous. For on Tuesday we were visited by three men. The first was a slight, pale man in a black velvet suit faced with scarlet, and lace to his throat and wrists, and a scented handkerchief held delicately to his nose; this was Sir John Copplestone, Colonel in His Highness's foot and Lord High Sheriff of Exeter. The second was dressed all in sober gray and his wig uncombed these three days; this was Martin Noel, merchant and alderman down from London. If the third had accumulated any of this world's rewards, he did not betray it in his clothing; his bucket boots were muddied and unadorned, and his coat was grease spotted, and his black hair was his own and cropped close to his skull, and he owned shrewd blue eyes and a weathered face that betrayed the seaman and a roll to his walk that confirmed it; this was Henry Hartsell, Master of the *Edward and John,* merchantman out of Plymouth, cargo (on this occasion or others) powder, shot, muskets, pistols, mattocks, shovels, felling and broad axes, iron crows, sledges, single, two-handed, pit and whip saws, files, smithy tools, handbarrows, woolen stuffs, laces, powdered and salted beef, herring, wine, horses, mules, indentured servants from out Bridewell or Newgate, blacks from Guinea, or anything else, mineral, vegetable, or animal, that could be bartered

224

to advantage against the sugar, tobacco, indigo, or maize in Carlisle Bay.

I do not know what transpired in London that week. It may be that the Protector, with two hundred rebels under lock and key, most of us certain to be found guilty by his packed juries, found himself with an embarrassment of riches, more hangings than he had a mind for. But more likely palms were greased that week; Martin Noel had shares in the *Edward and John* and was a London alderman, and Desborough was Cromwell's brother-in-law and his greed a byword in the land, and men who would not fetch a sixpence if they were hanging from a Devon scaffold could bring a ton of sugar on the block in Bridgetown. But whatever the explanation, we were faced that morning with these three, and Noel had an order in hand to contract with Copplestone for forty prisoners now being held in Exeter Gaol, certain names only being excepted. And so these three entered the Common Side that Tuesday morning and lounged down against the bars and set to a study of us— Copplestone idly, his scented handkerchief held firmly to his nostrils, the other two not so idly, the other two looking at us speculatively, the way I have seen horse traders eye animals at a fair. And then, "Be this the lot o' them, Sir John?" the one in gray said.

"The lot of them, Mr. Noel," Copplestone said.

"Bid these move just there," Noel said, and read off the names of the excepted—Penruddock and Grove and Francis Jones and John Freeland and ten others. He watched gloomily as these moved to the far wall, for some among the fourteen were young and strong, some would have fetched a top price on the block in Bridgetown. Then Noel nodded to Captain Hartsell.

Hartsell's eyes, shrewd and blue and bitter, wandered among us. "Bid them strip, Sir John," he said.

"Strip?" Copplestone said.

"Aye. Strip, sir. Am I to purchase a pig in a poke, then? I would see them naked."

Copplestone gave the order and we obeyed it. We stood naked and shivering in a cell cold enough to freeze water while Hartsell walked among us, exploring with hands that knew little of gentleness and none at all of mercy our bodies, thrusting a dirty forefinger into our mouths to examine our teeth, examining privates for pox, rejecting

225

this one as too old and that one for too thin a chest, complaining under his breath that we were a poor lot and it were very miracle if we endured a long sea voyage to say nothing of performing an honest day's labor in the tropics. And when he had done with his choosing, Noel explained that once again the Protector, in his great goodness and mercy, had seen fit to tender us leniency. We deserved to hang, he said, but His Highness was Christian and so there it was; either we could stand trial or we could sign papers and take ship for the plantations, there to labor for five years in payment for our passage. And if any among us preferred to stay, let him step forward.

It was small choice he offered, trial before a packed jury or five years of chopping sugar in the Indies, death or slavery, but none among us stepped forward. And so by afternoon forty of us again found ourselves marching south under guard, this time to Plymouth. And a day later we had all been stowed securely in the hold of the *Edward and John,* together with sixty or seventy other wretches culled from out the workhouses and gaols of London.

I was among the last aboard the *Edward and John;* only Andrew, who (God alone knows how) had clung to me like a parent since South Molton, and Richard Munke, and four of our crew, and Captain Hartsell followed me up the ladder. I dropped leg over the bulwark and was prodded among the others who huddled there on the quarter-deck. Behind us thirty of the crew stood at the alert, eyes bright, hands to the knives in their belts. At the bulwark, two others lounged. One was a small man with a great nose and eyes that had known every waterfront stew from Lisbon to Virginia. The other had been born with a fault to his upper lip that pulled his mouth to one side and his left eye partly closed. Before us, at the mast, a third man faced us.

He was a man you would not mistake in a crowd. He was taller than I by two hands, but there were few among us who did not outweigh him; had he been naked, I think he would have seemed to have no flesh at all, only a taut skin stretched over ribs as sharp as naked sticks. His hair was black and so long it hung two inches below his shoulders; and against that hair, his face was a startling white, white as the face of a blooded corpse, white as a bleached bone lying against tropic sands, so white I found it incredible that

226

he had ever faced into sun or wind or weather. In that white, white face the eyes were so deep-set that when he stood against the light, they were but shadowed holes, like the blank, black sockets in a skull. But if you stood close and the light proper, you could see into his eyes, and they were the eyes of a man with a fever in him. I cannot to this day name the color of those eyes. But I can still remember my feelings the first time they rested on me, the prickle at the base of my scalp, the small leap of blood in my throat, the feeling that my heart had been touched lightly, lightly by a sliver of frozen metal.

He faced us thus in the thin, cold sunlight, the mast behind him thrusting up forever and forever above him; standing just so against the mast, he might have been some ancient martyr, gaunt and bloodless white and three days dead, just descended from his cross. Then Captain Hartsell's face showed above the bulwark. The bulwark presented a small problem to the Captain, for he had been drinking steadily and sullenly since daybreak. So it was a while before we could be certain that he would make it safely aboard; and once his feet found the deck, he swayed back against the rail, his merchant's eyes in that weathered merchant's face bleary and uncertain, his face puffy from the night he had made of it, specks of wine and vomit to his unkempt coat and soiled shirt, one hand thrust behind him in search of the comfort of the bulwark. "That would be the lot o' them, Mister Cole," he said thickly.

"Aye, sir." His voice surprised you, so deep and firm it was, and he looked at Captain Hartsell as a father might look on a wayward son, his head a little down, his eyes reproachful and sorrowing. "I believe ye are drunk, sir," he said gently.

Captain Hartsell grinned across the deck to him. "Why, so I am. Pissing drunk. Nigh falling-down drunk. And would ye ha' ought to say to that, Mister Cole?"

Mister Cole had nought to say to that. There was yet sorrow in his eyes, there was yet reproach. But he had nought to say.

"I ha' also committed fornication since last we parted," Hartsell said. "I spent my night in a Plymouth brothel. I rutted three sluts 'twixt dusk and dawn, and what say ye to that, Mister Cole?"

Still the mate said nothing.

"I further propose to stay drunk," Hartsell said, "this entire voyage an I so choose. And ha' ye nought to say to that, Mister

Cole? None of your sermons, sirrah? No bit o' prayer for a poor, damned sinner?"

Cole's head was a trifle down, but now he brought it up. "The night is far spent," he intoned, "the day is at hand. Let us therefore cast off the works of darkness. Let us walk honestly, as in the day, not in rioting and drunkenness, not in clambering and wantonness, not in strife and envying."

For a little Hartsell still grinned. And then he did not. Then there was no more a grin on his face, and he lowered his head like some tormented bull, and his voice was as thick as porridge. "Scripture," he said. "Ye choose to quote me Scripture, do ye?"

"Aye, sir. With all respect, sir."

"Well, do not, Mister Cole. Do not." He yet leaned drunkenly against the bulwark, and his head was yet down like something harassed, and his speech was yet thick. But it was no bottle that had put the glare in his eyes. "I ha' suffered your piety one voyage," he said. "I do not propose to suffer it another. And do ye mark me, sirrah?"

Cole's head was still flung back, and there was nothing of fear in either eye or voice. "Begging the Captain's pardon, sir," he said, "but I cannot believe that the Captain is in full command o' his senses, sir."

"Can you not, Mister Cole?" Hartsell lurched upright. He was ten feet from the mate, and once or twice it was a matter of some doubt that he would accomplish the entire journey. But he was yet on his feet when he thrust his face into the mate's. "Were I lying before ye, Mister Cole," he said, "just there, mark ye, and snoring afore I hit the board, mayhap I should not be. But until that day, fret not about my senses. For drunk or sober, mark me. Badger me this voyage and I promise you I shall ha' ye in irons, I shall ha' the skin off your back." He lurched past the mate to the companionway. "Now secure those forty below," he said.

"Aye, sir." The mate's voice was full of patience and pity and endurance, and I had no fondness for the sound of it. "Have I the Captain's permission to ask one more question, sir?"

"Why, ask away, Mister Cole."

"Be these all rebels, sir? The lot o' them?"

"The lot o' them. Aye."

"And would there be papists among them, sir?"

Captain Hartsell looked the four paces to his mate, his eyes bleary and shrewd and cautious. "The forty o' them for all I know," he said. "For I ha' not inquired into consciences intended for a Bridgetown block. Roman or Fifth Monarchy or Turk, they shall fetch their fifteen hundred pounds of sugar."

"An there be papists among them," Cole said, "an there be heathen idolaters here, have I the Captain's permission to pray for their conversion, sir?"

"Ye ha' not, Mister Cole."

The mate drew a slow breath. "Ye be the master here, sir."

"Aye. And I will ha' no more purchases spoiled for the market."

"Ye be the master here, sir. But there is another who is master over us all. And I would not have His countenance turned from us, sir. I but ask leave to pray—"

"Pray?" Hartsell laughed shortly. "Pray? I ha' seen your praying, Mister Cole. I ha' fed fishes wi' one or two o' your converts. And I will ha' no more of it."

He turned and felt for the companionway rail. He stumbled twice in his climb, the mate watching him the while. When he was out of sight, Cole turned.

"I would pray wi' ye," he said.

At the rail, the one with the fault to his lip started. "Begging your pardon, Mister Cole," he said, "but that were mutiny. 'Twere the Captain's orders—"

"The Captain's?" the mate said. "And what o' Almighty God's orders? Who fear ye the greatest, Mister Porter? Our Captain Hartsell, fresh from his harlotry, a'ready drunk and snoring abovedecks? Or Almighty God, who hath said, 'Drink ye, and be drunken, and spue, and fall, and rise no more, because of the sword which I will send among you'?"

The second mate's eyes shifted nervously to the mast behind Cole, to the dangling cuffs and the cat thrust into the loop of rope. "I know not," he said. "But I know the price for mutiny."

"And what price for mutiny against God? We ha' before us a long sea voyage, and hast ever felt the wrathful finger o' Almighty God?" Cole turned his eyes on us. "Let us pray," he said, and turned his white death's head toward heaven. We stood there a long minute, heads bowed, waiting. Then I opened my eyes, and Cole's eyes were fastened on someone behind me and there was triumph in

229

them, there was a quiet joy, there was something feverish and sick.

"Fetch that man forward," he said.

I dared not turn my head. I know not why, but I dared not turn my head nor scarce breathe. Then two of the crew were shouldering one of us past me to the mate, and I recognized the one who a sennight ago had swung the butt of a pike into John Dove's larded ribs. His name was John Biby, and he had worn a grin on that occasion. But he wore none now. He stood before the mate, a sailor to each side, and the mate bent those eyes on him, and he wore no grin this day.

"So I have guessed shrewd, have I?" the mate said. "So we do have papists among us."

"No, sir." Biby's voice trembled with terror. "No, sir—"

"Ye lie," the mate said. "I say ye are papist, sirrah. I say ye are an abomination in the eyes of the Lord."

"Nay," the man whimpered. "I swear—"

The mate did not interrupt him. The mate but moved a trifle, and the words were cut off as neatly as if Cole had put a hand to Biby's throat. "An y be no papist," he said, "why do ye kneel in prayer? Explain me that."

" 'Tis but how I was taught, sir, I—"

"Taught? An ye ha' been taught to bow and scrape and suchlike heathen practice, then ye must be untaught. 'Whereas my father did lade you with a heavy yoke, I will add to your yoke; my father hath chastised you with whips, but I will chastise you with scorpions.' "

He stepped aside and nodded once to the two sailors. He gave no order, nor needed to; the nod was sufficient. We watched while the two stripped Biby to the waist and dragged him to the mast. They stepped away, and one of them, the whip already in hand, looked his question to the mate.

"But a dozen," the mate said. "An God can temper justice with mercy, so can I."

And now Porter stepped away from the bulwark. "Lay a whip to that back, Mister Cole," he said, "and it shall be reported to Captain Hartsell."

"Shall it, Mister Porter?"

"Aye. And you ironed within the hour."

230

"Why, then, I shall be ironed. And let God judge between him and me." He smiled, gently, almost sweetly. "You can tack a course against a contrary wind," he said. "And can ye also plot one, Mister Porter? Know ye ought of compass, card, and log-line? Can ye determine latitude by use of a back-staff?"

"You know I cannot."

"You can furl a fore-skysail or lash down a whip-stock in a gale. And can you write sufficient to keep a ship's journal?" He smiled again. "So I shall be ironed, shall I? And who, then, shall manage this voyage? Your Captain Hartsell, drunk and snoring in his berth? And no other aboard with sufficient skill to land us within fifty leagues o' Carlisle Bay?" He turned away. "I think I shall not be ironed, Mister Porter," he said.

We stood in the thin and bitter sunlight and watched the whip coil slow and tender about John Biby's shoulders and back, hearing the first sudden gasp, watching the welts show and then the blood, quick and thin and bright against the white skin. A dozen lashes will not kill a man, not if he be a well one, and Biby was still to his feet when they led him back to us. He stood just before me while Cole again raised that white face to heaven; he swayed, standing there, and I would have reached out to steady him but for Andrew's sudden, fierce grasp on my arm.

We stood half an hour while Cole prayed to whatever God your saints pray to; while he prayed for fair weather and a safe, fast voyage; while he prayed that Almighty God in His infinite loving-kindness would lay His hand heavy upon the miserable and hardened sinners gathered here afore Him that our hearts might be softened and made contrite, that in the end, through pain and suffering and despair in this world, we might come to know His mercy and eternal love in the next. And then it was over and done with, and we were herded below.

The midship hold of the *Edward and John* was not the size of a twopenny chamber in a posting inn, but already seventy were crowded into it ahead of us. I had thought that the smell in Newgate's Common Side were intolerable enough, but my head was not a yard below the hatch before I knew I would have traded that for this and something over in the bargain. Pack seventy unwashed wretches from out London prisons and workhouses into a space not ten paces square and you will have the first ingredient for that smell. Sail those seventy rebellious stomachs from London to Plymouth and you will have a second. Compound with that four open buckets, unemptied this sennight, which served here for house of office and you will have a third. Mix in the flat, brackish smell of bilge water, and the sweet, thick, cloying smell of steaming, frighted horses in the aft hold, and other smells more delicate and mysterious, identifiable only by sea captains long engaged in human traffic, and there is your recipe, there is a stench will seem alive, will grip you by the throat if you do not breathe shallow until you are a little used to it.

The seventy watched bitterly while we were herded down the ladder, and they moved slowly and sullenly when our guards ordered them to make way, for we were nought to them save forty more in quarters already cramped and thinner rations of biscuit and water. Nine of the seventy were female—two, I noted, had escaped the rope by virtue of swollen bellies, and the others were but children, street urchins taken in petty thievery or at begging or for the crime of being orphaned, too young for hanging and no profit to the matrons at Bridewell and a charge on the state. Already, the women had found out companionship, warmth for the voyage against the savage cold of a ship's hold in winter, perhaps an extra sip of water or bite of biscuit if their favors proved sufficient. The two who had won them were lounged down side by side against the bulkhead, one with a head pillowed on his woman's breast, the other with a hand brazenly and bawdily beneath his woman's skirt. The one was a small man with eyes not to be trusted, and the other was large and bearded, and between them they had committed faults enough for two men, for they wore about them the marks of the pillory—ears bored through for drunken brawling or vagrancy, an *F* branded on the small one's cheek for forgery or fraudulent trading, a *P* for perjurer showing through the beard of the large one. Just now these two faces wore scowls as well, and I thought, These would be your understrappers here and we shall have a hard time of it once our guard is departed, we shall see brawling here and blood spilled ere this voyage is ended.

Our guard departed. The space here was not sufficient to accommodate twenty in any comfort, but somehow more than a hundred of us had already separated into two parties, the forty of us

232

to one side of the hold, the seventy of them to the other. Through the thin light admitted by the still open hatch, we faced each other thus, the silence heavy and sullen and prophetic between us. Then the small one removed his hand from the woman's thigh and spat between his crossed legs.

"Gord's guts, mytes," he said. "What ha' we here hast jyned us?" He spat again, between two missing teeth. "Gord," he said. "And be they not perty now, Bobby?"

The large, bearded one raised his head from his woman's breast. "Ar," he said.

"Fair 'n' perty," the small one said. "Nary a cropped ear nor a brand amongst 'em."

"They be rebels, I ha' heard tell," the large one said. "Rebels 'n' bloody gen'lemen, Willum."

"Think on that now. Gen'lemen all, Bobby? Like as ye see in fine carriages?"

"Ar," the large one said. "So I ha' heard tell."

The small one grinned and fastened his eyes on me. I returned him stare for stare, wondering at this one with the nervous eyes, for he was small, smaller than a twelve-year-old boy with his proper growth. And yet, if the woman was any test, he had wrested for himself the leadership here below. "What name ha' ye, lamb?" he said.

"Mordaunt," I said.

"Mordaunt. And be ye a gen'leman, Mordaunt?"

"I can hope so. Closer than some I could name."

He chuckled. "Think on that now." He turned his eyes on Munke. "And what be ye called, myte?"

"Munke."

"Munke. Think on that now. For ye look like none to me."

The large, bearded one waited a proper spell and then struck his leg with an open hand and roared out his appreciation. "Gawd, Willum," he gasped. "Gawd."

Willum was not one to laugh at his own jests. He lounged there, small and nervous-eyed and deadly as one of your tropical snakes. "I ha' heard tales o' gen'lemen," he said. "I ha' heard they be diff'rent nor thee nor me, Bobby. They frequent the house o' office, gen'lemen do, even as us common scum. But no stink."

"Gawd," the bearded one said. "You ha' heard tell that, Willum?"

233

"S'help me I ha,' Bobby." He yet lounged, no movement at all now in that small and deadly body, not even in the eyes. "Their blood be not red like as thine nor mine, Bobby. Blue, I ha' heard."

The bearded one shook his head in slow amazement, too full of wonderment at life's mysteries to venture judgment on that.

"Aye," the small one said. "Blue. But I ha' ne'er seen 'un bleed. Hast e'er seen 'un bleed, Bobby?"

The bearded one grinned. "Nar," he said.

I looked at Munke. His eyes were narrowed and he wore a smile I should not have liked had I been this pair. It was the same thin smile I had seen on another occasion, at half after midnight in the chamber of a London inn, with the offer of a ten-pound bribe lying between us and he advancing slowly on me, inviting me to make it twenty. "Hast a mind to suffer further insolence from these scum, John?" he said. He spoke not loud, but his voice was sufficient to carry the hold.

I returned him smile for smile. "Why, no," I said. "I think I have not, Richard."

"Hast a mind instead to instruct this pair in their manners?"

"Why, aye. I think I have."

We returned our eyes to these two. The small one's hand was hidden now beneath his shirt. "Hast a preference which o' these whoresons ye would play tutor to?" Munke said.

"None, I think. And you, Richard?"

"The small one. He would be quicker at his catechism than t'other, I would guess. And God created me a man of small patience."

"Take care," I said. "Five to one he hath a knife secreted 'neath that shirt."

"So I have suspected these five minutes."

We got lazily to our feet. They followed suit, the large one wearing a grin, the small one a snarl. "Well, whoreson," I said to the bearded one, "hast still a mind to have at me? Or is your insolence but in your mouth?"

He came at me then. He came at me exactly as I had thought he would, like one of your country wrestlers hurtling out of the crowd, head lowered and arms outcurved like some pitted bear, and I stood my ground. When he was on me, I brought my knee up into his face.

234

It was an error on my part. It was a small miscalculation in strategy, for I was unschooled in street brawling, and it proved very near fatal. I felt his nose go under my knee like an overripe melon, and briefly, I knew that were he to raise his head, his face would be blood-spattered from chin to eyebrow. And then his head rammed straight into the pit of my stomach, and I was flying backwards with him still on me, his arms wrapped tight about me now, and my mouth wide open, trying to gulp in air that was not there, and I trying to roll from under him but I could not for strength had left me with my breath, and above me, like some shadow in a dancing mist, his bearded face, with in it eyes aglare and lips drawn back over blackened stubs and stumps of teeth and a great splotch of red where his nose had been and his hands to my throat.

Then, as suddenly, the hands were not to my throat. There was yet a mist before me, but through it I could see Munke's face, still smiling thinly, and a hand in the bearded one's hair, and the bearded face wrenched back like a face dangling in a noose, and at that throat the point of a knife, nicely and delicately placed just beneath the chin.

"Well, sirrah?" Munke said. His voice sounded as if it came from a great distance. "Art still of a mind to see blood?"

The bearded one opened his mouth and then closed it again without uttering a sound.

"Or a baptism," Munke said, and glanced at the four naked and noisome buckets across the way. "Art an errant sinner, that is certain, and the font is to hand, and aye, a baptism, I think." And now the bearded one came to his feet, brought there by Munke's hand in his hair and the press of the knife to his throat. He stumbled once in his journey, and then he was on his knees again, this time with an arm twisted cruelly behind his back, and he said something choked and indistinguishable and not lengthy. For his face was straight over a bucket, and just as he opened his mouth, Munke thrust it into the filth.

Munke held it there a long time in the dead silence. His lips were moving silently; he was counting, I think, and he must have achieved ten before he jerked the head out of the bucket and gave one quick twist and the bearded one broke loose from him and stumbled and ended on his knees again in the middle of the hold.

235

Munke stood over him, looking down on him. "Hast remembered any forgotten manners, sirrah?" he said.

The bearded one knelt there, back to Munke, filth dripping from his beard. "Ar," he said, and strangely his voice was not sullen. It was amazed but it was not sullen.

"Then have the goodness to address me as sir."

"Ar, sir," the bearded one said and brought his face up. "S'elp me, m'lord, we meant no offense. We but intended a jest—"

"Do not jest further. Ye clearly lack the wit for it." Munke looked about him, at the ring of amazed and stony faces. "Are there others present have a mind to bait us?" He waited and then nodded curtly. "We sought no quarrel with you. Seek ye no further one with us." And now he turned to me. "Art hurt, John?"

I sat up. The breath stabbed back into my lungs. Across the hold the small one swayed and clutched a shoulder. A little apart from the rest of us—convict as well as rebel—the seven girls looked on, wide-eyed and amazed and frightened. Behind the small one, the two women looked speculatively at Munke; five minutes, I thought, and it will be bold invitation, it will be heigh-ho and off with the old and on with the new. I looked back at Munke. "I shall live, Richard," I said. "Though if I look at my belly a month hence, I think I shall still find cause to remember this," and then I hung my head like some schoolboy, for I was bitter with myself that he had had to manage the both of these with no help from me.

He grinned down at me; the grin was in his voice. "Do not take it so, John," he said. "You are unschooled in tavern brawling. And it was after all the small one I dealt with."

"Aye. With a knife in his hand. But I shall not make the same mistake twice. I promise you I shall not, Richard."

"I think there will be no twice. Not with these two. Not on this voyage."

"Do not be too certain. I do not like the look of that small one. He shall not soon forget this, I think." I came to my feet and stood there, breathing deeply against the sharp ache in my stomach, looking at the bearded one, still on his knees, then at the small one, on his feet now and his hand clutching his shoulder and his face twisted with pain. "He would have killed me," I said. "And so I thank you, Richard. But I think it not politic for either of us to sleep too sound this voyage. Not with yon whoreson awake among us." I turned from him then, for I was still ashamed of my part in this. There was a foot of empty bulkhead near the seven girls, and I moved to it and sat down and looked at these seven. They all of them sat hunched against the cold and damp here, not a cloak or coat or even a shawl among them, not a face that was not pinched from hunger or resigned to the ill-treatment of this world. I looked at these seven and smiled, and one of them, with a face that might have been pretty had it been fed this month or washed this fortnight, returned my smile, though shyly.

"Why, how now, child?" I said.

She said nothing, only dropped her eyes out of mine.

"Nay," I said. "You may speak me free."

She forced her eyes back up into mine. "Art a fine gen'leman as they say?" she said. "Truly, sir?"

There was such a grave wonderment in her voice that I could not forbear smiling broadly. "I have been called such."

"And ye abide in a great house?"

"I did once."

"And did ye ride forth in a fine carriage? Wi' four horses?"

"When I was a boy. Only it was six horses as I recall."

"Six," she breathed. "Think on that. Six."

"But that were long ago," I said. "Of recent times, save ye be rude and uncouth and a knave, the times have decreed against carriages and horses and suchlike."

Her eyes were very dark and very bright and opened wide. "I ha' ne'er seen a fine gen'leman afore," she said. "Not from this length."

"We are made even as you. Come closer an you would test that."

She pondered that hazard a moment. Then she closed the space between us and reached out and touched my knee. On impulse I put a hand to her cheek. Then I drew her to me. "Thou'rt cold, child," I said. "Thou'rt trembling from the cold."

"Aye," she said philosophically and looked up at me from under my arm. I have not often seen eyes fairer than hers; very black they were and bright and just now there was a smile in them. Were it not for a single thin and wretched garment, I thought, she would be naked to the cold, and I doubt that in all her life she had once known a full stomach, and she was not five years beyond babyhood but she could already describe the inside of Bridewell. But for all

237

that, those bright, black eyes had yet to admit to defeat or despair. "Are you not cold, m'lord?" she said.

"I wear a warmer coat than you, child."

She snuggled down under my arm. "Thou'rt kind, m'lord. Be all gen'lemen kind?"

"Why, you can answer that. Are all poor cruel?"

She thought awhile on that. But the puzzle was beyond her years, and so she gave it up and fell instead to toying with the points to my breeches. " 'Tis worse come night," she said. " 'Tis bitter cold i' the night."

"This night will be warmer. For tonight we shall share this coat, you and I. An you would have it so."

"I would have it so. And what o' the morrow, m'lord?"

"The morrow as well. The entire voyage an ye choose."

Her hand on the sudden ceased toying with my points and lay quiet on my knee. "Ye would not gi' me the lie, m'lord? Ye would not cozen me?"

"My word on it, I would not." I felt the tremor of her shoulder under my hand. "Dost doubt the word of a gentleman, child?"

"Should I not, m'lord?"

"Not an he be a true gentleman."

This time her hand fell to playing with a coat button. " 'Tis a long voyage," she said. "Two months, I ha' heard. Ye can tire o' me in two months, m'lord."

"Tire of you? Why should I tire of you, child?"

"When ye ha' known me."

For just a moment I felt the breath go thin in me and at my heart something like a small, sharp blow. Name of God, I thought, name of God. "Known you, child?" I said. "Known you? What mean ye, known you?"

"Why, known me, m'lord. As a woman."

I sat her up, more abruptly than I intended, and faced her about and looked down into those eyes. I still looked into the face of a child, but the eyes were no child's eyes. The eyes were black and serious and as aged as the Fall itself. "In God's name," I said softly, "dost know what thou'rt saying, child?"

"Why, aye. Do you not, m'lord?"

"Tell me," I said, "how many years have you?"

She shook her head. "I know not."

"Not eleven. I would stake my life on it. Not eleven."

And now there was something besides age and knowledge in those eyes; now there was something like fear. She was thinking that I had offered her the kindness of a warm coat against the bitter cold of a ship's hold, and she had in some way offended me, and she had not the wit to know why nor how to make amends. "Ha' no fear on that score, m'lord," she said. "Ye shall find me woman enough, I warrant you."

There have been times when I have wondered at the patience of the Almighty; times when I could not comprehend His infinite forbearance; times when, were I He, I should have laid wrathful hands on this my creation and destroyed it. "Have others found ye woman enough?" I said.

"Aye, m'lord," she said, and you would have thought I had asked her if she had eaten this day.

"Many?"

Suddenly she knew how she had offended, and she smiled. "Was it a maidenhead ye had a mind for?" she said. "I think you will find none here below, m'lord. Save it be Lotta there, and she ugly as sin—"

"I had not a mind," I burst out. "I had no thought—" And then I broke off and drew her to me again. She is but a child, I thought, and it is none of her fault, it is no world of her making. "I had no such thoughts," I said. "I swear I did not, child."

Beneath my arm she was now a child again, small and nigh naked and cold. "Ye are no more offended wi' me?" she said.

"I ne'er was, child. But at the world."

"And I may lie wi' ye this night?"

"Aye. And welcome."

"And for this ye want no kindness fro' me?"

"But one thing. Your comfort, child."

She fell silent. Then she sighed. "I find it beyond my wits," she said. "And passing strange."

"What?"

"Gen'lemen," she said.

ஐ *Fourteen* ௳

We weighed anchor that night. I have no certain way of guessing the hour, for already time to us in the hold was but light or dark, and before a sennight was out we could not even have told you what day of the week it was. But sometime that night I was jarred out of an uneasy sleep by the clatter of the hatch above us being banged to and secured, and muffled shouts in the rigging, and the distant bark of orders. Something later I could hear all about me the creak and protest of strained timbers, and so I guessed we were into the open sea.

There are those who had gone before us (and some after) will tell you that we had a speedy voyage and an easy one. There are those can tell you of the cruel voyages: of ships buffeted a thousand miles off course or becalmed a threemonth in the heat of the tropics; of plague ships and ships visited by gaol fever and ships on which the London disease was so savage that one out of two died of it and the other so weakened from flux he could not accomplish his feet and so tender he screamed when you touched his swollen joints; of ships commanded by officers more barbaric than ours, and of ships so old and rotten and foul-bottomed it was very miracle they ever cleared harbor. But ours was a sound ship and a fast one, and the weather fair and the wind firm, and thirty-four days after we set sail we were in Carlisle Bay. And of the hundred odd crammed into that miserable hold, only eight or nine died, and two of those old men, past fifty. And as for the rest of us, we were weakened only a little from flux or touched lightly by scurvy.

And so I must confess that fortune smiled that month on the *Edward and John*. And yet I have lived other months have passed more quickly and pleasantly than that one.

The details of the voyage I can recall only dimly. I can remember the beginning and the end, but the weeks between are as dim as a dream, vivid enough in the experiencing but already ill formed and confused within an hour of waking. In the beginning was the seasickness; we had scarce cleared Plymouth Harbor before the first retching began. That was with us three days, even after the little food we had eaten (the bread and water that morning in Exeter Gaol, the gray, watery stew that passed for fit diet for indentured servants here aboard) was out of us, even after the retching was but dry, empty agony. Enough of us those three days wished to die and could not. And on the fourth day one of the crew more tender than most for our miserable plight (or driven to kindness by the stench which must have risen to the very crow's nest) secured us leave to swab out the hold with salt water. And this day I recall because it was then I learned that Genesis is in the wrong, that labor is no curse visited on us at the Fall but the greatest of God's gifts to man.

But between the beginning and the end lay the forgotten days, the interminable twilight days that stretched forever from a forgotten dawn to a sunset as distant as Judgment Day; and after the sunsets the interminable nights, bitter cold the first fortnight out, then as stifling as some antechamber to hell itself. At first the monotony of our days was broken by quick and senseless quarrels, quarrels over such trifles as a man's right to a foot of bulkhead or a turn at the buckets. But later a terrible lethargy settled upon the lot of us. We would lie in the hold hour upon hour, waiting first for the noonday sun to appear briefly in the square of sky you could see through the open hatch, then waiting through all eternity for dusk and the moment when they would fetch us food and water. Or not food; it was not food we waited for with such terrible and anxious patience. That must have been well into the third week of the voyage, and the gnawing of hunger had long since left us, and if it had not, our gums were now sore to the touch and we dared not bite into a rock-hard, weevil-infested biscuit for fear of swallowing teeth. And so it was only water we waited for. We would lie there, staring through the hatch at the square of brazen, throbbing, tropic sky, panting (or imagining that we panted, though by now, in the stifling heat, our tongues clung to the roofs of our mouths), tasting hours before it was fetched the mouthful of brackish water, thinking of all the drinks we had tasted through all the days of our lives, waiting, waiting. It was during this period that five or six among us died.

Thus the bulk of that voyage. But I remember the end of it. I remember that sharply enough, and the manner of it was in this wise.

It began with another of those quarrels which would flare up between us and then as quickly die, gone out like some unshielded candle in a sudden draft. Again, the quarrel was between Munke and the small one. I do not recall what this exchange was about—the woman, perhaps, for these two had behaved abominably on more than one occasion; night or day, it made small difference to these two, and more than once Munke had abused them for their shamelessness. Or perhaps it was not the woman. We were in the tropics now, and the heat in the hold was like some great, throbbing oven; the heat in the hold was insufferable; we lay now as close to naked as our sense of decency permitted, our bodies slick with sweat, above us the open hatch and the brazen sky and no stir of air here below, our breathing in that thick, sullen, steaming heat short and quick and shallow and our tempers, for all our lassitude, abrupt as the fuse to a grenade. And so it may have been no more than the temperature that prompted the quick, angry words from Munke and the snarl from William in reply and then the end of it—or so we all thought.

But this time it was not the end of it.

The quarrel flared up in midafternoon. By dusk, when four of the crew fetched us our bucket of water and our basket of biscuit, Munke, I think, had forgotten it. But William had not. From his place beside the woman, he watched us, his eyes heavy and sullen, while we filed to the bucket and drank our drink. I should have guessed then that something was brewing, for courtesy was not one of William's failings, and that day he was last in line. When finally he took his turn, he swallowed his water and then stood there, the long-handled ladle forgotten in his hand, his head lowered and his eyes upturned and nervous and his mouth twisted and his voice fawning.

"Wouldst take me above, man?" he said.

The sailor stared at him, briefly amazed. Then he laughed. "Why, aye, Captain," he said.

William but looked at him, head bent, eyes upturned in that thin, snarling face. "An I were you," he said, "I think I should not laugh. Not I. I ha' a word for Captain Hartsell. He shall thank me for it, I promise you."

The sailor shook his head. "I think he would not. Since he is drunk and snoring in his berth. And sour as vinegar when awakened. No, I think he would not, sirrah."

"The mate, then. But fetch me above for five minutes—"

"Why, no. No, I think not." The sailor leaned. "Gi' me this word, sirrah. Let me be judge. An it be as heavy as ye say, it will be passed on—"

William's eyes darted once to us, then back to the sailor. He shook his head. "Nay, ye do not. There shall be reward for this. Ye do not cheat me out o' my rightful reward—"

The sailor shrugged and made as if to turn away. William caught his arm. "Nay," he panted. "Nay, I cannot, man. They be desperate men here below, I swear they be, and—"

The sailor but stood there, quietly, stopped in the act of turning away by the hand to his arm. He was not looking at this small, snarling one; he was looking instead to us, and disgust was printed on his broad, stolid, English face. "Take your hand fro' my arm, sirrah," he said.

William dropped his hand. Once more his eyes darted to us. You could read in them the hate he bore us, and you could also read the fear of a man who was engaged in the burning of bridges. Then he stepped back and drew a slow, deep breath. It is the breath, I thought, of a man who has reached a decision.

Which he had. "Go to, then," he said. "There be mutiny brewing here below, but go to, then."

The sailor stared at him. Then he glanced to his companion, standing by the ladder. Then he looked to us. He made a mouth as if to spit. "Mutiny?" he said. "Mutiny? These scarecrows?"

"Doubt me," William cried, his voice nigh hysterical. "Doubt me

243

now and doubt me later. Doubt me when they swarm up yon ladder i' the dead o' night, wi' that 'un i' the lead, and the knife in his teeth—" And he turned, wildly, and pointed straight at Munke.

The sailor's eyes obeyed the bidding of that gesture. He yet smiled his disbelief, but there was now a query in his eyes, and Munke shrugged his reply to it. " 'Tis the heat here below," he said. "He hath taken leave of his senses in this heat."

"Hath he?"

Munke shrugged again. "We be miserable men," he said. "But not yet mad. Could a hundred of us have any hope against eighty of you, bare hands against—"

"Ye might think so. Ye might entertain the hope. Desperate men may think desperate thoughts, and ye might try. I' the dead o' night. And as for the bare hands, what is this o' a knife?"

"But babbling."

The sailor yet studied him stolidly. "I ha' no great fondness for Mister Cole," he said. "Nor overmuch stomach for watching a man's back laid bare to the ribs. An ye ha' a weapon secreted on ye, gi' it me, man. An ye do so, this will go no further."

Munke spread his hands. "I have no knife secreted about me. But search me out if you cannot rest content with my word. It should not detain you long, man."

"Not about you, no," the sailor said. "But what o' elsewhere here below?"

"An there be, I know nought of any."

"I promise you," the sailor said, "an we conduct a search, it will be thorough. An ye ha' ought hidden here below, we shall find it." He paused again, his face honest and his eyes compassionate. "Gi' it me, man," he said. "For the sake o' the lot o' ye, gi' it me."

"An I could," Munke said, "I should. But I cannot produce what I do not have." And in his face, too, was the look of a man who had burned a bridge.

A moment longer the sailor studied Munke's face. Then he looked to his companion. "Fetch Mister Cole here below," he said.

He was confronting us within a quarter hour, was the mate. He was down the ladder and confronting a snarling and terrified scum from out a London cesspool within a quarter hour; with his long, black hair and white face and eyes like death, he might have been some old Hebrew prophet, come furiously and fanatically alive again, returned to another time, another place to wreak dispassionate vengeance in the name of the Lord God on the new cities of the plain. "What is this o' mutiny?" he said.

William told him. He was like some madman newly escaped from Bedlam, with his face twisted and his eyes darting hither and yon like something cornered and the words pouring out of him terrified and venomous and incoherent. But he told him. It was the pure truth he spoke, he told him. We had been hatching this plot a week now. We planned to swarm through yonder open hatch and seize the ship in the dead of night and cut every throat aboard and turn to piracy. . . .

"And what is this of a knife?"

And that the truth as well, William panted. Oh, he had seen it, and search that one out if he had doubts. He should find out who spoke truth if he searched that one out. . . .

And now the mate swung on Munke. "Captain Munke, is it?" he said. "I would have this knife, Captain Munke," and I wondered how a voice, pitched so low as his, could echo so loudly in that space.

Munke spread his hands. "Can ye not recognize madness when it confronts you?" he said. "The man hath gone clean out of his wits from the heat—"

"I will repeat myself," Cole said. "I would have this knife."

"And I tell you the man is mad. He hath chosen this lie to be revenged on me—"

"You are gifted with a faulty memory, I see," Cole said. "Ye have precisely thirty seconds to amend it, Captain Munke."

"Thirty seconds or thirty days, I cannot produce what I do not have."

To judge from Cole's face, you would have thought the man gone stone-deaf; if he heard Munke, he betrayed no sign of it. He stood there, just beneath the yawning hatch, his head a trifle down, his face in the shadow. From above, the brazen, pulsing light of a tropic afternoon fell on his dank, black hair like a halo. He stood thus for precisely thirty seconds; had I had a clock to measure by, I wager I would have found that interval of silence exactly thirty seconds. Then he bestirred himself and raised that bloodless death's face. In the light falling through the hatch, the skin to his face looked like bleached linen.

"Mister Porter," he called out. "I would have ten men here below, Mister Porter."

It was, as we had been promised, a thorough search. Before he was done with us, we had all been stripped naked, male and female alike, and our clothing examined article by article, and the hold searched inch by tedious inch. And in the end they found it. It was concealed behind a loose board in the bulwark, within arm's reach of where Munke was wont to lie at night, and in the light from the fading afternoon Cole stood, head bent, face shadowed, turning over and over in his hand the thin toy.

"Captain Munke," he said, "would ye know a knife when ye see one? Art acquainted with the shape and heft—"

Munke confessed that he was.

"And would ye call this a knife, Captain Munke?"

"It hath that appearance," Munke said. "Verily."

"But you have ne'er before laid eyes on this knife. Would that be the truth, sir?"

"Why, no," Munke said. "For I relieved yon whoreson of it. It was our first day aboard. He had a mind to murder me—"

"And so ye lied to me, Captain Munke."

"No," Munke said. "No, I did not lie."

"Not?" A flicker of pain flitted across Cole's face, a look like to a man experiencing some passing twitch in the gut. "Not, Captain Munke?"

"No," Munke said. "For it was gone within three days of my possessing it. I was relieved of it in my sleep, I think."

"So. And now shall we fall to talk of mutiny, Captain Munke?"

"There hath been no talk of mutiny. That scum lies—"

But the mate no longer attended him; he had turned a shoulder to Munke and was surveying the rest of us. "Would there be any among you would discuss mutiny wi' me?" he said. "I am a patient man, I can gi' ye one full minute to step forward." He waited, a patient and reasonable man, while some contrivance in his mind ticked off precisely one minute and no one of us stepped forward. Then he shrugged. "Very well," he said. "An that be how ye would ha' it."

"Mister Cole," Munke said. "Mister Cole—"

"Ye ha' plotted mutiny," Cole said. "On this I stand convinced. And one way or another, I shall have names—"

"In the name of God," Munke cried, "but look about you, sir. An you would see dead men, but look about you. I doubt ten among us could muster the strength to climb yon ladder unassisted, to say ought of engaging your crew—"

"I could take ye above and flog the truth out o' you," Cole said. "And hang what is left to the yardarm."

"So you could. Though it would not be the truth. A confession, but no truth."

Cole sighed. His hand went to his forehead; when it came away, he looked down at the slick of sweat on his fingers, his eyes and the bend of his head a brown study. "I find it unseasonably warm here below," he said, and he might have been passing the time of day with some chance acquaintance.

Munke seized on the bait. "Aye, 'tis warm. 'Tis like hell itself—"

"Why, no," Cole said, still conversationally. "Not with yon hatches yawning open to the breeze above."

His tone was still idle, but Munke no longer took it so. "You would not, sir," he whispered. "In God's name, you could not—"

"And why could I not? I am a patient man, Captain. And godly enough, I can hope. But patience can be stretched beyond all human endurance. And I will have the truth from you."

"You have it," Munke said hoarsely. "I swear to you—"

The mate only looked at him indifferently and then turned away. Munke considered that shoulder, the side of that face. "Very well," he said. "If you must have a confession, you have it. Hang me an ye must. But in God's name, do not—"

Cole smiled thinly. "Ah," he said cheerfully. "And who hath joined you in this business, Captain?"

"None."

The mate raised his face to the light falling through the hatch, a patient and reasonable and Christian man but put upon beyond all human endurance. "None? None, sir? A hundred desperate men here below, forty o' them confessed rebels? And not one recruit?"

"There is no spirit among us. I swear there is nought but despair—"

"Why, do not, sir. Your soul is already overmuch burdened with falsehood, and do not." His eyes dismissed Munke then, and made one more brief circle of the hold. Then he looked to one of his men, standing just at the ladder, and the man turned and started up the ladder and his companions after him. We watched them one by one reach the top of the ladder and pause there briefly, black backs against the dying light of a tropic day. Cole was the last to go, and midway in his climb he turned that white, cold, fanatic face upon us one last time.

"An there be some among ye would discuss mutiny wi' me," he said, "but call out. An ye scream loud enough, ye will be heard, I think. E'en with yon hatch battened down and your tongues swollen for want o' water."

William burst forth from among us. "What o' me, sir?" he cried out. "Ha' ye not forgotten—"

"What have I forgotten, man?"

"Why, me, sir. Am I not to go above wi' ye—"

"Above?" The mate's voice was heavy with amazement on the sudden.

William's face turned from something sharp and foxlike to something mindless with terror. "Aye. Above. Sure you do not intend—" He thrust out his two hands like some miserable supplicant without some hovel in a Southwark slum. "Name o' God, how ha' I offended? But tell me how, that I can mend—"

Cole smiled down on him. "Why, say I am not certain who it is lies here. Or say simply that I ha' no great fondness for you, sirrah."

And now William's face was not mindless. Now it was twisted with fear and savage. "And this my reward?" he said hoarsely. "This my reward—"

Cole smiled gently on him. "Have you not heard that virtue is its own reward, man?"

"These be desperate men," William screamed. "Leave me undefended but a quarter hour, they shall tear me apart—"

Still the mate smiled on him, gently and sweetly. "Be of good faith, man," he said. "Put your trust in the Lord and be comforted." Then he faced about and climbed through the hatch. William stood there, staring at the square of evening sky through the hatch, or at despair, or at nothing at all. Then he turned. He faced about like something doomed; he came about and retreated a step and then stood there, his eyes a glare and his back pressed hard to the ladder behind him and his hands outthrust. But no one made a move toward him. No word passed between us nor even any glance. We but faced him silently, between us the knowledge that this one would collect his rightful reward and no need for us to make him the payment.

We stood thus, while above the hatch clattered into place, and the light was blotted out like a snuffed candle, and the sound echoed and re-echoed like Judgment Day there in the almost darkness.

It required but a day for the first among us to die. It required a second for something close to madness to come among us.

I do not know when death visited us. The dead one was one of the debtors, a miserable wretch already half starved when they prodded him aboard and since reduced to dry, feverish skin and sharp bones. He was already far gone with scurvy, and it may have been the disease that carried him off and not the thirst that raged among us by high noon of that first day, not the heat that lay upon us like something physical, that was like trying to breathe through wet wool. I do not know. I but know that death stole among us a-tiptoe.

But madness did not visit us by stealth. Madness was fetched to us, a gift from the mate; and if it was compassion that prompted him, then Mister Cole, it would appear, was wont to sound trumpets before the synagogues to announce his charity, he was not one to keep secret from his right hand what his left hand did.

That was the second day. There had been, our first day without water, cursing and groaning enough—aye, and retching to boot, for near the end of that day some of us, more desperate than wise, had gagged against a palmful of our own water. But that second day a quiet despair settled upon us. We lay now in a stupor, the sweat dried on our bodies, our tongues thick and chalky dry in our throats, breathing a task we set our minds to, as a husbandman will put his mind to the boulder before he throws his weight against the crow. We lay thus, and death stood out there before us, and we looked him in the face and no longer knew fear.

And then the mate returned.

He descended the ladder with in his tow two men carrying the wooden bucket. At the foot of the ladder he relieved the two of their burden and set it down. Then he came to my corner. He stood over me but he did not look down upon me. He was studying the girl who lay beside me, her hand, small and hot and quiet as the end of some fatal illness, clasped loosely in mine.

"Give this one to drink," he said. "And t'other six. But not yon two whores."

I did not turn my head to watch. If you do not watch, I thought, you can perhaps endure; if you do not turn your head and see them swallowing and the water running down their chins, perhaps you will not go mad. So I watched the mate instead. He stood now just in the center of the hold, his eyes circling us, and I could see neither compassion nor fret in his face, only a faint pleasure when his eyes came to rest on the place where I knew William still lay.

"So," he said. "And art yet alive, then? Hast learned to pray since yesterday? Hast come to know God recently? And did I not say put your faith in the Lord and be comforted?"

Then he looked to the one with the bucket. "And one other," he said.

"Sir?"

"To drink."

"That 'un, sir?" It would appear that some among the crew shared our opinion of William.

"Why, no. The one I smell. Just there, I think."

"We are to gi' the dead to drink, sir?"

"His fill. The entire ocean. Fetch him above."

"Would ye pray over him, sir? Afore ye throw him over?"

"I think not. No, I think he doth not merit that courtesy."

The two struggled and grunted up the ladder with the dead one. The mate yet stood at the foot of the ladder, his head lowered, the bucket depending from his left hand. "And is there one among ye," he said, "would discuss this day the subject o' mutiny wi' me?" He waited his reply in the thick, hot silence. "None?" he said wonderingly. "None? Why, then, on the morrow, mayhap." He dipped ladle in bucket and raised it to his lips and drank of it, a long, leisurely drink; we lay and watched the ladle tilt, and watched him swallow, and watched the water run carelessly down his chin. Then he turned and climbed the ladder. We watched him through the hatch, and briefly there was a patch of blue and passionate sky where he had been. Then the hatch clattered to, and we lay again in sudden dimness, and the heat settled down upon us like something you could have weighed in a butcher's scale.

There had been silence before among us, but no silence like to this silence. It was like something physical come among us; it had a smell to it as plain as the stink of death that had just departed us, and it had a body to it like the heat that lay upon us. It was a silence as absolute as it is possible to achieve among a hundred people crammed knee to knee and shoulder to shoulder; there was the faint creak and protest of ship's timbers, and the lap of water against the hull, and that was all. It was the kind of silence in which madness is born.

In that silence there appeared, suddenly and without warning, a single figure at the foot of the ladder.

I did not immediately know him. By now a hundred of us were reduced to the anonymity of nakedness and dry, fevered skin and sharp bones and matted beards, and the light here was like the dusk of a winter's eve, and so I did not immediately know him. For the nonce he was a stranger standing at the ladder, some apparition created out of thin air by some devil's wish, some naked ghost with bearded face upturned, and eyes (gone raving mad, I thought) fixed on the hatch above, and one hand resting on a rung of the ladder, and a thin splash of sunlight, like a blob of bright paint, falling through a fault in the hatch onto a wasted, long-fingered, flour-white, blue-veined hand.

He stood thus for what seemed an eternity, and *'Tis coming*, I thought, *'tis coming. Let him but make a move or a sound,* I thought, *and it will be among us, the madness. Now,* I thought, panting, *now.*

Then he faced about.

He faced about slowly—but not heavily, not like a man wearied or sick, simply deliberately, as a man in full and perfect control of himself will face about. His head was a little down, his face in the shadow but not obscured, and in that instant I knew him. He had been one of us, a man they called Bernard; he had joined us at Blandford, an ejected minister turned to husbandry, I had heard; a man I knew but slightly, as you will know a face but not even the full name of one you nod casually to at morning muster. And yet I somehow knew that this man was not mad. I knew nothing of madness; I had never in my life gone of a long, dull Sunday afternoon to Bedlam, there for a penny ha'penny to watch the antics of poor, damned wretches possessed of devils; to the best of my knowledge I had never looked into the face of madness. But for all that I knew that this one was not mad.

He stood thus a little in the quiet. Then he spoke. He spoke at first as a man would who has not heard his own voice for a long time; he spoke cautiously and wonderingly, as if his voice were an instrument once familiar but since neglected, and at first his words betrayed the thickness of his tongue and the dryness of his throat. But the voice was not mad. *Prepare ye the way of the Lord,* he said. *Make straight in the desert a highway for our God,* and No, I thought, no, he is not mad. *Rend your heart, and not your garments,* he said, *and turn unto the Lord your God: for he is gracious and merciful, slow to anger, and of great kindness, and repenteth him of the evil,* and his voice was firmer now, his words bolder and more distinct. *The sacrifices of God are a broken spirit,* he said; *a broken and a contrite heart, O God, thou wilt not despise,* and now I recognized the call to morning prayer. *Is it nothing to you, all ye that pass by?* he said. *Behold, and see if there be any sorrow like unto my sorrow which is done unto me, wherewith the Lord hath afflicted me,* and now, so firm and steady was his voice, you would have thought him risen but an hour since from his comfortable breakfast table back in Wilts. And then

Let us humbly confess our sins unto Almighty God, he said.

I cannot tell you how we accomplished our feet and then our knees; I swear to you I cannot. But we did. There was his call to morning prayer, and there was, on the sudden, the comfortable knowledge among us that madness had brushed us by, that one had risen to throw down the gauntlet before Satan and Satan had not stooped to pick it up, and now there were forty or fifty of us on our knees, and forty or fifty voices joined in the general confession, while the rest looked on in absolute amazement.

Almighty and most merciful Father; We have erred, and strayed from thy ways like lost sheep. We have followed too much the devices and desires of our own hearts. We have offended against thy holy laws. We have left undone those things which we ought to have done; And we have done those things which we ought not to have done; And there is no health in us. But thou, O Lord, have

252

mercy upon us, miserable offenders. Spare thou those, O God, who confess their faults. Restore thou those who are penitent; According to thy promises declared unto mankind in Christ Jesus our Lord. And grant, O most merciful Father, for his sake; That we may hereafter live a godly, righteous, and sober life, To the glory of thy holy Name. Amen.

I can tell you about morning prayer. I can tell you of boyhood services where some starving curate, the poor nephew of an absentee rector, would carry us headlong through morning prayer—a call to worship, and the general confession, and an epistle chosen more for brevity than aptness, and no sermon at all, and a mumbled benediction—the entirety requiring not half an hour but even so the congregation restless and squirming, eager to be off to their dinners and their afternoon pleasures. And I can tell you of services conducted furtively behind barred doors; more seemly these may have been, and yet I doubt that God found any the more favor with them, for they were born not out of need but out of anger and rebellion against authority. But God came among us this day, of this I can bear you witness. We had for congregation that afternoon fifty naked and near dead wretches; and our priest had for robes but a rag about his loins and no surplice or stole at all; and all our sanctuary was a rude ladder for cross; and I doubt our altar faced properly east. And yet God came among us, He made His presence felt, and we were comforted when we joined voices in the *Our Father*, and when Bernard pronounced over our bowed heads the Declaration of Absolution and the Remission of Sins, and when, in lieu of gospel or epistle, he recited that passage from the service of Holy Communion:

Hear what comfortable words our Saviour Christ saith unto all who truly turn to him.

Come unto me, all ye that travail and are heavy laden, and I will refresh you.

So God loved the world, that he gave his only-begotten Son, to the end that all that believe in him should not perish, but have everlasting life.

Hear also what Saint Paul saith.

This is a true saying, and worthy of all men to be received, That Christ Jesus came into the world to save sinners. . .

Hear also what Saint John saith.

If any man sin, we have an Advocate with the Father, Jesus Christ the righteous; and he is the Propitiation for our sins.

Lift up your hearts. . . .

We were joined in the general thanksgiving when the hatch above us was thrown suddenly and violently open. Bernard had led us through the responses and the creed and the Twenty-third Psalm, and we were joined together in the general thanksgiving, *Almighty God, Father of all mercies, we, thine unworthy servants, do give thee most humble and hearty thanks for all thy goodness and loving-kindness to us, and to all men* when the hatch was hurled open and the mate's face appeared in it. Or we assumed it was the mate; the sun, red as heated copper, was just past noon and straight behind him, and his face was black against it. There were fifty of us on our knees when the hatch was thrown open, and truly I do not think a single voice among us faltered *We bless thee for our creation, preservation, and all the blessings of this life; but above all, for thine inestimable love in the redemption of the world by our Lord Jesus Christ; for the means of grace, and for the hope of glory.* Then the sun slid beyond that square of hatch, and we could see the mate's face framed against the noon sky, the face a livid white with rage and the eyes a-glare *And, we beseech thee, give us that due sense of all thy mercies, that our hearts may be unfeignedly thankful; and that we show forth thy praise, not only with our lips, but in our lives, by giving up our selves to thy service, and by walking before thee in holiness and righteousness all our days* and the mate shouted something to us but we heeded him not *through Jesus Christ our Lord, to whom, with thee and the Holy Ghost, be all honour and glory, world without end. Amen.*

And then the silence.

We were ended now, and the silence fell upon us. We yet knelt there, looking to Bernard, and Bernard raised his face to the mate's —or to the blue and serene and cloudless sky—and the mate made as if to speak but did not, for Bernard was pronouncing the benediction: *The grace of our Lord Jesus Christ, and the love of God, and the fellowship of the Holy Ghost, be with us all evermore. Amen.*

And then the mate and six or seven others were upon us.

❊ ❊ ❊

254

Mutiny, it would appear, he could abide, could the mate, but heresy he could not. He came tumbling and scrambling down the ladder with six or seven, and for a little all was unceremonious kicking and prodding as they got us off our knees. Then the mate turned on Bernard, and the threat of rebellion he had smiled on, but it was no smile he now bent on our priest.

"What call ye this?" he said. "What vanity is this?"

"Why, prayer," Bernard said, and his voice as steady as his eyes.

"Prayer? Ye call this Babylonian—this—"

"I would call it so. And I can hope that God—"

"God? Dare ye speak of God?" The mate made a mouth as if to spit. "I find ye an abomination. 'Tis a godly ship this, and God hath smiled on this voyage, and I find ye an abomination in the eyes of the Lord."

"I am a dying man," Bernard said quietly. "And a hundred with me. And so it is no more your opinion I value, sir, but the Almighty's."

The mate drew a slow breath. "Why, I think I shall put that to the test. I think I shall." He looked about for his men. "Take him above. And his congregation with him."

We had lived like moles for nigh a month now, and the light above struck us a blow in the face; it was bright enough, it seemed, to blister eyeballs; it was like looking into the face of eternity. We came blinking and stumbling out into that curtain of light, and the sun rode savage and pitiless in a pitiless sky, and the deck was hot against our naked feet. We stood out there on the deck, with sailors crowding the bulwarks, and watched through that downpour of pulsing light while they cuffed Bernard to the mast and the mate came forward to face him.

"Wouldst lead us now in prayer, priest?" the mate said.

I have in my travels in Italy seen a picture of the Christ hanging limp and forsaken on His cross and a great white light behind Him like an ill-formed halo. I was reminded of that picture now. They had cuffed Bernard backward so that he faced us, and his head was down, his chin sunk on his chest, and he swayed in a small arc with the sway of the ship, and his skin was as white as plaster, and I thought, *My God, my God, why hast thou forsaken me?*

"Come," the mate said. "I count it not charity if you refuse to share God with us, priest. Wouldst hide thy light under a bushel,

255

then? Come, here in God's bright sunlight, I would hear ye pray, priest." He dropped to one knee. "Bless me, Father, for I have sinned," he cried out, and a ripple of laughter, like water, ran along the bulwark.

"He hath no rosary, Mister Cole," one shouted out. "Can he pray if he hath no beads?"

"Why, I thank you," Cole said. "For I confess I am ignorant in these matters." A rope dangled from the yardarm, and the mate came off his knees and slashed a length of it free and hung it about Bernard's neck. "Pray, priest," he said. "A Pater Noster. A Hail Mary or two, priest." He waited in the white, hot silence. Then he freed the whip from its loop and laid the stock nicely and delicately just at the point of Bernard's chin and raised the head. "I would hear ye tell your beads, priest," he said.

Bernard opened his eyes, and sun or no sun looked unblinking into the mate's face. "I am no papist," he said. "Well you know I am not. But do your worst with me, for with God's help I can endure it."

"My worst?" The mate stepped back from him. "My worst? I intend thee nought save an afternoon here in the sun, priest." His back was to us and we could not see his face. But we could hear his words, and they were through his teeth. "Pray," he said. "For I would have God choose here and now between thee and me."

No whipstock now pressed Bernard's face into the sun. But for the nonce he did not lower his head. "I will call upon the Lord, who is worthy to be praised," he said. "So shall I be saved from mine enemies. In my distress I called upon the Lord, and cried to my God; and he did hear my voice out of his temple, and my cry did enter into his ears."

"Why, good, priest," Cole said. "Most excellent good. But louder. For the earth hath not shook or trembled; the foundations of heaven have not moved and shook, and mayhap God hath gone a little deaf this day." He glanced once, indifferently, toward the bulwarks, to where men stirred and murmured on the sudden and cast apprehensive glances toward heaven; sailors these men were and unlettered, but they could recognize Scripture when they heard it, and this foolery had gone beyond foolery, the spice of this was hotter on their tongues than was to their taste. "Wouldst match Scripture wi' me, priest?" Cole said. "Then hear this verse. 'Verily I say unto you, If ye have faith as a grain of mustard seed, ye shall say unto

this mountain, Remove hence to yonder plain, and it shall remove.'" He glanced toward the sun. "It yet lacks six hours to sunset. But I would hear ye bid yon sun to set here and now."

"I am no Joshua," Bernard said. "Nor never so pretended."

"But a small miracle, then. But a cloud to blot out the sun a little
and soften the heat."

"Not as I will, but as thou wilt," Bernard said.

For another breath or two the mate glared into the white silence
between them, the whip depending from his right hand, the strands
coiled like a nest of sunning snakes on the hot deck. Then he
shrugged and turned away. "Why, then, ye ha' the afternoon, you
and yours," he said, "to stand just here and consider your con-
victions. And if this be not Christian then let God frown upon it."

In that moment He did. In that moment the small miracle. In
that moment God chose.

No cloud appeared in that brazen and pitiless sky, and the sun
did not plummet into the sea. But God chose. Wonderful and
mysterious are His ways and beyond human comprehension, and
the instrument to His hand for the working of His will was the im-
probable and most ungodly person of Captain Hartsell, who appeared suddenly at the head of the companionway.

He was not alone. It would appear we had taken on more cargo
in St. Iago than water, for almost as if to flout his wickedness before
God and the mate, the Captain had a woman beside him. She was
a young Negress, not above sixteen an I were any judge. But none
of your field hands, none of your female blacks taken aboard from
out some slave stockade at Guinea or Angola, worth in Carlisle Bay
twenty pounds sterling for her skill at weeding and her fecundity
at breeding. This one would fetch twice that from some itching and
drooling planter and afterwards the investment dressed in silks and
protected from sun and elements. For this one was fine-featured,
and her breasts were not great and jutting nor her hips narrow as
a man's, and her hair was not short to her head but fell in soft,
black waves to her knees; in features, she would have caused some
of your reigning London beauties a twinge of jealousy, and in pro-
portion she would have pleased the painter Albert Dürer, and in
softness of muscle and curiosity of coloring she would have taxed
the skill of Titian. Had she been unclothed, she could have been
some pagan Venus just risen from out the sea; some heathen

257

priestess from out a distant time when men sinned and knew it not, with hair held above her ears by white ribbons, and copper pendants in her ears, and a bracelet of tooled and hammered silver on one arm, and all her concession to modesty a loose mantle of pale blue taffeta tied with a ribbon at her right shoulder and falling under her left arm so as to leave one breast exposed.

I looked at her through that throb of light, near dead from abuse but still with enough manhood left in me to envy our Captain. Then I looked to the mate. He, too, was looking up at these two, and his back was to us, and his thoughts were written in his stance, in his fists to his side. And more reason, I thought, than a few scraps from out the service of Common Prayer for his raging and fretting about the godliness of his ship. Captain Hartsell was not the first thus to relieve the monotony of a sea voyage; and if you could purchase such pleasure in one port and sell it at a handsome profit in another, why, what man, godly or no, was to say you nay? But for all that, I thought, just there beside the Captain stands a prime reason for our present condition.

A long moment these two faced each other, the mate below, the Captain above with his concupiscence boldly proclaimed beside him and his eyes pensively on this scene. Then the Captain came clumping thickly down the companionway.

"What ha' we here?" he said. "What sport goeth forward here, mister?"

"Mutiny, sir."

"Mutiny, is it?" The Captain looked through the haze of light to us. "Did ye say mutiny, mister?"

" 'Twas so reported to me, sir. Two days since—"

"Was it, now? Two days since? And I not informed?"

The mate looked once to the top of the companionway. "You were otherwise engaged, sir."

"Mutiny?" The Captain looked through the light to us. "Dost fear mutiny from scarecrows, mister? Do dead men threaten mutiny?"

" 'Twas so reported to me, sir. By one of them. And I good cause to trust his word in it, for I found a knife secreted—"

"A knife," the Captain murmured. "Would ye think on that now."

"Do not judge a fruit by its peel," the mate said stubbornly. "They be desperate men—"

"Why, I little doubt ye there. Truly I do not." The Captain moved

258

past Cole and stopped a foot from Bernard and looked him up and down. "How long since this one hath tasted food, mister?"

"A pair o' days."

"And water?"

"The same."

"And the same tale for those?"

"Aye, sir. I thought it—"

"So they be desperate, be they? But two days without food or water not sufficient to quell mutinous spirits, eh? You must whip them to boot, must you?"

The mate's eyes dropped to the strands of the whip lying against the white, hot deck. "I had not meant to whip him, sir. I but intended them to stand here in the sun an hour or so—"

"And for what offense this time, mister?" The Captain waited head down for a reply, and had I been the mate, I doubt I should have liked the set of his mouth just now. "What offense, mister? Riot? Murder?"

"No, sir."

"What, then? That they did not have the grace to die?"

"Not that neither, sir."

"For what great fault, then?"

"For praying, sir."

The Captain stared at him, speechless. And then, "Praying?" he whispered, and again, "Praying?"

Cole's head was a little back, his face very white in the sun. I could not read his eyes. " 'Twas not fit," he said. " 'Twas an abomination straight out o' Common Prayer, and unlawful—"

"Unlawful? Ye speak to me o' unlawful?" The Captain strode to Bernard and put out a hand and brought Bernard's head up off his chest. "A month since," he said, "when this one was in health, what might he ha' fetched in Carlisle Bay, mister?"

The mate shook his head. "I cannot say. I am no planter—"

"Ye had best say," the Captain said softly. "Ye had best." He waited, shoulders hunched, head lowered, in the white glitter. "How much, mister?"

The mate shrugged. "Mayhap a fifteen hundredweight o' sugar—"

"And were he papist, mister? But yet in health? How much?"

"The same."

"And were he black and a heathen?"

259

"Yet the same."

The Captain put out a hand again and raised Bernard's face into the sun. "Canst see this man clear, mister? Is the light fair and sufficient?"

"I can see him."

"Were ye a planter, how much would ye offer now for this man?"

"Truly I cannot say—"

"Why, I can. Nought. Save I were bat-blind. Or crazed i' the head." The Captain dropped Bernard's head. "What position ha' we, mister?"

"Position, sir?"

"Aye. Position. Ye ha' employed backstaff this sennight, ha' ye not? Between your sport—"

"Twenty-nine degrees," the mate said.

"Twenty-nine degrees," the Captain said. "Not three hundred leagues to the island. Not eight days if this wind hold firm." He turned and looked along the bulwark. "I do not see Mister Porter present."

"He hath the watch. He minds the whipstock—"

"I would ha' him fetched."

We waited while one ran for the second mate and another cut down Bernard and propped him against the mast and yet another fetched him water. Then the second mate appeared among us, panting from his run, his mouth pulled awry from the fault to his upper lip, his eyes uneasy as they slid from Captain to mate.

"I ha' some small tasks for ye, Mister Porter," the Captain said. "Think ye ye can obey them, and that something closer to the wind than this bastard?"

"I can but try, sir."

"They are to be given to drink," the Captain said. "These forty and those ye find yet alive below. Their fill. If the crew must go on short rations, they are to have their desire o' water between here and port. And half a pint o' rum a day. Dost attend me, mister?"

"Aye, sir."

"They are to be fed. Thrice daily, and bone meat once. Dost further attend me there?"

"Aye, sir."

"You are to exercise them. Twenty by twenty under guard from sunup to sunset. An it be daylight, I would see them marching. Dost further attend me there?"

"Aye, sir."

"An they so desire, they are to be permitted to pray. Established Church, papist mass, heathen witch's rite, they are to be humored in it. Dost attend me there?"

"Aye, sir."

And now, head down, the Captain was looking again to Cole. "As for you, mister," he said, "you are to go above and make an entry in the log. To wit: 'On this day, which was Friday, the twenty-third day o' February, in the year of our Lord sixteen hundred and fifty-five, at two of the clock i' the afternoon, was Martin Cole, first mate aboard the *Edward and John,* by order of Henry Hartsell, Master, relieved of his duties and ordered in irons. And on this day was Robert Porter, second mate, named first mate i' his place.' Canst repeat that, mister?"

The mate stood there, head flung back, tall and gaunt and his face like death in the sun, looking at Hartsell. Then he turned and directed his eyes above, to the top of the companionway; the girl had disappeared, but he looked to where she had stood. Then he looked once, indifferently, to us. And then he was looking again into the eyes of the Captain.

"Verily, I say unto you," he said, "that the flesh lusteth against the spirit and the spirit against the flesh. And I say that the works of the flesh are these: adultery, fornication, uncleanness, lasciviousness, idolatry, witchcraft, seditions, heresies, drunkenness, and such-like: of the which I tell you that they which do such things shall not inherit the kingdom of God." Again he glanced to the top of the companionway, to where the girl had a little before stood. "Thou'rt a wicked and godless man, Captain Hartsell," he said. "And irons or no, I would not change places wi' ye. Thou'rt rotten and corrupt, ye stink in the nostrils of God, and the day shall come when ye feel the anger o' the Almighty heavy on you. Mark me but ye shall. And when the day comes, may God ha' mercy on your soul."

The Captain looked at him, head down, while along the bulwark the crew stirred and shifted uneasily. And then the Captain grinned.

"Why, do thou pray for me, then," he said.

ະ⊲ *Fifteen* ⊳ະ

We drove down upon the island eight days later. We sighted the island early in the morning, the day fair but the light curious, for the sun was obscured by a thing which is neither fog nor mist and which the sailors call *haze*. In that light we crowded the bulwarks and looked off larboard to the island.

"Is it not fair?" Munke said. "And shall I offer you philosophy? For I have heard of life on this island an ye be servant or slave."

"Do not," I said. "I have eaten well and drunk my fill these eight days, and I can march about this deck an hour in a noon sun and not faint, and do not." I looked at him and then beyond him to Andrew; I was thinking that we had clung together through a rebellion and a sea voyage, but by afternoon we would be standing on a slave block in Bridgetown and by night God alone knew what or where. "I could endure slavery the better," I said, "were we to be purchased together, we three."

"Mayhap we shall be," he said. "God willing."

I looked again toward the island. It was not three leagues distant now, and I could see plain the ships crowding Carlisle Bay, and other ships flung all along the coast, and the coast falling away to the north. I placed elbows on the bulwark, and the island from this distance looked fair indeed, like some Eden flung down by the Almighty in a moment of compassion for His erring and lost creation. On my left hand, the sun burst forth as it will in these parts, all at once, and you could make out the shape of this side of the island, long and narrow and rising steadily from shore to center, a little the shape of a loaf of English bread; and along the windward shore the beaches, white as sheets spread out for drying on an English common, and the breakers roaring in like avengers and then dying gentle and frothy against the sand, as if the sea too knew this place and found it good; and far to the north the cliffs rising sheer and straight toward a sky that only this minute had gone from misty white to a pale gray-blue; and down to the very edges of the cliffs the plantations, neat, green squares of crop and pasture and wood, built one upon the other up the slopes so that no man on the island, it seemed, was denied his prospect of the sea. Fair indeed, I thought, and then turned my head and looked over our bow into Carlisle Bay.

"I have never seen so many ships," I said. "More nor in the Thames. And has all the world converged on this place?"

Munke, too, was staring at the ships riding at anchor in the great bay. "I have heard the rumors," he said. "And were they more than idle gossip, then?"

I looked at the side of his face. "Rumors?"

"Of a great fleet building in Portsmouth. Of the Protector determined on war wi' Spain. But all the talk was, these were intended for the Mediterranean, under Blake." We were but a long halloo from the nearest ship now, and I could hear above and behind me the bark of orders in ratlin and shroud and the rattle of block and tackle as our sails were furled, and on the distant shore, before the town, a dozen small boats were putting out to us. "Aye," Munke said, his eyes on the nearest ship. "The *Swiftsure*. And yonder the *Marston Moor*. And so it is Spanish islands he hath a hunger for, is it? And I wonder."

"What?" I said, but even as I put the question, I knew the answer. "Pressment," I said. "Now, by God. Pressment."

The look in his eyes—speculation, hope, whatever it was—faded. "Nay," he said. "They could not. It would be the ruin of every planter on the island were their servants mustered. Yet he is an ambitious man. And if ye would conquer, ye must have armies. And I would guess that your planter would not by choice trail pike o'er foreign soil to the risk of life and limb. But servants now . . ."

"Aye," I said. "Servants now." I looked out across a league of water to the rude line of warehouses tumbled down along the west shore of the bay like an afterthought; to the clutter of houses behind them which was the town; to the wherries and skiffs racing toward us. The boats were already half across the bay, one of them ten lengths in the lead, two naked Negroes bent into the oars, the wherry close enough that I could see the ripple and crash of shoulder and chest muscles under the wet, slick, glistening skin, in the stern, face obscured by the sweep of a hat brim, a figure slight as a boy's. Aye, I thought, servants, and I leaned on the bulwark and watched this race, knowing what the prize for winning would be, knowing as well that Munke had hit on the truth, that ashore servants had been pressed into the Protector's army and that cane rotted in the fields and that planters had been ruined. And standing there, with the sun bright and hot in my face, I was, on the sudden, smiling.

The lead wherry coasted alongside the *Edward and John,* and we fell back from the bulwark, and Captain Hartsell clumped down the companionway, his blunt face slick with sweat from the heat of the morning or the wine in him, and the boy, lawn shirt open at the throat and riding breeches and bucket boots and all, climbed aboard. For a little his face was still obscured by the hat brim. Then he raised his head and we saw with a start of surprise that it was no boy but a woman, the first white woman I had even seen dressed so immodestly.

It was a woman, young, not above twenty, with a heart-shaped face that would not have shamed an angel. "Well, Captain Hartsell," she called out, "what gallows bait hast fetched us this voyage?"

Hartsell grinned. "It stands afore ye, ma'am."

She threw us a quick, indifferent glance. "Why, I believe ye ha' fed these twice or thrice," she said. "Damn me if I do not."

"They ha' been fed," Hartsell said. "And seasoned a little. I ha' had them marching in this sun a sennight."

She glanced over her shoulder at the boats approaching. "I require nine or ten," she said, "afore that rogue Mudiford climbs aboard and bids up the price. Would ye have a carpenter among them? Or a smith?"

"I cannot say, ma'am."

"Twelve hundredweight apiece for your first ten, Captain."

Hartsell grinned dryly across the span of deck to her. "Did I hear twelve, ma'am? And for your pick?"

"You will find that the rate this week an they be prime."

"Ah. Then ye must mean *white* sugar, ma'am."

"Why, no. Muscovado. But Jim Drax's muscovado. Worth six pound the barrel—"

Hartsell still grinned that dry, amused grin. "An that be the rate, methinks I shall sail on to Virginia, ma'am."

"Eight hundred leagues? And against a contrary wind? And for woody tobacco at the end of it?"

Another face appeared above the bulwark, this one forty years old and lean, with skin burned black and hair bleached white from the sun. He was speaking even as he threw leg over the bulwark. "Now, by God, Elaine," he said, "I wish those blacks o' yours were mine. Now by God, I do. Three boats in as many weeks and thrice beaten. The day may come when I shall pay your price for them. Now by God, it may." He looked gloomily at Captain Hartsell. "What hath she offered ye, Captain? I can go fourteen hundred for my pick. A thousand for first culls."

"Doubtless," Hartsell said. "And I can offer you fifteen shillings for an unclipped sovereign."

Another face appeared above the bulwark, and then another. The one was fat, the other lean. "A thousand for first culls," the lean one said.

"A thousand," Hartsell yelled. "A thousand. Now, by God, wilt cease the jesting, gentlemen—"

" 'Tis no jest, Captain," the one they called Mudiford said quietly.

"A thousand," Hartsell said. "I have realized a thousand on men of fifty. But last year girls of ten—"

"That were last year. Those ships were not in the bay last year."

"Ships? What ha' ships—"

"Search out the *Marston Moor* an you would ha' the answer to that," the girl said. "Search out Jackson's regiment aboard the *Swift-sure*—"

"Mustered," Hartsell whispered. He turned abruptly and stared at the warship two hundred yards astern. "Mustered," he whispered again. He swung back to stare at Mudiford. "They could not," he said. "They would not dare. 'Twould be the ruin—"

"It hath been," Mudiford said. "Ye will find planters here with not a white male left them, and their fields within a week of ripening—"

Hartsell still stared at him, head lowered. "Mustered," he said. "And ye still buy at all? When a thousandweight o' sugar today may be drilling with pike and musket tomorrow?"

Mudiford shrugged. "Oh, they ha' locked the stable now that the horse hath strayed. They ha' passed laws in the Assembly. No servants within nine months o' freedom to be pressed. Any officer who fails to return a runaway within twenty-four hours to be cashiered. Runaways to ha' their service doubled."

"Then the price should be up. Desperation doth not depress a market—"

Mudiford shook his head. "Servants can yet swim, Captain. And officers with short rolls can look the other way in the dark of midnight. Fourteen hundred for your first ten. No more. I swear it."

"Twelve," the girl said. "Twelve o' Jim Drax's sugar against fourteen o' Mudiford's. And that madness. But I have five acres must be milled and boiled within the fortnight."

Other faces had appeared on deck now, and Hartsell looked to them, waiting for higher bids, getting none. Then he looked gloomily to the girl. " 'Twill ruin me. I stand to lose—"

"We ha' been already ruined, Captain. If you would recoup your losses this voyage, bring us blacks your next."

Hartsell sagged a trifle in the shoulders. "Choose out your ten, ma'am," he said.

She swung on us. We stood sweating before her, stripped to the waist and barefoot, bearded and burned. "I find them something o'erdressed for choosing," she said. "A pocky servant is a dead servant in this clime. I would have them out o' those breeches."

So once again we stood naked before fifteen or twenty pairs of eyes, male, and one pair, female. We stood naked and sweating in the sun and felt no more shame than had we been oxen at a fair; we had been human once but servants a month, and a man can lose the knack of it in a month. We stood with eyes fixed straight ahead and faces set while she came up the line, pausing now and again to bid someone step just yonder. There were a score clumped at the mast when she paused before Andrew.

"Know you ought of smithing?" she said.

"I was a gardener, ma'am. But I can shoe a horse."

She stepped back a pace and looked him up and down. "Art as sound as ye look? Sound enough to work from six to six in this clime?"

"God willing," he said stolidly. "I think I am in health, ma'am."

She nodded. "Step just yonder," she said, and then she was looking at me. "Why, how now, Captain," she called out. "And ha' ye *one* among this lot doth not dodder? *One* is not food for worms ere I can fetch him ashore?" She stepped back, and I permitted myself one look at her face, a flick of the eyes, no more. Then I again fixed my attention on the horizon. "What years ha' ye?" she said. "Three and twenty, mayhap?"

I could feel her eyes, cool as any man's, immodest as the clothing she affected, surveying me up and down. "Eight and twenty, ma'am," I said.

"And what skills can ye claim?"

"None I can think on."

"None? What mean ye none, sirrah?"

"I am gentleman born. I ha' no skills."

Her eyes were on my face now; I could feel them, cool and speculative, on my face. "Save insolence," she said softly. "Ye ha' your fair share o' that, ha' ye not?"

"Why, no," I said. "Not by intent."

"Not? Then look me in the face when thou'rt addressed, sirrah. And frame your replies wi' respect."

There was a warning in her voice, and I dutifully lowered my eyes. "Aye," I said. "Ma'am."

She smiled slightly, and the smile was a further warning. "I think your youth will do," she said, "if your manners will not. And skills can be taught and manners corrected. Step yonder wi' the rest, an ye please."

Then she looked at Munke. "And you? Art another o' your gentlemen?"

"No, ma'am," he said. "Not I, ma'am."

"And ha' ye any gifts, then? Save a skill at picking pockets?"

"I think I can count one or two, ma'am. I can write a fair hand. And keep accounts. And"—and he flicked a look at me—"I have some small knowledge of carpentry."

267

"Have you, now?" She, too, looked briefly at me, standing there against her bidding, and then her eyes fell on his hands. "Have you, now? For you have not the look of a carpenter."

"Why, no," he said. "Nor you the look of a planter, ma'am."

She smiled at that, briefly, against her will. "How small?" she said. "And do not lie. Not an ye value the skin to your back."

"Why, small, ma'am. I can set you a level ridgepole. Or distinguish between a plumb line and a drawknife."

So Munke, too, was commanded to the mast, though I hoped for his sake that he were not soon called upon to prove the skill he claimed.

In the midst of her culling out ten from the score she had assembled at the mast, she stopped abruptly and looked above us to the bridge, and all along the bulwark there were, on the sudden, tongues running over lips and sucking in of breaths, and I did not have to turn my head (though I did) to know that Captain Hartsell's St. Iago acquisition had made an appearance.

The girl stood there, one hip just touching the rail, nothing above her waist this day to disguise her charms save a rope of black hair that lay passionate and disquieting against one brown breast. She stood thus and looked down upon us, and Mudiford said, "God A'mighty," and there was awe in his voice, and Captain Hartsell glanced once to the girl and then, head lowered again, grinned across the deck.

"Comfort for a man's declining years, gentlemen," he said.

"I can believe ye there," Mudiford said. "Were I twice five and thirty, I could believe ye there. Now by God, I could. And would she be for sale?"

Hartsell grinned sleepily at him through the hot, sleepy heat. "'Tis a lonely life, the sea, Colonel. Gi' a man two months and no sight o' land, he can grow a hunger in his gut for such comfort as that."

Mudiford returned sleepy grin for sleepy grin. "Agreed," he said. "And thou'rt a larcenous rogue, Captain. And ye ha' but to say me aye or nay. Would she be for sale or would she not?"

"Why, as to that," Hartsell said, "I know nought that is not, Colonel. Comfort for the hunger in a man's gut, or honor, or life itself, so the price be sufficient. 'Tis the nature o' the times we live in."

"And what price would ye term sufficient?"

Hartsell looked again to the bridge. "Great comfort I ha' found her, that one," he said. "For she was born wi' instincts, gentlemen. Skills may be learned. But instincts now"—and he sighed—"instincts are a gift from God, gentlemen. Or the de'l." He smiled, slowly and sleepily, as if, standing there in the sun, he were recalling some slow, sweet, recent dream. "Fifty pounds," he said then. "I would say fifty pounds, gentlemen."

Mudiford pursed his lips as if to whistle. "That were two thousandweight o' sixpenny muscovado. The price o' two prime blacks, male and female—"

"Why, no. That were sterling, Colonel. Fifty pounds sterling, sir."

Mudiford stared. Then he laughed shortly. "Sterling? On the island, Captain?" He laughed again. "She must go a-begging, then. An there be a planter on the island could buy a keg o' nails wi' sterling, I would ha' his name—"

"There would be one," the girl said. "The Draxes can afford that purchase, Captain."

Mudiford laughed once, a kind of silly giggle, and then broke off as sharply. "You?" Hartsell said. "You, ma'am?"

"And do ye find that cause for staring, Captain?"

"Why, no," he said. "No, ma'am."

"Or you for laughter, Colonel?"

"Why, no," Mudiford said. "Not I, Elaine."

"An ye do," she said, and her face was the face of a twelve-year-old girl's and innocent as Eden, but there was, in eye and lip, a quiet fury which, were I servant or planter, I should not willingly have faced—"an ye do, but say I have need for a maid. To lay out my clothes of a morn and brush my hair at night."

Mudiford shrugged. "An ye choose to squander fifty pounds sterling for what ye could have for twenty at barter—"

"Or say," she said, her eyes on Hartsell, her eyes intending him some challenge—"say I am trader at heart, and the girl a venture."

Hartsell smiled blandly. " 'Fore God, ma'am," he said, "an ye ha' the purchase price, I am not one to ask further questions."

"And what o' you, Colonel? What further questions have you?"

"None," Mudiford said. " 'Tis live and let live on the island, as you have reason to know, Elaine. 'Tis only"—and he paused, while his eyes slid delicately out of hers—" 'tis only that I have known you these five years, and I had not thought—"

"Thought what, Colonel?"

"Nought," he said. "Nought, Elaine."

"An ye had one," she said, "I give ye a second to lay aside it. I have a brother. Who found it inconvenient to be present this day."

She let that lie a little in the bright heat, food for thought for whoever would taste of it. Then she was looking again at us. "Him," she said, nodding at one of us. "I shall take him. And that would be my ten, I think, Captain."

This were Bridgetown in the year 1655. A ragged line of rude warehouses, crudely fashioned from the native mastic and redwood and a curious stone on the island, so soft you could cut it with a two-handed saw; and a swaying, wooden native bridge which spanned Indian River and joined warehouses to town and gave the town its name. The town a single street of shops and dwellings, the dwellings so low that the eaves were eye level, no windows or doors to the east since during the typhoon season the rain was driven from this direction, the dwellings sweltering hot ten months of the year. Flung down among those strange houses, as though fetched here stone, mortar, and timber from out County Wiltshire, an English church. Coming down that dusty street four camels, the first I had ever seen, great, shaggy, ugly beasts picking their way as delicately as rope dancers to the bridge, their humps buried beneath leather bags of sugar. Before one of the town's two taverns a team of oxen hitched to a two-wheeled cart, heads hanging in the sleepy heat, the oxen out of Ireland and the cart out of Surrey. Before the church, crouched down against the stone steps, a naked Negro woman giving suck to a child, and another walking toward us with a basket on her head, singing of land crabs for sale. Standing in the shade of the smithy an Indian girl, brown as a mulatto, her concession to modesty a thin girdle of beads about her hips. Emerging from the tavern a man straight off a London street, very drunk for two in the afternoon, his suit silver on blue and his shirt lawn and his boots cordovan and his hat beaver, very fine. And suspended over all like some invisible blanket the dust and the shimmer of heat. And the smell, a smell like to the stink of plague, the smell of stagnant bog, for every spring the tides wash over the town's banks, and the rest of the year the backwash festers beneath the tropic sun.

The Drax plantation lay eight miles west of the town. We were two hours on that march, the blacks in our van singing a strange, tuneless chant in some heathen language as we went, the march not so hard as others I have known, for the grass-grown wagon track we walked wandered much of the time through shade. We came to the plantation just short of sunset.

And this a Barbados plantation. The plantation house a long, low dwelling built by a nervous man, a man distrustful of his slaves, for all before and about it for fifty yards were lines and bastions and earthen bulwarks. A hundred yards from the house a whipping post standing black against the evening sky, mute warning to all disobedient servants or rebellious slaves. Beyond that, fading off into the evening, the scattered outbuildings, ingenio and boiling house and filling room, cisterns and still house and carding house, stables and smith's forge, storerooms for corn and maize and bonavist. In the distance, atop a brief hill, the long, low quarters (like English pigsties) for servants. And three miles below us the sea—the gentle fall of field and wood and pasture, and the long, curved heel of white sand at that place called Maxwell's Bay (the ships here, too, their rigging black against the evening sky), and the blood-red sun hanging six yards above the horizon (an hour hence and it would plummet into the sea as if it had been cut from a string), and the sea before it more colors than I own adjectives to describe them.

And at the whipping post, still as a statue when we marched toward it, a man a-horseback.

He was as tall as I and as dark as his sister was fair, and neither horse nor man moved a muscle, not the entire while we were marching to him, not even after we were fetched up just short of him and his sister spurred around us and wheeled her horse and came to rest beside him. Even then he sat there motionless, his eyes reflectively above and beyond us, while from three paces I looked up into a face scraped clean of all save a fragment of a mustache, the face very dark and regular and handsome; the teeth behind the faint curl of smile very white; the eyes just now serious but most times given to easy laughter; the mouth self-indulgent but not weak. A man you might get drunk with, I thought, but one you would not insult, not even in jest, not if you owned wits and had given the matter a moment's reflection. The kind of man, I thought, for whom a sister might purchase a young mulatto wench, provided he owned that kind of sister.

271

"Well, James," the girl said. "And have I not done well?"

"Most excellent well," he said. "What paid ye for her, Elaine?"

"Fifty pounds. Sterling. Hartsell would have nought but sterling."

"Fifty?" he said, and whistled softly. "And sterling. And what your interest in her, sister? For I had not thought your tastes—"

"She is intended for you. A birthday gift from your sister. Though I may teach her to brush my hair of a night if she prove to have any idle time."

"I thank you, Elaine," he said dryly. "And aye, I would say you have done well."

She smiled faintly. "I did not speak of the girl, James. Are they not sturdy rogues, think you?"

For the first time he favored us with a glance. "As to that," he said, "I cannot say. Would there be a bastard amongst them can swim, think you?"

"I neglected to inquire that out." She looked briefly at the side of his face. "Did we recover none of them?" she said softly. "None, brother?"

"Four. Four in fourteen. Two I found aboard the *Paragon* in Spyke's Bay; ask me not how they managed t'other side of the island. Two Jackson delivered up his afternoon. Of his own free will, he reminded me, though if truth were known, I think his reason was he cannot abide a Quaker."

She glanced at the whipping post. "And so we have been busied this afternoon, have we?"

"Why, no. No, we have not."

"Not? But you swore—"

"That were this morning. And spoken in heat."

"And this afternoon?"

"The afternoon is for sober reflection."

"What sober reflection?" she cried. "To let runaways escape scot-free—"

"They have had their terms doubled."

She laughed shortly. "Much that will profit us. When the next moonless night—"

"Do not fret, sister," he said. "They shall know some sore backs. But in due time. For I have five acres of cane ripe for cutting. And I must have men fit for labor." And now he leaned through the dusk, so far forward that one elbow rested on the pommel of his saddle, for the first time favoring us with a full look. "If ye fail to follow this argument," he said, "we are debating ships, my sister and I. But turn your heads, ye will see them there below. And after a day in the fields, they may prove a temptation." He paused, long enough to permit us to read the curl to his lip, the smile in his eye which was no true smile. "I would not let them," he said. "I tell ye, I would not. Ask about the island, they will tell you James Drax is a good master. I have yet to flog a servant save for laziness or insolence, and none other on the island will provide you with a clean shift of drawers when you return sweated from the fields, or bone meat once in every other week. But my word on it, let not yonder sails prove a temptation. As my name is James Drax, I would advise you, do not." And now, on the sudden, he smiled. "The morrow is the Sabbath," he said. "We require nought of you on the Sabbath. An ye wish, ye may wash and scrape your faces and trim your hair and attend the reading of morning prayer." He nodded to the black who stood just before him. "Ye may show them to their quarters now, Tom," he said.

The servant compound—the slave quarters, a hodgepodge of tiny huts with thatched roofs, and gray, dusty, trampled turf, and swarms of flies and armies of ants, and quantities of small, black, big-bellied children, were on another part of the plantation—the servant compound lay a quarter mile from the plantation atop a small hill. It counted three shelters, long and narrow and so low a man must stoop to enter them, the walls fashioned of raw tree trunks and plastered with mud, the roofs thatched with plantain and palmetto leaves, the floors dirt. Coming as we did upon the compound through the dusk, you would have thought you had wandered upon some native village, like some trader in blacks off the Guinea coast, ashore for a day of bargaining. The black who led us thither stopped before one of these structures and stood aside while we entered. When we emerged on the morrow, we would find him there still, sprawled out naked on the naked ground, his eyes wide open as we stepped over him, his face still impassive, no more expression on it than if it had been chipped by some heathen and unskilled artist out of some rare, black stone.

We entered. It was satin dark within, the air still thick from the lingering heat of the day, though in the night it would turn cold enough to prompt a man to wrap his arms about his chest in his sleep. And not until the next morning would I learn that one of Drax's four runaways who that day had been recovered was an old acquaintance of mine.

He was standing, his back to me, before the hut next when I stepped forth into the milky light which is dawn on the island. He was wearing loose, white drawers, and he was burned the color of brick, and he was bearded where once he had been clean. But even before he faced about, I knew him.

"Fox," I said. "Somerset Fox."

He came about and stared briefly. Then, slowly, that great, knobby, homely face softened. "Why, Mordaunt," he said. "Why, lad."

"Fox," I said, and closed the distance between us, and he put a hand on my arm and I a hand to his cheek, and for the moment that was all I could think of to say to him.

But later we talked at greater length and to more purpose. We were fed at eight, a thick, cold pudding made of maize pounded fine in a mortar and boiled to the thickness of our English frumenty; it was called loblolly on the island, and together with potatoes and a yellow, pulpy, sweet root called yams by some and bonavist by others, this loblolly was the staple of a servant's diet. At nine James Drax read us morning prayer, the first time in five years I had heard an Anglican service conducted in the open and without fear, for England was far away and Independency but a word out here; only two years ago, Cromwell must send a fleet here to force the planters to swear loyalty to the Commonwealth, and even now the words *Cavalier* and *Roundhead* were forbidden on the island on pain of a stiff fine. After the service a dour-faced overseer issued us clothing—a straw hat, two shifts of drawers, a pair of shoes each, the shoes made by the Indians of pigskin and mangrove-bark thread, the soles very soft and without heels, the most comfortable footwear I have ever worn.

And then, in a locust grove beyond the compound, we talked, Somerset Fox and Andrew and Richard Munke and I.

From where we sat we could look straight down on the white slice of sand and the blue, blue water which was Maxwell's Bay and the ships riding at anchor there; and between us and the bay a file of blacks emerging from a grove with bunches of grass-green plan-

274

tains on their heads; and on our right hand, in the yard before the plantation house, an ancient Negro crone crouched over a treadle-and-wheel like to a grindstone—at work, Fox said, grinding cassava roots against the making of bread. And taking our ease there, Fox told us of the life of an indentured servant. The work was hard, he said, he would not deny us that; but save at cutting and curing time, no harder than for some at home who called themselves free; you worked from six to six at felling trees or clearing new land, at building or mending fence, at digging or harvesting. You would not be given work that was beneath or beyond you; weeding was for black women, and tending fires in the boiling house, where the heat could kill a white man in a day, for the blacks who could endure it. You would be fed thrice daily on food you would learn to abide—loblolly and bonavist, cassava bread and plantains; for drink, water, or mobby, a drink made of fermented potatoes which tasted like Rhenish wine in the must, or another made of spring water and sugar and orange juice which was called beverage; once in every week a mackerel or turtle tasting of sand; and when an ox or a horse died, servants got the bodies and Negroes the head, skin, and entrails. We would find the first month cruel, for we were unseasoned to the clime and the next fortnight cutting and curing, a time when master and servant and slave worked the clock around. But there were worse lots than being servant to Colonel Drax; he lived in riot and debauchery and his sister as wicked as he, but he treated his servants kinder than most; and if we survived the first month, we would find the greatest hardship coming sweated from the fields. Or, he said—and batted at a fly the size of a drone bee—the varmints. Mosquitoes that at dusk could drive a man mad. Or meriwings, whose bite swelled bluish to the size of a pease. Or cockroaches that bedded with you at night and bit deep enough to fetch blood; he had seen blacks bitten to the breadth of a man's two hands and the skin raised as if by a currycomb. Or the fleas they called chiggers that burrowed beneath toenails and laid sacks of eggs as big as tares; he had himself wakened of a morning with ten swollen toes; the Indian women had a trick with these, they thrust a needle into the hole and wound the point around the sack and so drew it out.

"And yet," Munke said, "ye went a-swimming."

Fox looked at him, puzzled. "Eh?"

"This James Drax," Munke said. "A good master, you say."

Better than most, Fox said; he could name you masters who flogged servants but for the pleasure it afforded them, or who starved them, or who treated a Negro kindly (for they were purchased for life) but worked a white till he dropped (for his term was but five years).

"A good master," Munke said. "Yet ye attempted escape."

Aye, Fox said, for a madness seized on the island when the ships came. The fleet appeared the last day of January, and within three days the rumors had spread like fire in a cane field. It was a great fleet come to relieve Spain of her islands in these parts, that was all the talk, and General Venables was drumming in the square in Bridgetown for eight thousand men, and not a servant on the island would not trade his five years here for one year of trailing a pike. And so the madness—masters setting blacks to guard servants and servants knocking them in the head; cane fields fired and outbuildings razed; on one plantation the servants, armed with handbills, rising in broad daylight, leaving the overseer in the field for dead; marching on the plantation house and slaughtering master and mistress and two small sons; the masters crying in Assembly that they were ruined, and Venables agreeing only this week to enlist no more servants. A madness had seized on the island this month, Fox said, and he had caught it with the rest. But he would not attempt escape again.

"But I shall," I said. "And if I know Munke, so shall he."

Munke smiled thinly. "You know me," he said. "Oh, aye, you know me, John."

"I would not, lad," Fox said. "They shall double your term—"

"They must catch me first."

"They shall. They return them from the ships every day. And Drax hath lost ten since the ships came, and his patience at an end. 'Tis very miracle I ha' not already been whipped."

"You shall be," I said. "I heard him so promise his sister." I read the bright panic in his eyes just before he lowered them. "But first things first," I said. "And he hath cane to harvest this week and need of all his hands."

"I shall labor my hardest this week. Mayhap that will mollify him."

"Mayhap," I said.

276

He raised his eyes into mine. "An I am whipped and thee a witness, I do not think thee will attempt escape, lad."

"I have seen a whipping. I think I will."

"With a cat. But hast ever seen a leaded bullwhip laid on by a black with a gift for it? I have seen five ribs broken in as many lashes. And welts raised to the thickness of a woman's wrist—"

"Nonetheless, I think I will."

He spread his hands. "Why, lad? In God's name, why?"

"Say I have no fondness for this pap they call food, this loblolly."

" 'Tis no matter for jesting."

"So it is not. And so say I will not be the first Englishman hath risked death or worse against liberty."

"Five years," he said. " 'Tis but five years. That were no eternity."

"It were," I said. "For I have a score to settle in England. And I lack the patience to dawdle here five years before paying it." I looked down the hill to the ships. "They have been here three weeks. How much longer before they sail, think you?"

"Some say a week. Some say a month. No one knows."

"But what think you?"

He shrugged. "Some say there are yet companies at half muster. I have heard that. Some say General Venables and Admiral Penn are at odds on place and plan, I have heard that. Some say they came ill provided with weapons, and this I can believe. For thee cannot get a horse shod or a wagon repaired these days; every smith on the island is busied at other work. Were I guessing, more like a month than a week, I would say."

"I shall pray you are right," I said.

He looked sadly at me. "I shall pray I am not," he said.

We were roused out at two the next morning, and marched by starlight a mile, and set to loading shides of wood into oxcarts. At daybreak, already so weary that I staggered when I straightened, we were led from thence to the cane fields.

It was barely day out, so early the dew still stood in great drops on the long, narrow leaves of the cane. But the fields were already alive with animals and folk—our overseer with a thick stick to hand; our master and mistress a-horse; quantities of small, black, grinning children; black girls with great, hard, jutting breasts; black women with the babes they call pickaninnies strapped to their backs; a scattering of Indians; in the lane the small, patient asses, wearing pack saddles such as you will see in Dorset, waiting heads down for the faggots of cane which they would carry half a mile to the ingenio and then return and all without being led by any human. There we were provided the small, curved handbills for cutting and then paired off, one black or Indian with one servant, the tutor and the unlearned. Me they paired off with an Indian girl.

She wore about her hips a thin girdle fashioned of tape and fish shells which hid nothing, and that was all. Her hair hung loose to her knees, and her breasts were neither child's nor woman's, and her cheekbones too high and her forehead too low and her nose too flat for beauty. But she owned the fairest eyes I have e'er looked into, brown and soft as a spaniel's. I thought at first that we spoke no common language, for she but motioned to me when we were paired off, and I followed her into the field, and she showed me the trick of cutting a cane—chopping it off six inches above ground, hacking off the top knob, then holding it in her left hand and stripping off the leaves with three swipes of her handbill, all the time nodding and smiling brightly at me. I was awkward at first; then I caught a little the knack of it, and again the nod and the quick, bright smile, and then we set to work side by side.

For those who are wont to complain of the hard lot that life hath dealt them, I can most heartily recommend labor for a pair of hours in a field of cane; it is a certain cure for self-pity. There is a constant breeze on the island but no stir of air at all in a crop that grows to three feet above a tall man's head, and the sun glowers down on you as merciless as God's disfavor, and the sweating stings you blind and leaves you weak and limp, and the long, thin, sharp leaves will draw blood if you do not grasp the cut cane with proper respect, and the constant stooping and straightening will fetch shrieks of protest from your back, and each time you stagger into the lane with a faggot, you are amazed that a field of but five acres can stretch forever and forever before you, to the horizon and beyond, like the sea when you have departed the sight of land. An hour in that field and I was cursing with each breath I drew Oliver Cromwell and John Thurloe and My Lord Monson and John Penruddock and the stupidity of rebellion. Two hours and my good will had fattened to embrace our overseer, who walked up and down the lane, stick idly swinging, eyes seemingly everywhere and nowhere, and my mistress, who had taken a fancy to me for I knew not what reason, and the Indian girl, who worked indefatigably beside me, or who, each time we squatted to bind another faggot, would nod cheerfully and smile shyly across the bundle. Three hours and (curses having purchased me nothing) I was wondering, each time I staggered into the lane with another faggot, what would happen, how savagely a man would be beaten, were he to fall down in the field and refuse to rise again.

The morning was well advanced when our mistress rode again down the lane. She stopped at our ass and examined the last faggot I had thrust through the crook of the pack saddle. "Daniel," she called out, and the overseer strode down the lane to her. "Whose cutting this?" she said.

"The Indian girl's," he said. "And do ye find some fault—"

"Fault? Fault? 'Sblood, examine it, man."

He did so. Then he looked across the stubble to us. "You," he called out. "Nina. Girl. Come ye here."

The girl had not ceased in her labor. But she was not unaware of the two in the lane; I caught her furtive, sidewise look when she stooped to chop off a cane, and when she straightened, her eyes were on them and not on the task at hand. And I saw the look that came into her eyes when he called for her. It was not fear, but it was something very like; it was as if a veil had fallen over her eyes, it was as if something within her had drawn up into a small, tight ball.

"You," the overseer called out again. "Come you hither, girl."

She crossed the stubble to him. I have never seen a back straighter or a head higher. When she was to him, he pointed with his stick to the faggot and said something I could not hear from this distance. She but stood there motionless. He waited. Then he struck her, once, with the stick, across the upper arm.

I could not see her face. But I had no need to, for I could read her back. She stood before him, back straight and head high and arms to her sides, and she made no move to defend herself; she did not duck her head or cringe or bring her hands up; she did not even clench her fists. He raised the stick again, and still she did not move. And standing there, looking across the stubble, I could imagine her face just now. It would be as impassive as stone, I thought, and the eyes would be elsewhere than on the overseer, they would be staring beyond him to something far away, and they would yet be veiled and unblinking.

And then, without thinking what I did, I was crossing the stubble. "Nay," I called out. "One moment an ye please."

The overseer's stick froze. The two of them, overseer and mistress, turned their heads slowly and looked at me, eyes wide and mouths agape, when I stepped down into the lane. "That were my cutting," I said. "An there be any fault in it, deal with me. But do not beat the girl."

The overseer still stared, amazed. "Your cutting?"

"It is. And is it not as the girl showed me—"

"Your cutting?" the overseer repeated, and then, soft and wondering, "Now, by God," and then he looked at my mistress. "And wilt explain this mystery, ma'am?" he said. "A servant that will step forth and ask for a drubbing to spare a naked Indian?"

My mistress was also staring at me. And then she was not. Then the amazement faded from her eyes, and she smiled a thin smile, and her eyes went to the girl's. Her eyes traveled slowly up and down the girl's body, and what was now in her face was something I found less to my liking than amazement. "Why, no mystery, Daniel," she said. "Is there, sirrah?"

"I know not what your meaning, ma'am," I said.

"Why, I mean love. I mean you are young and possessed of an itch that cries out for scratching. But one morning in the fields and art already courting, sirrah?"

I looked unblinking into her eyes. "Had I any thoughts of love, ma'am, they were for nought save simple justice."

She yet smiled that slight, knowing smile, and her eyes were as bright as if she had some fever in her. "And do I find you insolent yet, sirrah?" she said softly.

"Not by intent, ma'am."

"Not? Yet ye stand afore me covered?"

I removed my forgotten hat. "An you will instruct me in what fault I have committed," I said quietly, "I shall endeavor to amend it, ma'am."

"Fault?" She leaned and pointed to one of the canes in my faggot. "What color hath that?"

"Popinjay. I should call it popinjay, ma'am."

280

"And this one?"

"No color. Or if any, more yellow nor straw."

"Excellent. Now this one"—pointing to the popinjay—"this one were ripe. But this one were not. Dost know what a single green cane can do to a batch of syrup?"

"This would be my first week on the island, ma'am."

" 'Twill sour an entire cistern. Did not the girl so instruct you?"

"No, ma'am."

"And hath she not earned a beating, then?"

I was on the sudden a little mad, I think; it may have been the sun. "Why, aye," I said. "For plainly she hath one or two grave faults."

"I would ha' ye enlarge on that, sirrah?" Her voice on the sudden was soft in warning.

"She hath no command of English."

"And what other?"

"Other, ma'am?" The recklessness was now gone out of my voice.

"Ye named two. What other?"

I dropped my head. "No other, ma'am."

"What? Instruct me in what other, sirrah."

I drew a slow breath, the recklessness gone clean out of me, only the panic remaining. "She is not as fair as another of your purchases," I said. "I doubt she would fetch fifty pounds sterling—"

"That were enough." Her eyes in that fair, dainty, heart-shaped face had been bright before but now they were brighter yet, bright as the sea glittering in the sun below us and passionless as glass. "Ye go too far," she said. "Now, by God, but ye do."

"You bid me speak out, ma'am. I but did as you commanded me."

"And I have a mind to have you whipped for it." She paused, very briefly. "Look me in the face when thou'rt addressed, sirrah."

I did as she commanded.

"I shall instruct you in manners," she said softly, "an I have to shred your back to the bone. I vow I shall. An we had not this field to harvest, I should order it done this instant."

I ducked my head. "I thank you, ma'am."

"Do not. Thank God, rather. Or a field of ripe cane. Or ten servants made off this month." She glanced at the Indian girl. "Ye lack instruction in many things. Among others in the laws against bastardy here. They are very strict an ye be a servant."

"I shall bear it in mind, ma'am," I said. "I promise you, I shall."

She looked to the overseer. "Keep a close eye on this one, Daniel. An he pause once this day in his labor, but for a single instant mind you, do you not spare that stick."

She touched heel to horse, and the overseer's eye fell on me, and we turned, the girl and I, and went together back into the field.

I saw her face when she turned. And I saw it later when we faced each other across a faggot of cane. It was very serious; she no more smiled her quick, shy smile when she looked into my eyes. But her eyes were not now veiled, and there was a softness about her mouth, and the look she bestowed upon me contained a kind of wonder, like the gaze of a child who has never known anything but blows and then, one day, receives a caress instead.

"She whip you," she said, and for a moment I could not be certain she had spoken, for her lips moved not at all. "She whip you bad, I think."

I stared at her. "You speak English?"

She nodded. "*Si.*" She read my frown. "Yes-s. English." She pronounced it *Inglayza,* and I thought, They have fetched her people from the mainland, and would it have been Spanish or Portuguese, for I commanded neither tongue. "She whip you much," she said.

I bent over the faggot, my fingers slow and awkward with the knot. "I think she will not," I said.

"She whip you," she repeated. "For me."

I glanced once, quickly, into her face. "Not for you. For other reasons, mayhap. But not for you."

"For me." There was no uncertainty in her tone; she spoke a simple fact. "I be your woman now," she said. She reached out and touched one finger to my arm. "Hot," she said. "Like fire."

I shook my head. "It doth not pain—"

"Tonight," she said, "hot. You very sick. I fix."

I smiled at her. "I should be grateful."

Her hand dropped to mine, helping me with the knot. "Nina be your woman," she said. "In the night."

"I would not," I said. "No, I think I would not, girl."

"Young," she said. "Much man." She made a small movement with hand and hip; in another it would have been obscene, but for reasons I cannot give you, from this naked and doubtless heathen

282

girl it was somehow not. "I come to you in the night," she said. "I be much woman. You see."

I staggered to my feet with the faggot. "An you do," I said, "we shall share a whipping, I think."

She too came to her feet and reached out and relieved me of my burden. "I your woman," she said.

And in that there was no gainsaying her. At noon we halted work and I dropped where I stood and was immediately asleep. I awoke to her rubbing oil from out a small leathern bag on my shoulders and arms and legs. I do not know where she came by it or what it was; it smelled thick and faintly rancid. But I know it cooled my skin. And if it did not save my life, it at least spared me a night of discomfort. It is not uncommon on the island for men to die after a first day in the sun; no one among us did, for we had been a little seasoned on deck the *Edward and John*. But I alone, among the lot of us, slept the night through; and I alone, the next day, did not own a back and legs that were not blistered and raw and festered.

And in the night she came to me as she had said she would. At dark we staggered home, too weary to more than taste the food that was put before us; too weary to care overmuch whether we e'er opened our eyes to another day. But in the night I awoke and moved a hand and the girl lay beside me. A black guarded our door, and I do not know how she came there, and when we were roused out at daybreak, she was gone. But it was no dream, that she lay there beside me in the night.

No dream; she was my woman whether I would have it so or no. But not until later would I know how mysterious the ways of God, how wondrous the workings of a providence that had prompted me, foolishly and without thought, to step this morning forth in defense of a slave girl whose name I was not even certain of.

ᛚᚨ *Sixteen* ᛝᚢ

Whenever these days I am required to lay out tenpence a pound against good muscovado sugar, I remember my first fortnight on the island and do not begrudge the price. For never was commodity purchased more dearly. We were two days that first week at cutting cane and a third gathering the leavings for the livestock on the plantation. That accomplished, we were put to work in the barbion, a railed platform of ground without the ingenio; here the cut cane had cured two days and our task to fetch it twenty yards to the ingenio, where small asses plodded at the treadmill and where two enormous, sweat-glinting blacks fed the cane into great rollers and the juice splashed into a large flat tray beneath the machine and was then conveyed by lead gutters to the cisterns in the boiling house. We worked by both sun and lanthorn light now, for the liquor must not stand long enough in the cisterns to sour; we worked until we could work no longer and we slept where we dropped. And on Friday and Saturday we must gather wood for the fires under the great coppers in the boiling house, thirty of them all in a row, a black at each copper to skim and another to tend the fire, overseer and master now laboring with us shoulder to shoulder, for it was a strict law on the island that no one could be worked on the Sabbath, and a sea of liquor must be boiled and skimmed before that were upon us. By Saturday midnight it was done, the liquor moved in great iron ladles from one copper to another through

284

five boilings and skimmings, thence lugged in buckets to the still house to lie in the cisterns until it turned a little sour, for until then it would not, as they said, come over the helm.

But the second week was easier. We rebuilt fires Monday morning and fetched the liquor in the still house back to the coppers; now a temper was added, made of ashes and water, then the syrup boiled until it kerned, a word they use to mean that the liquor turns ropy and clammy, that it cruddles and separates. They call this boiling the tache, and the work was not hard now; much of the time we but stood about, watching the slow boiling and keeling and drawing up, waiting to lug the molasses back to the cooling cisterns. Once cooled, we poured it into wooden curing pots, these pots wider at top than bottom, in the bottom a hole the size of a man's thumb plugged with plantain leaves, the pots standing row upon row in stanchions in the curing houses; here it would stand three days a-sugaring, then the leaves pulled out and the molasses let drip a month into pans below each pot; later they would make of the drippings a cheap muscovado they call "penniless." A month hence they would drill through each pot with a long bit to vent the last of the molasses, and a day later take the pots to the knocking room and knock them hard on the floor and the sugar would come out all of a piece, the top brownish and frothy, the bottom dark, heavy, still full of molasses, the center dry and light brown and very sweet. Most planters on the island sold it just as it was knocked out of the pot for three pounds ten a hundredweight. But James Drax sliced off top and bottom and sold only the center, and this brought double the price.

By Friday sundown we were done with it—ten tons of sugar curing in the pots and Colonel James Drax richer by three thousand pounds; the skimmings from all the boilings souring in the cisterns and already smelling high (they would later distill these into a drink they call kill-devil, the most powerful I have ever tasted, strong enough to bring tears if you swallow it recklessly); sand thrown on the fires and the coppers scrubbed; ingenio and boiling house and still house swept, and servant and slave plodding homeward in the dusk with Saturday a holiday as reward.

And the Indian girl falling in beside me as I walked.

I was a straggler that evening, and midway to the compound she fell in beside me, her bare feet padding in the dust of the lane, her eyes looking a question into mine, her smile quick and bright and shy. "Why, Nina," I said. "You are called Nina?"

She nodded, pleased. "Nina. Yes-s. White name. Nina."

"White name?"

"White. Not Indian. Nina. White."

There was pride in her voice, and I looked at her and understood. We brought your people at sword's point from the mainland, we whites, I thought; we fetched you in chains across the great waters, and now we work you like dogs in our fields that a white man can take his ease and yet amass a fortune. And yet, I thought, you are proud of a name that is white and not of your people. "I am called John," I said. "That were a white name, too." And whatever was in my voice, it was not pride.

She said the name over, a little beneath her breath, her lips cautious but still unsuccessful with the *J*. And then, "Master much happy," she said.

"Why, aye," I said. "I should be too, were I richer by ten tons of sugar."

"Master much happy," she said. "Black not work one day. Indian not work one day. You not work one day." She dropped her eyes. "Nina your woman?" she asked.

I answered her carelessly. "An you would have it so."

"Tonight Nina your woman?"

Now I did not answer so carelessly. "Why, as to that," I said, "it hath been a cruel week, child. A weary week."

She seemed to falter in her stride an instant. Then she was looking sidewise at me, her head a little down, her eyes puzzled. "Wear-ry?"

"Tired," I said. "Sleep."

That word she knew, and she frowned. "Not walk wear-ry. Walk strong." Her eyes searched out my face. "You not want Nina be your woman, I think."

I stopped abruptly and faced her, there in the dusty lane, there in the dusk, and looked gravely down into her wide, grave eyes. "We have been warned, you and I," I said.

"You 'fraid?"

"Yes," I said softly. "Yes, I am afraid. For you as well as for me."

She shook her head. "Not be 'fraid. Not see, not hear, not know. You see. Dark I come."

286

"Nina," I said helplessly. "Look ye, Nina, she promised us a whipping, and there shall be a black guarding us—"

"No black. Black not work tomorrow. Black dance tonight. You hear?"

"I hear," I said, and I did—the first throb of the drums in the slave quarters, floating like some witchery across the dusk.

She nodded and smiled happily. "No black. You see. Dark I come."

I stood there in the thin side of dusk, with the last splotch of gaudy sunset pasted against the western sky, and the drums throbbing in the distance like some ancient and nameless rite, and the first of the night chill just settling about my shoulders—I stood there and looked into her eyes and would have said "Do not" but did not. For I knew not how. Her eyes in mine were not bold but neither were they shy, they were proud and firm and unashamed, like to the eyes of a wife who hath just invited her beloved and lawful husband to share her bed this night; and looking into those eyes I could hit on no arguments to advance that would say her nay and make her understand. Do you say to her, I do not love you, do you say that, I thought; we were slaves, and do oxen, then, know love? Do you say that sweet her delights might prove but you feared a whipping more than you desired to taste them; this girl had stood head high in a dusty lane and had not flinched to a stick about her shoulders, and did you confess to that? Did you say that ere another fortnight were out, you intended to be free of this place, and you would not leave with your bastard in her belly? For what did this girl, as innocent as Eve before the Fall, know of sin or law? Later, I thought, later will be time to tell her these things and others, slowly and carefully, and in a darkness that would hide from me her face. And so I told her nothing, only turned a little from her and shrugged small.

"Very well," I said. "If you would have it so, child."

"I come," she said.

And so she did. She had guessed aright, no black guarded us that night, and I sat without the hut awaiting her. There was a quarter moon, and the glow of a huge fire in the slave quarters a mile distant, and the sounds of drums and the sad, tuneless wailing of the blacks coming through the dark, and then I saw the flit of her shadow at the edge of the compound. She made no more sound than the night breeze might make in the parting of two blades of grass; and when she was to me and I arose and found her hand in the dark, I knew how it was that guard or no guard she had come to me that other night.

"I would walk a little, child," I said.

She made me no reply, only kept her hand obediently in mine while I led her to the grove of locusts above the compound. On the path I thought I could feel her hand tremble a little within mine, like some trapped bird. At the grove we sat down, and now I could smell the smell of her—not the stink of labor but a thin, clean, sweet, faintly musky smell. Days later she would tell me, in her abominably halting English, that it was the custom with them for a maiden on her wedding night to anoint herself all over with a perfumed oil they make; it was thought to have magical properties, for the smell of it would arouse desire in the lover and fertility in the beloved. I cannot vouch for the fertility, but for the other I can. We sat there, shoulder just touching shoulder, I looking down the hill into the darkness toward the ships that had still been at anchor there at sunset; and I smelled the smell of her and knew the stab of desire and thought my thoughts.

Which were these. Four hours since, we had talked, Fox and Munke and I, of this girl. They made but indifferent slaves, the Indians, Fox said; they died in captivity for reasons beyond the understanding of white men; some said they sickened simply from hunger for freedom, others swore that once enslaved, they could will themselves dead. Or, more often, they ran off, and no one ever successful at recovering them, not even dogs able to follow their trails; the caves and wilderness to the north were thick with such runaways, but you could search the place out inch by inch and ne'er a trace of hide nor hair of them. There they lived on wild pork and berries and suchlike. Or they built small boats they called can-o-as, and fashioned nets from a creeping weed on the island called *withs*, and fished off the rocky north coast. And just there in Fox's narrative, Munke came sharply upright and said "Boats," his eyes bright, and then he looked at me.

And I looked into the brightness in his eyes, and no need for words. Three of us meant to escape this place—a fourth if we could yet persuade Fox to join us—and the ships in Maxwell's Bay were anchored half a league offshore. And of the three of us, Andrew could not swim a stroke, and Munke and I but indifferently. But the Indians owned small boats, Fox had just said that. And an Indian girl had declared herself my woman.

And so, there in the dark, I said "Nina?" and she said "Yes-s," in that way she had of pronouncing the word, sibilantly, and I said, "I would talk with you, girl. Of your people. Dost know where they are to be found, the free ones?"

"There," she said. "Where sun go down in water. Much far."

"Nay. I mean your people here. The ones who have run away."

"Run away," she said. "Yes-s. Work in fields, white man whip, sick. Run away, not whip, not sick. Free."

"Aye," I said. "And could you find them out, think you? Could you take me to them?"

"You sick?" she said. "You run away?"

"Yes. I am sick. And I would run away. And three with me."

She pondered that a little. "You run away, I run away," she said. "Live with Indians, not work in fields, not sick. I be your woman. Much boy child. You see."

And there the rub, I thought wearily, there the rub. "No," I said. "No, we would not live with your people. We would have a boat from your people, we would go across the water, very far, many days."

"Boat?"

"Boat. Can-o-a."

"Can-o-a? Can-o-a much small. Can-o-a not go far on great water. White go in can-o-a, white die."

"I think we would not," I said. "For we would go but to the ships out there." I paused briefly. "To the great can-o-as. Out there."

Her hand moved in mine. Then it was very quiet on the sudden, and I knew she understood me. "Will you do this, girl?" I said. "Take me to your people?"

Still she was silent. It was not for very long, no longer than a dozen heartbeats, but it was long enough. And then, "Tonight?" she said, and I heard the sadness at the edge of her voice, and I was glad that I could not make out her face. "You run away tonight?"

"No," I said. "But soon. Four nights. Five nights."

Again she fell silent. Then she said, very simply, "I take." And then, "Nina be your woman now?" she said.

289

And in God's name, I thought, have you understood none of this, then? "Look you, Nina," I said, "I mean to be gone from this island. And do you not understand?"

"Not gone tonight."

"Not tonight. But soon."

"Not tonight," she repeated. "Nina be your woman tonight."

"Nina," I said, very patiently. "Child. I will be gone from this place within the month. And I would not leave with my child in your belly."

"Yes-s," she said, and for the first time this night her voice was happy. "Child," she said, and she turned full to me, her breast brushing my arm as she did so, and "Boy child," she said. And then, "No more talk now," she said.

That was long ago. But there are days when I find myself thinking back to that night, when I still hear in my memory, faint as some distant and uncertain echo, the sadness in her voice, when I smell the smell of her and feel the brush of her breast on my arm. And I do not welcome that memory, and I would tell you why if I could, but I cannot. For to speak truth, I do not know myself. There is an Indian girl yet on the island, and a child as well, I would guess; she was naked and heathen and I suppose godless, and I can name you divines who would reassure me that her soul is of no great consequence. And yet what I did that night I did not do in clean conscience. I did not take her simply because she was my way of escape; I did not take her coldly and expediently; God does not have to forgive me that sin; there was heat, there was passion; at the top of the fray she was, as she had promised me, much woman. And yet that were naked lust, for I bore her no true love. I think perhaps the island was in my blood that night. For it is not England, the island; life is different there, it is in the very air you breathe, the sun that falls hot on your back, the breeze that strokes the sweat from your cheek, the lush and brazen moon. It is a world where sisters with faces like angels' buy young mulatto girls for their brothers; where nakedness is a commonplace; where of an afternoon the sons of planters, the blood hot and high in them, will ride into the fields and bid an overseer send him this girl or that one, and an hour hence the black girl will emerge from the grove, breasts hard and jutting and eyes rolling and white teeth flashing, returned with scarce a second thought to her weeding. It is thus on the island, for slave as for free, and this was a tropic night, and the morrow was declared a holiday, and in the turning to me her breast brushed my arm, and I knew the hard, thick drive of lust. And for this, I think, would I know forgiveness, for heathen this girl may have been but she was innocent as well, none of your common whores, and so my act was betrayal.

I do not know. But this: this I know. When I left her, false dawn was not an hour off. But I could still hear the throb of drums from the slave quarters, and so I crossed the compound boldly and carelessly, certain that no black guarded us this night. And then my heart leaped within me, for on the sudden a shadow blocked my way. And then a voice and it was Munke's.

"Nay," he said. "No cause for fright, man." He stepped another step forward and thrust his face to within a foot of mine, trying to search out my face in the poor light. "Didst sound her out, your Indian girl?" he asked.

"I sounded her out," I said.

"And what her reply?"

"She will take us to her people."

"Good," he said. "Most excellent good." He fell silent. Then he chuckled. "And never escape purchased at sweeter rate," he said. "Eh, John?"

I heard his chuckle, and I read the slyness in his voice, and I knew on the sudden the bright flare of rage. This was Richard Munke who stood before me; this was my friend and we had walked through hell together. And it were none of his fault; the girl was but a naked savage; not ten men in England, I suppose, but would have thought as he. But for all that Munke never knew how close he came, just then, to being returned a blow he had once made me gift of.

"Eh, John?" he said again.

"Dost think so?" I said harshly, and I shouldered rudely past him. And then I turned back. "If you think so," I said, "I would the purchase had been yours."

And I cannot say what prompted that, neither.

Saturday was declared a holiday, but the day was not wholly ours. For four among us had attempted escape, and there was a whipping long promised and long overdue. And so late in the morning we were marched out to witness it, ten lashes apiece laid on by a black who was most consummately skillful at this, and Drax and his sister sitting their horses and watching—Drax indifferently, as if he had more pressing business to attend to this morning; his sister less indifferently, her eyes as hot and bright as if a fever burned within her and her lips a little parted and her breathing quick and shallow. And when it was over and done with, Drax wheeled his horse about and looked down upon us, his seat in the saddle a slouch but his eyes not so indifferent as I had thought and the lips beneath the mustache as thin as a scar.

"Now mark me, the lot o' you," he said. " 'Twere a light punishment I exacted here, a Christian punishment. But the next among you who would go a-swimming will not so easily escape; if I must bury him afterwards, he will not." He paused, and his eyes strayed westward toward the bay. "I doubt I should have ordered this," he said, "had we no more the company of those sails. But they are to be with us a fortnight longer. And they are a temptation, I confess to it. But if they should prove too strong a one, remember this day and be not foolish."

Munke and Andrew and I aided Fox in his slow walk back to the compound, and there we ministered as best we could to his poor back. He had been cut down within the hour, but already the welts were swollen to the thickness of my thumb and turned a dark purple where the skin was yet unbroken. We bathed his back in cold water fetched from the nearby spring, Munke's hand as gentle as a woman's but Fox still flinching when he was touched. And I crouched there and watched, and the rage within me was so thick and sullen that it was a sickness, it was as if I had gulped down some strong vomit.

Then someone touched my shoulder, and I turned my head and looked up into the bright, quick, shy smile of the Indian girl.

"He your friend?" she said.

"Yes," I said. "He is our friend, Nina."

"Then I fix." She touched Munke on the shoulder, and he looked around, and Munke looked at me, and I recalled the oil that first day in the fields and nodded.

Only this was something other, some kind of salve out of a small, round, wooden box, yellow as beeswax and soft as butter. A thing they called Negra oil, Fox told me later, a stuff most miraculously good for wounds and bruises. Very rare, he said; so rare it were a mystery how an Indian girl had come by a box of it; it was fetched here from the Barbary Coast, and ingredients lacking on the island to make more, and so the blacks who owned a bit of it guarded it jealously. A very great mystery how an Indian girl had come by it, he told me, and I think it was the salve and not the flogging or the nine more years of slavery he faced that made him decide, something later, to join Munke and Andrew and me in escape.

Rare the salve might have been, but the girl did not use it sparingly; Fox's back was a yellow film when finally he sat up. "Were that better?" I said.

There was yet sweat on his lip and forehead, but he managed a smile. "Aye," he said. "Though I think I shall be sleeping face down a night or two."

"And tell me this," I said. "Art still of a mind to endure this further, Somerset Fox? For nine more years to endure this?"

His eyes strayed to the girl. "That were Negra oil, I think," he said.

"I know not," I said impatiently. "Answer me. Art still—"

"I can endure ten lashes, lad. But next time it will be fifty. I doubt I could live through fifty lashes."

"And do you call this life? This?"

" 'Twere not death, lad."

"Is it not?"

Again his eyes strayed to the girl. "Negra oil," he said. "An she hath the wit to come by a box of Negra oil, she hath the wit to lead us away from here."

"Never doubt she hath."

"I know not," he said. "I must think on it a day or two, lad."

"Do so," I said. "For we have a fortnight. Drax said—"

But he was not attending me. "Negra oil," he said, as if to himself, and there was a kind of wonder in his voice.

Come Monday we were again in the fields, this time at planting. You plant cane by first burning off a field and then digging trenches six inches wide and six inches deep from one end of the field to the other; that accomplished, you lay ripe, fresh-cut cane in those trenches, two canes side by side. It is onerous work and felt in the back when you trudge homeward at night. But it is to be preferred

293

to cutting; there is much stooping to it, but there is none of the press to get the work done by this day or that one, and we were now seasoned to the sun, and in a plowed field there is a breeze.

The week was well advanced when our mistress rode into the fields. She drew rein in the lane and her eyes swept slowly over the field of kneeling blacks and whites. She had changed her ways, for she did not this day affect breeches and a man's shirt and bucket boots; she was dressed in a woman's riding habit, long skirt and modest bodice and dainty boots, and she sat her horse sidesaddle as was proper. Her only rashness was that sun or no sun she was uncovered, and her only immodesty that she wore her hair loose down her back. She was even fairer than I had thought, for almost her hair was the color and glint of silver in the sunlight, and briefly and idly I wondered at this change in her.

She sat her horse there for perhaps five minutes before the overseer crossed the field to her. They spoke together there in the lane, she still looking over the field of kneeling figures as if she were searching someone out, he standing at her horse's head, face raised to hers. Then he swung about and his eyes also swept the field.

"You," the overseer called out. "You are wanted here."

I knelt there and looked across the fifty feet of field to him.

"Aye," he said. "You, sirrah."

I made my way to them, then. I did not this time forget my hat, and I think I ducked head and touched forelock humbly enough.

She seemed to hold a like opinion. "It would seem," she said, and her voice softer than was her wont, "that someone hath lost his insolence this week."

"You may depend upon it, ma'am," I said. "For I have been at my lessons."

"Have you so? And who your tutor, may I ask?"

"A certain black, ma'am."

"A black? And what lesson taught he you?"

"It was a chapter on the art of whipping, ma'am."

She took no offense, only smiled the softer on me. "I think you have a quick wit," she said. "I can hope your memory is as long." And then her eyes wearied of this conceit. "Would you prefer another task to planting, I wonder?"

"But name it, ma'am."

"I would go a-riding. And I would be accompanied. I think you will not find it onerous."

"I can only hope I am worthy, ma'am." And now I dared a smile in return. "It sounds something easier on the back than digging."

"You may find it so," she said, and curiously she no longer smiled. "You may find it so," she repeated, and her voice short enough on the sudden that I wondered what new liberty I had just taken. And then she wheeled her horse about, more savagely than was needed, and set off down the lane; and for a short distance I must trot to keep her company.

The way she took led us two miles or more to the edge of the Drax plantation, to a grove of palmetto royals and one of the few streams on the island. Just where it exited the grove, the stream formed a pool shoulder-deep, and it was shady and cool here, very welcome after my hot, dusty walk. Save for the curious trees, it was very like a spot I could recall from boyhood, a place on the River Ouse where once Henry and I had swum and fished.

She had drawn rein just where the turf fell softly to the edge of the pool, and I was standing with my shoulder just touching the flank of her horse, and she was looking down upon me, and her eyes were a brown study. "Do you hope to escape me, man?" she said.

I returned to this world. I may have started guiltily. "What? What, ma'am?"

But she was smiling. "In your thoughts."

I ducked my head. "I beg your forgiveness, ma'am."

"You have it. So you but tell me where you have just been."

"Home, ma'am. There is a pool very like this one in Bedfordshire. My brother and I were wont to amuse ourselves on it of a summer's day." I smiled. "We fashioned us a pair of rafts one summer, and we used to quarrel as to who should be Sir Francis Drake and who the Spaniard. Then we commandeered young Tom Dykes, son of a groom, and after that he was the Spaniard and I Sir Francis and Henry our great-grandfather, the Lord High Admiral."

"The Admiral? You are a Howard?"

"My mother is."

"And your father?"

"The Earl of Peterborough, ma'am."

A distance came into her eyes. "So you did not lie to me. So you are gentleman indeed. And I have owned you nigh three weeks now, and still I do not know your name."

"It is John Mordaunt, ma'am."

A trifle longer the distance stayed in her eyes. Then she held out her arms to me, and I swung her out of the saddle. She stepped back from me and crinkled her nose.

"Faugh," she said. "You stink of the fields, John Mordaunt."

"No fault of mine, ma'am."

"It were if you do not shed your drawers and go bathing in yon pool." There was a bead or two of sweat to her forehead, and she brushed at it. " 'Tis uncommonly warm for March," she said. "I think the heat of the summer will be upon us early this year." Her eyes were very bright, as bright as another time I had looked into them. "If you will avert your eyes," she said, "I will join you a-swimming, John Mordaunt."

I did as she commanded me, turning my back and walking to the water's edge, my eyes on the shadowed pool and my thoughts on her eyes. For she had just now smiled sweetly on me, but her eyes were as hot as if she were possessed of some fever, and I had seen them thus another time while she had watched a flogging, and I was, on the sudden, afraid. Or if not afraid, uneasy; standing there, I knew a feeling like to a premonition, and I wished I were elsewhere than where I was.

And then to my left a flash of white and a splash, and the shimmer of her under water, and her face emerging, the silver hair all wet and the mouth laughing. "Come," she called out. "Come, John Mordaunt."

"I would you could forgive me, ma'am. For I cannot swim a stroke."

" 'Tis not all that deep. And if it were, I should rescue you. For I have a sweeter fate than drowning in mind for you, John Mordaunt."

I would have turned from her as I stepped out of my drawers, for her eyes were as bold and hard and curious as they had been the day she had studied my nakedness on deck a ship; and I would also have plunged into the pool as she had. But I did neither, only deliberately undressed and walked steadily and stiffly into the water.

We sported half an hour in the water. I was the first to call it quits, to walk forth from the pool as I had entered it, my back straight and stiff. I turned and watched her emerge from the water, young and boyishly built, and no command now to avert my eyes. But I dropped them nonetheless.

"Ye may stare an ye would," she said quietly.

"I think it not seemly, ma'am," I said. "For you are who you are, and I am who I am."

"And if I command you?" I raised my eyes, and she smiled as softly as she spoke. "Dost find me fair to look on, John Mordaunt?"

"Should I, ma'am?"

"Should you not?"

"I cannot know. I ha' been bought and paid for. Should one of your cattle find you so?"

"I find that no true argument. Servants are still men unless they have been gelded. Dost find me as fair to look on as your Indian girl?"

"Fairer, ma'am."

"Why, good." She was close enough now that I could have reached out and seized her, though I did not. "She is heathen and I Christian," she said. "But you may find me as wanton, John Mordaunt."

I looked into her smile, soft and seductive as sin, and into her eyes, hot and bright and fevered, and now I was afraid, more afraid than I had ever been within memory; the fear was as thick as phlegm in my throat. "What would ye of me, ma'am?" I said.

She laughed lightly. "La, now," she said. "Thou'rt no gelding, my eyes testify to that. And I had not thought you fool, neither."

"Nor am I," I said. "But I am a slave, and I stink of the fields, and my face not scraped and my hair not trimmed. And I think you are no wanton, ma'am, no whore, though your smile would have it so. And so what would ye of me?"

"If you are no fool," she said, very softly, "you will fence with me no longer, John Mordaunt."

And so I did not. I was doubtless damned if I did, but I was certainly damned if I did not, for the warning in her voice was plain. And so I ended the prattle and reached and seized on her.

I looked the while into her face. Her eyes were closed, and her mouth was twisted as if she were being put to the rack, and small, furred, muted sounds from deep within her throat, and I looked the entire while at the tortured lips and at the small, white, even teeth behind them, and I found no pleasure in this but only a thick, sick fear within me, like a hair ball lodged in my throat.

And then she opened her eyes sleepily and placed a finger to my lips and traced them out. "And did I not speak truth?" she said. "Am I not wanton, John Mordaunt?"

"Aye," I said.

"Wanton," she murmured. "And you no gelding. And what think ye of your Indian girl now, John Mordaunt?"

"I would not know, ma'am. For I know not of what ye speak."

She traced out my lips again. "Ye lie," she said softly. "Ye lie most brazenly, John Mordaunt. And so I think I must have you whipped." She searched out my face with sleepy, lidded eyes. "Doth that not surprise you?"

I shook my head. "I had expected little else at your hands. Not for an hour now. Though what pretense you will forward I cannot guess."

"I require none. But if I did, it would be your new-found humility. I can suffer insolence on occasion. But humility I cannot abide."

"Then I shall endeavor to amend it," I said, and I closed my eyes against the sight of her face.

"Fifty lashes, I think," she said.

"An ye hope to hear me beg and whine," I said, "do not. I have made you gift already of what pride I can spare. And if I cannot escape this island one way, I may another."

"Fifty lashes," she repeated. "I am resolved on it." She put her two hands to my chest and pushed me off her. "Avert your eyes from me," she said.

"I already have, ma'am," I said.

Five times in a pair of months I had watched men jerk and jump under the whip; five times I had thought that almost I could feel the lash myself as it snaked and coiled about a man's ribs or shoulders. But there is no imagining a flogging; you must experience it to know. The first lash is like the blow of a bludgeon in the small of the back; it will drive the air out of your lungs in a great whish, and afterwards you will swear that your spine has snapped, and you think, I will not cry out after all, she will not hear me cry out, it is not unendurable and she will rot in hell ere she hears me cry out for

298

I can feel nothing. And then you can. You begin to count, a second blow about the shoulders and a third coiling about the buttocks and a fourth crisscrossing the first, and suddenly your back is on fire from shoulders to knees, it is as if you had been stung by a thousand wasps, and you think, I will not cry out, do not let me cry out, oh, Christ, let me not cry out.

And then you know you will not. You count now through a haze, eight and nine and ten, and you know she will sit her horse forever and ever, until Doomsday and beyond, her eyes bright and hot on you, and you will not cry out.

And then, blessedly, you can feel almost nothing. There is the haze, growing thick and thicker, your count no longer certain for all the buzzing in your ears and the fog about you as thick as six o' the clock of a London morning. And then there is only darkness, like sleep. There is the fog, very thick now, and you lower your head and plunge into it as you might plunge into water, and on the sudden the fog is darkness, like the dead of a winter night, like the hour between false dawn and sunup, like thick, soft velvet. And you laugh aloud.

You laugh aloud. For you could take your oath on it that you had not cried out.

When I swam back into this world, I was sprawled face down on trampled and dusty turf, and a murmur of voices all about me, and fingers, very gentle, on my back, and I thought, Did I not die, then? My back was afire from shoulder to knee, and I thought, Fifty lashes and I did not die? Then I moved a little, but one hand an inch or so, and then I decided abruptly against any more of that.

"Softly," a voice said. "Softly," and I thought a little and it was Andrew's voice.

"Did I not die then, Andrew?" I said.

"Why, no," he said.

"Fifty lashes," I said wonderingly. "Fifty lashes and I did not die. And were that not a very miracle, man?"

"Not fifty." That were another voice, Munke's voice. "She called a halt to it at thirty. Lie quiet, man, till the girl hath done wi' your back."

"How bad is it, my back?"

"Why, bruised a little, John. Bruised a little."

"The truth, Munke," I said.

"Bruised," he said. "And bloodied. But I have seen worse."

I lay quiet awhile, grateful for the gentle hands, the feel of the Negra oil, like cool mud. And then, "Munke," I said. "Art still there, Munke?"

"Here, John."

"I would escape from this place now," I said.

"Why, aye," he said. "In a day or two. When your back—"

"Not in a day or two. Tonight."

"Nay, John," he said softly. "You could not walk a mile with that back."

"Not in a day or two." I moved an arm, and it was not comfortable but neither was it unendurable, and so I set my teeth and got to my hands and knees. I stayed there a little, head hanging, swallowing down the sickness. "I can walk a mile," I said, "and yet another," and then I came to my feet. I swayed a little there in the thickening dusk, but I was on my feet, I was by God on my feet. "Tonight," I said.

ᚷᚪ *Seventeen* ᚦᚷ

It yet lacked an hour to sundown, and so we hugged the rocky, wind-swept shore closely, I sitting rigidly quiet in this curious and nervous boat they called a can-o-a, watching the lean of the girl and the flash and dip of the paddle, still marveling after three hours that any human would dare breathe overdeep in a craft as treacherous as this, let alone paddle it.

"Would that be it?" I said. "The bay? Beyond that point, Nina?"

She frowned. "Bay?"

"The anchorage," I said patiently. "Ships. Big can-o-as."

"Yes-s," she said, and I sighed, for ten times since we had set out she had delivered me this same answer.

Only this time she spoke the truth. We drove down around the point, and suddenly, in the angry flare of the setting sun, Spyke's Bay lay before us and the ships all riding at anchor, ten or a dozen of them.

I gestured and she ran the can-o-a ashore. I winced when I stepped out, and she looked at me, her eyes troubled, and I smiled and shook my head.

"It is but stiff from too long sitting," I said. And that the truth, for it had now been six days since my whipping; six days since we had left a black with a bloodied head sprawled in the compound and fled north. We had floundered for two nights through water to throw off the dogs, twenty miles to the caves and cliffs on the northern tip of the island; and afterwards I had fought my bout with fever. But I

301

had since walked for three days on the beach in the sun, and Nina's Negra oil was indeed a most miraculous healer, and now there was only the stiffness and an occasional twinge to remind me.

I helped beach the can-o-a. Then, from behind a rock, I studied the ships. This was the windward side of the island and the anchorage tricky, and most of the ships were small and close in. But one was not small. One was a frigate of fifty guns and anchored further out. And that would be the *Paragon*, I thought, with Major General Heane's regiment aboard, Heane still beating the drums in Bridgetown if the Indian could be relied on, his regiment still at half muster if I were in luck.

"That great one far out," I said. "Canst get me through the others to her, think you? In the dark?"

"Yes-s."

I looked at her, and she was smiling brightly, and I thought wearily that even after a month I could still make almost nothing of her expressions. For five days we had not been out of each other's sight, I thought, but give me that many years and I would still not be able to read her thoughts in her face nor even be certain when she understood me.

"It must be just that one," I said. "And in the dark with nought but their lanthorns to guide me. Dost understand me, Nina?"

"Yes-s," she said. "I take. You see." She reached for my hand. "We sleep now?" she said, and there was sadness at the edge of her voice. She was smiling, but there was sadness in her voice.

"Yes," I said. "We sleep. Until dark."

"I fix back," she said, and there was the look in her eye, like eagerness, which was always present when she could serve me, and there was the grave sadness in her voice, and I turned a little away from her.

"It doth not require it, Nina," I said shortly. "It is near healed."

There was no moon that night, and the stars provided no very certain light. But the sea was calm, thanks be to God, and the frigate carried lanthorns fore and aft to guide us. From fifty yards off I whispered to the girl to cease paddling while I listened; it was so quiet aboard the frigate that I knew her regiment must be ashore, only the idle lap of the water against her hull and the muffled tread of the watch and a vague, bulky shadow in the almost dark left behind to tell me she was there. I listened and then I called out, having no great desire for a sudden challenge and a musket ball fired down my throat, and a call came back, asking me to name myself.

"Friend," I said. "Come to help you fight the Spaniard."

Two of them greeted me when I threw a leg over the bulwark; the one thrust a lanthorn into my face. "Another one, Nick," he said. "The second this week, and this but Wednesday."

"I think," the second said, "that ye ha' stepped foot aboard the wrong frigate, man."

It seemed to me that I had heard this voice somewhere before. "Am I not right for General Heane's regiment?" I said.

"Ye might be."

"And is not the General still beating up the drums in Bridgetown?"

"He might be. For anything save women and ancients and runaway servants."

The voice was familiar, I was certain of it. "Art so certain I—"

He laughed. "Dressed thus? In those drawers?"

He laughed, and the laugh was as familiar as the voice, and I searched my memory and found the time and the place. "Would you take me to him?" I said.

He laughed again. "The General retires early."

"For auld lang syne?" I said. "For memory of shared bottles of wine? Would ye but take me to him, Nick Swiftsure?"

There was, I think, a full minute of silence, very deadly. Then it was Nick's turn to thrust the lanthorn into my face. "An I know ye," he said, "I cannot say from when or where."

I reminded him and he cursed softly. "Now, by God, but ye ha' changed. Ye ha' added years. 'Sblood but ye have."

"'Tis very likely. Hast e'er chopped sugar, Nick? But a quarter hour with your General, man."

He shook his head. "It would be to no purpose. They shall be aboard searching you out afore noon to—"

"I think not. For I ran off a full week ago, Nick."

"The General is a godly man," he said. "And honorable. And he has firm orders. Any officer who knowingly takes on a runaway to be broken—"

"Godly were one thing," I said. "Numbers were another. Art at full muster, Nick?"

"Not three quarters. But still no room for runa—"

"But take me to him, then. I shall ask no more of ye, Nick."

He shrugged. "An I do, ye had best have a lawyer's tongue in your mouth."

"I need none," I said. "An he be godly, I ha' but to tell him a small tale."

Major General James Heane was a great hulk of a man, a head taller than I and three stone heavier, with a broad, blunt, honest face and uncompromising eyes. And, as Nick had fairly warned me, a godly man. He had not yet retired when I was brought before him, and he heard me out for the length of one sentence and part of another, and then he said no. He said no at some length. His regiment numbered but seven hundred, he said, and he charged to raise it to a thousand before the week was out; but if it numbered not half that, he would have none of me, for he had no humor for runaway servants. They were nought but thievish, lazy cutpurses and cheats, your Barbados servants, he said, for this island was the dunghill whereon England did cast forth its rubbish; and if they were not, they were worse, they were Cavaliers who had ne'er won a battle at home and would not help to win one here. There were enough of our kind already in this army, he said; he had been ten years a soldier, and he had ne'er laid eyes on a more unmilitary crew than he now commanded—profane to a man, and debauched, and scorners of religion, very bold to do mischief but not to be commanded as soldiers or kept in any civil order. And he would compound the felony no further; his orders were to keep me under close guard the night and to return me come dawn, for he would have none of me.

I heard him patiently out. And then, very humbly, I asked him to grant me but five minutes of his attention.

He studied me. "Ye have it," he said. "It is small enough request, and I shall not deny it you. But you get no more from me than this."

"I ask you but to look at my back," I said, "and hear how I came by it. For I think it may test your godliness, sir."

He heard me out, hunched far down in his chair, his eyes on the papers that littered the table before him, his great, broad face brooding and gloomy. "You have a smooth tongue," he said, when I had told my tale. "A lawyer's tongue. I cannot trust so oily a tongue, I think."

"It is honesty coats it so," I said. "And I do not lie to you, sir. If you would have me take an oath—"

"An oath?" he said dryly. "You admit to being a follower of this pretended king, this known whoremaster and suspected papist, this Charles Stuart? And ye speak to me of oaths?"

"We are some of us men of honor," I said. "Even as some of you. But if my word fail to satisfy you, I can produce three witnesses—"

"Three?" he said softly. "Three? Do you mean to tell me that four o' you—"

"Aye. One an ex-captain of foot in your own parliamentary army, and an honest man. And the second a Quaker and godly. And if your men are as bad as you say, you can use Captain Munke. And me, I can hope."

"What?" he said. "A king's man, but you would spill your blood for the Protector?"

But in the end he was persuaded. He had his orders not to muster servants, he said, and he warned me fair that should they come in search of me, he would give me over into their hands. Nor were we to think that the expedition was all plunder and no fighting; we should be put in the thick of it, we should be under his eye, we should be hanged out of hand if we but wavered an instant. He could name you men he would have preferred to a cashiered parliamentary captain and a seditious Quaker and a confessed king's man, he grumbled, but this business was already doomed, it was in the hands of rogues, men not fit to further the Almighty's purpose in these parts, and so you must work how you could with what the Lord put into your hands. And so in the end he was persuaded, for he was still three hundred short of muster, and I would guess that he detested debauchery even more than disobedience.

Abovedecks again, I called out to Nina and she answered from twenty yards out. "Go back," I said. "Tell Munke it is all right. Tell him the fleet still waits for their supply ships to come up. But if they do not, we sail within the week."

That was my farewell to her, and the last time ever I saw her.

There was an army, if you could call it such. In numbers it was the bravest ever sent into these parts by any power, Spain included

305

—fifty-five ships transporting seven regiments of foot, nine thousand men if you counted our hundred reformados, and our sixty horse, and our fifty artillerymen, and our hundred and twenty firelocks, and a hundred wives, come along to nurse the sick and wounded. But all the bravery of that army lay in its numbers. From England had come five regiments of five hundred each, and not one in twenty had e'er seen service or even drilled more nor thrice; the lot of them were raw fellows drafted out of the Protector's Irish regiments; or hectors, knights of the blade, very forward were it to come to plunder but as quick to run in the face of danger as the next man; or slothful, thievish servants; or runaway 'prentices; or common cheats and cutpurses out of Newgate and Bridewell. And those they drummed up in the Barbados were as abject—broken planters hoping to recover their fortunes in the sack of Santo Domingo, or debtors fleeing their debts, or servants escaping servitude. Nine thousand we numbered, and I would have traded the lot for Drake's thousand and given you something over in the bargain.

There was an army and it was supplied, if you could call it such. Desborough had had a hand in the victualing of the fleet, and he had not looked sidewise at his profits; so rotten were the biscuits and oatmeal and salt meat that General Venables had refused them out of hand at Portsmouth—only to have the Victualers of the Fleet send them ahead of him to the Barbados and the price doubled when the fleet arrived. As for brandy, that was gone before the fleet arrived at the island. For firearms we had two thousand ancient, rusty matchlocks instead of flintlocks, half of them unfixed if not totally defective, for the gunsmith tools were all aboard the supply ships that never came. We had few pikes and no lances at all; pike heads there were but no shafts, so we must be content with half or quarter pikes fashioned, for lack of ash, out of cabbage stalks cut on the island. For ammunition twenty tun of ball and ten tun of match would have been no overabundance; we had a tenth that, not fifteen shot or two foot of match to a man, and our powder was English and spoiled quickly in this climate. For artillery we had two drakes and a mortar. For pistols and carbines we had one for every fortieth man; and of linen for the chirurgeons or tents or blackjacks—leather bottles for carrying water on a forced march—we had none at all.

There was an army, so constituted and so supplied, and the command of it was in this fashion. The Protector had given the execution of the "Western Design" into the hands of five commissioners. And from the start the commissioners were at odds on every vote, Edward Winslow siding with Venables, General of the Army, and Daniel Searl siding with Sir William Penn, Admiral of the Fleet, and Captain Gregory Butler siding nowhere but only sniffing out how he could foment further trouble—"the unfittest man for a commission I ever knew employed," Venables said of Butler. "Truth is, I know not what use he is, unless it be to make up a number."

There was as well bad blood between our commanders, for each was jealous of the lengths of his command and each grudging of what credit the other might realize from this business. By Hispaniola it was unfeigned war between these two. By then Penn was saying openly that Venables' only quality as a commander was the very great caution you could expect in a man who had brought along his wife; the accusation was a half truth, at least. Venables in turn accused Penn of hoarding supplies against the army in order to undo him, and that was the entire truth, for in a fortnight at sea the army was on half rations on all the meat days and on fish days we tasted only biscuit and water, and we never tasted brandy once, and we were put ashore with but fifteen shot and a foot of match and a handful of powder apiece.

As for our staff officers, the tale was even sadder. Major General Heane of the second regiment was a stout man and godly—the finest soldier in England, some would have it—but he was sullen because Cromwell had given Venables the command. And Fortescue of the third was also ne'er accused of cowardice, though he was overfond of the bottle. But Colonel Carter of the fifth was a fret, a sot, and a very great curser and swearer, with the worst-disciplined troops I ever saw; and Colonel Buller of the fourth was vain and pompous and knew not how to obey an order, a trait that was to cost us dear. As for Adjutant General Jackson, he was to cost us dearer; a drunk and a whoremaster, with two known wives in England and a third on the Barbados, with forgery and perjury in his past and rank cowardice in his future, he was to cost us dear indeed.

There was an army, so constituted and so supplied and so commanded. And on the last day of March in the year of our Lord 1655, we fired off a gun and loosed the fore-topsail on the Admiral, signal for the army to come aboard. A fortnight later, on the thirteenth of April, we hove to before Santo Domingo on the island of Hispaniola, an exceeding great force sent into these parts not to pillage but to plant, not to plunder but to propagate the Gospel and the only true Word of God among the heathen and the papists who lived under the flag of Spain.

Had we been veterans of Cromwell's Ironsides and not gallows bait, we would still have been an unfit army to relieve King Philip of one of his fairest islands. For we had lived on half rations the entire voyage, and the men were half starved and so weak that when they were put ashore the next day, they fell down in the water under the weight of cuirass and pack and seventy-pound muskets, and three drowned. And by now it was common gossip that the command of this business was divided. And so there was no longer any brave talk that Friday afternoon of Drake and his thousand men, who had taken Santo Domingo seventy years before and held it a month and then sold it back to the Spaniard for seven thousand pounds sterling. We lay before Santo Domingo, a fair, large city set down in the middle of a great savannah or plain, with a wall to the west and a river to the east and a thick lime hedge to the north and six new bronze guns commanding the harbor, and our talk was not of Drake but only of whether the command would choose to assault the city from the sea, or land at the mouth of the River Hina and storm the town from the east.

They held a council of war aboard the *Swiftsure* that afternoon. When Heane returned and climbed aboard, his face was black enough that men stepped out of his way to let him pass. Which meant they had again discussed the landing and Heane again overridden, I thought. Thrice now in as many days they had debated the place of landing, and by now the fleet bristled with rumors. Heane had argued in council that the army was half starved and unable to endure a long march, and if Penn would sail in before the town and batter the walls, he, Heane, with but the sea regiment and five hundred of his own men, would land on the town quay and clear the way to the very gates. That plan Penn opposed because of a supposed boom blocking the sea road into the harbor. And Venables was for landing at the River Hina, provided we were unopposed there; and if we were, then he was for landing ten leagues east of the city, at Point Nisao.

Only this day they had not debated the landing, as we were to learn the next afternoon. On Saturday we sailed east up the coast, the Vice-Admiral and its squadron, going in close enough at the River Hina to see the ditch and the mounted guns and so sailing on to the place they called Point Nisao. Here seventy-five hundred of us landed unopposed, and they drew us up in order, by regiment, and General Venables stepped ashore between two aides. He was a gray-faced man, once given to portliness but a little wasted away now by two sea voyages and the weightiness of this business and the demands of a young wife; and it did not pass unnoticed that he had been the last to step ashore where Heane had been the first. Now, while we stood in rigid order under a sun that not a quarter of us were seasoned to, with the sweat already itching under doublets and breastplates, and muskets and pikes and packs already a burden, we heard our General announce the newest policy to come from the commissioners, which was the policy of no plunder. Twenty-five hundred of us had had no pay since Portsmouth, and the rest had had none never, and we had lived two weeks on wormy biscuits and rancid water, and we had endured the gibes of the seamen—they had lately taken to calling us dogs—and we had been put ashore with one day's rations and unserviceable weapons and fifteen shot and but a pinch of uncertain powder in our bandoliers, and now we heard that there would be no plunder. On pain of death, Venables said, in a voice as light and dry and gray as his complexion, for we landed here not to spoil but to bring the true Word of God to heathen and superstitious papists. And so the commissioners had voted that all goods and plate and money was to be delivered into a public store for the carrying on of the design and the use of My Lord Protector. We should have six weeks' pay the day we took the city, he said, but there would be no plunder.

There were no murmurs; we heard him out in stony and sullen silence. When he was done, I looked to Richard Munke on my right and to Nick Swiftsure on my left, and if what was written on these two faces was written on all, it boded no good for the success of this business.

"Is he mad?" Nick said. "Are those five that call themselves commissioners gone clean mad?"

"Why, no," Munke said. "Rather they are all secretly king's men. And they have chosen this way to undo the Protector."

309

"For the carrying on of the design," Nick said. "What means the bastard, for the carrying on of the design?"

"It were politeness," Munke said, "for the pockets of the commissioners. And if any should be left over, that were for pockets at home."

"If you fight at home," Nick said, "you fight for pay. That I have heard of. If you fight abroad, you fight for pay and plunder, that also I have heard of. But I have not heard of men spilling blood for neither." He looked at me, his face livid with anger. "There shall be hanging ere they enforce that policy," he said. "Mark me but there shall be."

"Or running," Munke said. "We had best not be opposed on this march, not by so many as two hundred, else there shall be running."

"And I in the van of it," Nick said.

He was prophet there, was Nick Swiftsure. They were both prophets there.

But for three days we were afforded no cause. For three days we but marched, four miles the first day, eighteen the second, twelve the third, and our only enemy was the country itself. The first day was but a minor trial, for we marched only two hours in the cool of the late afternoon and bivouacked the night in a large savannah; here was a pleasant river and a single, rude dwelling belonging to one of the island's cow killers, and Captain Pawlett's firelocks burned it and then very bravely swaggered back to our fires. But the second day was another tale. We marched ten miles that Sabbath morning through country burned up with drought, with the sun flaring down like the wrathful countenance of Almighty God Himself, and the broad, sandy road scorching our feet and so white it could blister eyeballs, and the savannahs along the way burned off by the Spaniard to drive away the wild cattle, and at the plantations the wells stinking with the dead animals the enemy had thrown into them. By ten in the morning we were raging with thirst, and men and horses would fall down and die on the spot unless you poured a mouthful of liquor into them, and a blind man could have followed our trail, for all behind us the way was littered with muskets and shovels and pickaxes that the men had thrown away as they marched.

310

But afternoon was better. Near noon we came to a small, grassy plain with a river channel cutting through it, the river dried up save for muddy water standing in a few holes. The forlorn shouted out when it came upon the river, and then the van cried out, "Water! Water!" and the regiments behind taking up the cry, and then the men breaking ranks, with Venables standing in the middle of the road and screaming out to them to maintain order and then leaping aside else he would have been trampled, and weapons hurled down, and for a little everything a wild, mad scramble as men plunged over the bank and fell to fighting like animals over who would wet tongue first in those puddles. We rested here an hour.

A mile further on and we came to a grassy lane, seven miles long and all arched over with orange trees. The oranges were green, but the men plucked them nonetheless and sucked them as they marched, and now there was singing in the ranks, and at three in the afternoon another rest and a half hour of sport. The reformados had the forlorn that day, and they it was who found the monastery. They had been sent out to forage for horses, and one of their number swaggered back with a statue of the Virgin on his head, very richly clad and the Christ Child in her arms. He set up a shout when he stepped into the lane, and fifty gathered around him and seized on her and stripped her naked and then fell to making obscene jests, while Venables stood grayly by, not liking this but not putting a stop to it neither, and Heane must finally step forward and order them to cease else he would have them whipped for the foulness of their tongues. They were none of Heane's regiment, but they looked at him and ceased the bawdry. But one let fly an orange at her, and then they all must take up that game, pelting her with oranges until she was battered and dripping and ruined.

We did not join in that sport. The five of us, Munke and Fox and Nick and Andrew and I, lounged down in the shade and watched, and Munke's face was dour and brooding. "I have seen rabble they called armies," he said. "But ne'er the like to equal this. Were I Venables, I should already be regretting the weight of this business. And hath he not the force nor the wit to call a halt to such blasphemy?"

"Blasphemy?" Fox said. "Thee call it blasphemy, Richard? When it is nought but a superstitious image and idolatrous—"

"To the Spaniard," Munke said, "it is blasphemy."

"Do not speak foolishness, man," Fox said. "It is Romish superstition thee speak of and a wickedness in the sight of all godly."

Munke looked at him. "We shall see," he said, "when we are engaged."

"Engaged?" Nick laughed. "Engaged? We are near ten thousand to their one, and mark me, we shall not be engaged. Not an we march to the very walls—"

"We shall be," Munke said, his voice stubborn. "Whatever else ye may lay to the Spaniard, he is no stranger to courage. And when they close with us, yon ruined lady will be fighting with them. And let us then mark which makes all the difference."

"Which?" I said. "What mean you which, Richard?"

He looked gloomily at me. "Numbers or heart," he said.

We bivouacked that night in a burned-over, desolate, waterless savannah. We had long since eaten up our allowances of biscuit and boiled beef, and there was no water and no more oranges, and in the night you could hear the men whimpering in their sleep for thirst. And that night the bloody flux came a-visiting. It was brought on by a fortnight of bad diet and green oranges and no brandy, and the next morning there were stragglers as well as articles to mark the line of our march, with men dropping out every ten steps to run into convenient bushes and drop breeches. Near a hundred of us must have died that morning, most of them from the glare of sun overhead, or from thirst, or from the twisting and griping in their guts. But some were murdered, for the cow killers on the island were now with us. They were men who hunted the wild cattle on the island with lances two feet longer than any we carried, and they would come upon a man squatting in the bushes, and they would lance him through and through before he could stagger to his feet or even cry out in sudden and final terror. A dozen of us must have been so dispatched, and by noon the cow killers were coming boldly into the road behind us to work their work upon us. But we were so spent and dispirited that we did not offer them chase or waste our small store of powder and ball on them; we only plodded grimly on, our eyes fixed on the road at our feet, our only thought the desperate one that if we should fall out, we were dead men, too.

* * *

We came up to the mouth of the River Hina Monday afternoon. We had marched for three hours into the dull, distant boom of naval ordnance, and now we learned the cause. For Rear Admiral Dakin's squadron rode in the bay there; freed from the doubts and caution of Penn, he had that morning run the *Martin* galley into shore and fired into the breastwork, and the Spaniards had all fled, and he had landed Buller's regiment on the east bank of the river. He had also landed food; we stood on the west bank, our guts growling from two days' fasting, and looked across to the barrels of boiled beef and the canvas bags of biscuit a half mile out of our reach.

And to no army. Where there should have been a regiment, there was but one man, a sergeant who stripped and swam the river to us with intelligence. Buller had landed at ten that morning with strict orders to wait until we came up. But Colonel Anthony Buller was an ambitious man. Colonel Anthony Buller had a hunger in him for glory. And an hour after he had landed, a Negro had come to him with a story of every Spaniard on the island cowering in quaking terror behind the walls of Santo Domingo. There were not two thousand Spaniards on all the island, the Negro said, and half those women and children and terrified priests. And so Colonel Anthony Buller, with the smell of glory and advancement strong in his nostrils, had marched off to take the city, with fifteen hundred men and a Negro sent him from the enemy.

And with him our only guide, the man Cox.

So we stood on the west bank of the river, seventy-five hundred starving men, with food a bowshot away but still as distant as England for all the good it did us. For without a guide we knew not where to ford the river. In these parts of the world, the sea current will build a sand bar across the mouth of every river; you have but to know of it and you can cross any river on any of these islands and never wet knee. But none among us was acquainted with these parts. And so at five that afternoon we were marching again, this time up river in search of a ford.

We found none all that night. Indeed, by ten we lost the river itself, though we stumbled on a plantation. Its wells, like all others within twenty miles of the city, stunk with rotting horses and dogs. But we found sugar to gnaw on and a grove of lemon trees. Here we bivouacked the night, while search parties stumbled about in the dark in search of the river, and got lost in the woods, and on

313

occasion fired on one another. Our men wounded four that night, none of them the enemy. And at camp another dozen died of thirst or the flux or, perhaps, simple despair.

At dawn one of our parties found the river again and a ford as well, and by midmorning we had crossed the river. We had marched that night seven miles out of our way.

The east side of the river was a crisscross of lanes and roads going every which way. Within an hour we lost the river again, and thrice before noon we found ourselves marching west by north rather than east by south, and we must turn about, the entire army, with rear and van reversed and no forlorn to scout the way. It was afternoon before we heard the distant, hollow roll of Buller's drums. An hour later we stumbled on a search party who led us to Buller's regiment, and to the guide Cox, and to the news that the enemy had finally engaged us. The city of Santo Domingo lay a mile and a half straight ahead, Cox told Venables, but the road was commanded by a fort which was called Fort Geronimo.

Just where we stood, the road was so broad that twenty men could march abreast and as hard and white as Surrey limestone. We stood in that road under a tropic sun and itched and sweated under breastplate or buff coat and thought on water and shade, while Venables and Cox and Heane and five or six field officers held a council of war. They stood not twenty feet from me, and Cox was a man whose voice carried, and I heard all his argument. He knew this fort, he said. It was a small fort, boasting only seven pieces of ordnance, and it was unflanked by breastworks or other forts, and give him four hundred resolute men and he would promise to take it. But let it stand and it would gall us as we marched past, for just where it stood the way narrowed; and if we did pass it and secured the savannah before the city, we would find ourselves in a cross fire. Venables heard him out, his face gray and gloomy and irresolute, and then he must mull over the meat here a little, like some cow chewing her cud, and then he could not rest content with Cox's word but must send his engineer to scout the fort. That required an hour; and when the engineer's report supported Cox's, Venables, still not content, must take a detail of fifty and go see for himself.

That slaughtered yet another hour of daylight, and when he returned, his face grayer and gloomier than before, he commanded us to draw up in order and prepare to march. And no need to give

314

reason for the command. For he had already squandered most of the daylight left us, and if he now chose to take the fort, then we must bivouac here the night without victuals or water. And so he chose to have at the city instead. He chose to march nine thousand ten abreast past seven pieces of enemy ordnance in order to be at the city before darkness fell.

Now the way of it that afternoon was in this wise. The reformados had the forlorn, and next were Captain Pawlett's firelocks, and next the sea regiment, and our regiment in the van of the army proper, with Heane and Venables leading us. And the way narrowed just as Cox had said, with the fort on our right hidden by a thick growth of young wood. There was some confusion when the reformados reached that place, for where the way narrowed one line of twenty must become two of ten and the reformados were but indifferently drilled. But the reformados passed that place, and the firelocks passed it, and the sea regiment came abreast of it.

And exactly then the fort opened fire, all seven guns crashing out at once, and the front line of the sea regiment staggered, and in the same instant the road ahead was full of bearded, roughly dressed, shouting men carrying long lances. They seemed to come from nowhere, and they made for our forlorn and then as one they all dropped to one knee. A curious maneuver, I was thinking, until I heard the roar as the forlorn and the firelocks fired, five hundred muskets all at once and every shot, I think, over their heads. And then they charged. Those lances were twelve feet long, with heads the size of beef hearts, but you would have thought, to watch them feint and then thrust home, that they handled walking swords. Our regiment had halted in some disorder, though before us Heane had come about to scream something out to us; and in that moment before we were again advancing, I saw the way these cow killers did it, how they would feint at a man's throat, and the man would throw up half pike or musket to ward off the blow, and then the lance head would drop and you would watch it disappear into a man's groin.

For perhaps a pair of minutes the reformados held their ground. Then they were diving headlong into the woods on either side of the road or they were running back upon the firelocks, and then the firelocks broke. But the sea regiment did not break. The first volley from the fort had killed all ten men in the first line and their Cap-

315

tain Catts as well, but they only staggered and then re-formed. And at first they were marching stolidly forward as before, and then they were running, for the cow killers looked once at them and then turned and fled. But they left forty of us dead behind them, among them the guide Cox.

The sea regiment chased them to within sight of the city. Our General came shamefacedly out from behind a tree and joined Heane; thereafter Venables no more marched in the van of any army he commanded. And all that afternoon the army marched in good order past that fort, though the guns played on us the entire time.

An hour before darkness the entire army sat before the town, between the guns from the fort and the guns from the town. We sat there without water or brandy, without bread or meal, without artillery or scaling ladders, with not four charges of powder or six inches of match or five balls to a man. Out in the bay Penn's squadron rode serenely and safely beyond cannon shot from the town; now and then a frigate would come about, and you would see the puff as she fired, and then you would see the ball splash into the bay, fifty yards short of shore. There was food and water aboard those ships, and ammunition, and our mortar and drakes, and ship's carpenters to make us ladders; and had the squadron been Dakin's, he would have run in close and shelled the town and landed supplies under his guns. But the squadron was not Dakin's, and so there before the city we must have another council of war. Venables chose to hold it within earshot of half the army; in the fading, violet light his face looked gray and sick, and Heane's was white and angry. Heane was for storming the city now, while there was yet a spark of life left in the men and a little light to see by; and if night fell before the business were accomplished, why, then, darkness would prove as much our friend as theirs. But Venables argued that we lacked artillery to breach walls or ladders to scale them, and besides, most of us were dying on our feet for lack of food or water.

"And will they be less thirsty come dawn?" Heane said. "There are wells within the town. If they be thirsty enough, let them earn their drink."

"It will be dark soon," Venables said. "In the darkness, we cannot tell where a wall is well defended and where ill."

"I can answer you that," Heane said. "The same answer I have given ye thirty times these four days. To the north. There is only a hedge—"

"In the dark? We are to circle the town in the dark—"

Heane looked wearily at him. "And what do ye then propose?"

Venables licked his lips. "I think we must retreat."

"Retreat? To where?"

"To supplies. To food and water for the men, and ammunition—"

"And where would that be, pray tell?"

"At the Hina," Venables said.

Heane's eyes flicked to Buller. "Do you mean to tell me," he said, "that you would go the entire way back that we have come up? Six miles each way for but a mouthful of water and a ship's biscuit when food and drink is within sight?" And now he was leaning into the thin and fading light. "I have come to think," he said softly, "that there is something about a wall ye cannot abide, General. Three hours ago it was a small fort. Now—"

"Are ye calling me coward, sir?"

"Am I commanded to answer that question, General?"

There was a silence between them. And then, "I have a mind to break you for that," Venables said.

"Why, do so," Heane said. "To a very private in the foot. For I vow I should prefer that to bearing any responsibility for the conduct of this business."

A little longer these two locked eyes and wills. Then Venables' eyes wavered, and he was looking at all of them in this party; he had not even the force, I thought, to reprimand a mutinous officer. "Mark me, gentlemen," he said, and you would have thought them all equal now, for you could hear the wheedle in his voice, "mark me. I have watched two rams fighting. I have watched them come up and I have watched them go back. And after their first going back, they came up with a great deal more force the second time than the first."

"And do you call this a reason?" Heane said. "This?"

Venables but looked at him, grayly.

"Look ye, General," Heane said. "Ye need not lead this an ye lack the stomach. But give me the sea regiment and my own men, I shall storm—"

"I yet command here, I think," Venables said. "And I am for retreat."

317

And so we rested before the city another hour, until full darkness. And then we began the long march back to the Hina. We in the van arrived there just at dawn. But this was no proper tropic dawn, no orange flare of sun. Dawn this morning was a cold, despairing light and a thin, chill drizzle of rain. And give us another week, I thought, and the rainy season would be upon us in very earnest.

For six days we lay at the Hina, the pretext for the delay the landing of necessary supplies, and further councils of war, and needed rest. As for the third, I little doubt but that such was the case with Venables, for he lay comfortably aboard the *Swiftsure* beside his lady. But for his men rest meant panting through the heat of yet another day, or sleeping miserably in the sand in pouring rains. For the army rest meant eating the food that Dakin managed to land— boiled beef so candied with salt it would drive a man mad with thirst; ship's biscuits, brown and moldy and soggy, the filthiest bread I have e'er set teeth into, so bad even the worms had deserted it; oatmeal that wriggled with weevils. And after the second day there was not even this, for now the sea broke so far out that Dakin could get no more small boats through. And so by Saturday we were driven by growling bellies to foraging; we would go out in parties of six, and sometimes we would return with a wild cow or a shirtful of oranges, and sometimes we would return empty-handed, and some of us did not return at all but were stumbled upon later, lying in the bush, lanced through and through by the cow killers who lurked all about the camp. And so by the end of the week, enough of us had made the acquaintance of fevers or the bloody flux; one in four, at least, had been seized by the awful cramps in the gut, and breeches were dropped fifty times a day, and between morn and night a man so taken would be so weak he could not stand unaided.

The sixth day we marched again, those of us who by God's mercy could still stagger to our feet. We marched now with all the impedimenta of storm and siege; we brought up on this march a mortar and two drakes and scaling ladders; and in addition to snapsack and musket or pike, each able man now staggered under the weight of shovel or pickaxe. The artillery set the pace on this march; since we lacked harnesses for the horses, the field pieces must be drawn by men, ten to the mortar, six each to the drakes, turn and turn about every quarter hour. And so we accomplished but three miles

318

that Tuesday, and behind us the cow killers came boldly into the road to kill our stragglers, and equipment littered the way behind us, and men would fall out and make water into the palms of their hands and gag it down and vomit it back up and then stagger on, and with every step we prayed for nightfall, for darkness would bring rain, and the only thing else that kept us going was fear of the enemy behind and all about us.

On Wednesday, at about three in the afternoon, we came again to that place where two ways formed a fork, with Fort Geronimo a half mile beyond. For two days Heane and Buller had argued that this time we must divide the army, one half to march past the fort, the other to come on the city by this new way. But Venables had over-ridden that. His reasoning was that with our guide dead, we had no certain knowledge that this second road led to the city, and besides, he did not think the enemy would twice lay an ambuscade in the same place. And so we paused here and were put in order. Heane was in command now in all but name, for Venables had been taken with the flux three days since and was so weak he must be supported by two men as he marched. And so he but looked grayly on while Heane chose out twenty men from each regiment for the forlorn and put Adjutant General Jackson in command of it, and ordered the reformados to march next, and after them Captain Pawlett's firelocks and Captain Carpenter's horse, and in the van of the army itself our regiment.

And again it fell out as before, only more disastrously, for now the army was demoralized from sleeping five nights in the rain, and from bad food, and from marching a full day without a taste of water, and from memories of the last time we had attempted the city in this wise. Again the forlorn set off; once out of sight, we would learn later, Jackson ordered Captain Butler to the head of the column and himself marched very discreetly in the rear, from whence he could come up if there were glory to be gained but not if there were danger; he also put his horse in front and his pikes to the rear against all reason; and he flagrantly disobeyed Heane's orders in that he did not put out wings to beat up the woods for ambuscades. And again the forlorn passed the fort without drawing a shot, and the reformados passed it, and the firelocks, and the horse. And then we were upon it.

The five of us were in the very front of our regiment. There is a

319

small turn in the road just before you come to the narrowing of the way where the fort is, and we swung around it in very good order, marching shoulder to shoulder and to sword's point. Ahead the road was straight for a quarter mile, and we saw the horse a stone's throw away. We also noted that the enemy had cleared a fire lane, ten feet wide, from fort to road, and I felt Andrew on my left and Munke on my right stiffen (though they did not break stride), and over the tramp of boots and the clank of gear I heard the sharply indrawn breaths, and so I knew that others expected what I did, which was that the Spaniard had saved us for his gunnery practice. But our only show of cowardice as we passed the fire lane was that to a man we marched with our eyes on that white fort squatting at the end of the line of stumps. But we passed the swathe and no crash of cannon, and the second line passed it, and the third and the fourth, and now I was wondering what the devil the enemy was about, whether he had abandoned the fort and dragged his ordnance to the city, or whether he lacked powder and shot, or what.

And then my answer. Then the roar of a single gun, and the brief whistle (grape, I thought, they are using grape and small shot today and not case or round shot), and behind me I heard a single, high-pitched scream like a woman's, and ahead a volley of muskets.

"Ambuscade," Munke cried out. "And in the same place. And the fools ha' fired all at once," and out in front of us Heane wheeled his horse about and raised his sword, and we halted and readied our pikes, awaiting his orders.

I cannot tell you what happened up ahead save by hearsay. Later they said that that one gun had been a signal for two hundred cow killers to burst out of the woods onto our forlorn, and again the firelocks had fired all at once and without taking aim, and Captain Butler's horse behaved handsomely, taking the enemy's charge and then wheeling about in very good order, but Jackson took one look and fled and all his pike after him, and the forlorn ran around the reformados, and then forlorn and firelocks together ran into the horse, and the horse in turn came down upon us. That, they said, was the way of it, but the first thing I saw was sixty horse charging straight down upon us, with Heane in the very center of the road beating at them with his walking sword and the horse swirling all around him, and then the horse almost upon us, and Munke leaping straight at one in front, his pike clubbed in his two hands, and he swung, and one horse was suddenly riderless before my eyes, and then Munke was diving for the ditch to his side of the road and I was diving for the other and rolling, my eyes still open so that I saw the blur of a horse's hoof pass not two inches from my right eye. And then, from the ditch, I raised my head, and in that instant a crash from the fort, six guns gone off as one, and the whole regiment behind me a tangle of plunging, screaming horses and some men already trampled and others hurling away their arms as they ran; and when I looked the other way, our men were bearing down on us, mouths open and eyes mad with fright, and Heane still planted in the very middle of the road, beating at them with that pitiful sword as they streamed past. And then, just as suddenly, the whole road between Heane and the enemy totally emptied save for the scattered arms and a few twisted bodies, and a quarter mile ahead the reformados, a pitiful twelve or fourteen still standing, still trying to hold a square and beat off with broken pikes or muskets or bare hands the hundred cow killers that encircled them, and Heane standing in his stirrups and twenty cow killers bearing down on him.

He shouted out, and I heard his words very distinctly, "Stand and we shall rout them." He looked behind, to his regiment in full flight, and shouted again, "But a hundred of you stand with me, and we shall rout them." Across the way two men staggered up into the road and made for him, and one was our ensign, with our colors still in his hands, and the other was Munke. By now I too was to my feet. There were a God's plenty of weapons scattered about, and I stooped for a pike, and when I straightened with it, the first cow killer was on Heane from one side, and his ensign was to him from the other, and Munke was running toward him, and in sudden horror I saw that Munke's hands were naked of any weapon. And in that same instant the first lance disappeared into the shoulder of Heane's horse, and Heane was out of his saddle, and while he was in mid-air his sword disappeared into the fellow's neck, and he landed on his feet like some traveling acrobat, and he shouted out again, "But ten stand with me and we shall rout them. Nay, but five, and we shall, I promise you." And then one of the cow killers turned to meet Munke, and Munke threw up his hands (grabbing, I think, at the lance head as it threatened his throat), and the lance head dropped

321

and disappeared into Munke's groin, and he seemed to bend forward, very slowly and deliberately, almost as if he were bowing before someone, and then I was running toward him.

I took two steps before something hit me from behind. A shoulder, it seemed to me, and I twisted about to face it, and then something hit me again, this time no shoulder, and that is the last I knew for a while.

When I came to, I was lying face down in a thicket, with a body atop me and a hand clamped cruelly over my mouth. In the near distance I could hear the steady roll of drums and the sound of cannon, single hollow booms, one following briefly on the echo of the other. I lay quiet a little, watching the slow progress of a black ant just beyond my nose. Then I tried to twist free of the hand. But it was not to be surprised, and so I set up a violent threshing, and now there were two hands, one over my mouth and the other at my throat, and a voice an inch from my ear, "Nay. Quiet, man. In God's name, lay ye quiet a little," and the voice was Andrew's.

But I would not, and so he let me loose, and I sat up and stared at him. "So it was you," I said. I achieved my feet. "Munke," I said. "I saw Munke—"

"And I," he said. "And nought to do. Save die with him."

"Munke," I said again, and Andrew stepped a step to me and laid a hand gently to my arm. "Do not," he said. "Do not go out there yet awhile, Mas—"

I struck the hand away. "But lay a finger on me to hinder me," I said, very quietly, "and I shall kill you, Andrew. I swear to God I shall."

When I came out onto the road, the sea regiment was marching past very gallantly, Vice-Admiral Goodson leading them and the drums rolling and the men swinging by in close order. I waited until they were by and then ran toward the three bodies lying in the road. I saw as I ran past him that they had lanced Heane through a half dozen times, and all the blood in his body, it seemed, had seeped out into the dust of the road. I ran past him, and past his ensign, lying dead as he, all wrapped around in the regimental colors. Then I was to Munke and I flung myself on my knees beside him.

He lay on his face a scant yard from the ditch, and I gently turned him over. His face, through the sunburn, was the color of wetted wood ashes, and his eyes were closed, and the blood was all down his right leg, from hip to ankle. But he yet breathed, and as I bent over him and put a hand under his head, he opened his eyes and recognized me and smiled.

"Why, John," he said. "And is there one in this army did not run, then?"

I thought he mocked me, and I swallowed against the bitterness in my throat. "I did not run, Richard," I said. "But Andrew must knock me in the head. He must make me coward against my will—"

"Nay," he said. "I know you did not. For I saw you come up out of the ditch." He closed his eyes again. "If someone should make me the offer," he said, "I think I should barter my immortal soul this instant for but a drop of water."

"Patience," I said. "It is near sundown. It will be raining again—"

"I mind not dying," he said. "But to die in such a cause. And among such rabble. There is little distinction in that, I think."

"You are not dead yet. And if I can do ought—"

He smiled faintly. "You can pray. Little else."

"I am already engaged in that," I said, and then I heard drums again, and I looked down the road, and Fortescue's regiment was rounding the turn. "I must get you off the road," I said. "And see to that wound. As gently as I can, Richard. And pray you forgive me if that be not gentle enough."

I got to my feet and stooped for him. But I was shouldered aside, and it was Andrew who picked him up, and Munke gasped once and then fainted. Andrew stood there with Munke limp in his arms and looked a question across the body. But I said nothing, and he carried Munke to the ditch and laid him gently down.

He was not dead yet, but I was filled with a numb despair when I ripped his breeches and laid eyes on the wound. He had twisted about to protect his groin when the lance came at him, and the lance had entered the thigh and scraped along the bone, and the white bone all exposed and the tendons in shreds. I stared at that hole, and Oh, dear God, I thought, oh, dear, merciful God, have mercy, and then, to spoil it all, I must fall to thinking bitter thoughts of an army that traveled without even enough water to give a dying man to drink or to bathe his wounds. But I did what I could; I ripped up my half shirt and bound the wound as best I knew how. And then I sat down beside him. I sat there until dark, holding his head in my lap, looking into his face and praying for him, and once, just at sundown, I permitted myself to weep a little.

He was still alive the next afternoon when we came back to the Hina, though only God knows how or why. The sea regiment secured the ground before the fort yet that afternoon, and they worked all night in a chill rain, throwing up a breastwork at the fire lane and planting the mortar, for Venables was finally convinced that we must swat this buzzing fly off our backs. But with the dawn the men in artillery refused to work the mortar, for the guns from the fort still raked the road; and even had they been forced, the officers were agreed that this sullen and terrified army would never storm a city wall. Fortescue was for making up a company of officers and attempting the city and so dying an honorable death. But Venables would have none of that. Instead, just at dawn, he ordered the mortar shells buried and the gun carriages burned and the dead buried and the army back to the Hina.

Andrew and I sat by Munke all that night, catching rain in our caps to give him to drink, and bathing his wound, and keeping him as dry and warm as we could, and at dawn fashioning a rude stretcher of young trees and wild vines and clothing on which to carry him back. For part of the night he was sane and thanked me courteously for the water. But toward dawn the fever came upon him and he raved a little, and when we lifted him onto the stretcher, he set up a furious struggle and then fainted. For most of the bitter way back he was mercifully dead to this world; he would groan now and again at the jolting we gave him, but he came full awake only twice to beg for water and then not even long enough for me to tell him that there was none.

It was a terrible march back; we left five hundred dead at the fort, and thrice that number died on the retreat. But for me those six miles will remain forever vague; I was near dead myself from hunger and thirst, and I walked the walk in a stupor, my mind on nothing except forcing one foot ahead of the other, my eyes fixed on Andrew's back as he plodded ahead of me, my shoulders numb as death under the dead weight of the stretcher and my arms total strangers. I remember that, and I remember cursing Andrew whenever he stumbled (for then it was that Munke would groan), and I remember cursing myself for the same sin, and I remember falling once to my knees, and Andrew pausing but nothing else, not even looking around, only standing there head down, like some spent, broken beast, until I staggered to my feet again. That I remember, and also coming finally to the river, and that is all.

Save for our rear guard, we were the last to come up to the river. When we did, we could see the army camped all along a mile of it, and the beach was covered with our wounded, and small boats were plying back and forth, for Dakin had converted the *Torrington* and the *Portland* into hospital ships. You could hear for a quarter of a mile the groans or screams or crying out for water of those poor wretches, and when we staggered onto the beach, some of them looked around at us, their eyes wide and terrified, as if even here they expected the enemy to fall on them. We set Munke down, and then I staggered to the river and fell on my stomach and plunged my face into the water. It was still salt this close to the sea, and I spat out my one foolish mouthful. Then I found my way through the sprawl of bodies to a small boat drawn up on shore and touched the officer in charge on the shoulder. "I have a dying man," I said. "Just yonder."

He looked over his shoulder. "Why, more fortune his," he said grimly. "For he can bid farewell to this before you or I. And he shall have God's own plenty of company to show him the way to heaven."

He was young and almost beardless, and he owned very full, red lips, and I hated him on the sudden. "He is an officer," I said. "And I must have a mouthful of brandy for him. But a mouthful."

He stared at me, speechless and amazed. Then he threw back his head and laughed.

"He stood with Heane," I said, "when all the others fled. And have you no brandy, then? Not even for the dying?"

"Why, yes," he said. "A rundlet or two. On those ships out there."

"Then fresh water."

"No lack of that. You will find your fill just there."

"Salt," I said. "For a quarter mile up river. Do you mean to say the Admiral hath not even landed water?"

"Nor intends to," he said. "An they cannot fight for victuals, let them starve for them. His very words." He looked curiously at me. "Stood with the Major General, did he?"

"Very bravely. He had not even a weapon, but ran on them with

325

his naked hands. And would you take him with you this next trip—"

"There?" he said. "Out there? You would have me take him out there?"

"Are there not chirurgeons out there? Will they not care—"

"Care?" He laughed shortly. "Care? Shall I tell you what care? He will lie on an open deck without shelter from sun or rain, and no wound dressed for that we have no linen, and no water because there is none, and worms will breed in his wound by the morrow. It is a greater hell there than here, sir." He fell again to a study of my face. "Stood with Heane, did he? And dying, you say? Art certain he is dying?"

"Not certain. He hath a hole the size of my fist in his hip. But he may recover. With a taste of brandy, and a decent dressing—"

He nodded. "Take him upstream. Bathe his wound and give him to drink. I shall return here in an hour. If I can, I shall fetch back a pint of brandy for him."

When I returned to Munke, Andrew was on his knees and bent over him, shielding him from the sun. "He yet breathes," he said.

I bent and touched his face. "Christ," I said. "The fever rages in him."

Munke opened his eyes only once that afternoon, near dusk, and I managed to force a thimbleful of brandy between his lips. He smiled, and his eyes were sane, and when he spoke, his voice was stronger than I had thought it would be. "Dawn?" he said. "Already dawn, and I not dead yet, John?"

"Afternoon," I said. "Nigh sunset. And you not dead yet, Richard."

"Now that were an unconscionable time to be at dying," he said. "Wilt forgive me that, John?"

"I pray you do not speak so, Richard."

He smiled softly. "Would you grant a man a pair of dying wishes?"

It was on my tongue to say that he was no dying man, but I did not say it. It were no charity to lie to the Richard Munkes of this world at a time like this; dying is above all other times the time you speak them truth. "If it be in my power, Richard," I said.

"Item," he said. "Would ye forgive Andrew his trespass? He hath been guilty of very few, John."

I looked down into his eyes. "And what other?"

"Revenge me," he said. "Build me but that monument. Revenge me."

"That I shall grant you."

"Both," he said. "Both, John."

I looked a little longer into his eyes. Then I nodded. "Both," I said. "And ha' ye any other requests, Richard?"

"One other," he said. "But that of God. Think you I die in a state of grace?"

"I am certain of it. As certain as that I breathe."

"I can hope I do," he said, and then he closed his eyes and was asleep again.

That night the winds came down upon us from out the mountains, and they drove before them the rains, rains such as I have never seen before or since; it was as if in sudden anger God had forgotten His pledge made long and long ago. The rains came all at once before the winds, and our fire was instantly out, and we were as instantly drenched through and through, and the rains were icy cold. In five minutes I was sitting in water ankle-deep, and Munke's head was cradled against my breast, and in the darkness I could feel his teeth chattering.

I cannot tell you exactly when he died. I sat there in the raging darkness with his head cradled in my arms, and with the first gray betrayal of dawn the rains let up a little, and then there was a light you could see by, and his face was the color of the wet sand out there on the beach and his lips were blue and he was dead. And just at dawn we buried him. We had no shovel, and we must dig his grave with sticks and with our bare hands. But we yet dug it deep, and save for the matted tree roots, the digging was not hard.

Another seven days the army lay at the Hina—long enough for the fleet to water and repair; long enough for them to hang a sergeant for cowardice, with his crime written on his chest, and to court-martial Jackson and break his sword over his head and send him aboard the *Torrington* to swab decks for the wounded; long enough for me to meet Somerset Fox and Nick Swiftsure once again, and to curse them quietly but fervently for their cowardice, and then to turn a shoulder and so dismiss them from my life; long

327

enough for interminable councils of war aboard the *Swiftsure* and for rumors to circulate that we were next for Jamaica; long enough for the army to be reduced to two thousand men still well enough to fight. For all that week we lay in pouring rains at night and in thick, oppressive heat throughout the day, and the men sickened of fevers and flux, and the men died. For two days hunger drove the men out to forage, for Penn had indeed said that if we would not fight, neither would we eat, and he sent no bread ashore all that week. But after an ambush or two, the men huddled on the beach and ate what meat was to be found on this side of our outposts; they ate all the horses, dogs, rats, apes, and asses in the camp; some ate land crabs, and these were poison, and they died; let a trooper but tie his horse to a bush and go off to ease his body, and he must be nimble else the beast would be quartered and half roasted on his return. And at night only the dead slept, for our sentries spent their last powder and ball on fireflies, which they thought enemy match, or on land crabs, which would rustle in the dark and which they mistook for the rattle of bandoliers.

On the fourth of May the army was shipped and the fleet set sail for Jamaica.

I was not present when, on the tenth of May, we took Santiago de la Vega, which is the only city on Jamaica; I only heard of that action from Andrew a long time later. How Penn said he would no more trust this business to the army but would perform it himself. How only volunteers went ashore this time, and how Penn waited for a wind to his back before ordering the landing, for then the boats could not turn back, and how officers marched in the rear of every company with orders to kill the first man to waver. How at the landing Venables stood on deck the *Swiftsure* with his cloak pulled up about his ears and his hat pulled down over his eyes, and the men going past in small boats waved their caps and cheered, as was the custom, and he only turned grayly and sullenly away. How they marched the seven miles to the city with Fortescue leading and Venables trudging behind, and not a shot fired on them; and how the Spanish governor, so ridden with pox he must be carried hence in a chair, met them and surrendered the island to them. But that is none of my story. For on the second of May, Penn ordered two ships, the *Selby* and the *Grantham*, to stay behind when the fleet sailed. They were sister ships of twelve guns each, and they carried a crew of a hundred sailors and forty soldiers, and they were to sail the coast of Hispaniola for five weeks, to direct any English ships that came up to join the fleet at Jamaica; and after five weeks they were to sail for England with dispatches. Fortescue now commanded our regiment, and I cannot tell you why he chose me out for duty aboard the *Selby;* it may be I was the first his eye fell on in all the regiment who was still on his feet. But I do know that not twenty men in all that army but would have given five years of his life and one limb at least to have traded places with me.

And so on the third of May I stood on the beach and looked out into the bay, watching the boat come toward me which would take me out to the *Selby,* and I would not look at Andrew, who stood beside me. Not until the boat had beached, and then I did. "Well, Andrew," I said.

"Well, Master John," he said.

"Why, farewell," I said. "And may God go wi' ye."

He cast down his eyes and was a little silent. And then, "I would ye could find it in your heart to forgive me," he said.

"Why, I forgive you," I said. "For was it not a dying man's wish?"

"Nay," he said. "Nay," and he swallowed against something caught in his throat, and I looked at him and tried to think of Richard Munke, lying in his lonely grave. But I could not; instead I was thinking of a moment long, long ago when Andrew and no other had stood by me, when he had freely offered me himself, his life and fortune, which was a shilling or two short of seven pounds; and of another time, when he had preferred hanging to deserting me. I have known but three other men in all my life could equal Richard Munke for courage and stern integrity and inner sweetness, and one of these was Sir George Booth and one was Sir John Grenville and the third was John Penruddock, and none of these did I ever truly love. But Munke had said that Andrew's trespasses were not many (and none of them, I thought, performed in self-interest). And so, I thought, let us let the dead bury the dead. And so I stepped a step to him and embraced him and kissed him upon the cheek.

"I forgive you, Andrew," I said. "Truly. With all my heart. And if I did not, why, I yet love you, man."

"God bless you for that, Master John," he said.

I smiled. "And may He see fit that we shall meet again," I said. "In England." And saying that, I could not know that Andrew would go through the Jamaica campaign and the bitter year of settlement to follow and still return to England but a little after me.

ᘓ *Eighteen* ᘔ

Fifteen months later, on the last day of September, 1656, the *Selby* staggered into the Thames. From the first the voyage had been fraught with ill fortune. It began by giving chase to a Spanish sloop and running aground on a Godforsaken rock off Hispaniola and ripping a great hole in our hull. We were two months patching that sufficient to keep us afloat and a month at St. Kitts careening. We were thrice becalmed. We were blown a thousand miles off course by a winter gale, and we were six months beating our way up the length of Africa. Now, in a ship so foul-bottomed it was very miracle she still floated, with masts broken and sails in rags and half our original crew dead from scurvy or smallpox, we crowded the bulwarks and looked in very amazement at a city we had despaired of ever laying cyc on again.

For a little, as I walked up Fish Street, it seemed that London had changed not a whit. There was about me the same hurry and hub-bub, the same strident and hysterical hawking of wares from stall or basket, the same shouting out of greeting or bawling of oaths. And in the Cheap, pretty women still fingered trinkets, and young knights of the blade still measured the swagger of possible opponents, and coachmen still cursed carters. And yet the city seemed not the same; methought I could sense something sullen and waiting on the faces that brushed past me. Before Mercers' Hall two solid and sober merchants stood deep in conversation, and I heard the word "parliament," and then one threw me a look, and the look

331

was suspicious and conspiratorial. And at the Great Conduit, a hawker of ballads sidled up to me, asking but a penny for the latest ballad, all about the sad martyrdom of James Naylor, Quaker, and he offered his sheet in a whisper, as if it were treason he peddled. Which is little enough to go on, I thought, but nonetheless, John Mordaunt, I think there is something not healthy in the city this year, and I would know what it is.

Well, I thought, there is a place you may find it out.

On Ludgate Hill, I hesitated a moment before the Belle Savage, for this was a two-shilling ordinary and I was browned and bearded and just off one of His Highness's ships and not dressed the part. Then I crossed the innyard impudently and as impudently entered the inn. The ordinary was not as deserted as another time I could remember—two merchants at a side table; a travel-stained squire at another, a dish of smoking salmon before him; at the great center table a young hector who eyed me arrogantly and distastefully as I entered, then dismissed me as beneath him. And Mr. Doyle, his face as nondescript as ever, coming across the ordinary with a bottle under his arm, his eyes lidded and hostile. "No alms here, sirrah," he said.

"I require none," I said. "But a little news, Mr. Doyle."

"If you have money, I shall serve you in a little. When I have finished other duties here."

"I am possessed of an abundance of patience. And half an afternoon left me."

His expression changed for the better; he did not recognize me, but my language gave the lie to my appearance. He served the young hector and returned. "Should I know you, fellow?" he said.

"Three years ago come April," I said. "Just here. A man named Alan Brodrick. And a certain Sir Richard Willis—"

His eyes narrowed. "You," he said. "You." And then, "Get thee gone from here," he said.

I looked down into his eyes. "Two years," I said. "A long time to bear a man so great a hate, Mr. Doyle."

"Return in thrice two years, I shall still bear it."

"I wronged you," I said. "And I have suffered for it. But you also wronged me. And so cannot we call the tally even for but a quarter hour?"

"What want ye of me?" he said sullenly.

332

"But a scrap or two of news. Of your daughter, first."

"Married. To a mercer. A good match, though no fault of yours. And two strapping sons. And do not inquire me out where she dwells."

I was silent a little, digesting this, thinking that some mercer in London were a luckier man than I. And then, "I have been absent from England near two years," I said. "And I am starved for news."

"We have a new parliament. That were news."

"Better than the Rump I left England with, I can hope."

He shrugged. "His Highness excluded a hundred and forty this week. His old friends this time. Haselrig, Scot—"

"And so no news there," I said. "Unless it be that the shoe pinches a new foot. What else, Mr. Doyle?"

"All known royalists have been banished the city this month."

"And nothing changed there, neither," I said.

"All the talk is, it will be King Oliver the First before Christmas. This time they say he will consent. And John Lambert in a pout, for he hoped it would be King John and not King Richard."

And that was news, I thought. For if Richard Cromwell did succeed, John Lambert might act, and with an army at his back. And so heigh-ho once again to civil disorder, I thought, and yet again, until they bring back the king. "Ought else, Mr. Doyle?" I said.

"They debate the Decimation Tax this month, I hear. And the Major Generals fearful they will be voted out—"

"Decimation Tax? Major Generals?"

He looked strangely at me. "You do not know? Of the nation divided into tenths, and a Major General over each canton? Of every king's man in the land paying a tenth of his estate yearly to bear the charge of the army—"

"Now, by God," I cried out. "Is there no end to the impudence of this upstart? And will the people forever endure—"

"Hush," he said fiercely. "In God's name, hush."

"Aye," I said bitterly. "Hush." And then, "Mr. Doyle," I said, "I would work again for the king. But I know not how—"

"Nor I. I am no more in that business."

"But a name. There is talk in places like this, and you have ears."

"Do not ask me. I have paid enough already—"

"You shall pay no more for this. I swear you will not."

His eyes drifted about the ordinary, then returned. "Try the

Feather's," he said. "In Cheapside. Inquire out a Mr. Hungerford. But mark you, I know nothing, only what I have heard—"

"This Hungerford. Would that be his true name?"

"I know only what I have heard," he said.

"And what have you heard, Mr. Doyle?"

"That his name is Edward Sexby," he said.

That first night I found no Mr. Hungerford at the Feather's in Cheapside. But I did the second. He was in passing conversation with another when the barmaid handed him my note, and he read it, and then the two turned and stared across the ordinary at me, and I recognized the moon face and sleepy eyes of my old friend, Sir Richard Willis. Then Willis moved on.

"You desire a word wi' me, fellow?" Hungerford said, when I came up.

"I do, sir." I stared curiously down at him. He was a man of medium height who contrived to look smaller than he was, and he wore this week a black periwig and a quiet, shabby suit, and he owned the hottest, most baleful eyes I have ever looked into. If this were indeed Sexby, I thought, he could put off that periwig for his own hair, and he could grow a beard, but he could do nothing with those eyes save only lid them. For I had heard of Colonel Edward Sexby, as who in England had not—this head of the Levellers, that sect which preached that if a man owned ten sheep, nine should be given to nine who had none; this one-time soldier in Cromwell's own regiment; this master of disguise who, since his break with the Protector, came and went into and out of England at will and in the teeth of anything John Thurloe could do; this writer of poisonous pamphlets and plotter of assassinations and planner of Spanish invasions; this republican malcontent who had worked four years for the king's return and who would work as unceasingly for his exile again were Charles Stuart ever recalled. "I do," I repeated. "And have I your leave to sit, sir?"

He nodded curtly, and I sat. He heard me out, his eyes hotly searching my face the while, his eyes full of distrust and something very like hatred. Then he dropped his head and set to playing with the wine glass before him. "Mordaunt, is it?" he said. "Brother to the Earl of Peterborough, is it? And you would work for the king, would you?" He looked up from the wine glass. "And what skills ha' ye, Mordaunt?"

"Skills?"

"Aye. Skills. Can ye prime, load, and fire pistol? Canst lie and cheat? Canst cony fools and outcozen cozening knaves? Canst perjure, steal, and forge?"

"Some of those, an it be necessary."

"What of killing without honor? Canst lie in wait and shoot a man i' the back? Poison his food? Bribe guards and slit the throat of a man asleep?"

"If I must."

"And why come ye to me?"

"I was sent. Mr. Doyle—"

"I know no Mr. Doyle. Nor ever did. And so name me some more names, John Mordaunt. Of honest men who can vouch for your honesty."

"I cannot, sir. Not in London. I have but my word—"

He laughed shortly. "Your word? Every third man in the kingdom trepanning these days for John Thurloe, and you offer me your word?"

I flushed. "I am sorry to have troubled you, sir," I said stiffly.

"And I sorrier."

I looked steadily at him. "Were I not honest," I said, "this place would be full of soldiers by now."

"Would it, now? And for what cause, pray?"

"Why, come for you," I said quietly. "Come for you, Colonel Edward Sexby."

His hand to the wine glass went very still on the sudden, and he lidded his baleful eyes. But not quickly enough; Mr. Doyle knew only what he had heard, but this time it would seem that he had heard sufficient. Then the eyes came up again, and I smiled sweetly into them, and I read there what was to be read. Which was that I had just been guilty of an indiscretion. Which was that I prove my honesty or I were a dead man within ten minutes of leaving this place.

"I intend no threat," I said.

"Why, no," he said, and his voice as sweet as mine. "Why, no, I am sure you do not."

"If my word will not content you," I said, "there is one yonder can speak for me. Sir Richard and I have shared a Newgate cell together."

"Willis? You are known to Willis?"

"You had best ask him, sir."

He turned and caught Willis's eye, and Sir Richard crossed the room. "My congratulations, Sir Richard," I said.

He frowned down at me. "Indeed? For what, pray?"

"Why, for your luck, that they have not hanged you yet. And for your courage. For are not all known king's men banished London this month?"

"Do I know you, fellow?"

"You do. But you must look behind two years to find me."

He did so, and his eyes widened. "Mordaunt!" he said. "Now, damn me but you have come down in the world, man."

I shrugged. "Would you tell Mr. Hungerford here that I have suffered for the king? And can be trusted to suffer again?"

Willis looked at Sexby. "An honest man, Mordaunt," he said.

Sexby fixed baleful eyes on me. "And a witty one," he said. "A very court jester. And near dead for it. He knows not how near."

"I think I do," I said.

He glared at me, baleful and bitter. "Honest, are you? And would work for the king, would you? And I wonder—"

"Nay," Willis said sharply. "Not he, Edward. Not for that business." He looked at me. "The king recruits an army in Flanders," he said, nervously. "For five hundred a year you could command a captaincy there. I will write a letter will make you known to Mr. Hyde. If you go abroad, go through Dover. Inquire out a clerk of the passage, one Robert Day. He will pass you through for twenty shillings."

"Five hundred?" I said. "Five hundred? And what can I command for ten shillings, Sir Richard?"

He winced. "You are afflicted with the royalist disease, then? I mean poverty."

"Aye. Though write me that letter nonetheless." I rose and nodded agreeably into Sexby's baleful eyes and smiled into Sir Richard's. "And while you pen it, you can tell me what business it is I am unfitted for."

"Do not ask me that. For it concerns you not."

"Mr. Hungerford here spoke of poison. Also of shooting in the back. Also of throats slit in the dark. Would it be assassination again?"

"You have been lucky once tonight," Sir Richard said softly. "But I would not play out another hand, were I you."

"If you say so, Sir Richard." But then I looked back into Sexby's baleful eyes, and I could not resist the temptation, the brief salute of finger to forehead.

"Happy hunting, Colonel," I said.

I swung up the drive at Turvey on a fine, bright, cloudless October afternoon. No one was about, but for all that Turvey did not seem this time deserted; I noted that the place looked prosperous again, the turf and hedges clipped, and the gardens weeded and neatly walked, and on the grass in back, sheets spread out to dry. And new sheets at that; my mother hath finally gotten her new holland sheets, I thought.

Mary answered to my knock on the buttery door. For an instant she had it on her lips to bid me begone, no scurvy beggars welcomed here. Then her eyes widened and her hand flew to her mouth and she cried out, "Master John! Oh, dear God in heaven, Master John," and I swept her into my arms and kissed her full on the lips, and then she was sobbing against my breast.

"Mary," I said. "Why, Mary."

"Master John," she sobbed. "We had gi'en ye up for dead, and—" She pushed away from me. "Let me look at ye a little."

"Your fill," I said. "But later. Would Henry be at home?"

"Abovestairs. Closeted wi' your mother."

I kissed her again. "I have been half around the world," I said. "But yours the fairest face I have seen in all my travels."

"Not a pound lighter," she said. "Nor a day younger. And so go to. Off wi' ye, rogue."

I grinned and slapped her on the bum. "They are in his apartments?"

"Hers. In the new wing."

Turvey had been built in the time of the second Henry, but it had been new fronted in Elizabeth's time, and both grandfather and father had added wings. I found my way through the great medieval hall, and up the staircase with its painted arabesques, and into the new wing. I stood in the gallery briefly, listening to the murmur of their voices through the heavy oaken door into my mother's apartments. Then I opened the door without knocking.

A small fire was burning itself out in the grate, and they sat before it—my brother, his back to me, in a brocaded chair that looked new, my mother on a settee that did not. Henry was punctuating some point with his hand when my mother's eyes betrayed my presence, and Henry came about.

He did not at first truly see me, only the red coat and cap of the mariner and an unknown face above it. And so he came passionately to his feet. "Now, what—"

"You will pardon my discourtesy in not knocking," I said. "Brother."

He had not yet taken his first step toward me, only bent into it, and in that posture he went stock-still. My mother gasped once and then put a hand to her mouth. I strode to her and bent over her hand. "I am glad to see you are in health, Mother," I said. "And you, Henry."

"John," he said. "John. We had thought you—"

"Dead," I said. "I know. And are you not greatly relieved?"

"Why, aye," he said, and only a tinge of doubt in his voice. "Truly. But where—"

"Half about the world. But now I am come home."

His eyes wavered. "For good? You mean to stay, John?"

"Why, yes. Where else have I? And am I not welcome, brother?"

"You know you are. It is only—do they still search you out?"

"I would not know. I have not trumpeted my return. Nor inquired that matter out of Mr. Thurloe at Whitehall."

His eyes were still nervous. "You have been absent from England. Do you know what this year has been like for us?"

"Something. Major Generals. Decimation Taxes. I have heard a little." I dropped onto the settee and fumbled and found my mother's hand. But I did not look into her face, not yet. "What would you of me, Henry?" I said. "I have not a shilling, and what would you?"

He wetted his lips. "If they find you here, it will be more than a tenth I shall pay. It will be all I own in the world—"

"I heard in London," I said, "that the king recruits an army on the Continent. I could go into Flanders."

"Why, yes," he said eagerly. "Yes. I could spare you passage money—"

"For five hundred a year I could maintain a captaincy there."

He stared at me. He knew on the sudden why I was at Turvey, and he stared at me in amazement and dismay. "You are mad, John," he said. "You know that were impossible—"

"Turvey looks prosperous this year," I said. "It had that look as I came up the drive. Doth it still bring in four thousand a year, Henry?"

"No. And taxes—"

"Do we still have Drayton Manor? And our Addington lands?"

"Mortgaged. Like Turvey, mort—"

"Another three thousand. And still an acre or two in Sussex—"

"I cannot," he said. "I swear I cannot—"

I lounged down before him. "If you cannot," I said, "why, then, you cannot. And so I must abide here, must I not?" I grinned at him. "Would there be plots in Bedfordshire this year?" I said. "For I mean to work for the king. Here or abroad I mean to work for the king this year."

For a moment I feared he would choke. "Blackmail," he said.

"Why, yes," I said. "It is, Henry."

"Blackmail. And you a very rogue—"

"Why, yes," I said. "I am, Henry."

"Blackmail," he said yet a third time, and then, "Have you not done enough, John? Have you not persecuted me enough?" And then, "Very well. Five hundred pounds."

"A year," I said. "Until the king is brought back."

"Agreed," he said. "Five hundred a year."

And now I allowed myself to look into my mother's face. She still affected the sober, high-necked dress of ten years ago, and in the severe, composed face her eyes betrayed her relief that I still lived. But behind that look, her face was also troubled. Severe and Presbyterian my mother was, and so her eyes must reproach me for what I now did. I suffered that look a little, and then I smiled into her eyes.

"Nay, Mother," I said. "Do not look at me so. For I am still your son."

❉ ❉ ❉

339

All that bitter year of 1656-57 Charles Stuart resided at Bruges. For almost a decade he had been hounded from Edinburgh to Paris, from Paris to Aachen, from Aachen to Cologne, from Cologne to Bruges by the fortunes of war or the implacability of the Protector's treaties or the temerity of European princes. For almost a decade he had lived on reluctant promises and little else—a small pension from Mazarin, irregularly paid; fifty pounds a month from his sister Mary, Princess of Orange; what few shillings the royalists at home could scrape together and smuggle past Cromwell's port authorities. At times he was so impoverished that a supper at court was but a single dish; that Ormonde or Rochester must pawn their last possession to pay an innkeeper's score; that a pack of hounds, sent him as a Christmas gift from home, must be given up because he could not maintain it; that, forced to depart this city or that one, he must leave behind his trunks and books and plate as security against the debts he also fled.

Now, in the eighth winter of his reign, there was war between Cromwell and Spain, and so Charles lived at Bruges in the Spanish Netherlands. He enjoyed a small pension from Madrid, and he had leave from the Governor, Don Juan of Austria, to raise four regiments against the intended invasion in the spring. His creditors still hounded him shrilly; his Chancellor, Sir Edward Hyde, must spend his days in writing testy letters to Don Juan asking for unpaid money; the house he occupied that winter was small and unfurnished. And yet the frayed and poverty-stricken Cavaliers who now haunted Bruges tasted hope once again. It would be brief enough; spring would bring despair again. But for the moment the news from home was good. The people in England were restless indeed this winter under the rule of the naked sword, rumor had it, and Cromwell's troops muttered and mutinied for their pay, and Presbyterians plotted with Anglicans to seize on a port for the expected invasion, and Fifth Monarchists preached openly before Whitehall for the destruction of Babylon, and 'prentices rioted and petitioned for a free parliament.

And so there was a God's plenty of English faces in European streets that winter. Some of them came to wait upon the king; these were the courtiers, and they formed cliques and factions in which Anglican distrusted Presbyterian, and Presbyterian feared Catholic, and Leveller plotted against the rest, and all were at one in

340

only one regard, which was the hatred they bore Hyde, the king's
Chancellor of the Exchequer. But these were the few, and the
many came to fight. All that year they streamed across the Channel
to enlist under Charles Stuart's colors, lured hither by the seizure
of estates, by the insolence of Major Generals, by the Protector's inhuman land policy in Ireland. They came by the thousands, and
they were loaned out to Spain and fought for Philip's bastard at
Valenciennes and Ardres and St. Ghislain, and they learned that
fighting for Spain meant vile quarters and no pay, and they deserted at Louvain as fast as they enlisted at Bruges, and in Brussels
they robbed churches and desecrated holy relics, and by spring
they had again tasted despair.

But despair was for the spring, and I came to Bruges in December. I arrived aboard a good horse, with a manservant, and thirty
pounds in my pocket, and a letter from Sir Richard Willis to Hyde.
At the Sign of the Emperor I learned that Mr. Hyde could be found
out at a Mr. Robinson's house, and thither I dispatched my servant,
with a letter stating my name and business and requesting an audience at his convenience. His convenience was three days later,
when I offered to buy him supper, an offer he refused once for
pride's sake and then accepted for necessity's.

I studied him while he attacked his supper. For all that he had
had practice these eight years at starvation, he was gouty and gone
to fat; the paunch he carried beneath his vile linen was a burden
to him, and his cheeks reminded me of a chipmunk who had discovered a goodly store of acorns and winter in the offing. But all his
character was in mouth and eye; his mouth, above the small,
pointed chin, was a thin, tight line, and his eyes were small and red
and bitter, and you somehow knew that not even a "good morrow"
would escape those lips without it had first received an hour's cautious deliberation, and even before he spoke, you knew why the
only man in all the world who truly loved this one was Charles
Stuart.

He finished half his leg of mutton and wiped his fingers on his
shirt before he favored me with his first question. His voice was thin
and irascible, a match for lip and eye. "John Mordaunt," he said. "I
knew your father. A very rogue."

"I bear his politics no love," I said. "But he was no rogue."

He glared redly at me. "General of the Ordnance under Fairfax,

341

was he not? An impudent rebel against his lawful monarch, was he not? And do we not agree on what is knavery, sir?"

"I am not here to argue definitions with you."

"Why, no. Thou'rt here to offer to shed your blood for the king. In the capacity of captain of foot." He bit savagely into his mutton while his small, bitter eyes memorized my features. "What fits you for such a commission? Save birth? And the villainy of a father? And a quarrel in the Cheap with someone's coachman?"

"I am no knight of the blade," I said. "And I have seen service in the field. I was with Penruddock at Salisbury. And with Heane at Santo Domingo."

He smiled—or I think he did. "You can satisfy in one particular, I see," he said dryly. "You have a talent for choosing the losing side. And what other qualifications, pray? Do you bring a company with you?"

I shook my head. "But one servant. And so I would be content as lieutenant. Or even ensign—"

"And what reward do you expect for such signal and selfless sacrifice?"

Had he not been close to the king, I think I would have struck him. Or abruptly taken my leave. "Reward?" I said.

"Aye. Reward. The word would be familiar to a Mordaunt, would it not?" He pushed his trencher aside. "Eight stivers per diem," he said. "That were a lieutenant's pay this year. Enough to live on if you sup but once a day. And rob churches now and again. And if it were ever paid. Which it will not be. Will that content you, sir?"

"It will," I said.

"You will be quartered in ruined barracks one fortnight in every two months. The rest of the year you will be provided no quarters at all. Will that content you?"

"If it does not, I shall lodge at some convenient inn."

"At half a patacoon a day, Mr. Mordaunt?"

"I can stand my own charge. I have five hundred a year—"

"Ah," he said. "Have you, now? And from what source, pray?"

I looked gravely at him, and I have spoken more sharply on other occasions. "Mr. Hyde," I said, "I have suffered your rudeness near an hour now. I do not propose to suffer it another. And so do not ask me what is none of your business, sir."

"But it is," he said. "It is. Hast ever heard the name Manning?

No, you would not. Henry Manning was a proper young gentleman, even as you, and Rochester pronounced himself ravished with his wit, and he was liberally supplied with money and generous in the spending of it. We were a year discovering out the source. It was straight from Whitehall, a hundred a month. And so we buried Mr. Henry Manning. The disease he died of was a bullet between the eyes."

Still I looked steadily at him. "I am no spy," I said. "The five hundred is from my brother. And all the reward I seek is leave to spend it in His Majesty's service."

"What?" he said. "No other? Neither before nor after?"

"Why, yes," I said. "One other, Mr. Hyde."

"Ah," he said. "I had thought so. And what would that be, sir? The return of estates? A place in the king's bedchamber? A monopoly—"

"Nothing so liberal," I said. "But I have chopped sugar in the islands. And so I have a scar to settle with one or two in England. And the king's return the surest way of settling it. And would you have a look at my back to prove that, sir?"

And now he did smile. It was little more than the smoothing out of one corner of a lip, but it was a smile, I could take my oath on it. "You will serve, I think," he said. "Aye, I think you will. We will put you in the Duke's regiment. Under Colonel MacCarty. Cormac is Irish, and he will be ravished by your company, I am certain of it. As much for your wit as for your money."

Had it not been for three things—Willis's letter to Hyde, a small service I did the Duke of York in the spring, and Hyde's tenacious memory—I would doubtless have lived out the next three years on the Continent, an obscure lieutenant in the Duke of York's regiment. I would have spent those years in endless marching and countermarching against the towns and forts held this month by the French, next month by the Spanish—St. Ghislain, Montmédy, Ardres, Mardyck, Dunkirk. Between the sortees and the sieges, the advances and the retreats, I would have endured the vile and ruined quarters which the Spanish provided us at Louvain or Lier or Damme. I would have idled away my time at standing drinks or suppers for my indigent fellow officers. I would have brawled in the streets of Bruges and been arrested for robbing churches. I would have contracted the pox from some slut in Brussels or gamed away two years' allowance at some table in Ghent. Near the end of 1657 I would have followed Charles Stuart from Bruges to Antwerp, where I would have whiled away a threemonth, loitering on the streets with the rest of His Majesty's ragged and penniless and starving army, waiting for word from England that the Sealed Knot there had secured us a port, waiting for Spain to provide us money and supplies and ships. In February I would have heard that we were again deserted by Spain and betrayed in England. The rest of that winter I would have squandered in winter quarters in Mechlin, cursing Spain for her broken promises, cursing the loose tongues of drunken royalists here and across the Channel, cursing the Earl of Ormonde his recent visit to England for that it had alarmed the Protector, cursing the Sealed Knot its irresolution and timidity, cursing John Thurloe and all his ilk, cursing the king and his advisers, cursing myself for serving the cause of one who, it seemed, had been born but for ruin. That spring and summer I would have been at campaigning again, this time against the combined forces of Louis and Oliver. In September of '58 the king retired to the vile little dorp of Hoogstaeten, and I might have been there when word came that the Protector was dead, and all the royalists in Flanders went mad for joy a little before they lapsed back into despair again. And two years later I would have followed His Majesty home, still buried in obscurity, one more of the hundreds who had starved with the king and hoped with him and despaired with him and bled for him, come home at last to an act of indemnity for Charles's enemies and an act of oblivion for his friends.

But there was Willis's letter, which vouched for my honesty and discretion. And there was a small service done the Duke of York. It was no great act of bravery in battle, no delicate mission delicately brought off; it was no more than the loan of twenty pounds—though that, God knows, was kindness enough in 1657, even to a king's brother. But it bought me an hour's very pleasant conversation with the Duke, and later, in a letter to the king, the humble suggestion that Charles might find a more profitable use for me than mere marching hither and yon for the greater glory of Philip IV and the increased reputation of Don Juan of Austria. And there was Hyde. Do not ask me why Hyde took a liking to me. Perhaps he did not; there was much talk around the council table in Bruges that year of the use the Presbyterian interests might be put to in bringing back the king, and I owned a father, now dead, and a mother, yet living, both of that persuasion. But whatever the reasons, in May I was relieved of my duties in order to wait upon His Majesty.

His Majesty received me in that house in Bruges which he had endured for two years. The house was "conveniently situated, being private and near all his business," as he sometimes (wryly and apologetically) described it. But it was small and meanly furnished, the furniture in the anteroom without the king's apartments battered and sad, the king's apartment itself owning to only a few ancient chairs and his bed and his great chest with a lock for his state papers and a dozen trunks for his clothes and bed linen, not even a carpet on the floor of his bedchamber, not even plate to eat on, for that was eternally in and out of pawn.

A servant showed me to the anteroom, but the king himself answered to the knock on his door—though that, I suspect, was not poverty but discretion. In the sitting room off his private chamber I uncovered and knelt and kissed his hand, and he raised me up and smiled a curious smile and very graciously invited me to sit. As I did so, I was thinking how very like the king and his brother the Duke were, and at the same time how little like. Charles was taller and leaner than James, but there was no mistaking the Stuart look, the same swarthiness, the same sullen length of nose and face, the same shape of mouth and jaw. But in Charles's face were lines not to be found in the brother's, lines of dissipation about the eyes and other lines about the mouth not stamped there by debauchery, lines that betrayed a cynical weariness with the world. And their smiles were not related, I thought. James's smile was that of a man who had lived easily and enjoyed his due of good fortune and knew the world not at all. But Charles's smile knew it all too well.

Now, in that sadly furnished room, with a summer sun streaming in through the casement, His Majesty lounged indolently down in his chair and from under his hat brim bent that smile upon me. "So you are fresh from the field," he said. "And how goes the campaigning, Mordaunt?"

"Hungrily, Sire. The Spanish have stopped our allowance of bread again. And the Duke is in a fret about quarters. And—"

It was a subject clearly painful to him, the vile condition of his

345

troops, and he waved it aside. "My brother speaks well of you," he said. "He confesses himself much taken by your wit."

"I fear me the Duke is too kind, Sire."

"Your Colonel, too. You were at St. Ghislain, I think. And you have courage, Cormac says. A pronouncement I value more highly, since he is a good judge of the one and my brother no judge at all of the other."

There had been enough talk that spring about the enmity between the king and his brother, and so almost I made no reply to that. But I did. "St. Ghislain was small test of courage, Sire," I said. "Since they but marched out and we marched in. And the Duke is a gallant officer and much loved by his men."

"I little doubt he is. And he is also a fool." His eyes wavered out of mine, for all the world like some petulant child's. "And so you have loyalty, too," he said. "Even at the risk of contradicting a king."

It was my turn to smile. "It doth not of necessity follow, Sire. For you might be baiting me a small test."

Now he laughed aloud. "Now, by God, my brother was in the right once in his life. You do have wit." He laughed again and then sobered. "Courage and loyalty and wit. Qualities not found in every man. And what worth put ye on them, Mordaunt? For on my faith, I would purchase them if I can spare the coin."

I looked soberly at him. "Mr. Hyde put me the same question," I said. "And I shall answer it the same. No need to purchase what ye already own."

"Nay," he said. "There is a price to all things. Gold or dross, there is a price. And so speak out, man. What rewards would ye have next year for starving in my service this? Lands? Have the rogues robbed—"

"Of a few acres in Surrey. No more. And I would not make those a condition, Sire."

"Some post, then. In my bedchamber, say. Or a title, mayhap."

"I am content with what title I have, Sire." I yet looked soberly at him, at the small, crooked smile, the lidded and lazy eyes, the indolent grace of his carriage, and for an instant I felt the brush of sadness, though I know not why. "I have no price, Sire," I said. "Or if I do, it is none your Majesty can promise to pay."

"But name it. That I may be the judge."

346

"Your return," I said. "When your Majesty is come home again, I shall have reward enough for any small sacrifices of mine."

He dropped his eyes out of mine, almost as if I had just shamed him in some way. "You are either a very great rogue," he said, "or a very great fool. I know not which."

"I know I am not the one. And I can hope I am not the other."

"Not? You offer to bleed and starve for an indigent monarch with but a whisper of a future. And all your reason love of my poor person—"

"I did not say I loved your person, Sire. But I do love my king."

He frowned. "Would this be some contest of wits? Some riddle?"

"No riddle, Sire. It is but that I love England. And so I must love England's lawful king. More than life I love her, and I would call her home again. But this place we now know, this thing of rags of law and scraps of whim and tatters of reason, this dunghill that Oliver Cromwell would call England, this were not England. I would know a land once again where decent and devout religion were other than subject for some bawdy tavern jest, where ignorance were not virtue and learning fit but to spit on. I would know a nation under law again, and I do not mean the law of the naked sword. I would know a country where villainy is not the first requisite for high place and nobility sole and sufficient cause for a pillorying. I would know a free England, and that will never be until we have again a lawful king and a free parliament."

He no more smiled that faintly mocking smile. He was studying me, intently and curiously and soberly, as one might study some stranger from some far-off land. "You have fewer years than I had thought, Mordaunt," he said.

I was, in point of fact, four years his senior. "I am thirty, Sire," I said. "We are near of an age, I think."

"When I was sixteen," he said, "I was older than you shall be at forty. But we have something in common. And so I think I shall learn to love you."

"I can hope you will, Sire. And that I will prove worthy of it. Though what you speak of I know not."

"Why," he said, "we are the disinherited, you and I."

"The disinherited, Sire? How disinherited? Is it lands you speak of—"

347

"I speak of the world," he said. "Is not honor dead in this new world? Hath not the Catholic vice of avarice become the Puritan virtue of thrift this year? Is not knavery crowned king and kingship martyred these days? We were born out of our time, you and I. But I have lost my innocence and you have not. And so I shall come to love you, Mordaunt." He arose abruptly and strolled to the casement and stood looking down on the streets of Bruges, bathed in the flat, bright summer light. "You are in the right of it," he said. "The price you ask is none I can promise to pay."

"England must someday regain her senses, Sire."

"Must she? And in my lifetime?"

"I am convinced of it, Sire. And I am rich enough in patience that I can afford to extend you credit." I paused, for I was uncertain about the extent of the liberties I dared take with him. And then I took the plunge. "I can hope she will do so without Spanish help," I said.

He turned and looked at me again, his face shadowed and darkened by his hat and the light behind him. "Why?" he said. "What fault find you with this way?"

"The price they ask, Sire, if it be your conversion to their faith, which I have heard. And if not that, it is still a sad cure for an ill disease. And so I would see England bring you home, not Spain. Your Englishman bears Cromwell no very great love, Sire. But he loves your papist less, and your Spanish papist none at all. And so I fear few of us would fall in behind that march on London."

I could not make out his face. But the incline of his head told me that I had not given him offense, that he but studied me thoughtfully. "And what of you?" he asked softly. "What if I landed at Yarmouth with a Spanish army at my back? Would you join our march, Mordaunt?"

"No," I said. "I think I would not, Sire."

"It is Hyde's counsel. The very same." He turned back to the view from the casement. "There is a slimmer way," he said. "The Levellers. Sexby is even now in England, gone over to kill me an usurper and secure us a port. And would you take kindly to those means?"

"I cannot say, Sire. Would Sexby have a price?"

"Indeed he hath. He would have England a republic. And I administrator of the law but not the master of it. And Parliament a single house, and all the power to lie there."

"Then I would as soon see you no king here as no king there."

"Almost you speak my own mind. And so we come about to you, Mordaunt. You are Presbyterian, are you not?"

"Not I, Sire. My father and mother, but not I."

He smiled at my small show of heat. "I shall amend that, then. You are known to Presbyterians in Surrey and Sussex."

"To many of them, Sire."

"No offense intended, Mordaunt."

"No offense taken, Sire."

He returned to his chair, and his eyes dropped to the hand lying on the battered arm, and with his forefinger he traced out the pattern of scars there. "The Presbyterians fret greatly under Independency," he said. "Some are grown so desperate they will even join with old Laudians to bring me home."

His smile was no longer mocking; it was infinitely weary instead, and I duly noted it. "And what would be *their* price, Sire?"

"That I subscribe to the old Covenant. That the Kirk of Scotland be made the Church of England."

"Have they learned nothing?" I said bitterly. "Near twenty years and have they learned nothing at all?" I dropped my eyes from his bent head. "Can nothing dissuade them from such a course, Sire?"

"Some are already dissuaded. Sir George Booth would bring me back without conditions. And others might be. And what say you to returning home again, Mordaunt?"

It was not, of course, unexpected; I had perceived his drift a quarter hour since. And yet I could not help staring at him a moment. "I am a man with a price on his head, Sire," I said. "And I have no more stomach for hanging than the next." Then I smiled. "But tell me how I can serve you there," I said.

There was a sameness to conspiracy, I thought, as I listened to him for the next hour. There were, to be sure, the small differences, for this man now languished in the Tower and that one had been executed and this one was now known to be in Thurloe's pay. But allow for the small erosions of history and there was a sameness—the same scheme for a general rising at the same hour that His Majesty landed at Hull or Dover with an army to his back; the same key counties named, the same towns betrayed or stormed, the same governors and officers bribed to come over; the same fomenting of mutiny in Black George Monck's restless Scottish troops or Lambert's unpaid London ones; the same fond hopes that Englishmen would this time fall in behind the king's triumphant march to Whitehall. It was '51 or '55 over again, I thought, and our chief hope that the disaffected elements in England had increased their numbers this year, that they were grown wearier under the Protector and hence braver. And that John Thurloe had for once grown careless.

As for my part, I was to head the rising in Surrey. I was to form a coalition there between old royalists and disaffected Presbyterians. I was the while to work closely with the Sealed Knot, that group of six who, since '51, had headed up all the king's interests at home. But I was not to be commanded by Sir Richard Willis or the others; the Knot had dillied and dallied for ten years now, advising only caution and circumspection and patience, and the king was grown weary this year of inactivity and timidity.

Such my assignment. As for the means, a fortnight hence I would board ship at Calais and land at Dover. There I would obtain from a clerk of the passage, one Robert Day, a pass to travel in England. I would proceed to London under an alias and lodge a pair of days in Drury Lane, at the house of a certain Roman Catholic surgeon. My second night in London, at precisely seven of the clock, I would be eating my supper in the victualing house of John Wharton in Blackfriars; I would find his place in Creed Lane over against St. Andrew's Church, and I would be wearing a white ribbon in my hat, and I would order cold beef and ale. My host would protest that the fare that night was fowl, and I would reply that it must be beef. If I behaved just so, I would be interrupted at my supper by one who would inquire out the state of my health and appetite; I would reply that it was better today than yesterday, and that I had hopes it would be better tomorrow than today. This would be one of our London agents, here to provide me with further instructions and a cipher, for no letters passing to and from the Continent these days were safe from Mr. Thurloe's eyes.

The next day I would set out for the south. Sir Francis Vincent, near Tonbridge, or Mr. Adam Browne, at Horsham, would extend me his hospitality. Thereafter, my course would be determined by my wits or by the instructions I would from time to time receive from here or from London.

At the end of the hour the king showed me to the door, so naturally and courteously that you would have thought he had lived his life without a servant. With my hand on the latch, I turned back to him.

"One last question, Sire," I said. "Suppose the Presbyterians will not be persuaded save on their terms? Suppose they cling to their demands? Am I to tell them that we shall move without their help? For I cannot conceive that your Majesty could consent, in good conscience, to the demands imposed upon your father."

"Could you not?" he said.

"Could you, Sire?"

And now his smile was twisted and wry and bitter. "Have I not said that you have fewer years than I, Mordaunt?"

"That were no answer, Sire."

"Were it not? Why, then, what of this? You may promise them what you will so you engage them. For our party, acting alone, can never bring me home. And I am grown exceeding weary of my travels. For but a single meal of more than two dishes, I verily believe I would sign a covenant with the devil himself. And are you answered now, man?"

I looked at him, and again I felt the brush of sadness, and this time I could name you the cause. For standing there I was thinking, for no good reason I can give you, of a moment long, long ago, of a chill, gray tropic dawn and the gray rain slanting through dripping trees onto my shoulders, and of a dying man cradled in my arms, his eyes open and his voice stronger than a dying man's had a right to be, his voice saying, "Build me a monument, John." And then I was thinking of Richard Munke lying in a lonely and forgotten grave beside a lonely river across the world. And thinking that, I felt the brush of sadness for something once owned and loved but now forever lost and gone from me. Or for something that never was, I thought; something that I dreamed was but was not. And so I turned away from the king's wry, bitter smile and opened the door and stepped into the anteroom.

In the anteroom, another waited upon His Majesty. He sat just without the door, his back to me, only a hat and a slice of cheek visible from where I stood, and I glanced once, indifferently, down upon the top of the hat. Behind me, His Majesty paused in the open door, and the man rose and turned, his hand to his hat. I was myself in the act of turning back to His Majesty when the man turned, and as I did so, my mind was on nothing except the formal bow of farewell I yet owed the king, and so my first full, fair view of that face was in passing, a face captured in but the corner of my eye. And then I interrupted my turn and looked again, and this time the look was not indifferent.

I stood not long in that posture, motionless in the act of turning to face the king. In point of fact, I stood not motionless at all, for I had that morning purchased a pair of summer riding gloves, and I was pulling them on as I stepped through the door, and I managed the left one even while I stared into that face. It was the same face, I was thinking, the very same; he had put off the clown's costume for something more severe, and he no longer sported love knots in his hair, but it was the same complexion, swarthy as the king's, the same gleam of teeth behind the same arrogant smile, the same hook to the nose. He has not aged a day nor changed a whit, I thought, and then, strangely, my mind fastened upon the glove in my left hand. It is a curious instrument, the human mind, and mine could have, just then, settled on things of greater moment— on the presence of the king behind me; on the humilities I had endured because of this one; on the vow I had taken that someday, somewhere, I would once again place a sword point delicately at that throat and this time I would not stay my hand. And yet, standing there, I could think of only the glove in my left hand.

It was his eyes that departed mine, not mine his. They moved— not nervously, not with any start of surprise or sudden fear—to the king, and "Sire," he murmured, and then the eyes returned to mine, and he bowed, very slightly.

"Your servant, Mr. Mordaunt," he said.

"And yours, Brodrick," I said, and I stepped toward him a half step and struck him with the glove straight across the mouth.

He did not even blink. It was no blow delivered in polite restraint; I intended no rehearsed and subtle bow, no small and courteous smile, no polished and delicate insult delicately delivered; I meant to draw blood, and if I did not, it was because the glove was intended

352

for summer wear and but light silk mesh. But for all the heat of that blow, he did not even blink, and the smile stayed to his lips.

"What?" he said. "Three years older but still at your brawling, Mordaunt?"

The remark was clearly meant for the king; you would have thought, to hear the stickiness in his voice, the note of injured innocence, of a wrong unjustly received but patiently endured, that he spoke through taffy. And so I turned to face the king.

"I crave your pardon, Sire," I said. "It would seem that I have forgotten myself."

I had seen the king's smile, mocking and cynical, and I had seen it infinitely weary, and I had seen it tender. Now I saw it silky in anger. "It would seem that you had," he said, and his voice as cold and silky and distant as his smile. "I had thought that I purchased this day loyalty and courage. But it would seem that discretion were no part of my bargain."

"If your Majesty would but hear me out—"

"I pray you," he said, "do not be at interrupting me while I am engaged in sermonizing, Mordaunt."

I bowed my head and fell coldly silent.

"You must render me a small service, Brodrick," he said. "You must find me out a tutor can school Mordaunt in his manners."

"Sire," I said, "but let me explain—"

"I also pray you, do not offer to debate with me. Like one of your damned Quakers, come before me uncovered."

"I do not so intend, Sire. I would but explain how this one hath wronged me—"

"I would not know. An he hath murdered your father and despoiled your mother, I yet would not know. I would but hear your apology."

"I have already offered it, Sire."

"I would hear it directed to Brodrick."

I felt a stubborn anger well up within me. "I beg you, Sire, do not ask what I cannot grant—"

"I do ask it."

"Your Majesty," I pleaded, "ask of me anything else, it is freely yours. My fortune? Take it. My life? I offer it ungrudgingly. But my honor—"

353

"This, too," he said. "This, too, if need be."

I looked at his expression, and then I looked at Brodrick's smile, and I did not speak. And now the king looked at Brodrick. "I pray you," he said, "have the goodness to show this fellow from my presence, Alan."

A little longer I stood mute. Then I bowed to the inevitable. "I ask your pardon, Brodrick," I said. I did not look at him when I said it.

"Why, for what, Mordaunt?" he said, and the cheerful triumph in his voice was only a little worse than a vomit, gagged down with a morning beer against a small fever. "That blow? It is already forgotten—"

"Not the blow," I said. "For my impatience. Were it not for that, I would have waited for you without in the street, where I could have put your cowardice to the test in privacy."

I had seen His Majesty's eyes and smile silky in anger. Now I saw the smile wiped from his face and the eyes flare in rage. "That were enough," he said. "By God, it were, and you gone too far, Mordaunt. And had I any thoughts of your service, they are forgotten. And so get thee from my sight."

I looked steadily at him, and my smile, I think, was a match for his in silkiness. Because for a moment he was no king, he was but another man, exiled and indigent, and so for a heartbeat or two I dared look at him so. "If you are dismissing me, Sire," I said, "then that were two servants you have lost in a single day. For I mean to kill this man. Provide him with a guard, nay, give him a company, I still mean to find him out and run him through and so rid the world of two hundredweight of dung."

What was in his face now was not anger but pure incredulity; it was the expression of a man who cannot believe what he has just plainly heard. Then he rolled his eyes upward in his head, and "Name of God," he said, and his voice a little choked, "name of God, was ever man since Job asked to endure what I must endure? Men have been set upon by their enemies. But was ever another man chopped and hacked at by his friends as well?"

There was something comical in his expression, in the way his mouth turned down and his eyes up, and almost I laughed. I did not, but I knew the impulse, and when I awoke from that, the anger was gone out of me.

"Your Majesty," I said, "I am sorry for that. And I would retract it."

He said nothing, only looked at me.

"Sire," I said, "there is but one other face on earth would make me so forget myself. And if you will forgive me this one indiscretion, you may ask of me what you will."

"I have asked it," he said. "I would hear your apology. Delivered to Brodrick without trickery or reservation."

This time I looked full at Brodrick, "I apologize, sir," I said. "As my king hath commanded me."

He bowed, slightly and coldly, and I looked again to the king. "I would also have your solemn oath," he said, "that this will never be repeated. In my sight or out of it. For I have use for both of you."

"Never, Sire?"

"Never."

"Never is a very long time, Sire. I cannot promise you that." The anger flared into his face again, and I plunged on. "I have sworn an oath to kill this man someday, Sire. If you knew the cause, you would respect the intent, I think. But I can promise that he shall come to no harm because of me so long as your Majesty hath use for him."

"It doth not satisfy me," he said. "But it must do, I suppose. And now you have my leave to depart."

"With your Majesty's forgiveness? Or without it?"

"I must think on that a day or so."

"If I find you gracious, Sire, you will find me grateful." I bowed and then turned on my heel. But at the door I turned back. "An hour ago," I said, "you asked me to name a reward for serving you. I could think of none then. But have I your leave to name one now?"

"You have. Though I cannot promise to grant it."

"It is nothing costly, nor beyond your powers. I would but have you ask Brodrick for the reason behind that blow."

He looked curiously at me. "That were indeed small request. Though I cannot see to what purpose—"

"Why, only this. That if he tell you but half the truth, you shall then know how much I love you."

A moment longer I looked into his eyes. Then I stepped backward and closed the door quietly behind me.

ᛤ *Nineteen* ᛥ

The Dover Custom House stands just beyond the gate which has been called Pennyless Beach for time out of mind. You step ashore on a pier built of beech pilings and sandstone blocks, and you climb the cobbled and walled walk that comes down from the town walls to the water's edge, and the great chalk cliffs ring you about from north and south, and the blackened walls and towers of Dover Castle gloom down upon you from the hill behind the town. If you stepped ashore thus in the fall of 1657, and if you were a king's man and bent on mischief, you climbed that walk with a feeling not of panic perhaps, but at least of tight, bright alertness in chest and throat, for along the wall were Roundhead soldiers, their eyes hard on you as you made the climb. At the top of the walk, just where the old sea gate once was, you would push through a turnstile—the first I had ever seen that device—and then the walk led straight to the Custom House.

It was, I thought, a building very like the government it represented. It had been newly built within these sixty years, and it was plain fronted and serviceable and pretending to no nonsense about beauty. But like the city itself with its breached breakwaters and silt-choked harbor, it was already battered by flood and storm, its sandstone windows and doorways blackened and crumbling, its brick decayed. And if symbol without, then doubly symbol within. For here it was all dark, narrow, twisted passages and rooms like

356

rabbit warrens and everywhere the scurry and scramble of rounded shoulders and ink-stained fingers and officious eyes. Time was when I thought that this new age that has dawned, this Commonwealth become Protectorate, this patchwork of rags of custom and scraps of law, this spawn of greed that talks much and does little about liberty—that this were an age of merchants, where men eternally haggled away lives in the market place and sold birthrights at a thirty per cent profit. But I subscribe no more to this. Now I think it is an age where the government clerk has come into his own, an age of scrawlers and scribblers where of the making of records there is no end, where if a man but cough injudiciously it must be duly scratched upon parchment and so preserved for the edification of all posterity.

That August afternoon in 1657 I faced one of these new men. We sat in a room the size of a cottager's scullery and no better furnished, I squirming on a chair vilely uncomfortable, Mr. Robert Day seated before me at a rude table. He was a man who made the most of his twenty pounds *per annum*, was Mr. Robert Day, Clerk of the Dover Passage; he wore fine holland and finer silk, and he did not deny himself at table, and had it not been for a certain dustiness of complexion, you would have thought him a hearty Bedford squire. Just now he was bent over my papers, and then he cleared his throat and looked up. But not at me. Not directly at me. At a point somewhere between my hat and the ceiling, and his expression was distant and his thoughts his own.

"So you deal in silks, Mr. Bentley?" he said. "From out Marseilles?"

"On occasion."

"And this one such?"

"Why, no. I am come from Bruges this month."

"Bruges?" He gnawed reflectively on his quill. "Silks from out Bruges? I had not thought—"

"I had not said silks."

"Ah. And what commodity, then?"

"Sedition," I said.

The devil demands his due, and I freely give it him; he did not even blink. He had been many years civil servant to His Highness, and he had issued clearance on stranger cargoes than mine, and his

357

eyes, fixed on some point beyond me, wavered not by so much as the thickness of my thumbnail. "I think I have no such item on my duty list," he said.

"Have you not? I had heard that you have."

"I cannot recall it. It may be it hath been placed on the forbidden list. Were this . . . commodity intended for the London market? You may find the London market glutted this season."

"I have heard to the contrary. I think I may yet find a purchaser or two in England. And if I am proved wrong, why all life were some hazard, were it not?"

He shook his head. "Glutted. Believe one who hath watched the demand daily shrink and the importers ruined. Glutted."

And now I bent into that abstracted expression. "Mr. Day," I said, "I find myself grown weary of this conceit. I require a pass to travel up to London. In the name of Joseph Bentley, silk merchant. And I would have from you the price."

His eyes drifted dry and dusty down into mine. "And I cannot give it you," he said. "This commodity is plainly forbidden this season, and I cannot clear your cargo nor issue you pass to travel. Not so far as from here to Cross Street."

I sat there in that vilely furnished room, staring into those dusty eyes set in a broadish, squire's face, feeling within me the first stir and prick of anger. "Cannot?" I said. "Why can you not, Mr. Day?"

"Say that I have taken a sudden liking to you, Mr. Bentley. Say that I would not see you committed to the Fleet a bankrupt."

"Or say," I said dryly, "that you are grown greedier this year than last, and your price higher."

"No. That were not it. I swear it were not." His eyes wavered. "Let us rather say that discretion were ever the better part of valor. And cannot we permit it to go at that, Mr. Bentley?"

"Do you mean to warn me, Mr. Day? If so, can you not do me the courtesy of but a moment's plain speaking?"

"Why, yes," he said. "There is a certain Foster, a searcher, here at Dover. Yesterday he was close questioned by Major General Kelsey himself. Today he languishes in Dover Castle. In irons and under guard. And would that be spoken plainly enough?"

I made him no reply.

"I can name you twenty," he said, "have been taken this month

358

for lesser offenses than this you ask. And would that be spoken plainly enough?"

Still I made him no reply.

"I would not be the twenty-first," he said. "And would that be spoken plainly enough?" And now his eyes drifted ceilingward again, and he pursed his lips prettily. "And so, were I you," he said, "I think I should on the morrow purchase passage back to Flanders."

"Very well," I said. "If you think this discreet, Mr. Day."

"Discreet," he said. "Yes. You put it well, sir. Discreet."

I arose and paid him the courtesy of a small, curt bow, and now I knew not the prick but the swell of anger. They are your true merchants, the Robert Days of this world, I thought; they sell what is given into their hands to sell to any who can pay their price for it; they will sell you clearance or pass, false identity or true, intelligence or gossip, loyalty or treachery, the means to make rebellion or the means to be forgiven it; they would sell you God Almighty Himself if they could but acquire a monopoly on Him. And so, I thought, they prosper. They dress in silk and fine beaver hats, and they deny themselves not at table, and week by week the store of coin accumulates in the thrice-locked strongboxes, and they know within themselves the swell and purr of inner peace. But there must be no risk, I thought; but let them sniff out the brief, distant, acrid smell of danger and they draw in their heads like turtles nudged in the street by some stray mongrel.

I stood there and looked down upon him and thought those thoughts. But when I spoke, it was very softly, very carefully. "His Majesty will be greatly disappointed," I said.

"Be so kind as to remember me to His Majesty," he said. "Tell him I regret the necessity for extreme caution—"

"I shall. And your services in the past will be remembered, sir."

He waved a hand. "Trifling," he said. "Trifling."

"Why, no," I said. "Were they listed before you, all the kindnesses you have done us these five years, the exact dates and the trifling sums you have asked in return, I think you would not find it so. Indeed, you may expect such a list presently, Mr. Day. Writ in His Majesty's own hand."

"Nay," he said. "His Majesty hath greater demands on his time—"

"His Majesty is never so weighted down with duties that he cannot prove his gratitude to his friends."

He perceived my drift; I was certain he did; it was in his eyes. "I protest, sir," he said, "that though I am warmed—"

"Of course," I said, "it would be most unfortunate were such a letter to be by some slip misaddressed to Mr. Thurloe at Whitehall—"

He perceived my drift, all right. "In God's name, sir," he said, "in God's name, you would not repay—"

"Why, no," I said. "It would be the fault of some slip of pen or memory, nothing more."

His eyes were now neither distant nor dusty. His eyes were opened wide, and there was a flush to his sallow cheek. "What is it you would have of me?" he said, and you would have thought, to hear the hoarseness in his voice, that he had been exposed the week to Dover's night air.

"But a pass," I said. "But your name and the day to a scrap of paper, nothing more."

"I dare not. I swear to you I dare not—"

I shrugged. "Why, then, you dare not."

"I tell you I am suspected," he croaked. "I am a watched man. And you. Depend upon it, you will be followed once you leave here. And closeted with Kelsey ere you have achieved five miles—"

"It is not ten minutes since," I said, "that I remarked in passing on the hazards all of us must endure in this life."

His eyes surrendered then, and he drew paper to him and scribbled out my pass and thrust it toward me. "Your servant, Mr. Day," I said, and I stepped to the table and dropped before him a handful of coins.

He stared down at them. "What would these be?" he said.

"Why, your fee. It would be twenty shillings, would it not?"

"It hath been. On other occasions."

"I have paid you thirty. I think thirty a more significant sum for these times. Do you not agree, Mr. Day?"

"Yours is the wit here," he said. "But I would have God judge which of us is the Judas."

I smiled softly down upon his raised face, his narrowed eyes, his soft clerk's hands lying before him on the scarred table. "Recall to mind your Scripture, Mr. Day," I said. "Take to heart the parable of the servants. Put this small sum to wise use."

"And what would that be?"

"Fence mending, Mr. Day," I said.

Mr. Day was in error in one regard: I was not followed in my ride to London. For Mr. Hyde was an old hand at conspiracy, and I left Dover following his instructions to the letter. In every detail, he had warned me, I must appear to be a plain country squire jogging up to London for a few days' pleasure; I must wear a plain, serviceable suit and a plainer hat, and if my host invited me to drink with him, I must accept, and at night I must sleep in my clothes, and I must lodge only at small country inns.

I stayed my first night in one such inn. Indeed, it was so small that no beds were available, and so I sat up the night, playing shuffleboard and drinking warm, stout Kentish ale with four maltsters. Come dawn, I was already an hour on my way. If there is anywhere on this earth a countryside as beautiful as that about Dover, I have never met with it, and that day I rode straight into the heart of as fine a summer day as you are lucky to meet with thrice in a twelvemonth. I jogged steadily along the king's highway toward Canterbury, through countryside so quietly lovely it caught you by the throat, with my portmanteau strapped behind me, and a fine, light dust filming my brown fustian suit, and a nightcap on my head and my head already itching under the unaccustomed peruke I wore. I was the ten miles to Canterbury before noon and beyond Rochester by nightfall. I stayed this night at an inn where there was a bed to let, though I had to share it with an unwashed carter who snored most abominably. The next day, in the very center of the afternoon, I rode into Southwark.

I crossed the Bridge without let or hindrance. That night I talked late with Dr. Honeywood, the Roman Catholic surgeon in Drury Lane, about the plans and hopes in England for a rising this winter; I discovered to my amazement that a papist could also be a loyal Englishman, for Dr. Honeywood was as opposed to an invasion by Spanish troops as I. The next night, promptly at seven, I sat down to my supper in John Wharton's victualing house in Creed Lane.

It was, I gathered, popular in and about Blackfriars, for the two tables in the ordinary were noisily filled, and I must part three curtains before I found an empty private room. In the first I startled an aged and wheezing merchant who was engaged in fumbling explorations of the charms of a woman whose dress was that of a fine lady and whose face was that of a slut. In the second I did not startle a lady alone, dressed all in dove gray, for she sat with her back to me. The third I entered. I was barely seated before mine host followed me through the curtain.

"Begging your pardon, sir," he said, "but this room were engaged." Then his eyes strayed to my hat and he coughed discreetly behind his hand. "Begging your pardon a second time," he said. "It is a busy night and I am grown unobservant."

"Unobservant?" I said. "Of what, pray?" For I would make no mistake about whom I spoke to.

"Of hats. Wouldst care to order, sir?"

"Sack. And cold beef."

"No beef, sir. Excellent fowl, hot or cold, duck or pheasant—"

"Beef," I said. "It must be beef."

He ducked his head. "An I must send to Ludgate Hill for it, beef it shall be, sir."

He backed out of the room. I lounged down against the wall behind me, prepared to wait out half the night for beef fetched clean from Ludgate Hill. At a table just without the curtain someone proposed a ribald toast to Mrs. John Lambert, may she continue to rest comfortable on her back, may she continue to be pricked by something blunter and sturdier than her husband's horns. That prompted a burst of laughter and much slapping of open palms on thighs. And then the curtain parted a second time.

But by no waiter and by no furtive royalist conspirator. My hat was far down over my eyes, and so all I saw at first was a skirt, dove gray, and gray shoes peeping from under it. For a little I considered through sleepy eyes the hem of that skirt. Then I pushed back my hat and raised my eyes. My mouth was already open, though I know not what I was about to say; something, I suppose, about not being in the market this night.

My mouth stayed open, but I made no such remark. I made no remark at all. For I was staring at the delicate complexion like pale country butter and the red-gold curls, the red lips, and the smoky gray eyes of Elizabeth Carey.

I know not how long I stared at her thus, my mouth dropped open like some country bumpkin's on his first sight of London Bridge, while she repaid my bad manners with a look calm and level and cool. Then she smiled, and the spell was broken, and I clawed my way to my feet and fumbled for my hat.

"Madam," I said.

"I thought it was you," she said. "And so you are alive, then."

The remark was edged with no ill intent, no shade of regret. And yet it was unfortunate, for it brought to mind My Lord Monson, lounged down in his great chair, with the bright square of sunlight behind him and his hand cupped over the fault to his cheek. "I am," I said shortly, and I did not add, "No fault of you or yours." But I had no need to; it was in my voice.

She sobered and something like consternation flitted across her face. But very briefly; it rested there no longer than the blink of an eye. "I find more years in your face," she said. "And your suit is in fashion this season, and your hat does not scream country."

"I find no more in yours," I said. "Though that gown whispers Presbyterian."

She smiled faintly. "Fashions change. And our new parliament hath been busy this year with decrees against female nakedness. And would I have your permission to sit, sir?"

"Pray forgive my bad manners," I said. "I fear they have been something blunted these three years."

I pulled out a chair for her. She dropped into it and cupped chin in hand and set to a study of my face, the gravity returned again to lip and eye. "Are you in London long?" she said. "And have you made your peace, then, with Whitehall?"

"Neither the one nor the other, madam."

"The name would be Elizabeth. To those I would call friend."

"And would I be one such?"

"If I confessed to it, would that make me forward?"

"If it would," I said softly, "then I would have you so, Elizabeth," and I looked as gravely as she into her eyes. "I am in London but until the morrow," I said. "And my name is Joseph Bentley this fall."

"You must know of the danger. They have little mercy these days for those who are at the king's business."

"Danger and I are no strangers. Indeed, I have grown some small appetite for it. Though I have not said I was on the king's business."

"And are you not?"

I was thinking that she had the gift to encourage rashness in me, did Elizabeth Carey; she had prompted one indiscretion on a spring road that staggered vilely into Dorking, with my arms loosely about her and her face turned smiling into mine and her eyes all alight. But I was enough older this year to have learned caution. And so I lied to her, the first lie that came into my mind. "The business I am on is my own," I said.

Very briefly her eyes strayed to my hat and something like bewilderment came into her face; just such an expression she might have worn had she come upon someone from behind and called out his name and then been faced by a stranger. "And soon accomplished, I can hope," she said. "For England is no safe place—"

"Very soon," I said. "It will require but a pair of days, no more."

Again her eyes strayed to my hat. "I cannot believe I am in error," she said.

"In error, madam?"

This time her eyes did no straying, though to judge from them, you would have thought I had just struck her. "You must forgive my prying, John," she said. "For I must ask you what this business would be."

I smiled crookedly, for I was remembering certain rash statements of mine on the topic of liberty of conscience. She must have read the smile for she frowned suddenly. "It is no idle curiosity prompts me, John," she said.

"I am returned to repay an old debt," I said.

"What debt? And to whom owed?"

I looked coolly into her eyes. "I mean to kill your uncle," I said.

Her eyes widened and she caught her breath. And then she smiled. "If you must sport with me, John, I pray you choose—"

"I have been more serious twice or thrice in my life. But no more than twice or thrice, I think."

"Then you are mad—"

"Why, so I may be. If a passion against vermin be madness."

"Mad," she said. "For you could choose no better way to ruin all. And for but a small, fancied wrong, and so long in the past it should have grown as cold as forgotten porridge—"

"Small?" I cried out. "Fancied? Would you care to see my back, madam? Have you the night to hear a tale?"

"Grave, then," she said, and her eyes flicked to the curtain. "Grave. And for the love of heaven, lower your voice—"

"Small," I repeated, though I heeded her sharp warning, I dropped my voice to a hiss. "Fancied. I was falsely accused of high treason, and all the cause was naked greed for another scrap of land. And when I would not confess, he must contrive my escape and so invent a pretense—"

Now it was her turn to stare. "Your escape? He contrived no escape—"

"Then who—" And then I broke off, staring, knowing the answer before she could offer it. "You," I said. "It was you. And why? Why?"

"Can you not hit on the answer to that?"

"No. I was a stranger to you, a country fellow with little wit and worse clothes, a clod you had known not two full hours. And so I would hear from your own lips—"

She dropped her eyes, and a faint flush betrayed itself against the white of her bodice. "You confess to a passion against vermin," she said. "I confess to one against injustice."

"You must have a very great fortune indeed," I said dryly. "That you can indulge a hundred pounds on but a whim—"

"I am in no great need. Though were I poorer than I am, I would yet make the purchase. Nor regret it later. For it was no whim, John." And now she raised her eyes again, and the flush was faint in throat and cheek, and if you could have gone untouched by the smile she bent on me, then you are less human than I. "I have squandered more in a single hour and purchased less," she said. "And you could discharge this trifling debt with but a single promise."

"Which were what?"

"That you will put away from you this humor for revenge."

I was but human, and the flush lay delicate and very pretty along throat and cheek, and her eyes and smile were soft. And yet the thought must cross my mind, warily and cynically, that she had owned a pretty face for enough years to have mastered something of the art of play-acting. And so the sullenness was still in my voice when I answered her. "He were less rogue than I had thought, your

365

uncle," I said. "But not greatly less. He must still quarter a troop on the Priory, he must still harry my mother from under a roof that was not mine. And so do not ask this of me."

"I do not ask it," she said quietly. "I command it, rather."

I smiled. "Yours is a pretty face. And I am in your debt for a hundred pounds and one life. But by what other authority do you command me? To this or ought else?"

For the third or fourth time this night her eyes strayed to my hat; it seemed to hold a fascination for her. When they returned, they were no more soft, and she smiled not at all. "Do I find you in health, sir?" she said.

I frowned. "Excellent. Though what bearing—"

"And what of your appetite, Mr. Mordaunt? Your reply to that, if you please."

I had been asked that question thirty times within the month; I had heard it so frequently from Mr. Hyde that my response was as unthinking as if I were an actor replying to a cue. "Better today than yester—" I began, and then I broke off. I had been served my share of surprises for supper this night, but this one was the most amazing of all, and so I broke off and for a second time within the hour my mouth dropped open.

She was smiling again. But not softly. "And would that be sufficient authority, Mr. Mordaunt?" she said.

"You are—" I stammered. "You are—" I twisted about on the bench, the better to face her, and I can recall that my two hands, lying before me, seemed on the sudden awkward and clumsy and much too large, as if I had sat down to dine unwashed. "You are niece to My Lord Monson," I said, "and kin to the Protector, and yet you would have me believe—"

"I am also daughter to Thomas Carey. Who died at Worcester. I am his heiress in more ways than one."

"One of us," I said. "You are one of us. Yet you plead for the life of this—this— You would think you were his daughter to hear you—"

"Not his daughter," she said, and now her smile was such as I had never seen on her face before and would not again more than once or twice, a smile that turned me as cold as if a wind had blown in from the street and the season not summer, a smile glittering and

366

hard and ruthless as the burnished and honed edge of a stiletto. "I shall weep no more tears over his grave than you," she said.

"Then why—"

"For that he serves some purpose at present," she said, as sharply as if I were a slow scholar and she my governess and come to the end of her patience. "He enjoys the confidence of the mighty. And I enjoy his."

Her eyes fell away from mine, and I looked at the side of her face, composed once again and gravely pretty in the candlelight. And what have they wrought, I thought, the jackals who sit in our mutilated parliament, the knaves who attend the Council of State, the usurper who pretends to nothing but love and devotion to this land, what in God's name have they wrought? Not ten years since a king died in the name of liberty and justice and the greater dignity of the subject, I thought, not ten years. And already is there anyone in the land is not at once betrayer and betrayed, cozener and cozened? And will there ever be an end to it, the dealing and the double-dealing, the buying and selling and trepanning? I thought that, my eyes bitterly on as pretty a profile as you will rarely see save in an ivory miniature, and then I bent my gaze onto my two hands, twisted awkwardly together on the table before me. We sat thus a little in a sullen and brooding silence, and then one hand was lightly over the two of mine. "What is it, John?" she said.

"Nought," I said shortly. "A private joke, and something too morbid for ears as delicate as yours."

"Or for ears not to be trusted? Which, John?"

I looked at the hand lying soft and ungloved over mine, the color of it under the uncertainty of the candlelight as delicate as tinted ivory. "I was thinking of a grave," I said. "It would be two years now since the night he died in my arms, in the rain, and he asked not much of me with his dying breath, and I promised him what he asked. But death is eternal, I have heard, and so I can hope that he hath more patience than the living." I withdrew my hand from under hers and opened it and looked at the fingers and then clenched it again. "It would appear I was not born to exact revenge," I said. "My stars must be wrongly in conjunction for it. I must to the latest fashion in astrologers afore I depart London—"

"Private, indeed," she said. "A very riddle. Or babbling—"

"It is," I said. "Though I shall perhaps tell you the tale someday."
I brought my eyes up into hers and smiled wearily. "Very well," I
said. "You have my word. Grave or no grave, vow or no vow, My
Lord Monson shall be permitted to stink up English air for yet an-
other year or two. Or if he does not, it will be no fault of mine.
And you have instructions for me, I was told."

She gave them to me, swiftly and clearly, her voice as distant
and cool as some veteran general's explaining a battle plan. She gave
me a cipher, a small, black book with enough names in it to hang
half the great in England, each name assigned a number (Charles
Stuart: 163; Hyde: 71; the Earl of Ormonde: 96); I was to write all
letters in cipher, and I must choose my carriers discreetly, for John
Thurloe was an artist at intercepting treasonous letters and a genius
at breaking ciphers. She gave me the names of those I was to approach—names of old loyalists who were still at large and still to be
trusted; names of Presbyterians who longed for the king's return and
without conditions; names of more fanatic Presbyterians who would
impose the old terms on him and who must be dissuaded from that
course—or, if they could not, why, then, promise them what I must,
for half the history of politics was a history of promises made and
promises broken. And she gave me a packet of commissions, some
filled in, some blank, all signed by His Majesty, all giving leave and
authority to raise troops in the name of Charles Rex. One of these
she dwelt on; it was issued to a John Stapely in Sussex. I would
find Mr. Stapely insufferable, she said; he was but twenty-three, and
both youth and arrogance sat heavy on him; he was, moreover, son
of one of the late king's judges. But he was certain that the king
would be brought back, and he was eager to make amends for the
sins of his father, and he was a member of parliament and carried
great weight with the Presbyterian party. And so I was to give him
what he asked for, even if it were commander-in-chief of all the
forces in the south. Which, she added dryly, it was like to be.

She finished. And, "One further question," I said. "That day on
the Dorking Road. Were you even then—"

She nodded. "Even then."

"And yet you betrayed me to your uncle—"

"I did not," she said. "I swear I did not. It was but something I
mentioned in passing—"

"But he made use of it. And is this, then, why you purchased my escape?"

"Mayhap. In part."

"In part? What the whole of it, then?"

"Are you all that dense, John?"

"Aye," I said. "I own no more wit than most country fellows. And so I would hear you say—"

Once or twice this night I had seen her face grave, and I had seen it soft and warm, and I had seen it ruthless. Now I saw it change again. She turned her face away from me, almost as if she knew that she was to best advantage in profile, and then she looked side-wise at me, out of the corner of her eye, and I was all at once reminded of one of your coquettes in the Cheap, with the young, crude, whey-faced, empty-headed rake boldly ogling bosom and ankle, and the invitation raw on his silly, dissipated face, and her fan fluttering before her lips and her eyelashes all a-flutter and her eyes proclaiming to all the world that she was a very harlot at heart. It was a look that became her not for it was wholly out of character, and yet she must employ it on me, and her voice when she replied was as light and empty as her expression. "You spoke out boldly against the present government that day," she said. "And so shall we say that I perceived some use for you? Even then?"

"I know not," I said. "Shall we?"

"Were this not as sound a reason as another?"

"Were it the truth, it were." I came abruptly to my feet and then stood looking down upon her. "Would this be the truth of it, Elizabeth?"

She returned my look, her countenance grave again, that empty, frivolous expression all erased in the time it took me to achieve my feet. "I think you know very little of women, John Mordaunt," she said.

I touched my hat to her. "Little enough," I said. "Even less, I would guess, than I know of men."

ᏖᎠ *Twenty* ᎠᏖ

It was one thing, I was to discover, to join a rebellion; it was quite another to head one.

It was a fall and winter of hope; it was a fall and winter of despair. The new parliament recessed in June, and that summer all the talk in London was of the Protector's new Council of State and of dissension at Whitehall. And there must have been fire with the smoke, for some of the mighty fell that fall, even some who had fought side by side with Cromwell in the old Ironsides regiment, even the great John Lambert, Major General in London and second in power only to Cromwell himself. Lambert had been in a pout the entire year, for it seemed now that he would not be named to succeed the Protector, and so he was sullen about the creation of the "Other House" as it was called, and about the Protector's new and greater powers, and about the oath now required of all members of the Council, that they would be loyal to the Protector's person and faithful to the government as established by the Humble Petition and Advice. And so in August he was relieved of all his offices and titles and retired to Wimbledon, there to potter among his roses and to work at the needle with his wife and maids and to await the storm which would recover his fortunes for him.

You had that meat to feed on were you a royalist in the winter of 1657-58, and we fed on it, waiting for a palace revolution, waiting for a mutiny in the army, waiting for any storm to break and for blood to stain the cobbles before Whitehall. But there was no storm;

the clouds scuttled a month or so and then blew over, and the Council submitted meekly to the will of the Protector, and the army pledged anew their allegiance, and nothing came of it that could be called advantage.

Then it was off with the old year and on with the new, and all the talk suddenly of the "Other House." For Cromwell was now determined that the land should once again have two houses in Parliament, after the old way. And so we waited and watched to see whom he would name the new peers of the land. Though we all knew; they would be honest and well affected, men with Christian and English interests at heart—which was Oliver's way of describing men who had procured their present possessions by their wits and were resolved to enlarge them by selling their consciences. Hence it was no surprise when Colonel Hewson, the shoemaker, was named one of the new lords, along with Colonel Pride, the drayman who had first purged an English parliament. Nor was it matter for surprise when old peers refused the Protector's invitation and declined to sit beside such jackals.

The parliament returned from its recess in January, its mood choleric and defiant. It opened with a debate on its prerogatives, a debate put to the test by the recall of the members excluded in the spring. That fetched back friends as well as enemies, old, inveterate Republicans like Haselrig and Thomas Scot as well as king's men like Sir George Booth. They trooped back, and they mumbled the required oath ("I shall heartily take the oath," Haselrig said; "I will be faithful to my Lord Protector's person; I will murder no man") and they resumed their seats while Cromwell looked sullenly on. That victory accomplished and they squandered a month in quibbling over the name for the new Second Chamber, while the Protector harangued them twice weekly in the Painted Chamber, one day pleading and the next threatening, one day urging them to their duties as patriotic Englishmen, the next commanding them to cease debating on what concerned them not but to enter upon such business as might be for the benefit and not the distraction of the Commonwealth—by which he intended the voting of money for his needs. And then, in February, the Protector ceased debating. On the fourth of February, at ten in the morning, he dissolved his parliament.

And now we more than hoped, now we openly rejoiced. For

Oliver was at his wit's end, it was said. The parliament had voted him no money, and his army was six months in arrears—the London troops walking barefoot in the dead of winter and Monck's Scottish troops starving—and he had four regiments in Flanders and not a sixpence to press the war there, and so desperate was the condition of the navy that the fleet must stay at sea for that there was no money to pay the sailors if the ships docked. Abroad he was deserted by his old allies, and at home half his regiments were infected with sedition. And English citizens were on the sudden grown bolder that winter, with 'prentices plotting riots in half the taverns in town, and merchants incensed at the unpopular excise tax; with Anglicans and Anabaptists and Quakers and Fifth Monarchy Men and Levellers all joined now in their common hatred of this latest tyranny; in Coleman Street the voices in the meeting-houses were all raised now to demand the death of the anti-Christ, and twenty thousand in and about London signed a petition to recall the Long Parliament and re-establish the Commonwealth and abolish both Council of State and the Protector's veto powers. And while all England muttered and grumbled, the king sat poised near Breda, with eight thousand flocked to his colors and twenty Dutch sloops and ten English frigates (deserters from Cromwell's own navy) in the harbor at Ostend, and only the lack of a port in England to give him pause.

The time had never seemed riper for bringing back the king. And yet it was a year of despair. We were two parties that year—one the old Sealed Knot, the other those in the land who were for immediate action. Brodrick was the king's principal agent for the Knot and I for the Action party, and our instructions were to work closely together. But no saint could have worked sweetly with Brodrick, and not even Job could have kept his patience with the Knot. For ten years now they had endured fines, decimation, sequestration, banishment, imprisonment, Major Generals, and general harassment, and now the heart was gone out of them. A half dozen times that winter I went up to London to wait upon Sir Richard Willis in his lodgings in Gray's Inn or to meet Brodrick in the Mermaid Tavern in Bucklersbury, and each time I must listen to advice to wait for Cromwell's officers to do our work for us, wait for his Council to defy him, wait for Lambert to march out of Wimbledon at the head of his old troops, wait for Oliver's death. Truly, for each letter

I posted to Hyde that winter urging immediate action, there was another from Brodrick or Willis warning him against my rash and impetuous impatience. I verily believe that had Charles landed that winter with ten thousand at his back and not five hundred still faithful to the Protector, the Knot would have stood at the gaze and done nothing until they had seen the outcome of the first battle.

As if this were not sufficient discouragement, the interests within our own party must add yeast to the devil's brew. There were factions enough that winter who were at one in their hatred of the Protector. But they were at one in nothing else; all was bickering and distrust and accusation and jealousy among us. Moderate Presbyterians could agree to bring Charles back without conditions, but they must be continually squabbling with old Anglicans over who was to command this county, who to captain that company. More fanatic Presbyterians would not exchange the young, debauched Charles for the old, tyrannical Oliver until they were promised no bishops, no episcopacy, the Kirk instead of the Church. The Levellers and Republicans would come in if we promised them no established church at all, no tithing, no bishops, and no power whatsoever in the hands of the king. And so all that sixmonth I— no politician—must be at smoothing the ruffled feathers of this cock, flattering the self-esteem of this fool, allaying the fears of that reformed knave.

And so by January, with weekly letters from Hyde ordering us to put ourselves in all possible and speedy readiness (for the king was now at Breda, he wrote, and the Spanish had finally granted him money and supplies, and the ships at Ostend were ready to sail on the instant), we were no nearer the mark than we had been in July. Indeed, we were further off, for Cromwell had not been idle. Even before his parliament sat in January, he was once again at his old work, sweeping up seditious preachers out of Coleman Street, purging the disaffected out of his armies, banishing all known royalists and papists to without twenty miles of London, the city streets all full of soldiers now and God have mercy on the man who was found supping in a tavern and who could not give a good and close account of himself, passes required if you would travel but from Ludgate Hill to Threadneedle Street, curfew severely enforced in the city and everywhere the guards doubled. And in the provinces the defenses strengthened in all the port towns, and soldiers on every highway, and in every county the militia warned to seize upon all suspicious persons. It was not the first time that Cromwell had owned to odds of ten to one and had faced them down and had triumphed. Nor was it the first time that he had had as much help from his enemies as from his friends.

Our affairs were in such a posture when, in January, I received a letter from Hyde, his news that the Earl of Ormonde would shortly land in England to meet with all the leaders of this business who were within a three-day ride of London.

There is an apothecary shop in West Cheap, belonging to one John Chase, and here we met that night of the fifth of February. The night was bitter enough to provide us excuse for walking the streets muffled to the eyes in cloaks and scarves, and we arrived by ones and twos, mounting the dark, narrow staircase and knocking thrice and whispering that we would speak to Mr. Pickering and being stealthily admitted. By nine of the clock a dozen were crowded into a room fitfully lit by a small fire in the grate and a few candles, the room itself all shuttered and draped and the door barred, the shadows from the candlelight playing in the corners of the room like nervous mice, the faces grouped about the table or lounging down in the chairs vague and uncertain and conspiratorial.

I was the last to arrive; the great clock at St. Paul's was striking nine and the watch crying out that it was the curfew hour when I mounted the stairs. Young, apple-cheeked John Stapely had arrived before me, with one of his newly commissioned captains, Henry Mallory; and Sir Richard Willis and Brodrick; and little Dick Pile, ridden all the way from Bristol; and a Colonel Roscarrock, here to speak for Sir John Grenville; and a Colonel Legge; and Ned Villiers, still wearing his prison pallor from the last time he had dared John Thurloe's displeasure by coming boldly up to London; and Sir George Booth, looking blunt and bluff and honest as ever, looking also very black, for he had sat in this latest parliament and the Protector's dissolution had struck only yesterday. When I entered, one of these rose from his place near the fire and advanced on me. "You would be Mordaunt," he said.

"And you Ormonde." I was, I fear, staring rudely at his hair, for it was streaked and mottled a fantastic variety of red and gold and orange and gray. "We met in Bruges. Though your hair was not then—"

He grinned. "I cannot abide a peruke. And Will Legge there took an oath he had a mixture would dye my own locks black as a raven's wing. Aqua-fortis, he said, that were the very thing—"

"It were the demned chemist," Legge protested. He was lounged down in a far, dim corner of the room, a thick man with great mustaches. "Demn me but it was. A very demned knave and I shall cut out his heart—"

"As to the color," Ormonde said, "that a man can live with an he look in a glass not oftener than once a week. But the stuff scalded my scalp. Now I not only cannot abide a peruke, I can scarce endure a hat." He still smiled, but he was looking at me with head cocked, his shrewd, cold, soldier's eyes in a face so handsome it was almost girlish searching out my face. "You were not followed here?" he said.

I shook my head. "I think I was not, My Lord. I was devoutly cautious."

He nodded. "Three times in as many days I have had to take to my heels. With search parties not five minutes behind. And how goeth the world in Surrey?"

"Apace. Treason flourishes a little if you can remember to water it. And abroad?"

"Better there nor here, I fear. More heart there than I find here."

"You will find heart here as well, My Lord, if you know where to search it out."

"Which would not be in this room, I think."

"You wrong us, My Lord. You cannot say so of John Stapely there. Or—"

"Why, no." He glanced to the table where sat Sir Richard Willis and Brodrick. Sir Richard's eyes were as sleepy as ever and Brodrick's countenance sullen and his lips a-pout. "Not of him. But of Sir Richard there. He is discouraged, is Sir Richard. He is all for postponement for another year."

"Sir Richard is a cautious man. It hath something to do with a certain nervousness about gaol fever, as I recall."

"Better caution than rashness," Sir Richard said hotly. "And I would remind you, My Lord Ormonde, we had heart once. We

375

had heart enough to betray us in '55. And there are enough say that the king's affairs go not so forward as we have been told."

"I have told you the posture of the king's affairs," Ormonde said softly. "And do you doubt my word, Sir Richard?"

"No, he would not, My Lord," I said quietly. "He would but tell you that you can count on no help from the Knot. They shall prove loyal enough once His Majesty is returned, but until then—"

"Now, by God," Brodrick burst out, and struck the table before him. "Now, by God, Mordaunt, that were enough. Do you claim a monopoly on loyalty? And while ye are about it, imputing the while an excess of timidity to the rest of us? As you have so imputed to me a sixmonth—"

"Longer nor that, Brodrick," I said sweetly. "Longer nor that."

"Impute, then," he said. "Impute and be damned to you. For I tell you we are already suspected—"

"In God's name," I said wearily, "canst name a day since '44 when we have not been?"

"—and betrayed," he said. "Betrayed. The Protector hath banished all known royalists to within twenty miles of London—"

"As he hath done thrice a year this decade," I said.

"—and but yesterday doubled the guards at all the gates—"

"His army is six months in arrears," I said. "He must provide them exercise will take their minds off the growling in their bellies and the frostbite in their bare feet."

"—and My Lord Bellasys in the Tower, and the guards tripled on Tower Hill, and Cromwell speaking openly about threatened alarums and invasions by the old, restless, brainsick party here at home and the popish inveterate enemy abroad. I tell you I am with Sir Richard, I am for postponement—"

"And I am not," I said. " 'Sblood, the town buzzes with treason. Listen but a quarter hour to the talk in any tavern, you will hear nought but the dissolution of the parliament, and Oliver at his wit's end for money and out of his head for fear, and the 'prentices never so restless—"

"Then let them do our work for us," Sir Richard said.

I swung savagely on him. "In the summer," I said, "your advice was to wait for the army to do our work for us. In August it was wait for John Lambert. In September we were visited by the malignant fever, this thing they call the 'new disease,' and now it was wait for that to carry off the Protector. What shall it be next year, Sir Richard?"

"You can rave and posture," he said. "You have no estates to lose. And you were conveniently gone from the country when we suffered under the Major Generals—"

I laughed shortly. "Speak not to me of suffering. Wouldst compare backs with me, Sir Richard?" I turned back to Ormonde. "I tell you, My Lord, if it is a rising the king must have, look not to the Knot for it. Come to Surrey if you would discover out a little courage—"

"We need more nor courage," Ormonde said. "We must have a port. The king cannot land an army save he have a port."

"I had thought we had one. Roscarrock wrote a month ago that Gloucester—"

"Aye," Roscarrock said from his place near the door. "For twenty thousand pounds."

"Why, promise it. Tell him it will be paid the day the king is returned—"

"It must be paid now. He hath been paid in promises before, he says. This time he hath a preference for gold."

From the draped casement, small, officious Dick Pile stepped forth. "It must be Bristol, then," he said. "You can count on three thousand—"

"If you listen to Dicky Pile, My Lord," Brodrick said, "you must have first mastered your mathematics, for any number of his must be divided by ten. Even then it is doubtful that the computation will be a modest one."

Pile puffed out his chest and thereby managed to look more foolish than usual; he was a small, pompous man with overlarge ears and a pointed chin, and just now he looked for all the world like a pouter pigeon. "Dost call me liar, Brodrick?" he said.

"Why, no," Brodrick said. "But a coxcomb, Dick."

"Nay," Ormonde said sharply. "Cease this." He bent his shrewd, cold eyes on Pile. "Three thousand, say you? All engaged by you, Pile?"

"Why, yes," Brodrick said. "For he hath put it out, My Lord, that he is the king's principal agent in all England." He was lounged down blackly in his chair, was Brodrick, and he now engaged himself in a gloomy study of the flicker of candlelight on his fingernails.

"There were four companies dispatched west this week," he said. "Wouldst match your imaginary three thousand against four hundred Roundhead regulars, Dick?"

"Shrewsbury, then," Pile said. "I still have hope for Shrewsbury. I—"

"Last week it was Hull," Brodrick said. "Ha' ye lost heart over Hull, Dick? And in but a sennight?"

"They have arrested Captain Gardiner—"

"So they have. And ten more. And so tell us now of Shrewsbury, Dick."

"I have felt out Colonel Mackworth—"

"Mackworth!" Brodrick lost interest on the sudden in his fingernails. "Mackworth!" He looked at Ormonde. "I tell you, My Lord," he said, "here is Pile, knows as much as you or I. I must confess it terrifies me to know so senseless a creature should know all he does. I swear to God it does."

"He is right, Pile," I said, as gently as I could. "You have as much hope of engaging John Thurloe as Mackworth, and you are a very fool."

"Now, by God," Brodrick said, "a very miracle. Once in six months Mordaunt hath agreed with someone other than himself. A very damned miracle, on my word, it is."

I looked at him. But I said nothing, only looked back to Ormonde. "What of Yarmouth, My Lord? It could be surprised, for there are not two hundred in the garrison there. And I can raise five hundred in Surrey. Give me leave, I shall attempt Yarmouth."

"You know the risk you run, Mordaunt?"

"I have run risks before, My Lord."

"If you fail, the entire business is ruined. If you succeed, and if by some misadventure of wind or tide the king cannot immediately sail, you will bring down a wasp's nest about your ears."

"Why, then, I shall be stung, shall I not?"

He smiled and then clapped me on the shoulder. "Bring this off and you shall know the king's gratitude. Believe me but you shall."

I glanced at Brodrick. "I shall ask but little, My Lord," I said.

He turned to the others. "We must have diversions," he said. "The king cannot face the Protector's entire army alone. What of the west, Roscarrock? What of Grenville?"

378

"He says he must have arms for five thousand," Roscarrock said. "And field pieces. He says he dare not move without those."

Ormonde looked wearily at Roscarrock a little, digesting that impossibility. Then he swung on Villiers, lounging negligent and indifferent near the fire. "What of Fairfax, Ned?"

Villiers shook his head. "Nothing, My Lord. He mutters some vagueness about My Lord Say, something about the old conditions—"

"God's name, you are his son-in-law, Ned, cannot you persuade—"

"I have no greater powers of persuasion than God granted me, My Lord."

"You had powers enough when it was your own skin," Ormonde said savagely. "You had powers and to spare when you must have Oliver's forgiveness." He looked now to Sir George Booth, and the look was that of a man who watched the cast of the dice and his last shilling at stake. "What of Chester, Sir George?" he said.

Booth had spoken not a word this entire hour. He sat near Will Legge, gloomy and preoccupied, and now his voice was as cautious as the broad, stolid set of his face. "I cannot say, My Lord," he said. "Shall His Majesty have Spanish soldiers to his back?"

"We must have foreign help, Sir George. You know as well as I—"

"Then do not count on Chester. Nor on me, My Lord. We are Presbyterians in Chester. We take our hatred of papists seriously. Particularly Spanish papists. Give me Oliver over Spanish papists, My Lord."

Ormonde's eyes swept the room around, bitter and contemptuous. "So that would be it, would it?" he said. "So not one of you save Mordaunt will stir off your cowardly arses—"

"I will, My Lord," Stapely said. "I and three hundred—"

Ormonde stared a little at this one, young and apple-cheeked as any schoolboy. "Three hundred," he whispered. "Three hundred. In all of England, three hundred."

"And I," Legge growled. "Three hundred and I, My Lord. If the king lands, you can count on a demned riot or two here in London. In the teeth of Barkstead's demned regiment filling the demned streets."

"Why, I thank you, Will," Ormonde said. "But clearly—" And then he broke off. For there was the sound of a commotion without, the sound of coach wheels on the cobbles, and feet running up the staircase, and a sharp and peremptory rapping, and Will Legge out of his chair and reaching to snuff the nearest candle. Save that he did not. For someone was crying out on the other side of the door, "Mr. Pickering, I would speak with Mr. Pickering," and it was a woman's voice, and Ned Villiers was across the room and had unbarred the door, and he swung it open, and Elizabeth Carey stepped through.

For an instant or two she but stood there, breathless from her run up the stairs. And then, "I think you are betrayed, gentlemen," she said.

If some of us were surprised enough to stand paralyzed a moment, Ormonde was not. For Ormonde this was but repetition, and he was to the door before she even finished speaking. "Betrayed, ma'am?" he said.

"Soldiers," she said. "At the end of the street. They will be searching this house within a quarter hour."

Ormonde turned back to us. "No great cause for panic, gentlemen," he said. "There is a back way. Follow the alley, it will bring you out upon Gutherans Street. You will not, I trust, impute any cowardice to me if I leave first. The Protector, I think, hath a very great hunger to lay me by the heels."

"I should not go by the back way, My Lord," I said. "If they should have the foresight, they will have seen to the back. I would go boldly by the front."

"Walk straight into their hands—"

"My lady hath a coach in front. It were shrewder to leave in her company."

"Flee from them in a lumbering coach—"

"Not flee. Do not hope to flee. Go boldly to meet them. But you shall be very drunk when they stop you. A rake on his way home with his latest conquest in his arms." I looked at Elizabeth Carey. "You must disarrange your clothing, my lady. That bodice were somewhat high in the neck for a slut's. And so disengage a button or two if you would."

Ormonde laughed. He was no stranger to danger, was My Lord, and his laugh was light and joyous. "Now, by God, Mordaunt," he said, "I think you have a touch of the rogue in you."

380

"It is the age we live in, My Lord. The price a man hits on for survival. One more question afore ye part from us, sir."

"Ask it. So it be short."

"Who else knew of these meetings save these present? Any servants—"

He shook his head. "The word was passed from one to the other."

"When you next have the leisure," I said, "write me who was common to these four meetings. For we have in this room a friend of John Thurloe's, I think, and if I do not swing first, I mean to find him out. And now Godspeed, My Lord."

He left, and I stepped into the doorway. "We must leave by ones and twos," I said. "You first, Pile. By the back. And see to it that ye walk, not run."

"Why Pile?" Villiers said. "And who gave you the authority—"

"It is reason," I said. "Pile is the most likely among us to babble. If not from fright, then from stupidity. As for the authority, wouldst contest it with me, Ned?" I waited, while Pile (not pausing to argue the nature of his character) sidled around me and Ned Villiers elected to hold his peace. "You would be next, Brodrick," I said. "And Willis with you."

"For the same reason as Pile, Mordaunt?"

"Why, no," I said softly. "It is but that if I am seized, I would know you are free. For I have not forgotten another questioning—"

"I mean to kill you someday, Mordaunt," Brodrick said, very low. "I have borne your insults a sixmonth, and the load is grown heavier than I can endure, and I mean to kill you someday."

"I mean to have you try, Brodrick," I said, very pleasantly. "But let us make it another night."

There were four of us left when the soldiers clomped up the stairs and entered the room. They were Stapely and Mallory and Jack Russell and myself, and we were marched off to the Tower and quartered in the Gatehouse. And this time my questioning was left to no subordinate. For a week later I was brought before the Protector himself.

I can still recall my start of surprise when first I laid eyes on him. I was questioned in Westminster; I was fetched in and bid to stand just there, with the Protector sitting stiffly before me in a stiff, high-backed chair like to a denuded throne; and on his right hand, one of his Major Generals—Goffe, I believe it was; and at a respectful distance on his left, hunched over a dainty desk like to my lady's, a dusty wisp of a clerk, his ear bent to catch our every word and his quill at the ready. I had seen likenesses of the Protector, and so I was prepared for his ugliness—the great nose, the warted forehead, the large, heavy, stern eye of the unbending and uncompromising Calvinist. But I was not prepared for the decay in his face. The hair was gone in blots and patches from his temples, and then behind, it hung down on his neck unkempt and brittle-gray and dry, like the hair of one who has fought a bitter bout with fever. The fever had touched down in his face, too, had dried out his lips and left his skin the color of neglected parchment. And standing there, I swear that I caught from three yards' distance the waft of death, flat and thick and sticky-sweet. The rumors had been thick all winter of the Protector's health, but we had shrugged them off; there had been rumors since '52. But now, standing before him, I thought in sudden surprise, He is a dying man, he is not after all immortal.

For an hour he put to me the questions they put, the questions asked in a voice dry and indifferent and somehow weary, put the way they will put questions when they have no trust in your reply but have not the knowledge, neither, to prove you false. I was John Mordaunt? I was, Your Highness. And I was member, was I not, of that restless, malignant, brainsick party which would plunge this nation once again into blood and insurrection? I know not what party that would be, Your Highness. I mean Charles Stuart's party, I mean the party would restore king and bishop and tyranny in this land; was I not member of that party? I am member of no party, Your Highness, I have no head for politics. And what your means of support, Mr. Mordaunt? I enjoy a small allowance from my brother, Your Highness. And I have friends. What friends, sir? A few, Your Highness. Would Mr. Hyde be one of these friends? No, Your Highness. What of James Butler, would James Butler, Marquis of Ormonde, be a friend? I know no James Butler, Your Highness. What of Colonel John Russell? Yes, Your Highness, I know Colonel Russell.

What is your present place of abode, Mr. Mordaunt? No certain place at present, Your Highness. But you have recently been in Surrey, have you not? I have, Your Highness. And before Surrey? I was abroad. Abroad? Where abroad? Was I in Bruges, perhaps? In the company of the rest of the riffraff and rabble that Charles Stuart calls army, the whoring, swearing, drunken, renegade Englishmen in his service? Not I, Your Highness, I was the other side of the world, in the Indies. And what do ye in Surrey, sir? Hunt during the day, Your Highness. And retire early in the night. Hunt, Mr. Mordaunt? Hunt what? Fox, Your Highness. And another time rabbit. Hunt fox, Mr. Mordaunt? Do they hunt fox in the dead of winter in Surrey? Some do, Your Highness.

And where your lodgings here in London, Mr. Mordaunt? In Covent Garden, Your Highness. Covent Garden? Colonel Russell also abides in Covent Garden, does he not? He may, Your Highness. And what your business in London, Mr. Mordaunt? Mine own, sir. Do I find you impudent, sirrah? No, Your Highness, not I. Then give me plain answer, sirrah, what business have ye in London? I am come up for pleasure, Your Highness. And to repair my fortunes if I can find a way. I believe you there, Mr. Mordaunt, on my word I do. And how mean you to accomplish this? By plotting for the return of this pretended king, this young, debauched Charles Stuart? No, Your Highness. Then how, Mr. Mordaunt? How mean you to repair these ruined fortunes? By marriage, Your Highness. Marriage? To what unfortunate heiress, pray? I do not know as yet, Your Highness, I have not found her out.

Canst read, Mr. Mordaunt? A little, Your Highness. Canst read a proclamation banning all of Charles Stuart's party to without twenty miles of this city? I am member of no such party, Your Highness. What? Were ye not taken, then, in the company of Colonel Russell? And is Jack Russell not a notorious and intractable member of that party? I would not know, Your Highness, we did not discourse of politics. Did you not, now? And of what, then, did ye discourse? Of nought I can recall, Your Highness. Small talk, I think. We but passed the time of day, so to speak. And James Butler? What did ye talk of with James Butler? I have already said, Your Highness, I know no James Butler. So ye did. And I have yet put ye the question a second time. What discourse had ye last Thursday night with James Butler, Marquis of Ormonde? No discourse, Your Highness. None, Mr. Mordaunt? None, Your Highness. What, and is he a mute, Mr. Mordaunt? Did he sit wordless among the lot of ye the entire evening? He was not among us, Your Highness.

At the end of that hour he was slumped far down in his chair, one blunt hand partly covering his blunt mouth, his heavy eyes fixed lowering as a November sky on my face. "I would put one last question to you, Mr. Mordaunt," he said. "And I would have from you the courtesy of one truthful answer this day."

"I have been nothing but truthful, Your Highness," I said. "This entire hour."

"Why, yes. And be so once again. Why dost hate me, Mr. Mordaunt?"

"Hate you, Your Highness?"

"In what way have I wronged you?" he said. "You are younger son, you were too young for the troubles of this nation, though your brother fought at Worcester. And does he not still enjoy his life and estates? And do you not enjoy your freedom? Have you felt my whips and scourges? Do you rot in a Newgate dungeon? Have you left your head on Tower Hill? And if not, why do ye hate me?" He came heavily upright in his chair and dropped his hand, and I thought, Aye, those are the eyes that looked on Drogheda, those the eyes that could order three thousand of us put to the sword and still close in good conscience come nightfall. "Why?" he said. "For I have not sought my present position. There was a House of Commons, and there was this thing they called the Petition and Advice, and no man living can say I sought it, he cannot. They petitioned me to undertake this government, and I told them the burden of it was too heavy for any creature, and I undertook it with reluctance. I say I did. I can say in the presence of God that I would have been glad as to my own conscience and spirit to have been living under a woodside, to have kept a flock of sheep, rather than to have undertaken such a place as this. But what I have undertaken, I have undertaken with integrity. I say I have. And I say further, what I have done, I have done for love of God and for love of England. And wherefore, then, do ye hate me?"

"And what I have done, Your Highness," I said quietly, "I also have done in integrity and for love of England."

"And do ye call this a reply, then?"

"Do you not, Your Highness?"

He sank back in his chair, and his eyes were again heavy and sullen and sick. "You may return from whence you came, Mr. Mordaunt," he said. "Which would be these lodgings of yours in Covent Garden. But I do charge you, you are not to stray from them."

384

For a second time within the hour I may have betrayed surprise. "I am free to go, Your Highness?"

"You are. So you are to be found again if we should come searching. For I do not rest content in you, Mr. Mordaunt."

Discretion, I have heard, is the better part of valor, and I did not trust myself to reply to that. I only looked at him once more, he slumped back in that chair, his blunt hand again covering his blunt mouth and his eyes heavy with some grave and sullen sickness. And then I turned and found my way out of that place into the bright, thin sunlight of February. And for all that it was cold enough to entertain a flake or two of snow in the air, it seemed to me that I could smell in the air the first, distant promise of spring.

६व Twenty-One ७२

I was arrested again near the end of March. They roused me from my bed in the dead of night and conducted me to the Tower and installed me once more in the Gatehouse. They locked me in a room with for furniture a curtained bed, a rude table, a single chair, and a tiny and most abominably ragged carpet that covered a square of the scarred stone floor like a bedsheet spread out on a village commons. But they provided me with the amusement of constant company. There was an officer in my room night and day, and two keepers stationed without my door. One of the officers, a Lieutenant Colonel Miller, daily offered to wager one piece against a hundred pounds that I would hang before I would escape this place. He also neglected to tell me what the charges were against me, though I put the question once or twice.

I was held incommunicado for a month. Then, early in May, Elizabeth Carey gained entrance to me.

I heard that afternoon the heated argument without my door, and then she swept into the room. It must have been spring in London with a vengeance, for she was wearing a taffeta gown so pale a lavender it was nearly white, and dainty white shoes and gloves, and a summer hat, and her bodice was a filmy gauze. She was flushed from her argument with the two keepers, and she stood in the doorway a moment, catching her breath, her eyes memorizing the lines of my face, the written leave to be admitted to this place fluttering from her hand. "John," she said. "John."

"My lady," I said.

"You look very pale," she said. "Have you been ill, then?"

"It is but lack of sun and air. They will permit me no exercise."

She turned her eyes on Captain Foster. He rose from the bed and bowed; he had the instincts if not the birth of a gentleman, did Captain Foster. "Captain Foster," he said. "Your servant, ma'am."

"I would speak to Mr. Mordaunt in private, Captain Foster."

He shook his head. "I have strict orders, my lady."

"He will give you his parole, Captain."

"His parole, ma'am? He hath been seized for high treason."

I glanced at the barred slit they called a casement here. "If my word will not satisfy you, Captain," I said, "sure my circumstances must. God's name, a mouse must have the ingenuity of a man and the agility of a fly to escape this room."

And now Elizabeth moved to him and laid a gloved hand on his arm and looked up into his face. Her back was to me and I could not see the look she made him gift of. But I could guess at it. "I pray you, but half an hour, sir," she said.

He smiled uncertainly. "I should be a rogue were I to refuse a request put thus, my lady. But I charge you, no tricks. If Mr. Mordaunt should leave this room and you remain behind, it will go hard with you. Smile or no smile, it will."

"Why, Captain," she said sweetly, "dost think he could squeeze into this bustle? Or that I could hope to cozen you with a trick the age of that one?"

Captain Foster closed the door softly behind him, and she turned to me. "Have they treated you scurvily, John?" she said.

"Why, no," I said. "Very civilly." I permitted myself another hungry look at her gown. "It would be spring in England," I said softly.

"It is very lovely in the country."

"And what news of the outside world?"

"That were not lovely. Admiral Montagu and thirteen English frigates have Charles's navy bottled up before Ostend. They say near all of Charles's army hath deserted him. And here at home three of every five of us rots in prison, and the other two questioned weekly and close watched between. And in London they trip over each other's heels to protest their undying fidelity to Oliver. And in the country, if you but wear the shirt of a gentleman and ride no

387

more nor a yard off your land, you are immediately secured. Once again, John, he carries all before him."

"All but one thing."

"And what, pray, would that be?"

"God," I said. "There is death in his face. I tell you I stood before him not two months since, not so far as from here to there, and I smelled death in the room. And so if we are patient—"

"You have not the time for patience, John."

I smiled wryly. "It would appear I have little else."

"You have not the time," she repeated. "For Stapely and Mallory have babbled. They have named you as the one who delivered them their commissions. And the Protector means to try you. For high treason. And so we have not the time—"

I was, I confess, not unprepared for that news; I had suspected something of the sort. And so I still smiled calmly at her. "We have nought else," I said. "Do not think to buy my escape this time, Elizabeth."

"I do not mean to. I mean to purchase the court, instead."

I briefly stared at her. Then I laughed, shortly and, I fear, rudely. "There comes a time," I said, "when hope were fondness, Elizabeth. And so do not suffer it to come near me. Give me a month to make my peace with God—"

"You are to be tried by a High Court of Justice," she said. "You, and a Mr. Slingsby, and one Dr. Hewet, a London minister. The names of this court were made public yesterday. I can name you ten can be purchased, for they know what we know, that Charles Stuart will come back. This year or next he will come back. And they mean to scurry for their holes if they can be shown the path."

"Ten were not forty, Elizabeth."

"We need not forty. We need but twenty. And there is a second way. They cannot find you guilty save they have two witnesses against you. This much of the law His Highness hath seen fit to cling to. And I am informed that Mallory is not so close held as you or Mr. Stapely. It may be I can contrive his escape."

"Elizabeth—"

"There is a third thing you must do."

"You have embarked on this tale," I said. "And so you have my leave to finish it. Name me this third thing, Elizabeth."

"You must marry me," she said.

388

I was turned a little away from her, and I heard that and turned back, very slowly. Her eyes rested firm and constant on mine, no waver, no down-looking, no coy flutter of lashes. I looked very seriously into the seriousness of those eyes. And then, without thinking what I did, I laughed.

" 'Sblood," I said, "but that were cure worse than the kill."

The look flitted into her face and then out again, and do not ask me to describe it. Shame, anger, shock—I know not what it was; I only know that I had done her a greater kindness had I struck her. "I had not thought," she said coldly, "that the price were all that dear, John Mordaunt."

"Nay," I said and took a single step toward her. "Nay. I did not mean that as it sounded, Elizabeth."

"Did you not, Mr. Mordaunt?"

"I swear I did not. I was not thinking of the price I paid, Elizabeth. I was thinking of the price you paid."

"And what price were that, sir?"

"A high one," I said bitterly, "for but a short ride on a spring road. First you put your fortune at my service. Now you would put yourself. And I with nought to offer you save a quick widowhood—"

"Have I asked for ought, John?"

"And have I not my pride?" I said fiercely. "And can I ask you to give all where I give nothing?"

"You said once that pride these days were a luxury only rogues could afford. And do not think that you will be giving nothing."

"And what shall I be giving, pray?"

"I do not know," she said. "I have not heard you name it yet."

"Then answer me this. What the reason for this? What advantage do I gain save your person? Which God knows were enough—"

"Why, two," she said. "One, I have an uncle. I think he is fond of me. I know he fears the return of the king. Were you my husband, and were you to promise to speak a word for him in the king's ear, I think he would approach your judges for us. For I cannot accomplish this alone."

And so there would go one of your monuments, Richard Munke, I thought. But this no time for thoughts of revenge. "And the second?" I asked.

"They have suffered me to see you this once. I doubt they will

389

give me leave again. But were I your lady, sure they could not refuse my request to join my husband here. Indeed, they might give me freedom to come and go."

I smiled down into her eyes. "You have named two," I said. "Would there be a third, Elizabeth?"

"There might be," she said, as softly.

"If there is, name it me."

Still she did not flush; still her eyes did not trip on mine. "I think there is some devil in you, John Mordaunt," she said. "Must you be forever and eternally at shaming me?"

I laughed. And then, finally, finally, I reached out and laid my hand aside her cheek. "And I wonder," I said, "I wonder which of us will be guilty of speaking the word first."

"What word would that be, John?"

"Love," I said and laughed again, and then I drew her to me. "Christ, but you are beautiful," I said. "Sweet Christ, but you are. And would you have me to husband, Elizabeth Carey?"

We were wedded that same afternoon. The ceremony was performed by Dr. Hewet, who occupied a cell near mine and who a month hence would be murdered on Tower Hill for the crime of high treason. Save for our disregard of the injunction regarding banns, the ceremony was a decent one, Dr. Hewet speaking the sacraments from memory from out the Book of Common Prayer, Captain Foster and two keepers standing witness. Afterwards, the keepers stood the company to a bottle of wine and we had a small celebration, very merry.

But at seven Captain Foster was relieved of his watch by Lieutenant Colonel Miller. One minute there was merriment in the cell and the next there was dead silence, for the door was flung open and Miller stood dourly in it. His eyes swept the room and seized upon Captain Foster. "I would know the meaning of this, Captain," he said.

"It is a wedding, sir. My lady and—"

"A wedding? Didst say a wedding, Captain? And ha' ye leave to permit this?"

"No, sir. I have not, sir. I thought it no harm—"

"You are not paid to think, Captain. You are paid to obey orders. Were not these orders to keep a close watch on this prisoner?"

"Yes, sir. And so I have done—"

"How, Captain? By permitting drunkenness—"

"None here is drunk, sir. We had but one bottle of wine for six—"

"Do not contest me, sirrah. I charge you, do not. And be so good as to clear this cell. I would have him"—nodding at Hewet—"taken back to his cell. And you, Captain, may conduct this—this lady hence from this place."

"Colonel," I said, "the lady and I are man and wife. And—"

"Man and wife, do you call it?" Miller glared at me. "Man and wife? This ejected and treasonous minister hath mumbled some popish superstition o'er you, and do you think this makes you man and wife, sir? Decently and properly?"

"Aye," I said. "I do, Colonel."

"Well, I do not. And so Captain Foster will conduct her out of here. And until she hath leave from the proper authorities . . ."

She obtained leave the next day; I think Monson had some of the doing of that. And she moved bag and baggage into my cell. And at seven that night Miller entered once again to stare gloomily at her trunks, her hatboxes, her few toilet articles. Then he gave an order to the keepers without. A quarter hour later the keepers fetched back a tick and some quilts, and Miller went sourly to work at making up a pallet in the corner of the cell.

We watched him, and I could feel the pulse of blood in my throat. "Canst explain the meaning of this, Colonel?" I said.

He did not look up from his work. "Ha' ye not eyes in your head? If I am robbed of half of your bed, I must sleep on the floor, must I not?"

"Do you mean," I said, slowly and carefully, "that you propose to sleep in here the night, Colonel?"

"I do not propose to sit up the night, Mr. Mordaunt."

"Colonel," I said, "this is my wedding night—"

"Why, so it is."

"—and can you then deny us the common decency of a little privacy—"

"Why, yes. Very cheerfully, Mr. Mordaunt."

"In God's name, Colonel—"

He straightened and swung on me. "You are already guilty of the sin of concupiscence, sir," he said. "Do not compound it with blasphemy."

"We have different understandings of both those sins, Colonel. My lady and I are decently and properly wedded in the eyes of God. And I intend no blasphemy. I but—"

"You were permitted this wedding, were you not, Mr. Mordaunt?"

"I was. And now I but ask what is usual and decent, I—"

"My orders are that you are to be close watched. Day and night. And I propose to obey them. You have your lady, Mr. Mordaunt. And would you have the entire world as well?"

I could feel the pulse in my throat, but my voice, I think, was still soft and reasonable. "Then grant us but ten minutes, Colonel," I said. "But long enough for my wife to prepare modestly for bed."

"Bid her sleep in her clothes," he said, and turned back to his pallet.

In the three weeks between wedding and trial, Elizabeth was not idle. She secured a copy of my indictment—do not ask me how, for this was never allowed in cases of high treason. She obtained advice of counsel, from that same Justice Rolle who, three years before, had stood on a Salisbury scaffold and who, like other judges in the land, had refused to sit on the Protector's High Court of Justice. By the day of the trial, she could promise fourteen judges who would not find against me. And at night, with a single sputtering candle to provide us light and Colonel Miller glowering from out the shadows where his pallet was, she would sit beside me at the rude table while I bent over all the papers, trying to wrap my slow wits around the precedents preserved in the strange foreign language which is the law, the cases gleaned from out Coke's *Reports* or Mantell's *Treatise.* Later, in the darkness, with the bed curtains drawn decently between us and the world and she in my arms, we would whisper of other matters more personal and private.

On the night before the trial, lying thus, she said, "I have fresh news for you, John."

She lay in my arms, and in the darkness her unpinned hair felt soft and fine as cat's fur against my hand and lips. "An it be bad," I murmured, "let it wait until the morrow."

"It is not bad, my dearest."

"But say that once again."

"Say what again?"

"My dearest. As ye said it just then."

"My dearest," she said. "My dearest dearest."

"That were good news enough," I said, "for a man who hath fallen in love with his own wife."

"Who is not his wife. Not truly. Not yet. And so shall we pause a moment, my darling, to damn our Colonel Miller?"

"With all my heart," I said. "Most fervently." We fell silent a little, the better to damn Colonel Miller, who, I am sure, lay in the far corner of our cell with his eyes open to the darkness and his ear bent and his lips pursed tight in disapproval. And then, "What other news, Elizabeth?"

"It concerns Mallory. Who will have escaped by now, I think."

"Mallory? Escaped? When—"

"Hush," she said. "Not three hours since, I think."

"You have not been absent from this room these three hours. How then can you know—"

She laughed softly. "I know. And now they sure cannot hang you. For they have not two witnesses against you. Think you they can hang you now, my darling?"

"I know not," I said. "It were but law. And law were what Oliver—"

"They say he dares tamper no further with the law. Think you he dares bend it further to his will, John?"

I pressed my lips to her forehead. "Why, no," I said. "I think he doth not, Elizabeth."

"And so you shall not hang," she said. "I could not bear it were you to hang now. Dost think thou wilt hang now, John?"

"No," I said. "I think I will not. For I think God hath other uses for me."

She laughed, very softly. "Have I not done well these three weeks?" she said. "Have I not, my dearest?"

I echoed her laugh. "I can only say, my lady," I said, "that I am devoutly glad that you are not on t'other side from me."

But lying there, my eyes open to the darkness, I could not be as sanguine as I tried to sound. For I would on the morrow be brought before no English jury, no judge sworn to uphold the Great Charter; I would be sitting before a High Court of Justice, forty men named by the Protector, instructed by the Protector, responsible to the Protector, fearful of the Protector. I would sit before them and before My Lord Lisle—the only judge in all the land who would have ought to do with this judicature—and I would dispute the lawfulness of the Court, as Rolle had told me I must do; I would dispute the commission by which they sat and the act of parliament which had created this court; I would demand my rights under the Great Charter and the Petition of Right. And if they override me, I thought, then we no longer live under law but whim, and why, then, should they blink at single witnesses?

No, my lady, I thought, I cannot be sanguine. If they mean to hang me, they mean to hang me, and no single rag or tatter of law they have left us shall say them nay. You have provided me with one more string to my bow, my lady, I thought. But lying there in the darkness, with my wife that was not yet my wife in my arms— that may never be my wife, I thought, that may be widow before she is wife—lying there, I could not make myself believe that a single bowstring had e'er decided the outcome of any battle.

A little after dawn, the curtain to our bed was thrust rudely aside and a keeper made free with my shoulder; when I inquired him out the meaning of this insolence, he replied that he but followed orders, and he watched me sullenly while I dressed and more sullenly when I bent over the bed to kiss my wife adieu. Without, the morning sun was a-glitter on the river and hurtful to my eyes. At the watergate the prisoners had congregated, as is the custom, and when they bid me Godspeed, Colonel Miller glowered at them and grumbled that they but wasted breath. "For never went out a man to his trial so sure to lose his head as this one," he said, and I turned in the act of climbing into the boat. "And art my judge as well as my keeper, sir?" I said.

It is a mile by water from the Tower to Westminster Hall, and when we swung out into the river, I could see the whisper of mist lying on the black surface of the water, and the turrets and battlements of the Tower loomed down upon me like a vague omen in some evil dream. Gliding up the river against the sighing current, I could feel the fear in my stomach like something ill digested, and then we rounded the bend and the Parliament buildings loomed down upon me. There were the usual idlers in Palace Yard when we disembarked—boatmen arguing on the wharf, and uncoifed Inns of Court students strolling in the Yard, and professional witnesses

lounging down at the conduit with straws in their shoes and consciences for sale; and as I came through the Yard with two soldiers
before me and two after and Colonel Miller holding me by the
hand, I could feel their eyes upon me, idle and indifferently curious, for they had seen their fair share of doomed men these ten
years. And as we entered the Hall, the great clock in the clock tower
struck the hour of ten, and the strokes echoed down upon me like
disaster.

Then we had entered the shade and shadow of the Hall itself.

I stood there at the lower end of the Hall, amidst the press and
push and babble, with along the sides the stallkeepers—booksellers
and law stationers and sempstresses—hawking their ribbons and
books and baubles, and in the center the lawyers in black gowns
and white taffeta coifs busily and officiously advising their clients,
and overhead, all the full length of the Hall, the banners and stand-
ards hanging from the oak beams, all the colors the Roundheads
had taken from us at Naseby and Worcester and Preston and Dun-
bar. There are four judgment seats in the Hall, and I was to be heard
before the King's Bench, which is at the upper end of the Hall.
Through the thin crowd of lawyers and gawkers from out the
country and idlers fingering baubles for their latest mistresses, I
could see, beyond the sad, limp banners, the place, the stone steps
leading up to the rail, and behind the rail the bar and jury boxes,
and the tables below. And for all that it was but ten in the morning,
the Court already sat; through the part and swirl of the crowd, I
could see the Lord President in purple robes leaning across the bar
to look down upon the black-robed Attorney standing below him,
and the jury boxes crowded with the forty judges, all in scarlet
robes and white coifs, and at one of the tables below, a single figure,
his back to me and his head down. From this distance the figures
looked as small as dolls, and I can remember thinking that those
robes and coifs on those forty were insolence, for these men had
been named from off the Protector's Council or from out the Commons, and not five among them, I would have wagered, was
learned at the law, not five had e'er seen the inside of the Inns of
Court. And then I was not thinking of justice in this time and place
but of other things. I was thinking of lying in the darkness with my
true love in my arms, and she saying softly, "And so they shall not
hang you. Dost think they will hang you now, my darling?" And I

was thinking of all those others who through all the years had stood just here where I stood. Of Sir Thomas More, and the awful and solemn sentence echoing against these beams, this stone. Of Protector Somerset, led from here to be drawn and quartered, and after him the Earl of Warwick. In Elizabeth's time Thomas Howard, Duke of Norfolk, and Robert Devereux, Earl of Essex. In James's time Guy Fawkes and forty with him. And in my own lifetime, the Earl of Strafford and after him His Majesty of blessed memory, Charles sitting covered before his judges, and leaning once to put the question, and pointing with the stick he carried, and the gold head of the cane falling off and clattering against the stone, and His Majesty staring down at this solemn omen. They had all stood just here, I thought, all the long line of the accused and the condemned, and I could think of none who had walked from this place a free man. There must have been the lucky ones, I thought, but I could think of the names of none of them.

At the upper end of the Hall, the Lord President made a sudden gesture (he is grown angry, I thought), and below him the Attorney General turned and pointed to the figure at the table. The figure made as if to rise but did not, and the Attorney General turned back to the bar, and the Lord President gestured again. This time the figure at the table rose. Then the Lord President was to his feet, too. And then six soldiers were come from somewhere, and they seized on the figure and pulled him about, and then he was being hurried toward me.

We passed each other in the center of the Hall. It was Dr. Hewet. He was given by nature to paleness, was the Doctor, but there was now no blood at all in his face, none at all, and his eyes were wide and black with sudden fright. I passed not five feet from him, and I called out and asked him how he was tried. "I refused to plead," he said. "It is no lawful court, for they would grant me neither jury nor counsel, and I refused to plead, and they have condemned me out of hand. But may God give you better fortune, Mr. Mordaunt."

Aye, I thought, as I sat down at the table, may God grant it. Behind me, as from a great distance, a nimble-tongued sempstress with a treble voice called out the news of her ribbons and geegaws. Before me the court crier cried out his "Oyez, oyez, oyez, we will have silence in this Court." From the bar Lord President Lisle looked down upon me. He was a smallish man but gone sweatily to fat, and his complexion was curdled and mottled and the color of cow dung in a summer pasture, and his eyes looked down upon me sadly and reproachfully, as if I had done him some grave personal wrong. About him in the jury boxes the faces of the judges, above those scarlet robes and beneath those insolent white coifs, looked all alike, and you could not separate friend from enemy. Beside me the sergeant at arms stood stiffly at attention. Then Lisle was looking to where the Attorney General sat at his table across the way and the Clerk of the Court beside him.

"Mr. Attorney," Lisle said, "what have you to say against the prisoner at the bar?" and the Attorney General said, "My Lord, I have prepared a charge of high treason against the gentleman at the bar, which I desire may be read," and the Clerk rose and said, "John Mordaunt, Esquire, stand at the bar and hear your charge," and the sergeant at arms touched me upon the shoulder and I obediently rose and the Clerk read off "a charge of high treason against John Mordaunt, Esquire, as followeth". . . .

I did not closely attend that reading, for I had read this document a hundred times, had crouched over it in the pale, lemon-yellow light which a slitted casement admitted to a Tower cell, or had bent over it as it lay cream-white in the light of a guttering candle. I had near memorized all the fine, high, obtuse, legal phrases which with great labor and greater repetition said that John Mordaunt, "minding and intending to embroil this Commonwealth in new and intestine wars and seditions . . . did traitorously, advisedly, and maliciously plot, contrive, and endeavor to stir up and raise war against Oliver, then and yet Lord Protector"; and that he did further "traitorously, advisedly, and maliciously declare, publish, and promote Charles Stuart, eldest son of the late king Charles, to be king of England . . . and did then and there traitorously, advisedly, and maliciously hold intelligence and correspondence with the said Charles Stuart"; and further that he "did traitorously confer with John Stapely, Esquire, and Henry Mallory, and others, how to alter and subvert the government as established"; and that he did further "deliver commissions to several persons in the name of and as from the same Charles Stuart, concerning the raising of forces and levying war against the said Oliver." That was all the sense of that document, and I was familiar enough with it, and so I stood before the stony faces of my judges and let the solemn and weighted phrases

397

of the Attorney General wash dreamlike over me. And then the Clerk was done and, "John Mordaunt," he said, "thou standest here charged with high treason against His Highness, the Lord Protector, and the Commonwealth. You have heard the charge read; the Court demands your positive answer thereto, whether guilty or not guilty."

The Lord President looked sadly down upon me. "Before you answer to that, Mr. Mordaunt," he said, "I would tell you that there is a respect due this Court which you have performed not. You have stood covered during the reading of the indictment, during the entire reading, sir. I therefore must charge the sergeant to remove your hat."

"It will not be necessary, My Lord," I said, and I removed my hat and laid it on the table before me. "If I have already misbehaved myself here," I said, "the error is the more pardonable because I have not had any counsel, and I dare not presume to have any knowledge in the law. I have not been told that this is the custom, My Lord."

"It is the custom," Lisle said.

"Have I your leave to sit, My Lord?"

"You have it," he said, and I sat down and made some small business of placing all my papers before me. "My Lord," I said, "I desire a copy of my indictment, and time to prepare my defense."

"It is never done," Lisle said. "For any indictment of high treason was never delivered to any prisoner."

I had expected that; Rolle had said that such would be their answer; it was the law. "My Lord," I said, "I am ignorant of the law, and I have heard these charges but five minutes since. But what may make no sense to my ear may to my eye. I do humbly crave a copy of my charges that I may place it but here before me."

"And I do deny it you. Your business, Mr. Mordaunt, is to plead to the charges, whether guilty or not guilty."

"Am I, My Lord, to plead to charges I do not understand?"

"An ye be innocent, ye have little to fear. An ye be not, your understanding is for nought."

I bent again over my papers. "My Lord," I said, "you sit there as judge. I desire I may hear the commission by which you sit."

"This were an irrelevancy," he said. "You are impeached of high treason. We require your answer."

398

"Under favor and with submission, I think it not an irrelevancy. I beseech you to let me know by what commission you sit there."

"Mr. Mordaunt," he said, "we sit here by a commission under the Great Seal of England, in pursuance of an act of parliament. That is our commission."

"I desire the commission may be read, My Lord, and the commissioners' names."

Something like impatience flitted into and out of his face. "Mr. Mordaunt," he said, "we know our own authority. It is not usual to read commissions to prisoners. The laws of England and acts of parliament are to be submitted to, sir."

"My Lord," I said, "I am ignorant in the law, I do confess I am. But is this the law of England, that I am to own every person that will sit to judge me? Will you take away that liberty that we shall not know by what commission we are tried and who are our judges? I claim it as my right, My Lord."

"It is visible who are your judges," he said, and he was grown impatient, all right; it was in his voice that he was grown impatient. "We are chosen judges," he said, "and are your judges by act of parliament."

"It appears you will be," I said dryly, "though I am not satisfied in it. Pray, My Lord, wilt answer me this? Doth this act of parliament specify that your commission may not be read?"

"The act doth not require it."

"But doth it deny it? If it do not, it followeth, it is my right. *Misera servitus ubi lex vagum aut incognitum.* I therefore humbly desire that this act be read."

Across the way the Attorney General came to his feet. He was a very tall man and very lean, and it took him a very great while to accomplish his feet; it seemed to take him an eternity; it was as if he did so only by some act of will. "My Lord," he said, "this young man doth protest his ignorance of the law, yet he pretends more knowledge than the Court." He turned and bent a long, pallid face upon me. "I tell you, sir," he said, "the Court are here and know themselves lawfully authorized to try you. If you please to give your answer, whether guilty or not, you will find the justice of the Court to be according to the laws of England."

I smiled gently upon him. "My Lord," I said, "this learned gentleman—I know his face though not his name—I little doubt this learned gentleman, who is so learned in the law, will be cautious what he doth against the law. But I do not desire to be judged by every person that would sit to judge me. Therefore, I demand this, that the act of parliament may be read, that I may know what I am lawfully permitted and what denied."

"The act is public," the Attorney General snapped. "The Court are not required to give you an account of their authority."

"My Lord, shall I not know by what law I am tried, nor by what act, nor by what commission? Have a care, My Lord, what is done here to the native rights and privileges of all Englishmen."

"We shall have a care," Lisle said. "We know what justice is. We need no instruction on it."

"Then I pray you, order the act to be read."

The Attorney General still stood, tall and lean as a shadow and stooped, one hand upon the edge of the table, his head bowed a trifle as if he meant to pray. "My Lord," he said, "I pray you let this young gentleman know what hath been done here but a little before him, to warn him. There was one before you, Mr. Mordaunt, that would not plead but must dispute the judicature of this Court, and the Court hath ruled it otherwise, and he hath received his sentence. If you will be pleased to answer whether or no guilty of these crimes, then you shall have a fair trial; if you stand mute, then you have brought judgment upon yourself, you have confessed." And now he raised his head and smiled fairly and kindly upon me. "Your papers were better laid aside, sir; you have, I think, been ill advised; they will prejudice you."

I returned him smile for smile. "With your leave, sir, I shall not quit them for yet a little." I looked again to the Lord President. "Shall I be overborne here too, My Lord?"

Lisle looked down upon me, his eyes patient and sad and reproachful. "I advise you to plead, sir. If you do not, I must warn you, it will be very penal to you."

Penal indeed, I thought; I had read the act, and penal indeed. For if I refused to plead, if I stood mute, the act instructed the Court to interpret this as confession of guilt and to proceed to conviction. And yet Rolle, who was a judge of the land, had advised me that I must dispute the lawfulness of this Court. "My Lord," I said, "wilt answer me this? Doth the act deny me right to counsel?"

400

"The law doth deny it you. There is matter of fact laid to your charge which amounts to treason; you are now upon matter of fact, whether guilty or not guilty; there is no law allowed in matter of fact."

"My indictment is matter of law, My Lord. And I humbly conceive that the lawfulness of this Court is matter of law. I desire I may have counsel assigned me, that he may argue with this learned counsel the lawfulness of this Court. If this counsel convince mine that this is a lawful court, then I will submit; if the contrary, what I demand I expect will be allowed me."

This time the Attorney General was to his feet something faster. "My Lord," he said, "this is the same ground we walked upon this morning. We have trod this path with Mr. Slingsby and again with Dr. Hewet, and must we—" He broke off and a little recovered himself; then he turned to me. "You seem to be a young gentleman," he said, and voice and smile all silk suddenly. "This way will lead you nowhere. I wish you would rather plead not guilty or make an ingenuous confession. You have been impeached of a very high crime, high treason; it may be a straying of youth; the first step to mercy is confession."

"My Lord," I said, "I humbly thank this learned counsel, but I shall not betray mine innocence by confessing to a crime. It truly appears that this gentleman is for the Protector; I am for myself and resolved not to lose my native rights. My Lord, I have asked that your commission be read, that I may know who sits in judgment upon me and by what authority. It hath been denied me. I have asked that the act of parliament be read, that I may know what is denied me and what allowed. It hath been denied me. My Lord, I am ignorant of the law, yet humbly I conceive there is matter of law here as to the lawfulness of this Court. But since I cannot obtain the having the act read, I shall as well as I can explain the sense of it. The act specifies the Commissioners of this Court to the number of a hundred and fifty; it names the Commissioners of the Great Seal, the judges of the land, and all members of the late parliament. Yet I do not see the number of a hundred and fifty here. I therefore humbly conceive that without the whole I cannot be tried."

"Mr. Mordaunt," Lisle said wearily, "you have urged the reading of the act, yet it doth appear you know the act as well as any man. I shall say to you only this, that the act specifies a hundred and fifty or any seventeen of that number; it requires but seventeen for a quorum; we have here to the number of two or three seventeens."

"My Lord, the words of the act are these: that the respective commissioners or a major part of them are empowered to meet or adjourn but not to try or determine. In seventeen is no major part—"

It were difficult when a man owned a face such as Lisle's to say whether he were grown angry or not. But I think he was angry now. "Mr. Mordaunt," he said, "you have been offered very seasonable advice; I wish you may be capable of it. For the Court, the quorum is seventeen, Mr. Slingsby and Dr. Hewet have already debated it, the Court hath ruled on it, it requires no further debate. For counsel, we are now upon matter of fact, whether guilty or not guilty; counsel was never allowed in matter of fact."

"My Lord, am I not to know whether this Court be a lawful judicature before I give in my defense? I have heard that the judges of the land are the best and proper expositors of the law; the judges are named in the act as commissioners; I cannot but wonder that I see none of them here. My Lord, if I am denied counsel, I desire that you submit it to the judges of the land whether this be lawful or no."

"Mr. Mordaunt," he said, "I do acquaint you that there is no judicature in England superior to this but the parliament immediately. Your business is to plead and stand debating this no further. I charge you, sir, apply yourself to matter of fact. The Court asks you again, whether guilty or not guilty."

And warning enough in that voice now, My Lord Lisle, I thought, warning enough. "I see," I said, "that I will be overborne here as elsewhere. Yet I desire a little patience. If I am denied counsel, then I desire to be tried by jury, according to the laws of the land."

This time the Attorney General did not trouble himself to rise or even to lift his head. "My Lord," he said wearily, "now is a second part of this same tune. I know there are many others upon the same string when this is resolved."

"If I try the patience of the Court," I said, "it is but that I am a little jealous of those rights and privileges which my countrymen hold as dear as I. If it be by the laws of the land that this trial should be by jury, I desire I may have that privilege."

Lisle smiled dryly. "We are all here your jury as well as your judges," he said. "We are here the number of two or three juries. You are to plead to your indictment."

"My Lord, the law gives liberty in cases of juries to the party accused to make his exceptions against the jury, which he cannot do here where you are both judge and jury."

Still he smiled. "If you have any particular exception to any man, Mr. Mordaunt, you may make it." And then he ceased smiling. "We are a very great grand jury, forty persons," he said. "And we have power upon a special act of parliament to give orders for a charge to be brought in against you. Acts of parliament make justice and law; they are both. Parliaments have great care for the rights of people, and if they think fit to change the customs of trials that have been in former times, then all persons must submit to it. And the parliament hath thought fit to make this Court both judge and jury. We are your grand jury, Mr. Mordaunt, and your petty jury, and your judge. All the people of England must submit to the laws of England, to the authorities of England; all must submit to My Lord Protector and acts of parliament. We did not call ourselves to be your judges. We are named your judges by act of parliament, and we have power to declare to you what the law is by that act of parliament, and I do declare it. I must require you to plead, Mr. Mordaunt."

"My Lord, if I am permitted counsel and my counsel doth say—"

"Enough," Lisle said. "This were enough, it were more than enough. You have offered very much concerning the jurisdiction of this Court; in conclusion you must acquiesce; I must put you to plead; you know the danger if you do not, being required."

"Or the judges, My Lord. If we may submit this to the judges of—"

"I do warn you, Mr. Mordaunt," Lisle said, very softly, "I do warn you, if I bid the Clerk enter it that you have been required to plead, and that you have abstained, you are greatly to be pitied, sir."

"My Lord," I said wearily, "I but pray this, that *you* will say this is the law. If you will but say under your hand that this is lawful, then I will proceed."

And now Lisle frankly stared at me. "I doubt this is insolence, Mr. Mordaunt," he said, and his voice was very soft indeed, you could scarce hear his voice, it was like something leashed. "I can hope it is not," he said.

"If it hath that sound, I do not so intend it. My Lord, if you will not say that this Court is lawful, I dare refer it to the counsel against me. If this learned counsel will but say under his hand that this Court is lawful, I will submit."

The Attorney General raised his head, very slowly; he also frankly stared. "I doubt this gentleman is in jest," he said. "Yet it is a little slighting of the Court to appeal from the Court to the counsel. But, My Lord, that he may forbear to say he is overborne, I have a word to inform him. I would not press anything against him which in my judgment I thought not legal. You shall have justice done, sir, if you will plead."

"And do you call this an answer, sir?"

"It is my answer, Mr. Mordaunt."

"Then I ask but this, that you name a precedent for this."

"You have been answered there, too. This Court sits by act of parliament. It requires no precedent."

"I have been answered nowhere. And I ask a precedent for it."

"Why, then, I will tell you a precedent for it. Mr. Slingsby and Dr. Hewet, they are a precedent."

"Is it a good precedent? If any give an ill precedent, is it reason I should not debate it myself? I am clearly resolved not to put myself upon a trial that never had a precedent. Neither am I so mean to do it, did I respect the liberties of my countrymen. If this Court sit by the act, then let it sit according to the act, and I will submit."

"This were beyond all endurance," the Attorney General snapped. "Your reason and my reason and all reason must submit to the law, and the single question is guilty or not guilty, and I have no more to say." He looked to the Lord President. "If you please, My Lord," he said, "this gentleman hath been required to answer to his charges, he hath been often required; yet he will do nought but stand here disputing. My Lord, I submit that this young gentleman is a young gentleman of parts and we may delight to hear him; but we have shown him patience enough. I must therefore do my duty, which is humbly to pray the Court to require him immediately to plead, and if he will not, then to proceed to sentence according to the act. If he will not own us, then we must own him. I have no more to say."

My Lord Lisle looked down upon me, and I read the dry impatience in his eyes, and I thought, So this is justice, so this is what

404

the law hath come to. "Mr. Mordaunt," he said, "you have heard the learned counsel, you have heard his instructions to the Court. I must require you to plead."

"In the name of justice, My Lord—"

"Mr. Mordaunt," he said, "I will tell you that many sit before you who have a prejudice to you and think you are loath to plead; I will tell you that you lose yourself mightily in saying this one thing so often, and we lose our time. I have called upon you often, very often; this Court hath been patient; it shall be patient no more; we must make our authority appear to you either by trying you or judging you. I require you a second time to answer, will you be tried? I shall not ask it a third time."

I sat there before him, looking up at this one who called himself a judge of the land; I was thinking that if this were justice, then purchased Court or fled witness, it were all for nought, for I could expect little more hereafter; I was thinking, with the fear in my stomach a small, tight knot, that I was intended to hang after all. I sat there, still saying nothing, while behind me was all the idle and indifferent murmur of Westminster Hall and before me English justice died. I sat there, and My Lord Lisle looked to the Clerk, prepared to bid him enter it that I had been required to plead and that I had stood mute.

And then one behind My Lord Lisle leaned and whispered in his ear.

He leaned, scarlet robe and white coif, and My Lord Lisle listened gravely a little. Then he looked to the Attorney General. "We have sat here long," he said. "It hath been requested that this Court recess until two of the clock. Have you objection, Mr. Prideaux?"

"None, My Lord," the Attorney General said. He looked at me. "It is to be hoped," he said, "that this young gentleman may come to his senses in that time, My Lord."

"I do charge you, Colonel Miller," Lisle said, "that this prisoner is to be held incommunicado. And I do declare this Court recessed."

I watched the scarlet robes file solemnly out the passageway which is at the upper end of the Hall. Then Colonel Miller touched me upon the shoulder. "Wouldst walk a little, sir?" he said. "Wouldst go into the Palace Yard, feel sun upon your back one last time?"

He made no very great effort to disguise the triumph in his voice, and I arose and looked distastefully into his eyes. "I shall pray for you, Colonel," I said. "For I do truly hope that God will reward you for your Christian kindness and charity."

He grinned. "It is not I who stand in need of prayer, Mr. Mordaunt."

I held his eyes another moment. Then I looked beyond him and Elizabeth was standing not thirty feet from me.

She stood before one of the bookstalls, and her eyes met mine, and she put down the book she pretended to examine and started toward me, and I could read the wide, tight fright in her lips and eyes. She made no effort to speak to me, only swept on past. Then I noted that one of my judges had remained behind. He loitered just at the foot of the stone steps, and Elizabeth made for him.

When I went out into the Palace Yard, Elizabeth and the judge were still engaged in close and serious conversation.

When I returned an hour later, she was standing in the entry and beside her My Lord Monson. As I came into the doorway, she stepped a step toward me. "John," she said. "John—"

The Colonel stepped brusquely between us. "Nay," he said. "Nay."

"Colonel," I said, "this is my wife. In the name of Christian charity—"

"In the name of nought," he snapped. "You are my prisoner, sir."

My Lord Monson stepped forward. "We must have a word with your prisoner, Colonel," he said quietly. "But five minutes—"

"I am sorry, My Lord."

Monson stared at him. "Do you not know me, man?"

"I know you, My Lord."

"You shall regret this, Colonel. I promise you, you shall."

"Then I shall regret it, My Lord."

The argument was brief. But it was not too brief. For in the midst of it, Elizabeth stepped around Colonel Miller, and her hand touched my hand, and that were long enough for her to thrust the scrap of paper into my hand.

I was still sweatily clutching her note when I came full into the Hall and noted the soldiers about the Attorney General's table. I noted them idly at first. Then I noted them not so idly. For as I came toward the bench, I saw the figure among them. He was seated at the Attorney General's table, and he was dressed all in sober black, and he watched me as I came toward him, watched me yet as I sat down at the table, and I dropped my eyes out of those eyes, and now the fear was like a cold ball in my stomach.

I sat at the table and unfolded the damp, crumpled note. It was in her hand and it said not much. *John*, it said, *oh, John, wouldst make me widow before I am ever wife?* And it said, *For God's sake plead, plead for my sake and stand disputing it no longer.*

I laid the note among my papers, and Oh, my dearest, I thought, my dearest dearest. Then I looked again across the way, looked to where the Protector sat, dressed all in sober black, come here this fair June afternoon to look upon justice done.

At two of the clock my judges filed back in, a few of them looking nervously to where Cromwell sat, and the Clerk called out for silence in the Court, and Lisle asked me once again, did I intend to be tried.

"My Lord," I said, "I have but little more to say. I desire to know whether the Court doth intend to try me by a jury."

"It doth not, Mr. Mordaunt."

"And doth the Court deny me counsel, My Lord?"

"The law doth deny it you, Mr. Mordaunt."

"Then, My Lord, seeing I am overruled, I shall demur to the Court and plead not guilty. And may God forgive what is done here this day."

"For one of his years," the Attorney General said, "Mr. Mordaunt is a man of many parts. This morning he would be the Court's solicitor. This afternoon he must be our conscience as well."

I turned to reply to that, for desperation had begotten a recklessness in me. But the Clerk was already speaking. "Mr. Mordaunt," he said, "you stand here charged of high treason. To this charge you plead not guilty. Do you stand to your charge, not guilty?"

"I do," I said.

"I could wish Mr. Mordaunt had done this before and made himself capable of more favor," the Attorney General said, and then he called his first witness and they fetched in John Stapely and swore him in.

And he is but three and twenty and not to be condemned, I thought. He sat there, young and apple-cheeked, with a whisper of sweat on his lip and his fingers a-tremble and his eyes too nervous

407

to meet mine. "We produce this gentleman to prove the charge," the Attorney General said. "I presume he is well known to the prisoner. I desire he may declare what he knows." He bent his eyes upon this one who would have commanded all the king's forces in Sussex, and Stapely's eyes met mine, very briefly, and his eyes asked my forgiveness. "Mr. Stapely," the Attorney General said, "what do you know concerning the discourses of Mr. Mordaunt, touching upon the bringing in of Charles Stuart?"

Stapely's tongue came out to wet his lips. "What I can say will not be much," he said. "Mr. Mordaunt did once tell me there was a design to bring in the king. He did ask me if I knew of such a thing. I told him no. He was pleased to tell me somewhat of it. I asked him if he was engaged in it. He told me he was not."

"What did he tell you concerning his being entrusted by the king?"

"He told me the king wrote to him to speak to his friends, that they should be ready to assist him when he should come into England with force."

"Did he say he had commissions from the king?"

"He did not tell me so."

The Attorney General paused, and Stapely's eyes strayed into mine, and mine told him that I forgave him. If indeed forgiveness were necessary, I thought; if indeed, Mr. Stapely, you do not play here as dangerous and delicate a game as I do. "Mr. Stapely," the Attorney General said, "did he encourage you thereto? What arguments did he use?"

"Only in commendation of the thing," Stapely said.

"Mr. Stapely," the Attorney General said, and there was a warning in his voice, "I would remind you that you sit here upon oath."

"I speak you the truth, sir."

"We would have the whole and entire truth, Mr. Stapely."

"I would speak no less upon oath, sir."

The Attorney General looked to where the Protector sat, his head broodingly down, his eyes fixed on his hands lying before him. The Attorney General looked down upon him as if to say that what was done here was no fault in himself. Then he turned and looked to where all behind us a crowd had gathered, drawn hither by the Protector's presence. "My Lord," he said, "if it please you, I would

408

have this place cleared of the distraction of those who have no business here."

Lisle so ordered it, and the Attorney General turned back to Stapely and came in upon a new tack. "Let us to other times," he said, "when Mr. Mordaunt did discourse with you upon this business."

"I cannot under oath—"

"To the best of your remembrance, sir."

Stapely looked once to me and once to the Protector. And aye, I thought, a dangerous and delicate game, John Stapely, and may God give you the courage. And if He does not, you stand forgiven. "There was a time at Berkshire House," Stapely said. "But at that time there was no discourse about the business at all. After that he was speaking to me about the times, losses of privilege, great taxations, wherein I agreed with him and wished they might be better. I asked him if there was a way to help. He said Yea; he said that Charles Stuart was intending for England, and that would be a fair opportunity to redress all grievances."

"When was this, Mr. Stapely?"

"It was—I cannot tell the days. It was since the last parliament. All our discourses were since the last parliament."

"And who was by?"

"Nobody was by. It was all private."

"And when and where else?"

"At Long Acre, there he was pleased to tell me something concerning Surrey, that there was a considerable strength in case the king should land. He did say he had delivered out three or four commissions, but to whom I know not; I dare not swear to it; but it is to the best of my remembrance."

"And this was all the times and places?"

"There was a time at the Half Moon Tavern in Aldersgate Street. There was Captain Mallory and myself and this gentleman, Mr. Mordaunt. He did ask us what readiness we were in in Sussex. I told him I did not know; I had not been in the country lately. He asked us to meet him upon a Tuesday next, at Crawley in Surrey, further to debate of things. I understood it was for the business of the king, but it was not so positively expressed."

"And these were all the times and places?"

409

"Yes. I think all. I can recall no other."

"And they were all private?"

"Save this once, when Captain Mallory was by."

The Attorney General looked down upon the Protector, thoughtfully, as if to say that Mr. Stapely was no longer his business but another's. And babbled you have, John Stapely, I thought, but you have not babbled all, and I felt the blood quick and hot in my throat. A little longer the Attorney General looked wearily down upon the brooding figure of the Protector. Then he looked as wearily to My Lord Lisle.

"I have done with this witness, My Lord," he said.

Lisle asked me if I had any questions I would put to this witness. I answered a few, My Lord, and I turned to play with John Stapely this game he had chosen to play. He sat there, young and apple-cheeked and less ready than I for death, and I thought, He hath used his wits, and now do you use yours, John Mordaunt.

"Mr. Stapely," I said, "at this time at Berkshire House, when ye say I spake to you concerning Charles Stuart intending for England. I desire to know who was by."

"Nobody was by."

"At that time you were pleased to ask if I were engaged in this business. What was my answer to you?"

"You said you were not."

"But this time at Berkshire House, this was the place where this encouragement was first made?"

Stapely looked to Lisle. "I do not know what he means by encouragement, My Lord. He only told me of it."

I smiled softly upon him. He did not return the smile. "This time at Long Acre, when I spake to you of commissions. That time who was by?"

"Nobody. We were private."

"I desire to know when that was, Mr. Stapely."

"I cannot remember the day. It was above half a year since."

"Canst remember the month, Mr. Stapely?"

"I dare not take my oath upon it."

"Canst remember the season? Was it harvest? Was there snow upon the ground?"

"There was no snow upon the ground. I recall no snow upon the ground."

410

"But you are certain this is the time when I spake to you of commissions."

"Yes."

"What commissions did I say these were? Were they for horse or foot?"

"I cannot recall. It was above six months—"

"Why, yes," I said mildly. "And you cannot even remember the season, whether it was harvest or frost upon the ground. And so let us to the subject of correspondence. Ye say I said to you that Charles Stuart had writ me to engage my friends. Did you see this letter?"

He shook his head. "You did not show it me. You but told me of it."

"You are certain I said it was from the king?"

It was a game we played and delicate, and there were rules and limits, and he clung to the limits. "I am certain," he said.

"And it was at Berkshire House I spake to you of this letter?"

He was about to say no. Then he perceived my drift and said yea instead.

"A little ago you said I spake but in generals at Berkshire House. There was no discourse at all about this business at Berkshire House, that is what you said."

He had his talents, did John Stapely, and one was a gift for play-acting. His tongue came out to wet his lip, and his eyes strayed nervously about him, and the sweat was a thin, gray shadow on his forehead. "I cannot re—"

"But it was the king writ me. You are certain I said the king."

"I think I heard you say so."

I looked to the Protector. His head was up now, his eyes fixed on me. I could still see death in his face. I looked to my judges. Two or three of them listened attentively; one nodded; I think he was the one who had spoken with Elizabeth. I looked back to Stapely.

"Let us to the Half Moon," I said. "When Captain Mallory was by and I did ask you what readiness you were in in Sussex. That was what I asked, was it not?"

"Yes."

"Readiness for what, Mr. Stapely?"

"I do not know for what. You did not say for what. I supposed it was the business of the king."

411

"And I asked you to meet with me the Tuesday following, further to debate of things?"

"Yes."

"At Crawley in Surrey?"

"Yes."

"My Lord," I said to Lisle, "I do not know this place. He says it is in our country but it is not." I returned to Stapely. "I desire to know whether I did meet at the place appointed."

"No. For I was sent for to Whitehall on that day."

"Was Captain Mallory also sent for?"

"I do not know."

"Was I sent for? Your being sent for, should this have hindered me from this meeting?" I looked once more to the Protector. Then I looked to Lisle. "I have done with this witness, My Lord," I said.

The Attorney General rose with a very great effort of will. "My Lord," he said, "there was a mention made of one Captain Mallory, whom we did intend to have as a witness. He was committed upon this design, being privy to it. It hath so fallen out that he is lately escaped. I desire that Major Ellison may be sworn."

It was done, and the Major testified that Captain Mallory had indeed escaped. Then a Mr. Scobell, the justice of the peace who had taken Captain Mallory's examination, testified that I had indeed plotted treason with John Stapely and Captain Mallory in the Half Moon, for Captain Mallory had so declared it upon oath before Major General Goffe and himself. Then Mr. Scobell stepped down, and the Attorney General said, "My Lord, I have exhibited a charge of high treason against the prisoner at the bar; I have shown that the prisoner was to raise force against this government, and that he did publish Charles Stuart to be king, and that he did hold correspondence with him." And My Lord Lisle looked to me and I arose to address to my justification.

"My Lord," I said, "if I speak but briefly to this that this learned counsel would call evidence against me, it is that it doth not merit length. For this second witness, for Mr. Scobell, I will say nothing; this is all *sotto voce*, it is hearsay, it doth not confront me with my accuser. For Mr. Stapely, he is pleased to urge against me that I said Charles Stuart writ me to engage my friends, but he says he saw not the letter or that anyone was by; he did not name the time or place but at random, and that I but said so.

"Being asked about commissions, he first denied I told him I either had commissions or delivered any. Then he says I said I had delivered out three or four. But he said it was only to the best of his remembrance; he did not say he saw the commissions; he knew not whether these commissions were for horse or foot; being asked the time, he could not even remember the season, whether there was harvest or snow upon the ground.

"He says at the Half Moon I spake with him and Mallory. He says we agreed to meet on the Tuesday following at Crawley, but says I was not there. My Lord, I do not know that place; he says it is in our country but it is not. He says it was not about any positive thing why I was to meet there but only to debate things in general. He says Charles Stuart was not mentioned, but he supposed it to be so.

"My Lord, this is but a single evidence; a man cannot be found guilty upon single evidence; if we have any law in England, we must have this law. But suppose it true, what Mr. Stapely says; suppose I do confess to it. Hath Mr. Stapely said ought save that I knew of an intended design to bring in the king? If this be treason, then I submit that this honorable Court is guilty of treason. Is there a man before me did not know of this design? Is there a man in England did not know it? If this be treason, then we must find the Protector guilty of treason, for did he not know of this design? If I am to be condemned upon this, My Lord, then let us dispense with pretense, let us speak no more of acts of parliament and courts of justice, let us hang men but upon whim and say so and have done with it.

"My Lord, I speak no more to these charges, but submit all to this honorable Court. Yet I desire leave to speak a little upon generals, upon hypothesis. And if I speak more boldly than is politic, it is not that I love my life less but that I love my country more. I stand here charged with high treason. I know not what this honorable Court would call treason, but I would call it betrayal of a man's country. But what is a man's country? Is it but a piece of land lying from here to there? We know that if the country be England, it is more than this, it is government under law, it is justice for all men, it is those rights and privileges which my ancestors have so often sweated and bled for in purchasing the Great Charter and the Petition of Right.

"My Lord, I have been told here that this Court sits by act of parliament, and that all men must submit to that authority. But

413

there was another parliament, and there was a king would have seized upon five men out of that Commons, and a great cry went up that this were a breach of privilege, and England fought a war over that debate. And is the exclusion of a hundred from their seats this year any the less a breach of privilege? There are those sitting before me would not submit to that authority; am I then to submit to this one? There was a thing they called Ship Money; it was a small thing; I have spent more on amusement in a single night than this tax cost my father in a year; there was a precedent for it. Yet they called this tax arbitrary. Are our taxes this year the less arbitrary? There was a court they called the Star Chamber, and it was claimed this were not justice but tyranny, and for it a king lost his head. Yet have I not been denied as much in this place as ever Englishman brought before the Star Chamber was denied? There was—"

And now behind me the sudden scrape and stir, and the Attorney General crying out, "My Lord, we must not suffer this," and I turned to face him. He had clawed his way to his feet, and, "I suppose you will allow this man all favor, My Lord," he said. "But this is a very ill precedent to the justice of England—"

"My Lord," I said, "I speak but upon generals, upon hypothesis."

"Mr. Mordaunt," Lisle said, "I pray you remember that text, 'He that seemeth to be religious and bridleth not his tongue, his religion is in vain.'"

"My Lord," I said, "whilst I speak for the laws of England, this is not an evil speech."

"My Lord," the Attorney General said, "his words, they are seditious, they show the spirit of the man. I have attended many, but I never saw the like in my time. You have had the patience to hear him oppose yourself, your authority, your persons, and now he would strike at the root of all. My Lord, this man hath condemned himself out of his own mouth, and I would have him carry himself with more respect—"

"My Lord," I said, "if this hath been a foolish speech, I crave the indulgence of the Court. I meant it but upon hypothesis, that I might ask but one question, which were this. If all this should be so, and if a man should say I will not endure this, I love that England that once was but I love not this England, I love life but I hate tyranny more, then is this man treasonous? And now I have no more to say."

414

A very great quiet fell upon the room when I was done. In that quiet the Attorney General stepped out from behind his table and approached the bench. "My Lord," he said, "I will speak to you very short. You have heard the evidence; it is certain there was a design to return this land to its old troubles; it is a happiness this business were discovered. And God hath seen fit that this man should betray his seditious spirit. Out of his own mouth hath he done this. Upon this evidence I leave it to your justice and as you shall judge. I shall say no more."

I watched them file down the great stone steps, and you could read nothing in those faces. But then a curious thing happened. For just at the foot of the steps, one of them suddenly stopped, and a look came into his face such as you will see when a man is astounded. He was not ten feet from me when he stopped, and I saw that look strike into his face, and then he gasped, so loud you could have heard it from fifty feet. And then he had fallen to the floor.

Four or five carried him from the Hall while I thought, *Who, I wonder who? One of the purchased or one of my enemies? Who?* And then from somewhere out of that clotted crowd I heard the word *Pride*. And *Pride*, I thought, *Colonel Pride, the purger of parliaments, Colonel Thomas Pride*.

It was then, I think, and not later, that I knew what verdict the Court would return. Near ten years ago, Charles had sat where I now sat, and he had seen his omen. And now I had seen mine. For of all those forty, Colonel Pride was the judge most certain to have voted against me.

They were absent two hours. Then they returned, and Lisle ordered Slingsby and Hewet to be brought before the bench for judgment, and it was done. Slingsby had pled, and him the Court found guilty and sentenced to death. Hewet had stood mute, and him they also sentenced to death. Then the Clerk bid me rise and hear the judgment of the Court, and I obeyed. "Mr. Mordaunt," Lisle said, "have you ought else you would say to this Court before I pronounce judgment upon you?"

I stared up at him in some surprise, for this was not usual. "I think I have not, My Lord," I said.

"I must tell you," he said, and now I noted the drawn nervousness in his eyes, "I must inform you that the vote hath been equal in your case, an equal number for guilty and not guilty."

And oh, God, I thought, it is up to Lisle to decide, and the Protector seated in this room, with those uncompromising eyes fixed upon Lisle's, and my judgment written in his face, undoubtedly my judgment written in his face, and Lisle delicately sweating. And so what do you say, John Mordaunt, I thought, oh, Almighty God, what do you say?

I said the one thing that came into my mind.

"My Lord," I said, "if I am permitted one word, it is only this, that there is death in this place."

He understood me, all right; they all of them understood me; they could have understood me no more clearly had I plainly said that the Protector was a dying man, it was in his face, he carried the smell of death about with him, and time, My Lord Lisle, for all rats to be scurrying for their holes. And standing there, watching Lisle's eyes stray to the Protector, watching the gray come into his face, watching his tongue flick out to touch his lips, I thought that I would not be standing here had I any choice, but neither would I be sitting where My Lord Lisle sat.

And then he had decided; then it was in his face that he had decided.

"I have a word to speak to you, Mr. Mordaunt," he said. "God hath appeared in justice, and God doth appear in mercy. As the Lord is just to them, so He is exceeding merciful to you. And I may say to you that God appears to you at this time as He speaks to sinners in Jesus Christ; for, sir, He doth clear sinners in Jesus Christ even when they are guilty, and so God cleareth you. I will not say you are guilty, but ask your own conscience whether you are or no. Sir, bless God as long as you live, and bless My Lord Protector by whose authority you are cleared."

I stood in that silence and heard that. And then, behind me, the Protector spoke. He had sat silent this entire afternoon, his great, sad, terrible eyes upon the proceedings, but now he chose to be heard. "My Lord Lisle," he cried out, "I am not satisfied in this."

"Your Highness," Lisle said, "it was but single witness. I—"

"I tell you, I am not satisfied. Single witness or no witness at all, I am not satisfied."

"Your Highness, whilst we have law—"

"Do not prate to me of law, My Lord President. I charge you, do not."

Lisle was a small man and gone sweatily to fat, and there was gray in his face, and there was agony in it. But he was also a judge of the land, and somewhere in this moment he recovered some scrap of his rightful dignity. "Your Highness," he said, "I have been faithful to you and your interests, I have long done your bidding, you well know I have. But I cannot find it in my conscience to find this prisoner guilty. If you would condemn him, Your Highness, it must be out of another mouth than mine."

A very little longer these two stared into one another's eyes. Then Cromwell turned from him. "I am not satisfied in this," he said. "And I do charge you, Colonel, to conduct this man back from whence he came."

"Your Highness," I said, "I have been acquitted. By your own Court have I been acquitted. And so may I know what charge I am seized upon this time?"

"No charge," he said. "I require no charge, sir." And I had not been present five years ago, when he strode in upon the parliament with thirty musketeers in attendance; when he called out to the Commons there assembled, "Your hour is come; the Lord hath done with you"; when he said, "I will put an end to your prating"; when he offered to lend the Speaker a hand to come down, and then, lifting the mace from the table, cried out, "What shall we do with this bauble? Take it away." I had not been present that day. But I think I now knew how it had been.

I was imprisoned the summer in the Tower. A week after my trial Mallory was again apprehended, and during the entire month of June my keepers asserted that double jeopardy or no, I would be brought to trial again, that the Protector meant to see me hang on one pretense or another. I know not why I was not; enough were, that bloody month; Hewet and Slingsby were beheaded on Tower Hill ten days before my third and thirtieth birthday, and in July the crowds about Tower Hill or in Cheapside could watch the drawing and quartering of four or five others. Perhaps it was as they said, that all London was so nauseated with blood that Cromwell must finally heed the murmurs and call a halt to this. Or perhaps it was that no judge, not even Lisle, would sit in judgment on me. But

417

whatever the reason, I was not, and by July Elizabeth and I occupied an apartment in the Tower from which we could look down upon the river in the summer sun. And by August I was near forgotten at Whitehall, and all that summer the outside world seemed very far away, and come August Elizabeth was with child, and we were very happy.

The third of September was a Friday, and Elizabeth was gone forth into the city that day, for it was the anniversary of Worcester and she had a whim to watch the celebrating in the Cheap. She returned very late, near dusk, and I looked up from the book I was reading—I recall that the volume was the *Reliquiae Sacrae Carolinae*, the works of Charles I, and I was rereading the *Eikon Basilike* —and I noted that she was out of breath from running up the stairs. And so I dropped the book and rose in some haste, for she was near three months with child. "Why, Elizabeth," I said. "What is it—"

"Oh, John," she said. "Oh, John, it is over."

"Over?" I said. "What is over?"

"Tyranny," she said.

I stared at her; I could suddenly feel my heart in me. "He hath landed," I said. "Charles Stuart hath at last landed."

"No," she said. "But the Protector is dead. He died but two hours since, and now it is over, my husband."

ᘓ *Epilogue* ᘗ

It was not over, of course; the Commonwealth would be eighteen months a-dying, a very long time. With his last breath the Protector named his son Richard to succeed him, and for six months Tumbledown Dick sat uneasily in his father's place in Whitehall, while all about him men hungrier than he for power maneuvered and intrigued for power. Even before the Protector was decently in his grave (for he lay in state until November) there was the vying. Before September was October the army presented a petition to make Fleetwood commander in chief of the army in place of Richard himself. On the Council, army officer intrigued against civilian for place and privilege. In city and nation, the major parties (Independent, Presbyterian, Anglican, Republican, Commonwealthman, Loyalist) watched for whatever would advantage them. In Coleman Street and in the suburbs, all the mad sects (Baptist, Fifth Monarchy Men, Millenarian, Behmenist, Visionary, Libertine, Ranter, Socinian, Seeker, Leveller, Quaker, God knows what other) scribbled petitions and preached heresy and rebellion. In the provinces, men publicly joined with the crowds to cry out, "God save the Protector Richard" and in private drank toasts to the return of the king. And in camps and port towns, soldiers and sailors muttered and mutinied for their pay.

But there was no pay. And so in December Richard must call up a parliament. The elections returned a hodgepodge of Republicans like Haselrig and Scot, and army swordsmen like Major General

Butler, and secret royalists like Sir George Booth. It was a Commons all at odds on every question save only three: a hatred of rule by the army, a conviction against rule by single person (be his name Oliver or Richard), and a detestation of purged parliaments. And so all that winter the parliament debated the Humble Petition and Advice, debated the "Other House," debated the question of succession, debated everything save money, while the army fretted and fumed and threatened. Then, in April, under the pretense that rebellion stirred in the land again, the army came to the end of its patience. The last week in April, the army officers forced Richard to dissolve the parliament. And now Fleetwood and Lambert and Desborough gave orders in Whitehall. And in May these three recalled the old Rump Parliament of 1653, and forty-two Commonwealthmen and old regicides trooped back to Westminster and sat down and waited unhappily for orders as to what they were to do.

The army was right about one thing: rebellion stirred in the land again, all right. While the parliament sat, we royalists were content to wait patiently for all to fall into anarchy and confusion and the land in desperation to recall the king. But with parliament out and army in, it was 1656 all over again—arbitrary arrests and arbitrary seizure of estates; ministers like Owen exhorting their congregations to return to godly living and the principles of the Good Old Cause; rogues in places of authority and honest men brought to account for their honesty; Cavaliers banished London, and in the country horse racing, cock fighting, and other "unlawful assemblies" forbidden; disaffected officers purged from the army and disaffected ministers turned out of their livings. And discontent seethed in the land, and royalists lit fires where there were none and fanned flames where there were, and rebellion stirred again.

Rebellion stirred, and again it was the old story—enough of us could agree that the king must be brought back, but none could agree on the way of it. There was a thing in the land called the "Sealed Knot," six men with the heart gone out of them; Brodrick headed this, and their counsel was now as always to watch and wait, let others do our work for us. And there was another called "The Great Trust and Commission," and after my release from the Tower in September, Charles named me to head this. And my counsel was that we must act now while all was in confusion. Wait, I argued, and within a month the old Rump would name Fleetwood or Lambert Protector, and then God have mercy on our souls. Wait, and it would be the Levellers or the disaffected Cromwellians like Dick Ingoldsby who would bring back the king—or George Monck in Scotland—and these would impose conditions, these would clip the king's wings, we would end up by having no true king but only half a one.

To Brodrick or Willis my arguments fell on deaf ears. But the king heeded them. I returned from Brussels in June, after an audience with His Majesty, and I returned with orders. Which were that we should rise on the first day of August. We would be ruined again, Brodrick cried out when I delivered the orders; that were harvest season, the generality of peasants would rather work in harvest for two shillings *per diem* than fight for nothing. And Willis, in that same meeting, must deliver a pious preamble of his own. The action was totally presbyterian, he affirmed. It was managed by rash, vain, giddy people (meaning me), he pleaded, and we should all see what blood and misery would ensue from this. But they knew the king's hand, they could read an order, and in the end they reluctantly agreed to obey.

I was not in England that first of August, when the drums beat at Warrington and Sir George Booth was up in the land. Nor was I present nineteen days later, when Lambert marched out of London at the head of five thousand redcoats and routed Booth's forces at Winnington Bridge and so broke the back of another rebellion. For a week before, in the thick heat of a July night, I faced, across a private table in a London tavern, a certain Samuel Morland.

He owned a pallid skin and sad, worried, fretting eyes; he looked like a clerk and rightfully so, for that is what he was; for ten years he had been John Thurloe's secretary. Of late years he had sniffed out the direction the political wind blew; he was privy to Thurloe's correspondence, and he had been selling us information for two years now. Which of recent months had not been much, for Thurloe was this summer *persona non grata* at Whitehall, he was out and Thomas Scot was in.

But he had information for me this night, did Samuel Morland. Information and a packet of letters.

"You must call a halt to this rising, Mr. Mordaunt," he said that night, across the candlelight.

"What rising?" I said, for I did not trust this man.

"I pray you do not fence with me," he said. "I pray you, do not. For the rising is betrayed, My Lord."

"My Lord?" I stared hard at him, for His Majesty had named me a viscount only weeks before, and the commission was not known to five persons as yet. Or so I had thought. "What is this My Lord, Mr. Morland?"

"I know of your recent viscountcy, sir. I know many things. As you will discover if you will read one or two of these." And he pushed the packet of letters a delicate inch in my direction.

There were three dozen or more in the bundle, all addressed to Thurloe, all in the same hand though signed by different names—Richard Watkins, Mr. Thompson, Mr. Steele, Thomas Barrett. Some were four years old; one or two had been written within the month. And it was all there, names and places and plans and numbers, all there for four years or more, all our schemes betrayed weeks before they were to be executed, explanation and to spare for John Thurloe's genius. I did not read them all, but I read enough, while the sickness stirred at the pit of my stomach, and I tasted bile in my throat, and I finally pushed them aside and looked again into Morland's fretting eyes.

"Whose hand?" I asked softly.

"His Majesty will know it," he said.

"Whose hand?" I repeated.

"Sir Richard Willis's," he said.

I moved a hand as if to seize him by the throat; I did not, but he read my intent, he flinched back from me. "You lie," I said.

He shrugged. "I have said it once, I will say it again. His Majesty will know the hand."

"You lie," I repeated.

"I do not lie, My Lord," he said quietly.

And I looked into those worried eyes and I knew that he did not. For it was too neat not to be true, it explained too many things too patly. The poverty-stricken Sir Richard neither transported nor hanged after the Gerard affair. Sir Richard privy to all the names and dates and places in '55, and all betrayed, Sir Thomas Harris betrayed, Grenville betrayed in Plymouth, Penruddock betrayed. Sir Richard lounging openly in London when I returned from the Indies, though all known Cavaliers had been banished the city. But a year ago, the Earl of Ormonde almost laid by the heels four nights

422

hand running, and Willis common to all those meetings. And I betrayed this spring, I thought, and sitting there I felt for an instant the rage, the urge to do murder. And then I did not; then I felt only the thick and sullen sickness, the tired nausea for all the trusts and all the betrayals over all these years.

I pushed back my chair. "I must get word to His Majesty," I said. "Who sails within the week. I thank you for this intelligence, Mr. Morland. I regret that we cannot pay you in weightier coin than thanks. Not immediately."

"Why, I can wait, My Lord," he said.

I dispatched yet that night riders throughout the kingdom armed with letters that would halt the rising. They carried no passes, and I could only pray God that they would get through. I left Elizabeth to manage the business I must leave undone. And by dawn I was flogging a horse toward Dover.

Three days later I was in Calais.

The king was not at Calais. He was at St. Malo, if he was not already embarked for England. Six of us, including the Duke of York, ruined six horses that day on the ill and rocky coast road between Calais and St. Malo. We reached St. Malo early in the evening, and I squandered no time on making myself presentable for entering His Majesty's presence, only burst as I was into the inn where he lodged, my clothes dusty and travel-stained, my face bearded, myself so spent I staggered. And no ceremony when I faced him, neither, only a brief bow and a "Thank God."

There were three in the room with him, the Earl of Ormonde and Hyde and Brodrick, and they all stared at me in amazement. "Thank God for what, Mordaunt?" the king said.

"That you are not yet at sea, Sire."

He knew; even before I explained he knew; he was no stranger to betrayal; he had known twelve years or more of it. "The rising is postponed," he said.

"The rising is betrayed, Sire." And I handed him the letters.

He carried them to the window. He spent not long over them. His face was normally swarthy, but it was something paler than usual when he looked across the room to me. "Whence came you by these?" he said.

"I had them at Morland's hands, Sire."

"I cannot believe this. He hath starved ten years in my service, and I cannot believe this."

"You cannot afford not to believe it, Your Majesty. He and Brodrick are good friends. Ask Brodrick if he knows the hand."

The king passed a letter to Brodrick, and Brodrick read it. And his face was not swarthy neither when he looked up; his face was as gray as cold wood ashes. "A forgery, Sire," he said tightly. "It must be a forgery."

"I think not," I said. "What hath Morland to gain—"

"Nought," Brodrick burst out. "But you have. You have been at odds with Sir Richard and me these two years and more. And only your word that you received these at Morland's hand—"

And then he broke off, though I cannot tell you why. I was staring at him, true, and no man could have more plainly called me rogue. And yet I remember no pulse of anger in my throat, and I betrayed none, I think, in my face. For I felt none, and do not ask me the why of that, neither. For five years I had lived to kill this man, but now, and quite suddenly, I no longer desired his blood, I no longer desired any man's blood, and I know the reason no better than you. Perhaps it was that I was a year married and father of a son; perhaps that can change a man. Perhaps it was that Brodrick had not after all betrayed us; for months now I had been certain it were he, and now I knew it was not; perhaps that was it. Perhaps it was that for three days now I had lived not with anger but with a thick, sullen, weary heartsickness for all the betrayals and the deceptions, the lies and counter-lies, all the loss of honor and integrity and honesty in this world of mine, and now I wanted no more blood, I wanted no more violence, I wanted no more hate, I wanted only peace. Or perhaps these were none of the causes. Perhaps it was only that hate can live but so long in a man, and then it must wither and die like an unwatered peach tree in an August drought.

Or perhaps, I thought, thinking now of a grassy, forgotten grave half around the world, thinking of a promise made a dying man and as yet no monument built him—perhaps it was simply that I, John Mordaunt, had not been born to exact revenge. But, I thought, what hath my promise to you, Richard Munke, to do with this man?

424

But whate'er the reason, I stood there, staring at Brodrick, and the words died in his throat, and I looked to the king.

"Sire," I said, and my voice as quiet and contained as if I but spoke in passing of the weather, "Sire, I have lived five years in anticipation of the pleasure I would someday derive of running my sword through this man's throat. But now I discover that it would give me no very great pleasure. Now I find I want no more his blood, I want no man's blood. I pray you, Sire, ask him not to make it necessary for me to kill him."

His Majesty looked at Brodrick. "I commanded Mordaunt to tender you an apology once," he said. "Now I command you to return the courtesy."

"He hath it," Brodrick said sullenly. "Until I can prove him a rogue, he hath it. And have I your leave, Sire, to return to England?"

"For what end?"

"To prove Mordaunt false, or Sir Richard, one or t'other. To confront Sir Richard with these, give—"

The king shook his head. "Later, mayhap. Not now. It is politic that he not know what we know. And I have other uses for you. And for Mordaunt here, who is for Scotland."

"Scotland, Sire?" I said.

"Aye. To Monck. I will send word to Grenville, he will meet you there. The two of you must engage Black George. He is our last hope now."

"Monck?" I cried. "George Monck? Monck loved Cromwell, Sire."

"So he did. And so he hath an army. The largest left in England and the best disciplined."

"He will impose conditions, Sire. It will be your father at Newport—"

"Then I shall accept them. For I am grown exceeding weary of my travels."

"Sire," I pleaded, "if we engage Monck, you will return no true king. You will return but half a king—"

"Why, half a king were better than no king at all."

I studied him, sick at heart suddenly and despairing. "Sire," I pleaded, "would you accept the Crown but let them take away the Miter? Some of us have starved and sweated and bled and died for your person. For twelve years some of us have. But more of us have

425

suffered for something else. Not for your person, Sire, but for king-ship. Not for a man but for government by law and not by whim, for custom and not for innovation, which were ever the better way. And were they all for nought then, all the bitter years?"

For a very little he studied the expression to my face, the hands thrust imploringly out before me. Then he was coming toward me through the evening light in that careless, long-legged, Stuart stride of his, his long, bony, swarthy Stuart face tired and sad in the way that cynicism is tired and sad. He came thus across the room to me and laid a hand on my shoulder. "I did say it once," he said, "and I shall say it again. We are the disinherited, you and I. And you more than I, John Mordaunt."

"I am not certain I follow your meaning, Sire."

"Why, no," he said. "I think you might not, John Mordaunt."

"Then if Your Majesty—"

"Say but this," he said. "Say that the times are out of joint. And neither you nor I were born to set them right. And so we must learn to live in them, must we not?"

"I cannot say, Sire. For enough years now I have chosen to fight—"

"Aye," he said. "Fight. And how often can a man endure defeat? How often?" He smiled, but it was no smile of happiness or con-tentment or peace or satisfaction. I know not what it was, but it was none of those, that smile. "One day," he said, "we must cease fight-ing, we must surrender instead. And then we must learn to live in the world as it is. And which of us better prepared for that, John Mordaunt?"

I did not reply to that. I was not certain that I followed his argu-ment, and so I did not reply to that. I am not yet certain. And he has never explained himself further to me.

But this, of this I am certain, this. I was not in England in August, when Booth met Lambert at Winnington Bridge and for the last time on a field of battle a Roundhead routed a Cavalier. Nor was I there later, when the Rump found leaders in Haselrig and Vane and refused to acknowledge the army as master, and briefly a new army and an old, mutilated, senile parliament glared at one an-other before the army turned one more parliament out of doors. I was in England not at all that winter when all was now anarchy,

with the milksop Fleetwood named commander in chief to forestall
the ambitious Lambert, and in London streets nought but rioting
and crying out for a free parliament, and rule now by the naked
sword and no pretense. For all that winter Grenville and I were
back and forth between Edinburgh and Calais.

But I was wrong in one regard: there were no conditions from
Black George Monck. There was nothing at all from taciturn, stolid,
seemingly witless Monck save tobacco juice spat at our feet, and an
occasional grunt that he was for parliament and against army rule,
and a reluctant admission that his dowdy slut of a wife was for the
recall of the king. He was all things to all people that winter, was
George Monck; not even in January, when he crossed the Tweed
and Lambert's army melted away from him and the way to London
was open, did we know Monck's intent. We did not know it until
April, with the Rump Parliament recalled one last time and one
last time dissolved, and the Convention Parliament elected, and
Monck finally declaring for the liberty of parliament and the ancient
constitution, and London gone mad, the bonfires in London visible
for forty miles, and rumps of beef roasted in the streets, and men on
their knees drinking toasts to His Majesty Charles II, and pamphlets
pouring from the press to prove that the ancient government was
the best government. And no conditions from the Convention Parliament neither; there all called out for a king, not a shadow of one
but a king invested with inviolable authority and power, limited
only by the ancient laws. And so the only conditions were from
Breda, where Hyde could not believe his new good fortune but
must play politician to the end, must grant concessions that were
never asked, must promise forgiveness to all the king's old enemies
and rewards to none of his friends.

On the last day of April save two, Grenville and I delivered the
king's letter to the new House of Lords. A month later I was at
Dover to watch His Majesty step ashore, to know for the first time in
half my lifetime a country at peace and with liberty under law.

And that was fifteen years ago, and this morning I stood with my
hand on the latch of a garden gate, and the morning sun glinted
pale gold on Elizabeth's hair, and my oldest son, sixteen years old
and already as tall as I, smiled down upon his mother and then

427

took a single step and bent and kissed her full upon the mouth. And for a little I did not lift the latch of the gate, for I was just returned from London.

And then I did.

The two of them smiled a greeting to me as I came across the garden. "A fair good morrow, John," Elizabeth said, and there was a lightness in her voice that befitted a morning as fair as this one.

"Aye," I said. "Is it not?"

"Our son is home," she said. "And hath he not grown tall, then?"

"And handsome," I said. "It is his inheritance from his mother." As indeed it was, for he was not swarthy like his namesake but blond, and he owned his mother's eyes. But he had inherited the Mordaunt stubborn mouth.

"And how found you London?"

"Noisy," I said. "Most exceeding nervous and noisy. As when hath it not been. I find my preference is for country life."

She was looking up into my face, intently, I thought. "I had not expected you home so soon," she said.

"He hath prorogued the parliament again," I said, and briefly I felt the return of the old, weary bitterness, the ancient, nagging fear. And then I looked at my son. "Well, Charles?" I said.

He was smiling. "Well, Father?"

"And how find ye Oxford?"

"I have not the bent for Greek that would content my tutor," he said. "But I am sound in mathematics. I am very good in mathematics."

"Your father's son there," I said. It seemed suddenly small and irrelevant, my son's bent for Greek, suddenly trivial and inconsequential like the absence of cake when a man hath no bread or meat on his table. "And what of politics?" I said.

"Politics, sir?"

"Aye. Politics. Have ye no tutor in that subject? To instruct you that the loyalty a subject owes his monarch is but the loyalty he owes himself? To draw out for you the price a land pays for treason and rebellion?"

He was frowning. "No such course of study ever was," he said. "To my certain knowledge. And so you must speak in jest, Father."

I held his eyes a trifle longer, the while I thought that I too had been sixteen once, and are you, my son, to inherit the same

428

world I inherited; the while I thought of Charles Stuart long, long ago, and *We are the disinherited, you and I,* he had said; the while the weariness in me was close to heartsickness. And then I dropped my eyes out of his.

"Aye," I said. "I speak in jest, Charles."

"Your tone is not in jest, Father," he said.

"And so I do not speak in jest," I said.

His eyes drifted to his mother, then returned to me. "Have I your leave to leave now, Father?" he said.

"To leave? You but returned home—"

"But into the orchard. For you would speak to my mother in private, would you not?"

We watched him depart the garden. He walked in the long, easy stride of the very young; it is the way they walk, I thought, when the world and life lies all before them, the way I walked once. I sat down beside my wife in the April sun. I did not look at her. "Wouldst tell me of it, John?" she said.

"Of what?"

"Of the noisiness which is London?"

"They found against me," I said bitterly. "They voted me libelous. The vote was two to one. They awarded Shaftesbury a thousand pounds' damages."

"It was a foolish thing to say," she said. "In public."

"And was it not the plain, unvarnished truth? I should say it again, for he is not for the king as he would pretend, he is for sedition and another Commonwealth."

"The truth," she said, "is sometimes a foolish thing to say. In public."

"And did they find him guilty of treason? 'It is but laying down my gown and buckling on my sword,' he said when the king dismissed him. His very words. And did they find him guilty of treason, and his Country party with him?"

Her hand now was lightly over mine. "It is no great fortune, a thousand pounds," she said. "We shall not starve, John."

"It is not that."

"What is it, then?"

"The times," I said. "The times." And I was thinking of this session of parliament, and of the last, and of the one before that; I was thinking of the king, forced by the Commons to retract his Declara-

429

tion of Indulgence, forced to accept the Country party's Test Act, and Hyde fallen now, Arlington fallen now, the Duke of York in exile this year, all the king's ministers and friends fallen now save only Danby, and he nearly impeached this session. And the parliament still not content, I thought; the king had given in to them at every turn, bent to every demand, and still they talked up the dangers from papacy, and Shaftesbury speaking out openly this session for his bill to exclude the Catholic Duke of York from the throne, Shaftesbury daily speaking his bold and impudent treason and sedition on the floor of the Lords and no one calling him to account. "I tell you," I said, "it is '44 all over again, Elizabeth. They call themselves the Country party, but they are nought but old Roundheads under a new name—"

"John," she said.

"—and they mean to climb back into the saddle. They mean to strip everything from the king save his title, and if they cannot, why, then, they mean to have a king's blood a second time—"

"John," she said again.

"I have lived out my youth under knavery," I said. "And must I live out my old age as well? In God's name, have they no memories of what it was like under Oliver—"

"John," she said. "Do thou look at me, John."

I did so. Her eyes were steady on mine, and her mouth was grave. But neither eye nor mouth was unafraid. "He said we were the disinherited, he and I," I said. "And I now know what he meant. But oh, my beloved, I would not leave to my sons the world I was left."

"John," she said softly, "while there are men, there will be rogues."

"But not eternally in the saddle. There have been times when they were a-foot. I know there have been times."

"While there are rogues," she said, "they will be at climbing. It is in their nature. But it is also their destiny to fall again. If you believe in God, you must believe that, John."

"To Him a thousand years is but a day," I said. "But I am only human and so impatient. And so when, Elizabeth, when?"

"Why, in His own time. For did not we recall a king, my husband?"

"Half a king," I said. "Half a king. And soon no king at all, if they have their way."

"Why, then, they shall recall another. As long as men live, they shall recall another. For as long as there are men, there will be honest men, too."

I looked into her eyes, the sweet gravity of her lips. "And our sons?" I said. "What of our sons? They shall leave us in peace mayhap, for we are grown old. But what of our sons, Elizabeth?"

"Why, their world shall decide," she said. "As ours decided. And would ye deny them that, John?" And I looked at the April sun lying pale and serene upon her hair, and I looked into the steady certainty of her eyes, and I thought of Charles, my son, striding from a garden into a world that lay confidently before him, and I thought, Would to God you were right, my darling. And then I could hope that perhaps she was.

DATE DUE

GAYLORD | | | PRINTED IN U.S.A.